In Somnis Veritas

In Dreams there is Truth

The Rosalyn Letters

S. Blake

Published by Blake Studio, LLC.
Written and illustrated by Sara Blake.
www.sarablake.nyc

First Edition Paperback 2024

ISBN 979-8-9863590-2-1

Contents

Dead Moon

Monday, April 7, 1997

Dear Nova,

It's been just over six weeks since we were last together. It's late, and I'm sitting at the kitchen table with that feeling like I'm waiting for something, although I couldn't say what it is that I'm waiting for. Maybe just for today's hours to end. Maybe I'm waiting for the sound of your footsteps through the house. Lately, I do this often, sitting in a daze, pretending I might summon the sound of your voice somewhere in the other room simply by wishing for it—but of course, that doesn't work. I couldn't tell you how many times I've sat quietly like this, waiting. Eventually, my back will start to hurt, and I'll shift in whatever chair or position I've found on the floor, still not quite knowing what to do next. Today though, I'm trying something new. I'll write while I wait.

It's strange staring down at this old journal after its empty pages have sat around collecting dust for so many years of my life. Maybe it's childish to expect that finally picking it up now will make any difference, but I don't know what else to do anymore. So here I am, writing to you. I've already tried all the other things that just seem like caricatures of what you think a person is supposed to do in a situation like this—the things people do when they hurt but aren't quite sure how to make it stop.

At first, there was nothing but anger. At least, I think it was anger. My whole body just felt hot, day and night. It didn't matter the hour, the amount of clothing I was wearing, or the thermostat setting in the house. I even took my temperature once to see what was going on. Ninety-nine point six degrees. Not quite a fever, but not quite normal either. The heat seemed to spill over from my body, and sometimes it took on a new kinetic form. I started slamming every door behind me, although I can't say I ever recall consciously choosing to do so. I threw the front door so hard in its frame I broke a window pane in the living room. It wasn't on purpose, but if the whole house had toppled over right then, I'm not so sure I would have cared. Later, in a repentant attempt at remediation, I duct taped the wide splinters of missing glass back into place, but I resented every tiny tear of silver tape. I felt like destroying things, not fixing them.

A few days later in the kitchen, without any prior awareness of the impulse, I hurled a plate at the wall. Then two more. I watched each one bounce, then shatter with a percussive clatter as they met the floor. And I just stood there waiting—waiting like I am again today. I stared down at the ceramic shards on the black and white linoleum as if I expected some kind of supernatural intervention, but of course, there was nothing. Instead, I just felt embarrassed, even though I was the only person in the house. At that moment, I prayed for something to come and interrupt the silence. Anything. You know how sometimes silence can just feel so loud? But not even so much as the draft that whistles through the gap under the back door came to my rescue, and finally, I just walked over and picked up the broken pieces one by one and put them in the trash as if nothing had ever happened.

Did it happen? Lately, I get confused. I ask myself if it's merely forgetfulness. Absent-mindedness. Sometimes I do things—meaningless things—but afterward, I can't be sure if I've only just imagined doing them. I swear I remembered putting my keys away in the bowl on the bureau. Later, I discovered them still dangling from the lock in the front door. I remembered taking the garbage out to the curb. Later, a stench from under the kitchen cabinet alerted me that I hadn't. When can you truly trust your own mind? If no one else bears witness except for you, how can you really be sure something is real? There's that saying. If a tree falls in the forest, and no one is around to hear... How does that go again? Did it make a sound?

The day after I broke our plates, I found a two-month-old expired carton of milk in the fridge, but instead of tossing it out, for no reason I can comprehend, I held it out perpendicular to my body, opened my hand, and let the whole thing drop to the ground. The cardboard fold popped open, and I watched what was left slowly glug out over the checkered squares as a sour smell filled the air. It looked like modern art. A Pollock. A de Kooning. Maybe even a Kandinsky. Was their art about order, or was it about chaos? And why shouldn't I be allowed to create a little of my own chaos too? Just a little. I didn't clean it up for several days, and by the time I did, the rancid milk had dried to a crust. I had to use steel wool to get it up.

When later that week I eventually decided it would be wiser not to demolish the entire house, I thought maybe I could try to exhaust myself instead. On the first day of this new notion, I walked all the way down Peninsula Drive and made an entire loop around the park and back. The parts along the water were especially cold, but I played mind games with myself enough to ignore both the shooting sting in my fingers and the full body chill that slowly transformed into a sharp ache around my joints as the day wore on.

I knew it would be chilly from the moment I closed the front door behind me, but I reasoned I'd warm up once I walked a few blocks. When I still wasn't warm by the time I'd gotten to the end of the neighborhood, I reasoned I'd warm up once the sun had fully risen. When I still wasn't warm by the time the sun had reached its crest, I reasoned I'd warm up if I could only walk a little faster. The brown and yellow Presque Isle State Park sign materialized from around the bend, and I considered turning back to stop at Sara's Diner for something hot to eat but realized I hadn't even brought my wallet. I kept walking. I veered left onto the shoulder of Old Lake Road, and the expanse of Lake Erie soon came into view through the trees at the entrance to Beach 1. It was apparent by then it was going to be one of those choppy, blustery days. It didn't seem to matter that we've lived here our whole lives—I still neglected to account for the possibility of wind.

We've been to The Peninsula a thousand times. You'd think I'd know how to dress by now, but when I'd put myself together that morning, my head had been somewhere else, floating far above the rest of my body, legitimately unconcerned for the well-being of the rest of its attached parts. I wore my hat, of course—that I would never forget—but somehow, I hadn't bothered with gloves, or a windbreaker, or even breakfast, which unsurprisingly resulted in spending the final two hours of my trek convulsing in shivers.

I reached the turn for the Coast Guard Station sometime in the early afternoon. I knew it would be wiser to keep moving along the loop, but I couldn't help myself from a detour to pay the North Pier Light a visit. I passed a flock of geese near Beach 11 and bid a silent "hello" to the houseboats on Horseshoe Pond. When the trees finally ended, and I spotted the concrete platform of the pier stretching out into the expanse of the harbor, my heart lifted. There's always something about the sight of the open water that has a way of calming you, even if only temporarily. I walked out onto the pier to look back over the entrance to the bay. The North Pier Light was just the same as always—weathered and slightly rusted.

Before they built that lighthouse in the 1800s, ships couldn't see the land at the channel's edges and would regularly run aground. One even destroyed the original lighthouse when it tried to enter the bay during a gale and crashed right into it. Over the years, they've moved it, extended it, rebuilt it, and reinforced it. Its lighthouse keepers cared for it. And now, all these years later, it's still active. You can see its light from miles out into Lake Erie. There's something about that old lighthouse's ruggedness that always has a way of pulling me out of myself and back into the context of the world, even if for only a moment. My mind feels free to wander far beyond the confines of my small life, venturing throughout all of time and history.

Before the lighthouse, there was just the peninsula, a young landform only about a thousand years old. And before the peninsula, fourteen thousand years before that, there was only the glacier that melted to form the Great Lakes. That lighthouse is already nearly a century and a half old, but it's only a tiny blip in the whole story of this place. If that lighthouse is just a blip, what does that make me? What does that make you? I can't tell if that thought is a comfort or if it makes me want to throw plates at the wall again.

By the time I'd made it along the bay-side road, out of the park, and all the way through town again, I must have walked twenty miles, but it was really only the last twenty blocks that were a true death march back to the front door. When I finally arrived back on the porch, I somehow managed to commandeer my inoperable fingers only just enough to grasp my keys and turn the lock. I flung open our door and stripped naked right there in the hallway. I left my clothes heaped in a pile by the stairs and dragged myself straight up to the bathroom like a frozen zombie. I must have stood in the scalding shower for over an hour, and when I eventually stepped out, I looked and felt not dissimilar to a boiled lobster. I drank a beer and put myself to bed without dinner. Just the thought of food made my stomach tighten. All those miles, and yet no appetite.

The next day, I over-corrected for my previous oversights. I wore two pairs of gloves and devoured three bowls of cereal for breakfast, but instead of some grand expedition to the water, this time I just made circles around our neighborhood so many times I started to get suspicious looks from a few of the older neighbors through their windows. I surrendered to the darkness only when it got too black to see the uneven sidewalk under my own feet. Each stride felt like stepping off a tiny cliff with a blindfold on. When I got back to the house, this time I drank two beers for dinner, then crawled into bed with my jeans still on.

It was still dark outside when I woke without an alarm the following day. I felt the physical exhaustion in my legs and a hollow ache in my stomach, but still, it wasn't enough to extinguish the anxious feeling in my chest, so I decided I'd embark on a more ambitious operation, this time employing the use of the car. I was out of the house an hour before the sun had even risen, and I drove to the Shell station and bought a half tank of gas, not remembering if it would be enough to get me all the way to Raccoon Creek State Park and back. I made good time and was at the park entrance no later than 8:30. I hadn't brought my rod, but I parked just off Raccoon Lake where we used to fish. My plan was instead simply to tire myself out on the trail. I locked the car and started picking up my feet.

When I'd passed the next trailhead and still felt unsatisfied, I kept going to its connection. And then to the next. And to the next. Forest Trail turned into Appaloosa, which turned into Heritage, and then back into Forest. I stopped somewhere along Heritage to have a drink from the springs, and I wondered how many times we'd walked those trails during the summers as teenagers. Now everything looks so different somehow. Had they changed, or had I never paid attention to what they'd looked like in the first place? It's funny how our memories can be so unreliable, even as their physical reference points are right before our eyes. Maybe it's only us that changes.

I had thought getting out of the house, some new scenery, and the endless miles in my legs would help chew through this god-awful feeling, but the only things that got chewed up were my feet. I got blisters so badly I bled through my socks on both sides and stained the toes of my Vans. When I took them off in the car, the heel of the inside lining was stained red too. Maybe I should have worn my boots, but I'm not so sure they would have helped in the end. Besides, in a sick way, I even liked it—peeling off the wet, blistered skin to reveal the raw, tender flesh underneath. Those unexpected moments of brief physical pain have been the most effective distraction I've discovered so far.

When I got back home just a little after dusk, I further inspected my damaged feet and made my own little first aid station on the bathroom floor. I used toenail clippers to trim back the excess rings of dead, bloated skin, but I accidentally clipped too far, and a bright red spot began pooling at my heel on the tile. At first, I didn't realize what I'd done, nor had I registered the color as blood, but after a few seconds, the pain flooded in. I didn't react. I just sort of noticed the feeling. Eventually, I fumbled for some Band-Aids, but as I pulled off the wrappers, I hesitated. I didn't want the bleeding to stop quite yet. A few droplets made their way into the recessed grout lines between the bathroom tiles like they were some kind of miniature crimson tributaries, and I thought about how much I wished I could have just taken some of your pain too.

I'm not sure how long I sat there on the cold tiles, but eventually, a faint voice of pragmatism whispered its command in the back of my mind. "Stop bleeding so you don't track red all over the house like a wounded animal and make another Pollock on the floor. Blood is tougher than milk to scrub up." I freed the sticky Band-Aid flaps from their coverings and wrapped the brown canvas as tightly as it would go around my heel. Slowly, the pain subsided, and the numbness returned. Not just to my foot but to my whole body.

Before all those miles, I could barely sleep, but by the following morning, at last, I'd sufficiently worn myself out. My legs no longer obeyed their commands. Now, I could sleep for days. I tied our old navy blue fleece blanket to the curtain rods to block out the sun completely, and I barely got out of bed again until I realized I'd started to smell.

Each day bled into the next. How long had I stayed there? Four days? A week? Occasionally, I'd wake up to realize I'd sweated clean through the sheets, so I'd peel off my wet T-shirt and roll to the other dry side of the bed naked. Inevitably though, I'd wake up beaded in sweat again, and do it all over, rolling back to the original side. I kept a thermos and an open box of cereal on the floor beside the bed. That was all I needed. A sip of water. A handful of Cheerios, here and there. Just enough to keep the old machine running.

I sincerely thought I might as well go on like this forever, but just as soon as I'd come to terms with living out the rest of my days as a motionless bag of warm flesh, my body again refused to do as it was told. How hard could it be to just lie flat and keep your eyes shut? But the sleep just wouldn't come anymore. So what else was left?

What would a "normal" person do with this feeling? Or this lack of feeling? They would try to soothe themselves, wouldn't they?

Would they wear soft clothes? Listen to classical music? Drink chamomile tea? I never liked the whole idea to begin with. Do I really believe I deserve to be soothed? Why should I be soothed when you can't? What does a soothed person look like anyway? The concept seemed so far away, but nonetheless, I decided that even if I didn't understand the likeness of a soothed person, at the very least, I could try to do my impression of one.

I stripped the sweaty sheets from my bed and stuffed them into a laundry bag while I let the bathtub fill with steaming water. I lit an old, dusty vanilla candle, rested it in the corner near the faucet, and poured in what was left of our shampoo to make bubbles. Slowly, I stepped in and lowered myself beneath the mountain of shampoo foam, feeling the pressure of hot water climb inch by inch over my skin.

This is me being "normal." This is me "soothing myself."

It didn't last for long. After so many days in bed, the sight of the insides of my eyelids for any period longer than a blink brought on a strange sense of panic and dread. As it turned out, trying to "soothe myself" just made me more anxious and claustrophobic. I soon gave up on all the soothing business and instead put out an entire book of matches, one by one, as I soaked, letting each tiny stick burn down enough to singe my fingertips. Finally, I opened the drain with my toes and screamed underwater to see if I'd run out of air before the tub ran out of water. It was about a tie.

I dried off feeling worse off than I had before but nevertheless went down to the kitchen to give this concept of comfort one last valiant effort. I haven't bothered making anything more complicated than peanut butter sandwiches or cereal since you've been gone, so I thought cooking myself a warm meal might be a long-overdue upgrade. Something simple. Scrambled eggs with cheese and toast. But when I opened the refrigerator door, my hand reached for a beer, despite my mind's command for the egg carton.

It's like some separate and more sensible part of myself is calling out from a distance in a tiny voice, offering to take over. I can hear it, pleading to help, but it's too far away—the chasm too great to bridge. So instead, I just keep coasting along as I have been, down the same old beaten paths I already know. My attempt at a warm meal ended with a bowl of Corn Pops and a PBR. This is me soothing myself.

That was the same day I first tried going into your room. I took what was left of my lukewarm beer upstairs and pushed open your bedroom door softly like I was afraid to make a sound and get caught. I know you hate it when I go in your room without an invitation, but I put everything back just where you'd had it, I promise. I still haven't packed up a single thing, yours or mine. I haven't told our landlord either. He still thinks we're staying through the end of the lease next year, but I don't know how much longer I can afford the rent on my own.

Officially, I got fired from Orly's, but mostly I just stopped showing up for my shifts. No one seemed surprised, though. A few days after it happened, Jack came by with flowers and a card that a bunch of the regulars had signed. He'd already gathered all your things from the back office, so I wouldn't have to. Your tackle box and orange bibs. Your green canvas backpack. Inside, an extra sweatshirt and baseball cap. Your buck knife. A broken pair of headphones. A half-empty pack of gum. A tube of string wax. Your gold hoop earrings. Sunscreen. Two scratched CDs: The Cranberries', No Need to Argue, and Nirvana's MTV Unplugged. Your spiral notepad with various scribbles: a grocery list for what looked like chicken marsala, phone numbers to record shops around town, and that staff music shorthand of yours that never made sense to anyone except for you.

In the very back, there were pages of imagined melodies, and I can picture your face thinking them up on your slow days behind the register, pretending like you're watching the customers, but really you're miles away in your own musical universe. Speaking of which, Jack even paid out both our last paychecks in full, even though neither of us had worked half of it. Instead of feeling grateful, I just feel ashamed. I hate feeling like I owe people things.

I spent almost a whole day last week just unfolding and refolding your clothes. I shook them out over your bed to see their shapes, then folded them back even more neatly than I'd found them like you'd be coming back for them. Your sweaters smelled like a combination of powder deodorant and that perfume you got over at Millcreek last year. I always thought it stank, but now I think it might be growing on me.

I ran my palms over the scuffed toes of your Doc Martens where you'd worn in the leather. I sat at your desk and leafed through your notebooks too, tracing my fingertips over all your little drawings and jokes in the margins where the ballpoint pen had indented the paper like inverted Braille.

And there it was again—that tightness in my chest. That feeling of anxious anticipation, but not understanding what for. What do I do now, Nova? What do I do without you?

All the breaking things, the walking, the sleeping, the screaming underwater, the folding and refolding your clothes, the shutting out the world. None of those things work. I just feel more restless and lost than I did before.

That's why I'm here. Here, in these pages, I mean—writing to you in this old journal on our kitchen table. And for the first time in twenty-two years, you're not here with me. You're somewhere else. You're gone. Without any reason. Without any answers.

That's what this letter is about, I guess. I thought I'd use my one last Hail Mary and try writing to you. I don't know what else is left.

I know you'll never get this letter, but "never" is a strong word. If our atoms were once the stars before they were our bodies, maybe we become the stars again. Maybe when your life left, your particles blew away in the wind and became something new. Maybe at this very moment, you can hear the vibrations of my pen scratching along against this paper, and you can feel my words in some other way that we don't understand yet with these five senses. Five is such a small number—just the fingers on one hand. Maybe you will get this letter after all. Maybe.

It's been six weeks and two days now since our last morning together—I've been replaying it over and over again. Do you remember? I'm not sure if thinking about it now makes me want to smile or go back to breaking things.

I wasn't even yet consciously aware that I was awake when my eyes met your face no more than a few inches from mine. You had rolled your eyes all the way back in your head, revealing nothing but their whites, and you were flicking your eyelids spastically like some sort of electrified demon. And although you were failing miserably, you were doing your very best to touch your tongue to your nose. My body jerked involuntarily in shock, just like it always has every time you surprised me like that, and the whole bed frame shook so hard the metal hinges squeaked.

You were, of course, delighted. How you've managed to slither yourself undetected over my blankets for so many years and strategically perch yourself like some kind of demented gargoyle to greet me from my slumber has always escaped me. You must have done some version of this ritualized prank hundreds of times since we were kids, but the true mystery of it all is how it still has never ceased to genuinely startle me. If I'd known that would be the last time, I wouldn't have scowled. I wouldn't have acted so sour.

When I asked you how long you'd been there, you just answered with your classic Nova shrug. Right eyebrow raised, both shoulders up at the same time, as if suspended on marionette strings. I miss that move of yours so much. So playful and mischievous. It's a gesture so unique to you, and somehow so distinct from me.

Over the past six weeks, I've spent more minutes than I can count remembering that image of you, sitting cross-legged there on the side of my bed, grinning to yourself, pleased with your prank's work. Do you remember our conversation too?

That morning you were so full of words. You asked me what I had dreamed about that night, and as you waited for my report, your litany of absurd suggestions filled my annoyed silence.

The ghost of Beethoven? Happy, fat pandas having a picnic on a pink cloud? Discussing the merits of dessert for breakfast with Edgar Allan Poe on a spacecraft? Kissing Trent Reznor while hanging upside down like bats?

You kept going and going. You had some even better ones too, but I can't remember them now. I wish I could. If I'd known that was our last morning, I would have held onto each word for safekeeping. And I would have thanked you too—for always making me laugh, even when you don't make me laugh. You know what I mean.

Your list of absurdities continued on until I interrupted to commend you on your excellent guesswork. Indeed, yes, I had dreamed about each and every one of those things—fat pandas and all. Sarcasm would have to suffice in the absence of coffee or adequate sleep. I told you that I hadn't dreamed in weeks, and last night was no exception. When I threw open the covers and swung my legs over the edge of the bed next to yours, you didn't seem satisfied. You always could see right through me.

That's what I keep thinking about now. That's what I've been thinking about every day now for six weeks. That was a lie, Nova. I did dream. I dreamed about you.

I don't know why I couldn't tell you that morning. Perhaps I just didn't want to think about it. It seemed so juvenile at the time, but I was scared. A stupid nightmare had gotten the best of me—I felt more like a child than a grown twenty-two-year-old. I just wanted to get on with the day, you know? I was never as forgiving or kind as you were, not just with others, but with yourself too.

You were always so willing to step back and take a deep breath, feel whatever it was that you were feeling. I, on the other hand, have always been so busy pretending to be tough and unbothered, shrouding myself in cynicism or sarcasm in an attempt to either postpone or deny whatever it was that needed to be felt. But your natural state was something different. A humble honesty and sanguine acceptance, so firmly rooted in the present moment. You always had that playful kind of smarts that only belongs to old souls. Sometimes I still don't know how we're related, much less identical twins.

Nova, I'm so sorry I lied to you that morning. I can hardly bear that my words to you on our last day together were anything less than the truth. The honest answer to your question is that my dream that night had woken me up in a cold sweat. I remember gasping aloud in the darkness, and I didn't think I'd be able to get back to sleep again. The dream had felt so real, but of course, when I opened my eyes and scanned the shadows for the outlines of my room, I knew it wasn't.

I stared up at the ceiling, listening to my own breath rise and fall, and focused on a slice of light from the street lamps cutting through the curtains, gradually giving the room shape as my eyes adjusted. My mind again found its grasp on reality. I was back in the safety of my bedroom, and yet some unnamed, nearby danger still clung to the fringes of my mind. It felt like more than just some kind of realistic nightmare—it was a bottomless agitation in my very being—the sinking feeling that something terrible was about to happen. I half expected a plane to fall from the sky and crash through our roof or for a masked intruder with a cleaver to slowly inch open my door. A fire. An earthquake. A ghost. Anything. But in the darkness of my room, there was nothing but silence.

When I finally dozed back off again, it was that wiry kind of sleep —the kind like when you've had too much caffeine and your mind is still wide awake, but your body is exhausted, so the two just sort of drift away from one another for a little while. Before I understood any time had passed at all, there you were on my bedspread with your eyeballs rolled back in your head and your tongue stretching toward your nose. It was already morning. The night had passed, and it was a new day that I hoped would wash away the foulness of the dream's residue all on its own.

But now I know it was my mistake to think that way. It was a mistake to try and ignore it.

Do you remember that stretch of summer when we were seven or eight? You kept having that nightmare about a beetle who came into your bedroom from under the door and transformed into a monster at the foot of your bed. You would cry and whimper in your sleep, and you kept Gram and me up for weeks. Every morning, Gram assured you that it was only a dream, yet every night you dreaded the moment she switched off our light. Neither of us seemed able to convince you to your satisfaction that there was no beetle monster in your room, and you were indeed quite safe. That went on night after night until that day Gram took us to the lake before school.

The sun had barely risen, and it was only the three of us on the beach in the crisp open air. It felt like we were the only people that existed in the whole world. What I remember most about that morning was that wolf who came slinking out of the trees ahead of us and how Gram seemed so moved. Sometimes I'm surprised I can still picture it all so vividly—we were only kids. Wolves hadn't been seen in Pennsylvania for over a hundred years, long ago trapped and hunted to extinction in our region. Thinking back now,

I'm sure it was probably only a large coyote, but Gram insisted on calling it a wolf. Either way, she told us that never in her life had she seen one this far into the city before—wolf or coyote. Yet there it was, staring right back at us across the beach. It kept its head so low at first, then raised its neck, gracefully twisting its ears like antennae in the morning breeze. We stood transfixed until it trotted away into the brush, disappearing like a phantom.

When the three of us reached our favorite fishing spot by the driftwood, Gram sat us down on one of the sun-bleached trunks and reached into her bag. She handed us our little black journals that she'd made for us by hand, the soft linen stitched around their floppy leather jackets, folded and fastened like fabric wrapping paper. On each of their covers, she'd expertly embroidered our names, the whimsical shapes of their threaded letters dancing together in an arc. Below, she'd sewn a single wide eye with thick, green, triangular eyelashes. "Your Dream Eye," she always called it. A sliver of a silver moon seemed to cradle the eye from underneath, and a tiny purple ladder emerged from a glowing hole in the sky below. It rested against the side of the moon as if some unexpected creature might climb up at any moment to perch upon its lunar lookout.

Seven tiny gold stars in the shape of small asterisks were nestled into the empty pockets of black sky—it always felt as though they might vibrate right off the fabric. A gray halo of moonlight surrounded our names, enclosing them with the moon, the stars, and our Dream Eye, as if together they were their own little celestial ecosystem, drifting like a crystal ball through space. The designs of our two journals were nearly identical except for the white threading of our names. Gram had even cut and bound the paper herself with thick mounds of enough blank pages to keep even Hemingway busy for a healthy stint.

It's only now that I'm older I can appreciate the care and intention with which Gram had conceived of our journals' anatomy. Their spines consisted of nothing more than a thin leather strip woven through four punched holes in each crease of stacked folded paper, creating a soft, movable tower. The binding was simple to untie, allowing for more pages to be added or swapped out as we grew older, even though we never took advantage of this feature. I wish I could have fully understood the depth of that thoughtfulness before she was already gone. She really loved us.

I'll never forget the look on your face that day. You were so enchanted. Your eyes were as big as the one on your new journal. That was the first time Gram told us her story of Astrid, the girl who could see things that others could not through her dreams. I know you already remember every detail just as well as you know our own faces, but somehow I think it might help me to write it. Things feel different when you put them down in ink. It's like you're telling the words that you mean them—that they matter and are worth remembering.

As the story went, Astrid was born many centuries ago, far away from Erie, in a small island village with tall wooded mountains that pierced the sky. Every day when Astrid was a young girl, after all her chores were done, she would descend her village's mountainside and walk to the water's edge to fish and gaze out over the green-gray sea as she let her mind wander. Astrid's village was small, independent, and self-supporting, as were the others just like hers scattered throughout the hillsides. It was never any challenge to find a new secret hideaway where she could be completely alone with her thoughts for miles in any direction—just herself, the water, and the plentiful animals that roamed the encircling wilderness.

By day, Astrid was a nimble explorer of her forests and beaches—and of her own imagination too—but when night fell, and the stars and moon shone bright above her family's thatched home, she became an unwitting explorer in an entirely new way. Her dreams seemed as vivid as waking life, both beautiful and horrifying alike. They took her to unknown places, and often they scared her—just like your beetle dream had scared you too. It was only after many weeks had turned into many months that Astrid began to take notice of the curious connections between her waking life and her dreaming one.

At first, the phenomenon felt coincidental—easy to overlook—but the more she paid attention, the more she noticed that all too often, after a particularly vibrant dream, she inevitably watched some version of it come true. Slowly, she began to realize that somehow her dreams were not just flickering scenes of her own imagination but an extension of her wakeful reality—tiny open windows into her past, present, and future, part premonition and part intuition.

Gram explained how sometimes Astrid dreamed of messages from wild animals or from beings from other dimensions—sometimes even from nothing more than a voice in the wind. In other dreams, she could see through time and space and into the underworld too. And though often it was all very frightening for a little girl, each strange dream was a new adventure and a fresh opportunity to overcome an unexpected challenge. Every morning when Astrid found herself still safe in her bed, she felt an overwhelming sense of relief—she was unharmed by the various menacing characters or perilous trials that she had encountered in her sleep. She learned to attune herself, and by the time she'd shaken off her drowsiness, she realized she possessed some new insight that hadn't been there before she'd closed her eyes the night before.

Astrid was still very young when she first began trying to chronicle everything she saw in her dreams. At first, she tried to hold onto the dream's scenes by recreating them as little drawings with a stick in the dirt, but within a few hours, the wind had brushed away her sketches, and by the end of the day, Astrid had forgotten all her dream's details.

Later, she tried sneaking berries away from her mother's basket as she cooked. She crushed them with a pestle to make a deep purple stain—if only she could find a way to create a more permanent depiction of her dream's plot, then surely she wouldn't forget. In between her chores, Astrid crept away into the woods with animal hides and linens she'd scavenged from her family's home, and under the cover of the forest, she painted her dreams with her finger like giant canvas pictographs.

But when her hidden enterprise was discovered, her mother and father only reprimanded her for making a mess and for ruining their nice things. As time went on, Astrid finally learned that the best way to remember those fleeting visions of her dreams was to invent little rhyming poems about the important parts so that her mind had something more enduring to hold onto. The music of the language helped her remember each scene's description, and that description helped materialize each detail as an image in her mind's eye. Both the words and the visual memory worked together, conjuring each other in symbiotic harmony.

Sometimes Astrid's dreams didn't seem to make any sense at all, but over time, she learned how to follow their coded meanings. Uncle shouldn't go hunting today because he'll get bitten by a snake. The horse with the white spots will go lame. With her poor eyesight, Grandmother will accidentally pick pokeweed instead of sumac, and she'll try to use it to make tea and get sick if no one checks.

And time and time again, Astrid's tiny dream prophecies came true. The horse did go lame. Uncle did encounter a snake. Grandmother did pick pokeweed. In the beginning, Astrid kept her fears to herself, but the more she observed how her dreams so often became reality, the more she knew she had to intervene. She could no longer stay silent and allow dangers to befall her home. Now there was something genuine at stake. Steadily, Astrid felt a growing responsibility to share her dreams' warnings to protect both her family and her fellow villagers from harm. She struggled to grasp how her dreams could possibly predict such truths, but more importantly, she knew she had to act.

Eventually, Astrid did muster the courage to share her predictions and fears with the others, but of course, they didn't believe her. How could they? They accused her of being a liar or an attention seeker. "There goes little Astrid again, trying to get noticed with her wild imagination, pretending like she's some kind of sage. Who does she think she is?" But Astrid knew the truth, and she had no desire for attention. In fact, she often wished she could be invisible. She took no pride in her dreams' warnings, but she couldn't ignore her sense of duty. She knew she had to use her mysterious knowledge to keep her village safe. The others simply weren't ready to listen to a silly little girl's ideas about pokeweed or lame horses. Not even her own parents believed her.

Astrid spent many days and nights feeling misunderstood and alone. She wished her dreams would stop and that she could just be like the other children. Why couldn't she just go about her chores and play with her friends? "I'll be good. I'll do everything I'm supposed to do if only these dreams would end!" she would think to herself. But although her dreams made her desperately lonely, they also made her fiercely strong. Despite the other villagers' disbelief, Astrid stood by what in her own heart she knew was somehow true, and guided by her dreams, she continued to watch over and warn her village as best she could.

What Gram always impressed upon us most was that Astrid's truest skill was very simple—it wasn't any heroic choice to protect her home—it was quite plainly her willingness to be attentive to her own dreams. How many others, Gram asked, had the very same sight but were too afraid to see?

One chilly night, Astrid dreamed of a terrible storm with spears of lightning so intense that they lit up the night sky more brightly than the sunniest of days. Claps of thunder collided above as if the heavens themselves might shatter into pieces and crush her and her family sleeping in their house below. A final deafening crash rattled over her village, and Astrid heard the sound of monsoon rain poundings against the surrounding forest's leaves in the distance.

The winds whipped more violently with every passing second. Her thin roof fluttered as if it might tear away into the night. Terror gripped her chest as the sound of rushing water grew closer and closer. Only a moment later, a torrential flood swept over her village so quickly that rivers seemed to emerge from the forest in gushing ribbons, and a surge of cold water ripped open her thatched walls, swallowing up her family's house.

Astrid fought her way through the rising water to escape her collapsing home, screaming over her shoulder for her parents and little sister. The night was pitch black, lit only by flashes of lightning, but Astrid managed to climb outside and found her way to a nearby tree. She clung to its branches for safety, calling out desperately to her family, but in the rising waters, they were nowhere to be found.

That morning when Astrid awoke from her terrifying dream, the air was crisp and pleasant. Her parents and her little sister were still sleeping soundly next to her, and a soft, soothing rain fell gently on their roof. But throughout that following day, Astrid's dream would not leave her mind. Eventually, she confided in her parents about what she had seen. She begged them to leave the village and climb to higher ground—at least just for the night. "A horrible storm is on its way, and it will drown us all," she pleaded, but her parents just told her to go about her chores. "It was a bad dream, Astrid dear. Look, everything's fine. You see? It's only a light rain." When her parents wouldn't listen, she ran outside to warn the other villagers, but they too only patted her on the head and chuckled to themselves. "You worry too much, child," one of the older men scoffed.

That night, after her parents had fallen sound asleep, Astrid woke her little sister and pulled her from her bed. Together, they crept out of their house with their blankets and shoes. Outside, Astrid gathered what she could of a few morsels of food and placed them in her satchel. "Don't worry. We'll come back soon," Astrid comforted her whimpering sister as they began their ascent into the mountains.

Together, they trekked all through the night and into the following day, climbing higher and higher until finally, they stopped to make a camp together as dark clouds rolled in from the east. And sure enough, that night, a horrible storm descended over the mountain, just like the one in Astrid's dream. Heavy rains pummeled the forest, and though she and her sister were cold and without shelter, they were at least safe from the overflowing waters rushing down from the highlands.

The next morning, after the rains had subsided, Astrid and her sister began their somber journey back to their village. They silently followed the markers Astrid had left on trees, fearing what they would find when they returned home. After many hours, they reached their village, or what was left of it. Only a muddy heap of timber remained where Astrid's thatched home had once stood. "Where are momma and papa?" Astrid's little sister screamed to a nearby villager, rummaging through the wreckage. He turned toward the two children staring back up at him expectantly. It was the same older man who Astrid had warned about the storm only the day before, but his eyes were not laughing this time. Instead, they were gripped by deep sorrow. "You were right, Astrid," was all he had the strength to reply.

After the great storm, it took Astrid's village more than a year to recover from the devastating losses of their homes and crops. But healing from their lost loved ones took much longer. Why couldn't they have listened? Astrid and her sister mourned their parents until they had no more tears left to cry, but little by little, and day by day, they became stronger and rebuilt their lives, as did the rest of their broken village.

It was only after everyone had their time to grieve that the other villagers could finally realize their newfound esteem for the child dream-prophet who had warned them of their fate, and by the time Astrid had grown into a young woman, she had earned the trust and respect of not only her own village but also of the surrounding villages too. She became revered throughout the entire island for her gift. Her nightly visions were both a burden and a blessing.

She predicted when to prepare for a season of famine or for enemy attacks from the sea. And she predicted, too, when times of peace, health, and bounty were on the horizon. All the people of the island finally listened, and together they governed their lives according to Astrid's guidance. No longer was her mystifying clairvoyance something to scorn, but rather something to stand in awe of—a mystical reminder that just because we can't always touch something, doesn't mean it isn't there. It humbled the people and showed them just how much is still unknown and unseen in the waking world.

Whenever Gram would get to the parts when Astrid retold her dreams, she always spoke them in that little nursery rhyme way that she must have worked out for us beforehand. I wonder how

long she had spent preparing those stories for us. Astrid's lines
would go something like this:

> A dark wind blew over our village
> as storm clouds gathered in the distance.
> "Please," I begged my parents, "dangerous rains
> are on their way," I repeated with persistence."

Astrid always spoke her dreams in poem form like this. Gram
explained how it was not only a method of remembering but also a
tool to peel back a dream's layers and come to understand them in
a new way. "Dreams are like poems too," Gram would say. "They
allow your mind to speak one thing while really saying another."
Astrid's poems were always our favorite part of her tales. A little
flourish of magic.

That day at the lake, when Gram told us Astrid's story for the first
time, we were so late to school we might as well not have gone at
all. Perhaps it was a grim tale for eight-year-olds, but we were no
strangers to tragedy in our family. It was Gram's ability to turn a
catastrophe into a hero's epic that stuck. Gram never deluded us
about what happened to mom and dad, not in a harsh way—just an
honest one.

We stayed there on the beach until Gram had finished asking you
dozens of questions about your beetle dream. What color was the
beetle? How many legs did it have? What did it sound like when it
grew into a monster? Did you try to run away? Were you scared
when it was small, or only when it got big? And when Gram had
finally exhausted every last detail with you, she taught us how to
shape a dream's story into a little poem too, just like Astrid's.

Line by line, verse by verse, we let the puzzle of its structure unfold. Wrapping our nightmares into language was a way to conquer them, Gram said. The rhythm and rhyme help transform our terrors into something more like a song. It forces our minds to slow down—to dissect and confront what frightens us most.

Gram told us to do this exercise each time we had a dream that felt important somehow, especially the scary ones. Writing a poem, she said, gives our waking mind time to understand the mysterious rules of our dreaming one so that we no longer have to feel afraid.

I know Gram's story was just a way to soothe the nightmares of children—and a way to trick you into being brave so you'd sleep soundly through the night. But even so, Astrid's story seemed to make each windy night in Erie feel a little less dark. When Gram tucked us into bed, she always wished us "sweet dreams" and told us to never be afraid, even if the sweetness went the other way instead. "Sometimes we can see more with our Dream Eyes than with our waking ones," she would say. "Your Dream Eyes will keep watch for you while your real eyes rest."

You always loved Astrid's adventures so much when we were small. You were so willing to suspend your own disbelief. I, on the other hand, never felt quite so willing. Maybe I was more like the other villagers than like Astrid. It just felt like believing in Santa Claus or the Easter Bunny, and at that age, I thought I'd already learned the truth about all that.

But you were always more imaginative and free than I was. You were so enamored with the idea that a human being could be like a watchtower into the past and the future to keep the ones she loved safe. It was better than Wonder Woman or Superman to you. And even though your nightmares scared you, you were delighted by the thought that maybe you could secretly be a hero too. That was Gram's genius. With one story, she turned your fear into a superpower.

I can still remember those mornings at the breakfast table like they were yesterday—you, with your tongue wrapped over your top lip in concentration and your eyebrows pinched together, scribbling away in your new dream journal. You barely even touched your cereal. You wrote down every dream you had, just as Gram had instructed, and by the end of that summer, your nightmares had stopped and sleep was once again restored to our household. Gram's story about Astrid had worked. Maybe that's all a story really is in the end—a little narrative to wrap around all our questions to make sense of a world that doesn't seem to make any sense at all.

I found your dream journal on your desk when I was going through your things again the other day—"Nova" embroidered in whimsical, white threaded letters, arching over that wide eye and slice of silver crescent moon. I stared at its cover for an eternity before I could even open it. Almost every page was filled, but I couldn't bring myself to read any more than the first entry. There it was—your beetle dream in your eight-year-old handwriting.

"I was safe in my bed when I noticed a little
    beetle bug.
He came from under my door, not under the rug.
Every time I blinked, he doubled in size,
until he was a million times bigger right before my
    eyes."

I hadn't been able to cry even once since you've been gone. It was still just all stuck somewhere. Your little beetle poem finally unstuck it.

That was when I got this whole idea—writing you a letter—even if I know it's just a way for me to cope. Comfort. Company. An imaginary friend. A place to write myself stories. A remembrance of our past. A little system to try and make sense of all the fragments of feelings and memories that don't seem to fit anywhere, no matter how hard I try to file them away.

I never used Gram's Dream Eye journal the way you had used yours. I'd forgotten where I'd even put it after Gram died and we moved to this house, but I knew it had to be here somewhere. Yesterday morning, I tore up my room for over an hour trying to find it. I opened every drawer and shoebox and combed over every shelf. I'd very nearly given up and, in my frustration, flopped down on my bed to wrack my brain some more. That was when in a flash I remembered the day we'd moved in. We were each unpacking our rooms, and you'd found my journal in one of your boxes. Do you remember? You flung open my door and tossed it onto my bed like a frisbee, but you overshot, and it thudded against the wall and slipped behind the bed frame. That's where it had stayed.

As soon as I remembered, I slid my arm down behind the mattress as far as it would go between the wall and the bed frame and swept my hand along the floor. I didn't find anything except an ancient piece of rock-hard, runaway sponge candy, and a dried-out ballpoint pen. My heart sank as I resigned myself to the possibility that it might be lost forever. I wriggled myself across my mattress on my belly for one final fishing attempt in the corner. Dejected acceptance was already creeping in when suddenly I felt the dusty edges of a linen book cover against my fingertips. I lured it up, and there was Gram's little embroidered Dream Eye staring back at me, my name dancing above in threaded letters. I hadn't written a single word inside. The edges of the paper had started to age, and every page was completely blank, except for Gram's inscription inside the front cover.

"Dear Rosalyn,
Use this journal and fill its pages every day.
Record your dreams here, for they will light
　　your way.
Remember, Dream Eyes never lead you astray.

Love, Gram
P.S. In Somnis Veritas—in Latin, it means
'In Dreams There is Truth.'"

Now, here I am, fourteen years later, filling the pages that were meant for a child. I guess it just took that long to have the kind of nightmare that made me feel like I really needed it. In Somnis Veritas. In dreams there is truth. How much truth?

I'm ready to tell you what I dreamed about the night before you were killed.

I feel haunted. It won't leave me. I have to confess what I saw that night. Somewhere, deep inside myself, I knew something terrible was on its way. I know it was just a dream, but it felt like more— like an intuition I just couldn't shake, and that anxious foreboding followed me around all that next day, from the moment you woke me up on the side of my bed, right until you walked out our front door and never came back again. Somehow that dream had been a warning, only now it's too late.

I remember the sound of the door latching behind you. I remember listening to the car start from the street and the rattle of the engine growing fainter as you pulled away. What if I'd asked you not to go out that night? What if I'd gone out instead? What if I'd just told you the truth? I had a bad feeling but didn't quite know why. Would that have been enough? Would you have stayed? Would you still be here now? Sometimes I wonder if Gram's stories had some truth to them after all. Is it all my fault you're gone?

You asked me what I dreamed about our last morning together, but I couldn't answer you then. I'm finally ready to tell you now. I'll say it in a poem, just how Gram taught us as kids. I feel like one, after all—small, scared, and confused.

I hope you get this letter somehow, Nova. I miss you so much. I feel like half of my own body has been cleaved away.

Love,
Rosalyn

Dead Moon

The moonless night was chillingly quiet,
save the waves that lapped at Lake Erie's bank.
Sitting alone in the sand, I sensed movement
from the brush, and my heart suddenly sank.

With a pain-stricken limp, a beast edged toward me
as the sky fell black with the palette of a heavy storm.
I'm not sure how I knew it, but I was certain
somehow this creature was Nova in a wolf's form.

As she stumbled closer, I discerned a glinting object
and realized it was the dead moon in her jaws.
And suddenly, the heavens shattered, and every star
fell from the sky and began gashing at her paws.

Arriving at my feet, she bowed
to rest the dead moon on the ground,
and throwing back her head, she opened her mouth
to howl, but only blood poured out—not sound.

In an agonized snarl, she pulled back her lips,
revealing her perfect fangs had been removed.
My wolf sister whimpered like a helpless
pup—how could she be soothed?

I took her in my arms as her
blood soaked both our hair.
"Give me your pain now," I said.
"It's too much for only one to bear."

I kissed her forehead,
pressed her brow to mine.
"I'll find who did this," I whispered.
"They will pay in time."

And at that moment, her wolf body
exploded into starlight.
A supernova of sparkling dust
burst up into the night.

Without the moon, the lake
was a flat glass plate—
no gravity to charm its swells,
no waves to undulate.

The new wolf stars lit my reflection as I
waded into the cold water, still as could be,
and there, from its mirrored surface, a dark,
terrifying form peered back at me.

Slowly, I bent closer to see its face was
not mine but some twisted version of my own.
I inhaled sharply to speak but realized I had
no words—I was so utterly afraid and all alone.

It was then my phantom reflection spoke instead:
"I have a message for you, if I may,"
the voice hissed back, "Beware, Rosalyn.
There's something foul and evil on its way."

The Tortoise and the Cobra

Thursday, April 18, 1997

Dear Nova,

It's overcast, and there's been a strange chill running through the neighborhood for three days straight. It's more than just cold air—it's more like a mood, and it doesn't seem to be moving on any time soon. I don't know why I want to mention the weather to you, but lately, I find myself telling you all sorts of meaningless things. Sometimes I say them out loud like you're there in the room with me. Observations. Questions. Should I wear my blue hat or my black one? Are we out of Cheerios? Where'd I leave the keys? Pointless things I might ask myself, but I know they're really for you. And each time my words pass over my lips, for just a moment, I actually believe maybe there's a chance you'll answer back. But of course, you don't. You can't.

I don't think we've ever written a single letter to one another before—there was never any need. We were always right there beside each other. The whole concept of a letter is such an unbelievable act of trust, nothing more than a blind hope dispatched into the world with no guarantee of a reply. In the 1800s, it took the Pony Express days and sometimes weeks to deliver a piece of mail. Transatlantic took more than a month. How long does it take from where you are? I know these letters to you are just stories I'm telling myself, but it helps to imagine you reading them on the other side.

I'm jumpy today. Irritable. Shifty. I think I might be finally losing my grip. How can you love something so much that's no longer there? When a thing goes, why can't it just take the love with it? Why must it still slink around like your ghost?

The police still haven't found anything. Are they even looking? Do they even care? It's been over seven weeks now. In two days, it will have been two months. No fingerprints. No footprints. No DNA. Not a thread of clothing other than yours. How much longer until they give up? I've already called the station five times this week, and each time the answer is the same: "You don't need to keep calling. We'll be in touch if we have any new information," the man on the other line always tells me. He's firm but with a softness in his tone like he doesn't want to shatter me through the phone line. He always adds some polite version of, "They're doing everything they can over here." Or "You'll be the first to know if we find anything." Then he gives me the same pitiful, "Ok, Miss Whitman?" as if to signify the call is now over. And each time I hang up, it feels like I'm getting the news for the first time all over again.

The great task of this week has once again been finding inventive ways to distract my mind. I started with all the obvious diversions. I read. (*Grapes of Wrath. Catcher in the Rye.*) I did the laundry. (I stained my jeans with bleach and lost a sock at the laundromat.) I watched TV. (A nature show about animals battling each other in the African savannah.) But mostly, if I'm being honest, I just shut myself in my bedroom and passed the hours by slogging through memories, trying to find ways back to you.

I tried to trick my mind into crawling slowly in reverse, peeling back the pages of our life's manuscript, chapter by chapter, to when we were still little girls listening to one of Gram's stories by the lake. I've passed so many hours thinking about those stories. Yesterday, I spent all afternoon just lying on the floor on my back, remembering the one Gram told us about how we got our names. "Star twins," she always called us—named for the stars.

After mom and dad died and we moved in with Gram, you'd ask her to tell the story of our names all the time. It went on for years. I remember how you'd wrap me in your arms with a hug and your big toothy smile and say, "Gram, tell us again—why's my name Nova? Why's Ros's name Rosalyn?" You're like that in almost every picture taken of us when we were little—you with your skinny arms thrown around mine, pinning them to my body while I just stood there, stiff like an awkward tree stump. Ros and Nov, the star twins. So different, yet also exactly the same.

Gram's story wasn't true, of course, but we were none the wiser when we were small enough. The fiction was far better than the underwhelming reality that our names were, more likely than not, quite an afterthought to mom and dad. They had enough to worry about with no money, no plan, and surprise twins. To them, a name was probably just a sound—something to write on the forms. Maybe Gram always felt like she had to make up for that. She told the story like you and I were some sort of heroes in one of her fairytales, adding her little dashes of mysticism and magic.

January 27, 1975. We had arrived to the world on a full moon brimming with light, and so, Gram said, we were named for the stars. As far as I know, only the full moon part was true. We really had been born on a full moon. I looked it up once in an almanac. I don't think I ever told you that before. I guess I just thought you would always still believe it anyway, whether an almanac proved it or not.

According to Gram's story, you arrived to the world just minutes after me. You wailed and beat your tiny fists so fiercely that you scared the nurses. You had a fiery energy from the very first moment you were born. And then, all at once, as they tucked you in beside me in our little hospital bassinet, the brightness that exploded across your face seemed to illuminate the whole room. For the blazing light created by colliding twin stars of a supernova, you were given your name. Nova Whitman was here.

My name's origin story, on the other hand, was a little more difficult to fabricate, but Gram was always so artful in her poetic leaps of imagination. She told us my name was not only for our closest star, the sun, but also for its counterpart, the moon. A marriage of light and dark that indeed seemed to fit my personality so well. I was named for Ra, the Egyptian sun God, and for Selene, the Greek moon Goddess, who each escorted their respective orbs across the sky to create day and night. Ra and Selene. Ra Selene. Rosalyn. Together, their sounds formed my name. Children love stories. I know it was all just an invention to enchant the minds of little girls, but in a way, I think it always shaped how I thought of myself, just like I know your story shaped you too.

I always loved the vision of Ra with his human body and falcon head, driving his sun chariot in an arc clean across the sky to the west, pouring out fields of life in his wake. And then, when he neared the heaven's edge, he carefully descended the firmament and disappeared behind the horizon to preside also over the darkness and all the demons who lived on the other side. He was the ruler not just of life but of the underworld too. Gram always loved that idea best. We are all governors of both our domains. I can hear her voice now. "The darkness, my dear, is nothing to fear, only something to tend to like its own sort of garden."

It's only now that I'm older I can see what Gram did with those stories was so wise, giving us each our own identities, distinct and individual from one another, even despite all that we shared. We may have been identical twins, but I have to confess—sometimes it felt like the only thing we shared was our reflection. Our personalities, our temperaments, our ways of seeing the world— they were all so different. Yet somehow, it was always our opposing forces that seemed to bind us so closely together. Rather than duplicates of the same person, we were more like two halves of one person that had been split apart, each receiving separate pieces. We were complements, not copies. I know you always understood this too, without either of us ever needing to say it.

Maybe it all made sense, in a way. For anyone who bothered to take a closer look, it was clear enough that we were opposites. Your blue eye on the right, your brown one on the left. Mine the other way around. Your birthmark spread from the middle of your hairline down your forehead to your left eyebrow, mine veering to my right. These details were simply the subtle external evidence of what we already knew was true on the inside. Gram told us we'd gotten our birthmarks when we were born as a shooting star kissed our foreheads while we passed from another universe into this one.

We were mirrored images, not clones, and to us, it was always so obvious how to tell us apart. How did others always seem to have such a hard time? At a certain point, you just stop correcting people and instead start resenting them for not even trying. How can so many look but still never really see? And yet they always had endless questions about our birthmarks. Was it a scar? Were we sick? Even ten-year-olds can figure out a baseball cap is a simple yet effective tool for avoiding incessant examinations of the same annoying topic. Hat on. No more questions. Easy.

Recently, I can't stop thinking about Gram's story of the day we were born. I know we'll always have each other—bound together by our sisterhood—but sometimes I'm so ashamed to admit that it could also feel draining moving through the world with a second version of myself. I always wondered if you ever felt that way too but were afraid to tell me—afraid I might misunderstand your meaning, just the way I was afraid you would misunderstand mine.

I had another dream last night that's been twisting my mind around all day. It was about you again, and I can't put it out of my head. I've never dreamed so clearly in my whole life. Our bodies were joined, attached at our backs, and fused together at our spines. The base of our heads butted up against each other, and if we moved too quickly, we cracked our skulls together like coconuts. It was nearly impossible to walk—an exhausting feat of strength even to just balance upright in any semblance of coordination. I felt trapped and stifled, and I have to admit, I wanted nothing more than to be free of you—even as I was consumed by shame. It was you, after all. My sister, my other half. Nonetheless, I would have given anything to disentangle myself. My only wish was to become my own person again, moving about the world unencumbered.

Maybe in a way, that's how it always felt to be a twin. Never an individual, just always part of a pair. I often wondered what it might feel like to stand on my own in the world, not without you—maybe just apart from you somehow. But I never imagined that question would be answered like this—by losing you completely. You were always my counterbalance, my levity and light when I felt so heavy and dark. And yet, in the dream last night, I felt none of that comfort.

The first thing I remember was trying to take a step forward. My stride lurched against the weight of your body, and your heels dragged in the mud behind me. My movement nearly toppled us both. I felt so clumsy and helpless, my weary knees collapsing under our combined force. How ironic that right now, I'd do anything to carry you like that.

As I struggled to stand, I heard a rustle in the surrounding tall grass, and an enormous king cobra as thick as my thigh emerged. He slithered up to our feet and coiled his long, smooth body tightly around ours in a stiff spiral. My breath became shallow in the pressure of his grip. His soft scales felt cool against my skin, and his eyes locked straight into mine. Then he spoke, his forked tongue tasting the air so close to my face I could feel its vibrations against my cheek.

His voice was no more than a hissing whisper, and his words seemed to hypnotize me, offering me what I most desired. He could separate our bodies, he told me. He could cut me loose from you and let me go free, but for a price, he said. The cobra wanted to keep you as his trade—for a meal, I assumed. Perhaps we were too large for him to swallow as a pair. I'm repulsed to write it now, Nova, but in the dream, for just a moment, I was tempted to consider his offer.

As I reckoned with his proposition, his scaly grasp constricted against our bodies, and I thought perhaps he'd just kill us both before I could give my answer. It was then I heard a second voice from somewhere just beyond my view, and immediately the cobra's grip slackened. An old, giant tortoise crawled out of the tall grass and arrived at our feet in slow motion. Her words seemed to creak out of her ancient body as she scolded the cobra as if he was nothing more than a silly old fool. It was clear who held the power.

I was relieved by the intervention but felt I had no choice but to confess to the old tortoise that I wasn't sure I had the strength to navigate the world with all your weight bound to my back. The cobra had indeed appealed to my weakness. I pleaded for the tortoise's guidance, and when I'd finished my lament, she stretched her long wrinkled neck out of her shell and raised her gentle head toward mine. She told me my solution was all very simple, although her words didn't immediately make any sense. She said I could find all the strength I would need each night in my dreams. I didn't know what that meant. It sounded like a line right out of one of Gram's stories.

When I awoke, I felt foggy, still stuck on the precipice of sleep. Had I been dreaming at all? I laid on my side under the covers, replaying the scene, wishing I could again be close to you, even if in the dream I'd desired the very opposite.

The longer I lay there, the more I began to wonder if I had misunderstood. Maybe that feeling of heaviness was not the weight of being bound by you—just the weight of loving someone so much. The responsibility. The constant paralyzing risk that you could lose the people you love in an instant—and to keep them close, you must suffer too. Maybe that's the real weight you carry when you love someone.

I rested under the covers on my side for what felt like hours, but I'm sure in reality, it was only minutes. As I became more conscious of the brisk morning air filling my lungs, I fought my way back to the dream, forcing my mind to hold on for just a moment longer. A few more nearly forgotten details surfaced from the depths of my psyche as I desperately attempted to paint them into permanent memory, and I fell back into the haze of the dream's scene, my heart racing as I lost all sense of my surroundings. I was no longer in my bedroom but back in the savannah with the feeling that you might still be right there, only just behind me.

I swallowed a deep breath and held it in, working up the courage to roll over onto my other side. Part of me truly believed that if only I turned over, I might find you there, still attached to me, your skin growing into mine.

I exhaled slowly, my eyes pinched shut as tightly as they would go, and finally, I shifted to my other side, expecting a miracle. When I opened my eyes again, I was still alone.

Love,
Rosalyn

The Tortoise and the Cobra

My body felt clumsy and out of balance
from some force I couldn't immediately see.
I tried to take a step forward, but
an unexpected weight arrested me.

In a shock, I looked down at my feet
to discover I had not two but now four.
And suddenly, I sensed a second skull behind
my own—although whose? I was not yet sure.

Then, at once, I realized it was Nova—our bodies
growing into one another's from our spine,
and for an instant, I felt reassured—safe forever
in this inseparable company of my own bloodline.

But only a second later, I was overcome
with a sudden jolt of overpowering dread.
I was ashamed that at that moment
I truly wished myself dead.

Forever joined back to back
to my identical human form—
not just my sister but my twin—I felt
only a foreboding chill against her warm.

For even though I am her,
even though she is me,
against the weight of her
body, I yearned to be free.

It was then a cobra emerged from
the tall grasses and stared me in the eyes.
I felt sure this was how Nova
and I were to meet our demise.

He coiled around us, only scales
and fangs as far as my eye could see.
Resigned to death, I waited for his strike,
but instead, in a hiss, he spoke to me.

"Surrender to me now, and
you'll be given what you're owed.
I can free you—never again shall you
have to carry such a heavy load."

"What's your price?" I asked,
nervously considering his proposal.
He looked over my shoulder, implying his meaning—
"Only that which you have at your disposal..."

It was then, from out of sight, that I
heard a slow and creaky voice speak.
"Excuse us, king cobra, but how
dare you presume her so weak."

A tortoise had appeared, rebuking our captor:
"Cobra, surely there's some other dupe you can find."
Then, turning her old head gently to me,
"Don't pay that nasty old scale-bag any mind."

"Tortoise," I pleaded, "I can barely stand.
Perhaps I really am too weak."
How am I to continue? Where is this
unwavering strength that I seek?"

"Listen carefully," she replied.
"I'll tell you all that you need to know.
Just remember, any challenge, after all,
is only an invitation to truly grow.

Yes, it's true. You bear a heavy load, though
you would surely mourn it if it were gone.
Never give up and surrender only to dreams, for a
replenished strength awaits you with each new dawn."

"Am I dreaming now?" I asked her as the
cobra released his grip and slithered away.
"How do I know?" she winked back. "I'm just an old
tortoise—that's something only you can say."

One Song

Friday, May 2, 1997

Dear Nova,

I'm still getting used to talking to you like this. It helps to feel like I can always reach you in these pages whenever I need. I never minded being alone before. I rather preferred it, relieved when we got back to the quiet of our home after hours of ingesting the exhausting blather of the world. Kids at school, customers at work, strangers in line at the grocery store. It all sounded the same. Solitude was always a reprieve. But these days, now that my solitude is no longer a choice but a mandate, I can't seem to bear it. I miss sharing my aloneness with you.

These letters to you are the only times my words feel honest. I store them up over the days so I can pour them out truthfully here. Better to sweep them together all at once than to whittle them down to toothpicks the way you always have to do for polite company until the words become so diluted and meaningless they no longer deserve to be spoken at all. Even if I wanted a genuine conversation, who would listen? Who else could understand?

I know I have no way of getting these letters to you, and yet, I'm compelled to pick up my pen. Is it an act of trust? Of hope? Of desperation? A desire for connection? A refusal of abandonment? It's as if the very gesture of committing these words to ink serves as some invisible contract—with whom, I couldn't say. These pages are a wager that somewhere out there, there's someone ready to receive them on the other end, even if I can't understand how. Isn't that why any writer writes?

Sometimes I wonder if you really might be receiving my letters. I wonder if you're out there, in some new form, feeling my words. Not as a ghost. Not reincarnated. Not in heaven. I'm not sure what I mean. But as I write this sentence, I think it out loud too, and I imagine you hearing it. I wish you could write me back somehow. Perhaps you already have, in your own way—I just haven't yet found your reply.

It's been exactly nine weeks now since you've been gone, and from where I'm standing, it doesn't seem like anyone resembling law enforcement is even remotely trying to get answers. If they are, I certainly haven't been privy to their progress. It's been nothing but radio silence and waiting. The morning after, it felt like the cops would never leave. Now, they won't even call. There must have been at least six officers here that morning, plus that detective, all of them practically crawling through every corner of the house. Where are they now?

Two more officers came by the house again the week after it happened, but it was only to return our car. They said they'd impounded it for evidence, dusted everything for fingerprints, and checked for signs of forced entry, but nothing unusual revealed itself. One of the officers told me that usually, they make you come to pick up the car yourself or pay to get it towed, but given the circumstances, they must have taken pity on me and bent the rules somehow. They knew we shared one car. I guess they thought it was the least they could do. "You're all set," the first officer said as he handed me the keys and a piece of paper. "You'll just need to fill out this change of title form to put the car all in your name and then take it over to Penn DOT to get it processed." I nodded in a trance. "Drive safely," the other officer had said as he turned to leave, like it was the only thing he could think of to say.

And that was it. That was my last and only other interaction with the police—besides the day they showed up with your news. No more visits. No more calls. Nothing, except sitting alone in the house on standby, trapped with my thoughts.

Then, finally, the day after I last wrote you, the phone rang. A deep voice I vaguely recognized was on the other line. "Hello, Ms. Whitman. I'm with the Erie Police Department," the voice began. But it wasn't a call to tell me they'd found something. It wasn't even to tell me they hadn't found something but were still working diligently. Instead, it was the same detective who'd come by the house with the news. Detective John Singer. He said he needed to ask me a few more questions. I thought I'd already answered all his questions before. I was the one with the questions now.

Singer's voice was flat and emotionless on the other line. He asked if he could come by the house to talk. He phrased it as a question as if I had a choice in the matter, but of course, I didn't. I knew he'd show up whether he was invited or not. His brown Buick was parked in front of our house only an hour later.

I didn't know how you're supposed to host a detective, so I just offered him some tap water and led him to the kitchen table. We sat facing one another in awkward silence until a tiny pad of paper and a pen materialized from his jacket pocket. He seemed to purse his lips together before he spoke, but it was hard to see the details of his expressions under his thick mustache. He's exactly what I always imagined a detective was supposed to look like. Maybe when you look like him, they just hand you a badge right out of the womb.

"I'm going to ask you a number of questions if that's alright with you," he said slowly across the table. "Some of them I already asked you before. Some of them may be new. We just find that when people are under immense amounts of stress from the kind of shock like you've experienced, memories can sometimes be…" he paused, searching for a word, "unreliable."

He looked across at me, studying my face for a reaction.

"OK," I said with my arms crossed, my line of sight only just barely clearing the brim of my hat.

"Baseball fan?" he asked, tapping his index finger to his forehead. I wasn't sure if the questions had officially started. I was confused about how baseball had come into the equation. It took me a second to register that I was wearing my SeaWolves hat with the navy visor and light blue crown. I still couldn't name a single player if you offered me a million bucks on the spot, but I always liked that pirate wolf logo.

"Not really," I answered flatly. Was he trying to be friendly? I felt on edge.

"First time I've seen you wear a hat. I thought you might be a fan," he seemed to elaborate. Was he making small talk?

"No more or less than the next person. It's just a hat," I offered. "We wear hats most of the time." By "we," I meant you and me, of course. It felt uncomfortable referring to us without you there, and even stranger using the present tense. My sister wore hats—past tense.

"You like how they look?" he pressed on.

"Not particularly," I answered coldly. Singer sucked in a slow breath through his nose like he was physically gathering his composure.

"Maybe they just make things easier for you, then," he said, completing his own thought since I was making no effort to do it for him. As soon as we'd sat down, I'd already decided I would only be answering his questions precisely as they were asked and no more. Maybe it wasn't fair of me, but I was angry. My patience had already run dry weeks ago. After all this time, and suddenly now he decides he has more questions?

"Yes, they make things easier," I repeated.

Singer nodded to himself gently.

"Because … you look different?" he asked.

"That's one way to put it," I answered.

"It's a birthmark on your forehead, is that correct?"

I nodded.

"Have you or your sister ever been bullied or threatened? Harassed? Anything like that?"

I lowered my chin, the brim of my hat shading my eyes from his. I took a moment to think about how I would answer his question.

The image of our lockers flashed across my mind, the words "WEDNESDAY FREAKS" scrawled in Sharpie, the rushed, adolescent handwriting stretching the full length of both our side-by-side doors. It only took one day in sixth grade of showing up to class in pigtail braids for them to latch on to a Wednesday Addams reference, and they didn't get bored with that nickname until halfway through high school. How exquisitely creative thirteen-year-olds can be. I never fully understood how the likeness was an insult, and even at that age, we appreciated how truly pathetic the taunt was, but it didn't make it hurt any less. School had it scrubbed off, but not a month later, two demonic caricatured versions of our faces appeared in its place. The bullies had taken the liberty of giving us long serpent tongues, and we had more of what looked like horns protruding from our foreheads than just our modest birthmarks.

Another memory flashed past, this time years later—our car covered in shaving cream. The ingredients had reacted with the paint somehow, and it left permanent wispy marks all over the hood—they even left the half-empty can resting shamelessly right there on our roof. Between the two of us, it had taken us a year and a half of overtime at Orly's to pay for that car, and even then, we still needed a little extra help from Gram.

Then another: a prank love letter from that boy who, of course, did not really like me at all. You got one too around the same time from another boy. Is it any wonder why we've always preferred our own company? Then another: a rumor that spread like wildfire around the school that you and I were secretly in a romantic relationship with each other. And another: that mom and dad hadn't died at all, but were forced to abandon us because we were cursed.

These things hurt when you're young. Sticks and stones, right? But how to answer Singer's question?

"Nothing that ever became violent," I said softly, assuming that was the relevant piece of the answer he was after.

Singer let a moment of silence pass. His upper lip shifted, bristling his mustache like a furry caterpillar.

"Let's get back to that night then. Do you remember what time your sister left the house?"

"Maybe around 6:30? 7?" I said. "I remember it was dark already."

"Did you hear the car start?"

"You can hear it from anywhere in the house. The muffler is shot and it takes a few minutes to warm up," I said.

Singer pursed his lips in concentration, his mustache fanning out like the bottom of a broom. "Why was your sister parked alone down at the lake? I thought you said she left for groceries. Does that seem unusual to you?"

"No," I answered bluntly. "We've been going almost every day since we were kids, and dusk is best for walleye. Sometimes we fish. Sometimes we just look at the water and have a few minutes of peace."

Singer scribbled on his pad.

Singer's inventory of questions continued for what must have been at least ten minutes—the same questions he'd asked the morning you were found. Maybe it's just protocol, but the repetition of his inquiry felt like an intrusion somehow. A violation. Why did he need to put me through all this again? He sat across from me in the very same way that morning, scribbling with his silver pen on that tiny pad of paper as I answered from my daze on the couch.

Had anyone been by the house earlier that day? What about earlier that week? Had we noticed anything suspicious? Anything out of the ordinary leading up to that night in general? No. Had we noticed any cars following us? No. Were we dating anyone? Ha! Absolutely not. Did we owe money? No. Has anyone been in a disagreement with either of us recently?

No. No. And no. We keep to ourselves. Nothing suspicious. No disagreements. Singer paused and took a sip of his tap water.

"What about you two?"

"What-about-us-two-what?" I repeated back, genuinely not understanding.

"Had you and your sister been in a disagreement recently?" he said, pressing the tip of his pen against his pad without moving it. "With each other," he added, sensing I still hadn't grasped his question.

What did he mean, "had we been in a disagreement with each other?" Of course not. "No," I told him with defense in my voice. You and I don't argue. We tease and joke but never argue.

"When your sister left, was she upset by anything? Did Nova ever act out in any way you are aware of?" Singer asked.

"What is that supposed to mean?" I asked back, feeling a rush of protectiveness.

"I mean, did she ever have any tendencies to rebel or find ways to let off steam?"

I didn't like where he was going. How dare he try to turn things around? How could he even suggest it? You're not the one on trial. Besides, you had been in good spirits all day, just like you always are. You're the most even-keeled person I've ever known.

"No," I said flatly.

Singer adjusted himself in his chair and scratched his mustache before scribbling down more notes. "You said after your sister left that you fell asleep on the couch and can't remember anything further. Is that account correct? Are you always such a heavy sleeper?" Singer's voice seemed twinged with suspicion. I didn't like how he asked it. I noticed my body tightening and wondered if my disdain was palpable. I felt the hot pressure of contempt bulging in my temples.

I told him I had barely slept the night before and was exhausted, which was the truth. Singer looked up from his pad with each question and studied my face as I spoke.

"Do you or your sister ever do drugs?"

At first, the question surprised me. Then it enraged me. Drugs? I felt like a child being accused of something I hadn't done. I didn't understand what he was getting at—all I knew was that if my eyes could burn holes, Singer's forehead would match ours.

"Drugs were never our idea of fun," I told him as calmly as I could, but with a deliberate defensiveness in my voice. Even if it was, we're not the criminals in this scenario.

"There are plenty of reasons people do drugs that aren't about fun," Singer pressed. "Maybe that's true," I scowled back, "but not us. Not Nova. At most, we have a couple beers at home. That's legal, isn't it?" I said with as much sarcasm as I could muster.

"It is," Singer answered dryly. "I noticed your sister kept some kind of diary when she was young. The black one in her room with the eye on the front. The entries ended in 1986. Did she keep a more recent diary that you know of? That could be very helpful."

"No," I told him.

Why was he asking these questions? His tone felt distantly accusatory. It was like he needed me to prove myself to him—like he thought I was withholding some secret that he wanted a piece of. What was he getting at? Something private? Something shared only between sisters? Something I wouldn't tell a cop? But I can't tell him more than what I know. And the only thing I know that Singer doesn't is something I wasn't about to offer freely. There was something out of the ordinary leading up to that night. I knew something awful was coming. I can admit it now—I felt it from the moment I woke up that morning. If only I'd told you about that dream, would I be writing this letter?

But dreams aren't evidence. There's no reason Singer needs to know about something like that. It would only make me sound delusional. Certain things are best kept to yourself.

Singer took a sip from his water glass, and we sat across from one another in tense silence. His questions were finally finished, and so were my answers. His face seemed strained. I could sense that he was not satisfied, and perhaps he could sense that I was offended.

But I don't owe him anything. He's the one who owes me an explanation. You're my sister, and it's his job to bring criminals to justice. It had been two months by then, and still, he had nothing new to tell me. Instead, he has the audacity to come to our house and imply that I'm the one who's done something wrong. Eat dirt.

"That's all for now. Thank you for your time," he said finally, signifying his visit was now over. I took Singer's glass to the sink and led him back to the front door. Singer paused on the porch, looked back at me, and said he'd "be in touch," whatever that meant. He handed me his business card. "Call if you can think of anything you'd like to add," he said distantly.

I shut the door after him and watched through the window until his beat-up brown Buick pulled away down the street. The instant he was out of view around the corner, I felt a wave of wild anxiety overtake my body. I had to sit on the floor just to keep myself from losing my balance, and that's where I stayed for hours, replaying Singer's questions and our last day together all over again. I re-lived as many details as I could conjure, but the more I tried to remember, the more I realized how little I actually did. My stomach clenched.

That morning, I remember with pristine clarity. Your prank, startling me awake on the side of my bed, and the ensuing uneasiness that followed as I recounted that awful dream—you as that wounded wolf and my ghoulish reflection in the lake. I remember you asking me what I'd dreamed, and I remember lying about it too.

We had the day off from work, but it was so cold out we decided to lounge around the house all day and relax. You and I hardly talked all day—we were just pleasantly alone together, each wrapped up in our own solitary activities. I remember you practicing your flute in your room for most of the afternoon. As the day wore on, I surrendered to my exhaustion, conceding that I wouldn't be of much use at anything productive. Nonetheless, I managed to stay awake on the couch with my book long enough to feel optimistic reading might be the one activity that wouldn't be a lost cause.

Somehow I made it through more than a few chapters, and before I knew it, daylight was done. The street lamps met the darkness with a soft, fluorescent glow through the gaps in the living room window shades. We still hadn't gone shopping for food, but we had plenty in the house to tide us over: half a batch of chili from Gram's famous recipe, a box of frozen waffles, and some leftover pepperoni balls. You knew I hadn't slept well—I was grouchy and lethargic, so you offered to pick up groceries on your own. Eggs, milk, and whatever else looked appetizing to fill our stomachs for the next few days. I agreed, but something about it immediately felt wrong, although I wasn't sure why.

Just before you closed the door, you shouted over your shoulder that you were heading to the lake for a quick walk before hitting Serafin's. You only had a little while before it closed—it would have to be only a momentary visit. I remember how the sound of the door latching behind you had sent an electrified shudder through my chest, and suddenly that same uneasy feeling gripped every inch of my body once again. "Something foul and evil is on its way," I heard a faint voice whisper in the recesses of my mind.

"You're just tired," I told myself. "Stop worrying again. It's nothing. You get jumpy when you don't sleep," I thought. "Read your book. A little distraction will cure everything."

That's where I start to forget the details. I remember the crocheted blanket over my legs, my toes poking through the loose weave. I vaguely recollect laying my book across my chest. I'd meant only to rest my eyes and wait for the sound of your keys in the door, but that must have been when I fell asleep. It wasn't until I woke up to the sound of heavy knocking on the front door and saw daylight spilling in through the shades that I realized it was already tomorrow, and I'd slept clean through the night.

I jolted upright in a flood of panic, but I didn't stand right away. A paralyzing fear swept over my body as if somehow I already knew what was waiting outside, and I couldn't bear to confront it. I could see the edge of the door's frame from where I lay on the couch and felt momentarily disoriented. I thought I'd fallen asleep facing the other way around. I must have turned around at some point in my sleep, too groggy and comatose to even remember moving. Finally, I rose to my feet and called out your name like you'd be able to hear me from your room upstairs, but I knew from the feeling inside my chest that you weren't there. When I opened the door to two uniformed officers, somehow, I already knew what they were about to say too.

I watched their mouths move, but I couldn't hear the words—all I could hear was the sound of my own ears ringing. Everything went woolly. Suddenly, I was not myself—rather a passive spectator to a scene in someone else's story, watching it unfold through thick, fogged goggles.

Maybe Singer understood that feeling well. He must see that sort of thing all the time in his line of work—one shell-shocked person after another. Maybe that's the only reason he stopped by again with all his questions—he needed to hear my answers a second time after the numbing shockwave had finished passing through me.

By now, I've replayed that day more times than I can count, as if securing every last detail might somehow change things. But change things how? Bring you back? Rewrite the past? Maybe I just need answers, just like Singer wanted answers from me. It's funny how the more times you relive a memory, the less its outlines seem convincing.

None of this makes sense. Why were you killed? Who could do something like that? And how is it possible that I could have such an unshakable feeling that something horrible was about to happen before it actually did?

Before a storm rolls in over the lake, all the birds get quiet on the beach. They know they need to brace themselves, and by the time the first crash of thunder rattles the sky, they've already found shelter in the thicket. They've learned to read nature's many signs. The wind, the sun, the smells. Mother nature makes sense. She subscribes to logic and laws. She offers tangible clues. But this was just a dream—just a feeling. How was I supposed to know it was more real than any storm? People have meaningless dreams all the time. If we all heeded the nonsense of our sleeping brains as if it were truth, the world would be a loony bin.

In a way, maybe Singer's suspicions are justified. Perhaps I do have a secret. But there's no way I'll ever tell him or anyone else about that dream. I can only tell you. Even if I could, I'd sound like a lunatic—or simply pitiful. A sad girl who will tell herself anything just to make the world seem a little less mad. But Nova, I swear to you, somewhere locked away in myself, I knew something foul and evil was on its way, precisely as my reflection staring back from Lake Erie's shallows had told me.

Why didn't I ask you to stay? Why didn't I go instead? Why can't I remember falling asleep after you left? Protection from my own guilt? The convenient shield of forgetfulness? A tool the mind employs to ward off pain and injury, no different from the swelling that defends a broken bone or a scab that keeps you from bleeding out. Self-preserving amnesia. How could I let you go? I knew something terrible was coming. I just wouldn't let myself believe it then.

And now you're gone. Is the universe truly so void of logic? Of laws? Or is life just inherently chaotic and cruel?

I feel like a few of my screws are coming loose. I'm always alone, my mind free to spin itself in circles. When I look in the mirror, I don't always recognize myself. My face looks unfamiliar. Longer. Older. Maybe it's just the drain of anger, the grief of brokenness, or the fatigue of constantly missing you. I feel myself changing a little more every day. I'm awakening into some other creature entirely as some kind of feral restlessness sets in. It's like I'm discovering some new dimension in my own nature that I never knew was there and can't yet put into words.

Another week passed after Singer came by the house with his stack of questions. I sat around anxiously all weekend, anticipating the sound of the phone ringing, but there wasn't a single call—not even from those Channel 24 reporters, all of whom I've refused to speak a word to. How could there still be no news from Singer after the theater of his inquisition at the kitchen table? Are they even looking? I've read the statistics. Every day without new evidence or a lead is a higher probability that a case will never close. By the following Monday morning, I'd made up my mind. Now I'd be the one to pay Singer a visit. It was time to make a trip to the station.

I'd never even once paid any attention to the police department building before, and I wasn't even sure if that's where I'd find Singer, but it certainly seemed like the best place to start. I parked the car across the street a few blocks away and made my way toward the front entrance. Two uniformed officers were leaving, and as we approached one another on the sidewalk, I watched how their faces changed, visibly spooked by my very presence. I'd left my hat in the car on purpose. I wanted Singer to see your face when he looked into mine. I realized right away that's what the other officers saw too. While no one seems to be doing anything about your case, by now, at least, everyone seems to know what we look like.

To them, I was you, walking around alive and well again, right before their eyes—and then, I watched the realization wash over their faces, one at a time, as they remembered you had a twin sister. A little light bulb went off behind their eyelids, and the look of surprise in their countenance shifted to pity. They each gave me an apologetic little nod as we passed. I didn't react. I just kept walking. I was too angry. What happened to you isn't their fault. I know that. But all this time without answers? Without any justice? That does seem like their responsibility.

Answers. Justice. That's what I was on the hunt for. And if I'm being honest, maybe I was also on the hunt for someone or something to blame. The lobby of the station was empty when I swung open the entrance door, and I marched right up to a man with thick-rimmed glasses behind what I assumed was bulletproof glass. "How can I help you, Miss Whitman," he said through a chrome speaker vent. He knew my name already. Maybe he was the same man I'd spoken to when I'd called so many times before. Still, I found it unnerving.

"I'd like to speak with Detective Singer," I said in as stern a voice as I could summon. "I'll see if he's in," the man said. "If you could have a seat on the bench behind you, I'll let you know if he's free." He picked up the phone but didn't immediately dial. I felt his eyes follow me as I walked away.

As instructed, I took my seat on a worn wooden bench fastened to the wall next to two rusted flagpoles—the Pennsylvania State flag closest to me and the American flag on the other side. Flags look so sad and perfunctory when hung indoors without wind to unfurl their full color and design. Instead, they sag motionless, collapsing in on themselves like wet towels hung up on a peg to dry. That was how I felt about Singer. Obligatory. For decoration only. Not observably useful.

Initials and obscenities were carved in messy knife hashes on the edge of the bench next to my knee, and I wondered what kind of person would have the nerve to vandalize police property with a potentially deadly weapon in a police station. Probably just the type of person who hangs out in a police station. The bulletproof glass at the dispatcher window suddenly made more sense.

A few minutes later, Singer emerged behind a heavy door. "Hello, Miss Whitman," he said from across the lobby. My legs straightened automatically. As I approached, I noticed a small gray patch of hair in his mustache, which somehow I hadn't observed the other two times we'd met. For whatever reason, that day at the station, my mind felt sharper—more attuned to absorbing the details of my environment for which I simply hadn't had the capacity before. How long had I been living in this fog? Singer's thick mustache appeared much longer than I'd recalled, and his strong eyebrows seemed to grow right down the bridge of his nose. He looked like a detective alright—but the name "Singer" didn't seem to fit somehow.

He gestured for me to follow, leading me into the belly of the station, and escorting me through a few meandering rows of desks littered with manilla folders and loose papers. Some had officers seated behind them, some without. A series of cork boards on the far wall displayed an assemblage of printed paper bulletins, photographs, and Triple A regional maps. We turned a corner and reached Singer's office at the back of the building. He closed the door behind us and requested that I have a seat. His eyes looked tired as they settled on a paperweight at the edge of his desk—a tiny version of the scales of justice suspended in glass. It seemed like he was avoiding looking at me.

My anger had already been at a low but steady simmer since I first stepped out of the car, but I hadn't fully noticed my temper swelling as I followed on Singer's heels to his office. By the time I sat in an uncomfortable upholstered chair facing his desk, a trembling rage had already overtaken my body, like a tea kettle with a broken whistle silently boiling over. I didn't acknowledge it outwardly. I just felt my skin flush with heat and my eyes grow wide without my permission. It seemed like I might be shaking, but when I looked down at my hands, they were steady. I didn't speak a word, but I'm sure Singer could read my face. He knew why I was there. I didn't need to say it. He knew I was the one who'd come for answers this time.

I crossed my arms, digging my fingers into my biceps as I waited for him to begin. I thought he owed it to me to speak first. There had to be some news. But instead, he just shifted in his seat, turning an empty paper coffee cup with his thumb and index finger in little circles on his desk like he was deciding about something. When the officers outside had looked at me, their faces lowered in pity and slightly nodded out of respect. Singer never does either. He always just seems to study me.

We sat like this, neither of us saying a word, until finally, Singer cleared his throat, made a face like something sharp had just stabbed him in the foot, and opened a creaky drawer in his desk's filing cabinet. He retrieved a brown folder and rested it softly in front of me. His face went blank, and his lips tightened under his mustache.

Singer must have known from the moment the dispatcher had breathed my name that there was no use asking me to leave until he'd given me something. I guess he still didn't have anything to give me besides what was inside that brown folder. I looked down at it, then back up at him. The words "POLICE DEPARTMENT HOMICIDE CASE FILE" were stamped in all capital letters on its cover below the Pennsylvania State seal. Names and dates were scribbled in rows over a half-empty gridded table. Singer dragged his hand to his face, cradling his chin and splaying his fingers across his cheek, partially covering his mouth. "If you need to look, you can," he said through his fingers, "but I strongly advise that you do not." His words were punctuated, graveled, and firm.

In an instant, I felt the anger drain from my posture, and all I could feel was my heart pounding through my ribcage. I knew why Singer didn't want me to look in that folder. Even at the coroner, they wouldn't let me look at you. They just handed me your little gold star necklace in a plastic bag, asked me to sign your release papers for the mortuary, and sent me home.

I reached out with my right hand, slid the folder into my lap, and opened the cover. At first, I didn't even know what I was looking at. I can barely write the words now. Your face was white as a sheet —like you weren't even a person—more like some wax sculpture from a museum. Were these pictures real? The cognitive dissonance was too great—it still is. It feels impossible to reconcile how I know you as my sister and the images staring back at me.

The rest of the world seemed to fall away, my chair suddenly nothing more than a clumsy life raft bobbing miles out at sea. My panicked mind struggled to fathom the scene before me. At once, the truth felt more real than ever. Nova, what happened to you? Your eyes were still open wide in a blank, expressionless stare. Your face was covered in dried blood—it dripped in thick streaks down your chin. Your cheeks were sunken like an old woman without her false teeth, but it wasn't an old woman's face—it was you.

Another faint memory from the coroner's flitted to the surface of my mind, and I remembered overhearing an officer whispering in the hall. My back was to him while I waited for the forms, and he must not have known I was there. If he had, I'm sure he would never have uttered the words. "The freakshow even took her teeth," he had said. I didn't know what that meant then. "Took her teeth." Surely, it couldn't have been literal—some sort of police jargon. Or about another case, I thought. It was too gruesome of a statement to make sense at the time. And, of course, I never let my mind go so far as to visualize it. But there in Singer's office were the pictures to match. What the officer had whispered that day was not police slang. It was true. It was real. And it was about you.

I'm not sure how long I sat there, transfixed and unable to look away, though still not understanding. I must have been in shock—I don't know how else I could have looked for so long. Picture after picture of a body I know as well as my own lying limp and cold in the sand. I thought my heart might break free from my chest and fling itself from my body. I vaguely sensed perspiration gathering on my upper lip.

I reached the last of the photographs, a closeup of your neck, your little star necklace still clasped around it. Whoever did this to you had no interest in gold. They left it right there for the police to find —left it for us to see that the violence itself was enough.

I don't know what happened next. I just remember two officers helping me off the floor several feet from the entrance to Singer's office. Singer was on his hands and knees next to me, hurriedly sweeping up your pictures back into his brown folder, glancing over at me with a look of remorse and shame. Maybe I shouldn't have looked. After all, Singer advised me not to—but then again, he also let me. Perhaps I should have listened, but I had to know what happened to you. I needed the truth.

When the officers finally got me upright again, Singer asked me if I felt well enough to speak for a few minutes longer in his office. An officer with a tight bun led me back to the same chair I'd been sitting in before. She disappeared around the corner and reappeared moments later with a flimsy white paper cup full of ice-cold water and placed it on the desk in front of me. I heard Singer whispering outside, and a few moments later, he reemerged, closed the door behind himself, and took a seat back at his desk.

My anger was gone, replaced only with overwhelming nausea. I reached slowly for the water but realized my hands had gone numb. Waiting for the blood to return, I squeezed and released my fists. Singer opened his filing cabinet drawer, slotted back the brown folder, and shut it with a clang. "Take a few minutes," he said calmly, "and then I'd like to speak with you briefly about what you just saw."

"I'm ready now," I said. Singer nodded politely but took his time. His eyes lowered to my hands in my lap, now a jaundiced shade of yellow from my knuckles down to my fingertips. I'm sure by the looks of me, I didn't appear ready. He raised his paper coffee cup to his lips again, even though I could tell it was already empty. He seemed to procure an imaginary last drop and tossed the cup into a trash bin behind his chair. He took a deep, slow inhale and leaned his elbows against his desk, lacing together his fingers.

His words came out flat and low like tired marching soldiers. "Your sister's case is more than a typical homicide," he began. "It was particularly methodical, but we have no motive. Your sister's wallet was untouched. She was wearing a gold necklace that was untouched as well. We also have limited evidence. No witnesses have come forward. We found only one set of fingerprints, but those belonged to your sister. There were parts of a boot print in the sand, but they were mostly brushed away. Without a complete imprint, we don't have enough to positively ID a size. And as you already know, there was no forced entry to your car."

Singer took a pausing breath and scratched his mustache before starting again. "The nature of your sister's murder shares many characteristics with a ritualized killing. Sometimes a killer may take something from the victim with them. As you saw in the pictures, many of your sister's teeth were missing," he said, studying me as if to gauge whether or not I had understood. I hadn't. What could he possibly mean by that? Ritualized killing. Take something with them. My hands were still numb, and the ribs just above my heart had started to ache.

"In other words," Singer continued, "we believe the killing itself was the motive—psychological gratification for an extremely disturbed individual. Rarely is a case like your sister's an isolated event. We strongly suspect that a homicide of this nature is connected to more. Quite frankly, we don't have the type of expertise or resources for serial murders in Erie, nor do we have any other files that match this profile in the state of Pennsylvania. We should likely be looking across state lines. The perpetrator could have been in Ohio or New York State within twenty minutes of leaving the crime scene. I know this is all difficult information, but I hope it can be of some comfort to you that we've been working with a federal unit from Pittsburgh that specializes in cases like your sister's. They've been putting together their own profile and will be taking the lead in facilitating cooperation between law enforcement agencies in other states. They'll be sharing any new information as it arises. That, I can assure you."

My mind felt incapable of processing the flood of new information into any logical reaction. Instead, it only conjured a more primal response. I felt another wave of anger beginning to bubble up. I didn't say anything back. I just scowled, not looking directly at Singer's face but just beyond it. I couldn't look him in the eye. A moment of silence passed between us. Singer cleared his throat. "Rosalyn, how did it make you feel to see those pictures of your sister?" The question caught me off guard. What did he mean, "How did it make me feel?" How did he think it made me feel? What kind of question was that? I didn't come all the way to the station to talk to him about my feelings, nor had he seemed to care much about mine thus far.

I didn't immediately have words that felt like an answer. If I'm being honest, I don't know what I felt. Instead of a feeling, a memory from Critter's farm flashed across my mind. I remember when Gram dropped us off for the summer, she got out of the car and gave him the tightest hug I'd ever seen her give anyone. "Teach them something useful in life, already," she teased with a toothy grin, the way only siblings can.

By then, Critter had already taught us everything there was to learn about our bows. How to replace our strings, how to wax them. How to disassemble our sight and stabilizer. How to inspect the arrows. Cracked nocks. Damaged fletching. How to stomp out and rotate our targets. We hadn't even gotten our bags to our rooms when he asked us, "How 'bout we get out into the woods more this year?" By that fall, we were back almost every weekend, hiking, creek fishing, or crouched behind a ground blind with a doe bleat listening to the sounds of the forest.

I remember the first doe I ever hit as vividly as if it were that day in Singer's office. You, me, and Critter tracked her for hours. My shot had been too low, and we all knew there was a good chance we might not recover her at all, but when we finally found an ant-covered pool of blood in the leaves, we knew we were close. By then, she'd had plenty of time to bed down and bleed out. The last of the dried November foliage crunched under our feet as we approached her fallen body. Critter was just behind me, and I was trying so hard not to let him catch sight that I was silently crying underneath the brim of my hat. "Remember how I showed you. This one's yours," Critter said as he squatted next to her lifeless head. "Thank her for her life, and dress her on up now."

I rested my hand on the doe's beautiful head, tears streaming down my face. Her big black eyes were wide open. I tagged her ear just as he'd taught us, and Critter handed me his knife. By then, it was no secret to him that I was crying. In my effort to suppress my tears, my chest had begun spasming, and I needed to gasp to breathe. I made the first incision under her tail in between my own little whimpers. And then, all at once, her soft pink flesh folded open, and I felt that same overpowering wave of nausea. The smell was putrid. My blood rushed to my stomach, and my eyesight went cloudy, then black. The next thing I remembered was waking up on my side with Critter down on his knees in the leaves next to me. Those are the only two times I've ever passed out—the day of my first kill shot with you and Critter and last week at the police station with Singer and your pictures.

What I saw at the station that day was more horrible than even the worst of what I could have ever let my mind imagine on its own. And yet it was true—with Singer's photographs to prove it. That was the only answer that arrived when Singer asked me how your pictures made me feel. Numbness, nausea, and the image of that beautiful doe, still warm to the touch, her wide black eyes, and the pink flesh of her open abdomen.

Of course, that's not how I answered Singer's question. "How do you think I feel?" was what I said instead. He lowered his chin slightly and squinted at me from his chair. "I just have one more question for you, Rosalyn. Can you tell me anything more about you and your sister's eyes and the marks on your foreheads? It may or may not be relevant for putting together a strong profile for your sister's case." I assumed he meant what everyone means when they ask about our appearance.

"Not much to tell," I answered under my breath. "A genetic feature, the same as that gray streak in your mustache. My sister and I are called mirror twins. Our features are flipped." Singer nodded. "I see. And your foreheads?" he asked cautiously. "I already told you. It's just a birthmark, as far as I know," I answered softly. "We're not sick or anything. We didn't get hurt. Nothing special, although other people sure seem to think so," I added. Singer nodded gently to himself as if I'd just said something he found mildly interesting.

Again, he pulled his pad of paper from his jacket pocket and started scribbling. "What other people do you mean?" he asked, looking up. His questions were again feeling intrusive. It didn't seem like the moment for another interrogation, but I suppose "Sensitivity" wasn't a course in detective school.

"Just people. Kids at school. Strangers on the street. Anyone," I replied obediently.

"Mirror twins. So you two are rare," he said like he was doing a lousy job complimenting me.

"If that's how you want to put it. Technically, you're rarer than me. There's only one of you," I answered contemptuously. He stared back at me blankly. I knew he was waiting for me to elaborate.

I still felt nauseous. My head was fuzzy. I wanted to go home, and this was the last thing I wanted to talk about. "Less than one percent of people have different colored eyes," I told him. "Look it up if you don't believe me. I'm sure you will. It's called Heterochromia," I said, again pausing to squeeze and release my hands. "Identical twins happen once in every two-hundred and fifty births, and twenty-five percent of those are mirror twins. So I guess you can do the math."

I gave him the very same spiel we give everyone. I might as well have told him a person is more likely to get struck by lightning a dozen times than be born with our features. Singer looked up with a deep sigh like we were somehow getting somewhere. "Heterochromia. Prominent birthmarks. The twin part makes everything mirrored. Am I getting it?"

"Not much to get," I answered, feeling exhausted.

"Is there anything else besides your appearances that's different?" Singer asked as if we were some kind of factory-issued replicas.

"We're different people, for starters," I shot back. I knew what he was asking, but I didn't like how he asked it. Though my patience was vanquished and my energy completely drained, my temper still felt wild and unpredictable. It seemed to spume from some unknown source. I knew I should cooperate with any information that might be useful, but Singer rubs me the wrong way. He always has.

Singer remained calm and undeterred. He began his question again, choosing his words more carefully this time. "Do you have any prominent or notably differing characteristics from your sister—besides your reversed physical features?"

"We use different hands to write and have different personality traits. Nova was outgoing and friendly," I answered, scowling—letting my delivery convey the fact that I considered myself neither.

We sat across from one another in momentary silence. Singer leaned back in his chair, uncrossed his arms, and tapped his ring finger on his desk like he was thinking. "Rosalyn, if there's anything else that maybe you're afraid to tell me, I understand, but we need to know the truth about every detail if we're going to make progress with your sister's case." There he goes again. I knew it. He doesn't trust me.

"I've already told you the truth," I replied insistently, but in the back of my mind, I pictured the dark form of my reflection in the murky water of Lake Erie. "Something foul and evil is on its way." I knew there was no way he could have meant the dream, and yet somehow, I felt guilty. I did know something more, even if it didn't make sense.

Singer flipped several pages backward in his little pad as if it were a prop to occupy his hands. He furrowed his eyebrows in thought before speaking again. "Rosalyn, we found ketamine in your sister's body at the time of death. We got the final toxicology back last week. I'll ask only this last time. Are you sure neither of you had done any drugs that night? If you can just see things from my perspective, I'm sure you can understand how it would seem strange that you were out cold on the couch for a full twelve hours at the same time that we have confirmation that your sister had a high dose of ketamine in her system."

What was Singer saying? Ketamine. I barely even know what that is, and he was accusing us of using it? The only thing I've ever known about ketamine came from a history book, and I must have read that years ago—something about medics using it to do emergency surgeries on wounded soldiers in Vietnam. Apparently, it was initially some sort of horse tranquilizer. I guess it would make sense people use it to knock themselves out now. But you would never do something like that without telling me—especially not by yourself. You could never hide anything from me.

I was immediately furious. Confused. How dare Singer accuse me, especially after what he'd just shown me? And even if I had done it, what would that have to do with anything? I felt a wave of nausea returning. What happened to you that night, Nova? My mind could barely process my new understanding of reality, and the shocks didn't seem to end.

By that point, my overwhelm must have been plastered across my face, and at last, Singer relented. We'd reached the limit for the day, and I watched him scratch the side of his head with his pen as he spoke like he wasn't sure what to do with his hands. "I'm going to give you a phone number for someone named Dr. Hilma Molina. It might help to have someone to talk to. A few of the guys from the department even see her sometimes." He slid open the top drawer in his desk and retrieved two index cards. One was adorned with a coffee stain and messy handwriting in blue ink. Its corners appeared worn. The second card was blank, crisp, and new.

I watched Singer transcribe the name and number from the worn card onto the new one, and he slid the new one across his desk in my direction. I reached out in a trance and picked it up, unsure of what to make of it. In all caps were the words "DR. HILMA MOLINA," a phone number scrawled below. With that, Singer stood up from his desk.

"Are you feeling well enough to walk?" he asked abruptly. I nodded. "I give you my word," he added, "we're doing everything we can to bring your sister justice." Singer's voice felt sincere, but his words brought no sense of peace or assurance. I rose from my chair too, feeling the room spin as I took my feet.

Singer stepped in my direction and extended a hand for balance. I didn't accept. "I understand all your next of kin is deceased," he said with his hand still floating before me. "Do you have any friends you can be with right now?" I shook my head "no," resenting his question. You and I have taken care of ourselves for years after Gram died. Next, Aunt Ivy. Critter went into hospice shortly thereafter with the loss of both his sisters. But no one ever asked us if we needed help then. Why start now?

"I see," he said, suddenly rotating his outstretched hand ninety degrees into a handshake as if out of habit. When I didn't offer mine in return, he withdrew his hand awkwardly, paused, then raised it to the top of my shoulder. He tapped me lightly, like he wanted to comfort me but didn't know how. It was as if he felt sorry for what he'd just shown me, yet relieved that I might now better understand why he couldn't give me the answers I'd come for.

"I apologize, but I have to go take care of something. If you can remember anything else that might be useful, don't hesitate to call." He pulled a white business card from his jacket pocket, and I lifted the card from his hand, remembering he'd given me the same card twice already, once after each visit to the house. Either he gives them out at the end of a conversation by habit, or he was trying to make a point.

Singer shifted his hips as if he were about to take a step but hesitated. "You know," he said, "just because we brought in the guys from Pittsburgh doesn't mean I stop doing my job here. Cases that make it to my desk stay there until we have an arrest. Your sister deserves that much."

No, I thought. You're wrong. Nova doesn't deserve any of this. I didn't say anything back.

"It's unnecessary to make another trip down here," he added. "The number on the card is my direct line."

Singer swung open his office door and held it ajar as I unsteadily stepped through. He escorted me back out the way we'd come in, and on our way, we passed another officer with that same look of pity smeared across his face, no different from the others when I'd walked in. "Are you sure you feel well enough to drive home?"

Singer asked once we'd gotten outside, but my back was already turned to him. I didn't answer, only slightly raised my hand to sign "I'm OK," and kept walking down the street toward the car. I wasn't crying, but a sharp, painful lump had formed in my throat. I was anything but "OK."

Somehow I made it back to the house in one piece without ending up tangled in someone's front yard. I must have driven ten miles per hour the whole way back. The world around me felt like it was moving at a pace three times faster than my own. My mind couldn't keep up. When I got home, I collapsed onto the couch and spent the rest of the day alternating between blank stares and rubbing my temples. A splitting headache had moved in to stay.

As I write you now, it's been five days since that day at the station, and perhaps it's no surprise to report that I've felt utterly infected with violent, tormented thoughts. At night I drift away, but it can't be called sleep. It's more like watching some old horror movie on a broken projector with half the frames cut out and stuck on repeat. Images of your bloody face flash across the walls of my mind. There is no narrative—just freeze frames straight out of a slasher film.

Should I have looked inside that folder? Why would Singer offer me those pictures of you—did he just want to see how I would react? And the ketamine—what was he talking about? Can that be true? Nova, what happened to you that night?

I've become obsessed with imagining your last moments. The first days and weeks after it happened, I wouldn't let my mind approach the subject, but now, after seeing those pictures, it's all I can think about. At first, my fixation was nothing more than raw, painful emotion steeped in feelings of rage, grief, and disgust. But after enough of this, you'd be surprised how quickly you start to go numb.

Before long, my thoughts had graduated into a purely analytical exercise—sterile and diagnostic as I tried to logically understand how it all happened. How could another human being conceive of such a thing? And then, again, I thought back to that first doe I killed. I thought about all the ones after it I managed to kill too. And after enough practice, not another tear was shed. Could that be all it is for a person like that? After long enough, maybe there isn't any emotion to it at all—just a calm practice of perfecting one's sport. How else could such a thing be possible?

Why you, Nova? None of it makes sense. I spin myself in one circle after another, always landing back in the same spot again— back to the dream about the wolf the night before you were killed. Back to the warning spoken by my reflection in the lake. "Something foul and evil is on its way." How could so much be the same between the dream and what happened to you? The wolf's teeth had been removed, just the same as yours. Even as I dreamed, I knew that wolf was somehow you, recreated in her form. I dreamed all of that before I knew anything was about to hurt you— even before I saw any of Singer's sickening pictures. I really think I must be losing my mind.

I've spent the last two days in a robotic stupor, mindlessly occupying my hands. I cleaned whatever I could find. I scrubbed the bathroom twice and wiped down every crevice and cranny in the kitchen. I even managed to slide out the oven from the wall and sweep out all the runaway dried-out blueberries and pretzel sticks that had rolled away over the years. I found the key to your bike lock in the back of the couch. I found the laundry card I'd accused you of losing. I was using it as a bookmark in the Carl Sagan book about the universe with that big orange nebula on the cover. I'd had it all along—I'm sorry for blaming you.

Yesterday morning, I'd run out of rooms to clean and thought I might embark on the grand mission of reorganizing our book collection when suddenly I felt I was about to lose the ground from under my feet. In an instant, I was overcome with aches, and every inch of my body started to sweat. The room spun. I don't think I was sick, perhaps simply exhausted.

I abandoned my pile of books and slumped down on the couch, assuming I'd just take a few minutes to regain my senses before getting back to the task at hand. But the next thing I remembered was a clap of thunder and the sound of heavy rain pounding the living room window. It was dark outside, and I quickly understood that I had slept through the day. I checked my watch. It was a little past 9 PM. I'd been unconscious for more than nine hours.

It took me some time to settle back into the waking world. I felt like I'd just gotten back from a long trip but couldn't remember for the life of me where from. I was desperately thirsty and stood up to get a glass of water from the kitchen when out of the blue, I got that feeling like you've forgotten a word, but it's just right there— right on the tip of your tongue. Or like when you're trying to remember an old picture but can only see its general features just at the fringes of your mind, its details hazy and remote.

I kicked off the dust of sleep and shuffled to the sink in a fog. I filled my glass and watched the tiny bubbles spin under the running faucet. The white pockets of air climbed to the surface and dissipated, the water slowly becoming clear. It was entrancing. I lifted the glass to my lips, but before I could take a sip, everything came rushing back. I remembered where I'd been.

The farthest corners of a vivid dream came soaring back into view—a dream that felt like it stretched on for centuries, millennia, chapter after chapter, act after act. It was as if I had been floating in some sort of womb of the universe with an omniscient narrator, and all I wanted to do was smile and melt into whatever was holding me. I can't remember the last time I'd felt so safe and whole, either in dreams or awake.

It's hard to explain now, but it was as if I was witnessing all of history compressed, starting with the existence of the first particle in our cosmos. The dream's plot line extended billions of years, yet I experienced an accelerated version through only its key scenes. There seemed to be no difference between the universe around me and my own body. We were one and the same. Was I dreaming or hallucinating?

The first thing I remember was a lonely form floating in infinite blackness. I couldn't say I saw her—it was more like I just felt and heard her. I became her. I don't know how, but somehow I knew it was a "she," even though the feeling was nothing more than a vibration. Maybe that's just the only language I know to describe it. It was like some energetic charge. She rocked back and forth in the utter emptiness of limitless space like a pendulum, and the waves of her motion made stringy shapes as if you were to shake a piece of rope over a slick floor.

I don't think I've ever felt more myself than I did as I felt her dancing alone in that expanse of nothingness. Her mission seemed so assured and simple. Just move. Vibrate. Why can't our human lives ever feel so straightforward and pure? Her only purpose was to rock her own form back and forth at a pace only she knew was right. That was all. It was as if all her challenges and victories were no more complicated than trusting her own rhythms. It was beautiful to experience. What was she? An atom? A quark? Something else we can't name?

The dream went on like this—strange and ethereal—a second vibration materializing from the edges of space to join her company. As the two met, their movements became chaotic and discordant. It was like watching two untuned instruments of novice musicians trying to play a duet. Their disharmony continued for what felt like a million years until, finally, their persistence paid off. Suddenly, the two fell into each other's movements, like two uniform waves chasing one another, rippling across the lake in tandem—or two voices singing the same note so perfectly you can no longer tell which one is which.

Soon their vibrations grew faster, tighter, and so condensed that eventually, I couldn't tell if they were even moving at all. It was as if their movement had transformed into a solid shape, like the optical illusion of a quivering rubber band taut between two fingers. The harder it vibrates, the more solid the ribbon at its center appears to your eye—its motion too fast for your brain to register.

I'm not sure how it happened, but the next thing I knew, the abstract forms had transfigured into images I now recognized. I watched a planet take shape like a wet ball of clay molded by an invisible sculptor. Its smears of reds, grays, and browns became canyons, mountains, and volcanoes. A feeling of suspense was building.

That was when time seemed to slow again, like the last few feet of a roller coaster inching to its crest before the drop. And then, it was as if I'd taken the first gulp of air in my life. The browns and grays exploded into a palette of greens and blues, and I watched every creature I'd ever seen in Darwin's *On the Origin of Species*, plus a thousand more I'd never seen at all, spill out across time.

It was surreal—like watching a genetic diagram of the tree of life animate across my mind in three-hundred and sixty degrees. I suppose the dream had a narrative I recognize objectively from science books. A creation story. The birth of the universe. But through the distortions of my dream, it was somehow felt—not told. I wasn't listening to it or watching it. I was feeling it and living it. Does that make any sense at all?

It was only just before I remember waking up that I heard some omniscient, otherworldly presence speak. I couldn't say where it came from, but it was a calming voice that seemed to tell me what to do and how to be. It didn't feel like a god—or at least how other people describe it—it felt more like Gram, and like you, and like me all wrapped into one. It was a voice telling me something I already knew but had never quite heard in such a way.

I stood at the kitchen sink, staring down at my water glass. I could feel the vividness of the dream already slipping from my mind's grip, like tiny grains of sand falling through my fingers. I wanted nothing more than to hold onto every moment, but all I could do was build a new conscious memory around it as if creating a plaster cast of a beautiful but fragile flower that will soon be nothing more than dust.

I rested my glass on the counter and sat down at the kitchen table, replaying the dream's narrative as if it were nothing more than the scene of a play. It was then I had a peculiar thought. What if we can see everything in life like this?

What if our past and future are laid before us in plain sight, just the same as we might look over our shoulders upon any valley behind us—or forward, toward a mountain that extends into the horizon? What if time is a three-dimensional form—our pasts, our futures, exploding and collapsing and reshaping their physical structures with our every breath in the same way that a storm shapes the coastlines or a volcano carves out the canyons? Perhaps as we sleep, the gentle push and pull of gravity quiets our minds and clears the fog of our noisy, conscious thinking just enough to finally see our truest underlying topography.

Maybe that's what Gram was saying all along with all her dream stuff, but in different words, with different characters, and in a way that children can understand. Maybe that wasn't only Astrid's world but ours too if only we listen closely.

I'm not sure what I'm even talking about—but something about this dream has me feeling different somehow. I don't know the right word. Open? Curious? Humbled. Awestruck. Even if only fleeting, I'll gladly accept any other feeling than the ones I've been left with since you've been gone.

We are all so unfathomably small in this universe of ours, stretched across all of time and space—but this morning, as I write, that feels like comfort, not a tragedy. It's nothing short of a miracle that any of us made it here at all. It's a marvel that twenty-two years ago, you and I, Nova and Rosalyn Whitman, split from the same embryo and nine months later met the world as mirror images of one another on a full moon somewhere in Erie, Pennsylvania.

I just never imagined our time together would be so short. I always took it for granted that we'd have each other forever. When you're young, you assume life has only just begun, and everything in front of you is still possible. Your past is short, your future is still so long, and you hardly pay any mind to the present because you haven't yet learned how to savor it. Perhaps you can only truly understand this once you lose something irreplaceable.

I'll leave you with my dream now. I hope a poem can do it better justice than I've done in this letter.

Love,
Rosalyn

One Song

(Part 1, First Mother)
In the old time, our first mother
was nothing more than a vibration,
singing alone in the night to what she
thought was only her own congregation.

At first, just a low quake that
gently rocked her being to and fro,
softly, according to her intuition—
a deep instinct that only she could know.

She felt such clarity in her design
to simply become her own motion,
only to hum with her energy against
the universe with perfect devotion.

Then sometimes, for no reason
at all that she could name,
she shifted on her axis,
and rocked herself all the same.

And just as she did, her vibration
accelerated to a new pace—
like her body was an instrument
and her audience, infinite space.

And though she was her song's creator,
she was as much its child too,
exploring her own orbits, each time
giving birth to herself anew.

Did her song unfurl her as it played,
or did she unfurl her song?
She made her home within herself,
a place to always belong.

A fresh lesson with each trough
and each crest of her every amplitude,
that each time she would return to herself
in the belly of its vicissitude.

It was a commitment to ride each
wave to its eventual resolution
that taught her a stoic trust
in her own steadfast constitution.

And when her song rose to shrill notes,
like an angry wind about to intensify,
she knew she needed only endure it long
enough to fall again into a lullaby.

(Part 2, First Father)
It was the lifetime of a thousand stars
that our First Mother sang like this
until, for the first moment in her
recital, she felt something amiss.

From the horizon of the universe, echoes of
an unknown song vibrated into her concert.
All other languages but her own still unexplored,
she became tense and wiry, afraid and alert.

How could this stranger's music
harmonize with her own?
How could this encounter forge
a melody they both could intone?

Would their wavelengths dance effortlessly
like choreographed ribbons in a maypole?
Or would they thrash and tangle like loose wires
in a storm, whipping wild and out of control?

At first, it was cacophony—she, unable to
temper her voice over his introduction.
And likewise, her new visitor offered a
meter that was only noise and commotion.

"Who are you? Where have you come
from? I thought I was the only one.
I'd only just learned to trust my rhythms—
what now am I to make of this new union?"

But slowly, clumsily, they negotiated
their harmonies with patience,
committing in tandem to the worthy
search for their shared cadence.

The indifferent universe grew ancient
around them, their tiny drama ignored,
as stars collided, black holes collapsed,
unconcerned with the pair's discord.

Together they bowed the instruments
of their bodies in unrelenting dedication,
until, at last, they awoke to one another's music,
together creating the song of their new coalition.

And at this moment, the chaos settled,
and their noise became melody once more.
Their frequencies now married, they relished
in their new vibrational rapport.

His push became her pull—
her vanguard, his slipstream.
His swell became her recess,
his temperance, her extreme.

And even when their flows
would draw them apart,
always, they returned both to themselves,
and to their new counterpart.

(Part 3, First Home)
As First Mother and First Father at last
mastered the notes of their duet,
their bridges and allegros created
the elements of their new alphabet.

With renewed confidence, now as a tandem force,
the two knew their song was how it all starts—
surrendering to the truth that their sum
was much greater than their parts.

Their notes grew so tight and rapid—
a twisting vibrational swarm,
that from the void, they became solid
shapes, singing themselves into form.

And so, together, they bore a child
through their unyielding incantation.
Her belly was an ocean, her bosom the bluffs—
so exquisite was their newborn creation.

Her infancy was marked by growing
pains of sudden tectonic tantrums,
reshaping her bones for millennia
in innumerable volcanic spasms.

And each time, her topography was
thrown into some new contour,
new paths emerged for winds to snake
her canyons and waves to crawl her shore.

Yet it would be a procession of
one billion trips around her sun
until young Earth was finally ready
for that which had never yet been done.

But always, she abided by some primal optimism
that her womb would be the eventual birthplace,
never abandoning the faith that one day she'd
meet her countless children's embrace.

And so it was, in the depths of her seas
and in the reservoirs of her geysers,
the ingredients for First Life
became tenacious improvisers.

Their tiny particles quietly hummed
in the oceans, swaying in gentle gyration.
And Earth's warmth tickled them until
they lunged into some new combination.

Then, at last, from the tonic of the seas
rose a single lonely organism,
brave to her new world, she would
have to practice unwavering stoicism.

She stepped over the barrier for all
lifeforms who'd tried but failed before.
Her only mission was survival, the battle
for her own life, her only war.

(Part 4, First Life)
It was a chapter written long before
humankind had begun its shift,
but finally, the history book's page turned,
and the universe delivered its ultimate gift.

And so the story of our evolution goes—
energy became vibration, and vibration became form.
But before First Life could truly thrive,
she'd be tested by a great many storm.

Though all future creatures depended
on her success, First Life was unafraid—
First Father and Mother's unyielding
resilience had prepared her for this crusade.

First Life would need to be strong so her
future children could be stronger still,
leaving even mightier versions of herself
to enact the very same powerful will.

In the early times, our Earth home
was a much less hospitable place,
but our primordial ancestors were fighters,
survivors—and they dared not lose face.

And so First Life kept her promise,
growing more hardy with every generation.
Little by little, she became more wise—
more complex—with every small transformation.

Then something miraculous happened—
her children grew into mossy greenery,
and before long, they learned to take root,
becoming flower, vine, and tree.

From the deep waters, wriggled worms
and sponges, mollusks, and fish.
Millions of new creatures exploded
into existence, and life began to flourish.

Our forebearers sprouted legs, learned to crawl,
then soon walked upright on solid ground.
Others grew wings and took flight to the skies—
foot and feather, the Earth did abound.

Warm blood coursed their veins, their
brains developed at an astonishing rate,
but their true mark of evolution
was their new skill to communicate.

(Part 5, In Somnis Veritas)
It was through the power of language
that our ancestors made their next leap,
speaking their new ideas not only with each other,
but in their own mind's eye, both awake and deep in sleep.

While it was our primate parents who led us
to the physical human form we all now know,
it was within the invisible depths of the mind
that allowed the human spirit to truly grow.

Stay close to your wild nature.
Let it remind you from whence we've all come.
But never forget that we all go back
to the same place when our time is done.

The deepest truth
has been with us all along—
we are all one family, and
we are all one song.

And if we ever forget this, our
minds will remind us as they dream.
There's a simple truth that can be found
by moonlight, which we must always esteem.

"In Somnis Veritas"—it means,
"In Dreams There is Truth."
Let your dreams light your way
and be your sayers of sooth.

From this day forth, let it be
your mission to use your Dream Eyes
to keep your spirit strong and brave,
free of the poison of doubt or lies.

First Mother, First Father, thank you.
Now it's our turn to be your troubadour,
for so long as we have sleep to dream,
there is truth to speak for.

The Door with the Face

Wednesday, May 7, 1997

Dear Nova,

Last night I set my alarm for 8 AM in a vote of confidence that today I might return to some semblance of a schedule, but when the buzzer went off, I lay in bed for hours and couldn't summon myself from the covers until sometime after 11:30. I felt like a beached whale. I stirred with the best intentions of moving, but a greater weight kept me flattened against my mattress. I pardoned my lethargy, feeding myself the fiction that I just needed more rest, but I knew the only reason I was still glued to my sheets was that I much preferred the darkness behind my eyelids to whatever daylight might have to offer.

It's already the second week of May. I say "already," but the truth is, the last few months have felt like a year. The sun is starting to set later, and tonight the moonless sky is pitch black. I somehow feel exposed when it's dark like this. Fragile, but sharper too—more attuned and responsive to the world around me, as if the setting reveals some hidden acumen I never before knew I possessed.

Since last week's strange dream about the universe, I've been feeling different in a way that's difficult to put into words. In the mornings when I look in the mirror, my face seems changed. I step out of the shower and wipe the condensation from the mirror, and as I squint into my reflection to study my features, I feel like I'm forgetting something and remembering something else simultaneously. Something unconscious is becoming conscious, while some other part of me seems to be falling away.

My daily existence still consists of little more than moping around the house, fueled only by cereal and the occasional beer. Still, when I find myself most morose and lethargic, my mind returns to the dream about the universe—when I picture those first two little vibrating particles singing against the edges of the cosmos, momentarily, I feel comforted.

Perhaps it's an odd reaction to feel comforted, but it has a way of bringing me out of myself and thrusting me into eternity. It reminds me that there is a vastness beyond you and me. I think about the formation of the first planets and stars—how old they are now and how old they may one day become. And I think about how all of us humans are so willing to believe in them, even though, of course, to us, they are nothing more than tiny specks glinting against the night sky. Up close, they may be brilliant fireballs, but from down here on Earth, their light can take years to even reach our eyes.

They are mere mirages, the shadows in Plato's allegory of the cave, the ephemeral flickers from which we build our understanding of our world. We all believe in the stars, and yet we've never visited them—never seen them up close. To our eyes, they might as well be gemstones in the sky that we can pluck right down and wear on our fingers.

We inherit our understanding of the world. It's expected that we accept the rules we've been handed down from our books and our scholars. We believe in things like the Big Bang and the cosmic Dark Ages, even though no one living today was around to see those things with their own eyes. Today, we take these facts for granted. We create our collected history from the aggregated teachings of the great minds who came before. We invent our concept of the world and then teach it in science class. We celebrate our geologists, our biologists, and our astrophysicists. We memorize the names and the order of the planets around our sun. But when I look up at the night sky, what evidence of my own do I have to reassure me that Jupiter is up there, somewhere just behind the moon? I'm not saying I don't believe it. Of course, I do. But what can possibly underpin such a prodigious trust?

It wasn't so long ago that humans simply assumed the universe revolves around the Earth. You could say it was, quite literally, a self-centered view, but what other information was there to prove otherwise at the time? It wasn't until Copernicus came along and proposed another idea using math. Heliocentrism. The Earth revolves around the sun. It was always my favorite bit of science history, and I memorized every fact. I think I mostly loved the underdog story. In 1514 Copernicus released a small commentary about his idea of heliocentrism, but only to his very closest friends. Even in 1532, when he finished his pioneering manuscript on the topic called "On the Revolutions of the Heavenly Spheres," he resisted publishing it for fear of criticism, not only from other astronomers but also from the Catholic church.

Now, almost five hundred years later, Copernicus is the one credited as the first to describe what is really happening up there in the heavens above. Today, we have endless gadgets and cameras and our dear friend Hubble to observe Copernicus's astronomical model in great technicolor detail—but before any of that, what proof did the rest of us have?

The true orbits of our solar system were always happening, whether the astronomers or the church or anyone else believed in them or not. The stars didn't care who understood. And from down on Earth, all we humans could really affirm was that there was ground under our feet, a bright orb keeping us warm by day, and a moon waxing and waning by night. Beyond that, well, there just had to be some mysterious force holding it all together, hadn't there? As it turns out, that mysterious force is called gravity. It wasn't until Archimedes of ancient Greece, or Galileo, "the father of modern physics," or Newton's law of universal gravitation that anyone had the scientific vocabulary for it. But gravity had existed since the birth of the universe—with or without those words.

Humans are such naturally curious animals, so eager for absolute answers, so reluctant to accept a mystery—and when presented with the latter, our desperate minds lean on science and on our gods and our folklore to explain away the gaps in our understanding. It's what Gram did when she bestowed us with her heroic stories of Astrid. We could conquer our bad dreams if only we knew they had their proper reasons. When we were children, it was a poetic survival skill. But I'm not a child anymore, and a fairytale isn't good enough. I need more than make-believe about a little girl who lives in an island village to explain away what I saw in my sleep the night before you were killed. Each new dream only feels like another tap on the shoulder, inviting me to pay attention. If I don't listen now, what else might be at stake? I can't shake this feeling, and you're the only person I have to tell—just like Copernicus, who wouldn't dare share his quiet theory of heliocentrism with anyone but his closest friends. At least Copernicus turned out to be onto something. As for myself, I'm not so sure.

I'm slowly learning in the most painful way possible that we aren't promised the "how" or the "why." We aren't promised anything at all. What do we do when our scientists and our prophets fail to give us the answers we long for? I suppose we worship the questions themselves. Sometimes they might feel like tiny gifts—the sanctuary of a mystery we protect with our lives—but mostly, they just feel like torment, haunting us like ghosts. All there is left to do is hold tight to the hope that maybe the answer is still out there somewhere, perhaps just out of our view, but still within our reach, if only we keep searching.

Why are you gone? How could I have known something terrible was about to happen before it really did? How is it possible that I dreamed about that wolf who was butchered in the very same way that you were only a day later? Her teeth torn away, her face streaked in blood? My reflection warned me in plain words that something foul and evil was on its way, only I was not me, but some dark, distorted version of myself. My reflection knew the truth—and though I refused to admit it then, somewhere deep inside myself, I knew that same truth too.

If I had told you, would things be different now? But how could I have known to trust a dream like that? The world would be in chaos if we all listened to our dreams just as we do the evening news. I'm so sorry, Nova. I'm consumed with guilt. But how was I to know it was real? How can any of us know what's real half the time?

Science proclaims inexorable laws govern our universe, yet we must admit that sometimes the world around us doesn't seem to abide by those laws one bit. Neither my five senses nor my empirical mind can explain that dream—all I'm left with are my questions and a flimsy faith that somehow I might find a way to their answers. Why are you gone, Nova? I wish you were here. Everything feels like too much to carry without you.

That lonely particle transformed herself into countless new forms over billions of years, eventually becoming the Earth and life itself. We are her descendants, made up of that very same stuff. Have you, too, found your new form? Perhaps you're not gone at all. I like to think you're still here in some other kind of way, vibrating at the distant borders of the universe. Or are you right here in this room with me now?

That little particle never really lived or died—for her, those would be irrelevant terms. Life and death are too small a concept for the vast kinds of metamorphosis that she endured. She merely changed from one energy into another and, in doing so, learned to speak the new languages needed to accompany her new state.

Maybe you can learn to communicate with me in some new language that you are just now learning to speak and that I am learning to hear and understand. It's a consoling thought. I find my mind turning over these ideas when our house is so quiet and the night sky is pure black. But inevitably, if I sit long enough like this, my mood eventually shifts, and I become overwhelmed with an awful sensation like maybe I've never really even noticed my own life. It's a quiet feeling—one that I might easily overlook if you were still here keeping me company, but in my newfound solitude, it's easier to detect. It's sharing the room with me now instead of you.

I've started noticing a difference in how I hear the world—small things—but it's the small things that make up the big ones. The house is so steadily undisturbed that every sound seems conspicuous, contrasting against the ballast of stillness. Even my own ruminations seem to scream, like my mind itself is the wall of an empty tunnel, and each passing thought is a backfiring car engine.

And then there are the real sounds. The buzz of the refrigerator. The chattering of birds outside, the patterns of their repeating calls. The creaks from the wood expanding in the house, the radiators, the wind, the dogs barking in the neighborhood. Even my own breath sounds different. I notice the quality of white noise around me. Each room has such a distinct fullness or flatness, sometimes a sharpness, depending on its shape and size. The silence itself always has a tone.

I've never had the time to sit like this and simply notice things. Who does? I'm finding this newfound attention difficult to articulate. It's like my very nature is changing. I'm changing. My observations, my reactions—and whatever it is that's pulling at the strings inside of me is clamoring for recognition and obedience.

But what does it want? What exactly is it saying? Has it always been there, just like that constant buzz of the refrigerator? Until now, have I just always managed to drown it out? It's certainly more manageable that way—easier not to allow yourself to hear. Otherwise, surely it would have driven me mad long ago.

I always thought I knew what our lives would become, but for the first time, I can't imagine a future for myself anymore. When I look forward, all I see is a heavy fog, and there is nothing to do but let its murkiness roll over me.

We always assumed we'd somehow find our way out of Erie one day. New York or Paris. From the safety of our imaginations, we indulged in the fantasy that we could go anywhere, so long as we did it together. Academic hermitude didn't do much to make us popular, but at least it might be our ticket out of here, especially in the absence of any other viable options. One day you'd be a famous musician, and I'd be a writer. In Paris, you'd play at the Conservatoire de Paris. I'd study at the Sorbonne. Or maybe New York would sweep us away instead. You would go to Juilliard while I might find my way into NYU. We could compare notes together in Central Park over coffee. Never mind the money or our acceptance letters. You don't worry about those parts in a fantasy. Anything is possible. Somehow I think that was the only daydream I ever allowed myself. And if my confidence ever wavered, you strengthened me. We'd be in it together.

Of course, that's not how anything turned out. But when we were teenagers, I would have done anything to make that life come true for us. I prided myself on that drive and discipline. I believed if I could strengthen my mind more than anyone I knew, how could I ever be led astray? Science. History. Logic. As many books as I could consume. I lived life abiding by the principle that nature is rational and that the universe is governed by laws of reason.

Even with mom and dad gone—and eventually Gram, Ivy, and Critter too—somehow, I convinced myself there was an acceptable reason for everything in life. Perhaps I just couldn't understand them all yet. But now that you're gone, how could I have ever believed nature is governed by such laws? I resent the stoics and all their phony principles. Where are my reasons now?

My only religion was a belief that with a logical mind, I could never get lost. But here I am, adrift nonetheless. I have no compass, only an aching, spinning head, my heart too atrophied for anything else but missing you. Maybe if I'd learned how to use my heart better when I was young, I'd know what to do now. When we were still so small and came to live with Gram, I remember feeling like we were silently watching Gram's heart break more and more every day in slow motion. And yet she never allowed it to fracture to the point that she couldn't take care of us. We had just lost our parents, but Gram had lost her child. It seemed like everyone in our household was just holding it together. Carry on. Be practical. Don't get too distracted. Don't let your guard down. If your heart breaks, you break. At least you managed a lightness of heart that I never quite figured out.

I always thought if I strengthened my mind enough, what use would I have for a heart? A heart is nothing more than a distracting annoyance, bound to get you into trouble at any time. The head is what gets you someplace in this world. Because what do hearts do? They only get broken and slow you down when you have to stop and pick up the pieces.

Besides, I knew I would always have you. You were my heart, and that was more than enough. There wasn't space left for anything else. Friends felt superfluous. I never even once entertained so much as even the possibility of a crush. And all that was just fine by me. I always managed to convince myself one way or another that the prospect of extraneous love was far too unpredictable and dangerous until the idea scared me more than it enticed me.

Now, all these years later, I still thought that somehow I could protect myself. I spent my life casting an immortal shield around my softest parts, but in the end, my heart still shattered into ash the day you never came home. I was wrong. A strong head is no protection from a broken heart. Maybe I just misunderstood what the stoics were saying all along. "Loss is nothing else but change, and change is nature's delight."[1] The Roman Emperor Marcus Aurelius wrote those words almost two thousand years ago.

Loss is change, and change is nature's delight. One season departs, and another arrives. The moon shifts its phases like clockwork. Geese fly south and find their mates. Flowers bloom, then freeze and crumble with the first frost. Change and loss. Nature evolved to let go of what's necessary and follow its instincts in order to persist. A bird can't cling to each passing season, or survival would be an impossibility. And when the time comes for change—for loss —the bird knows. It doesn't wait around on a tree stump all day wondering how or why it's time to fly south. It doesn't mourn the task ahead. It simply opens its wings and takes flight.

Maybe this is what Gram was trying to teach us when we were little girls—that same intuition that flowers and birds have. Perhaps she always knew how we might be tempted to try and harden ourselves as we grew older, and she didn't want our hearts to callous over completely. I always thought you and I were capable of protecting ourselves from anything. In many ways, it felt like we had raised ourselves after Gram got sick. But lately, I look back, and I wonder if all along, Gram was protecting us in ways we could never have imagined when we were young, preparing us for the day she'd be gone. Even when our household felt so full of heartache, she still tried to open up something more tender and fragile inside us that one day might save us too. Would it have saved you?

"In dreams there is truth," she told us. I wish I could ask her now what she had really meant by that.

Sometimes a dream arrives as a full storyline, complete with characters and scenes—but sometimes, it's nothing more than a feeling rising from your body like a chill or a fever. Intuition. Premonition. That feeling in your gut. I've never in my life paid any attention to my dreams, not even when Gram gave us our journals, but now it feels as if I no longer have a choice.

What am I supposed to do now? Where can I go? How do I even take care of myself? What use are dreams when you're barely surviving? I'm not sure I have the strength to start over again—at least not in Erie. There are far too many memories here, good and bad. Every street corner is a shrine to an apparition of our past. I can't stay. Every day when I walk down the stairs and pass our front door, I hesitate. What if I just turned the knob and left forever? But each time, I falter, stumbling backward into the deafening silence of our empty home.

What I had cleaned up around the house last week, I've again let return to shambles. A pile of dirty dishes is currently mocking me from the kitchen sink. This morning, after I finally mustered the willpower to drag myself from my covers, I towed my heavy body to the kitchen for some water. We'd run out of clean glasses on the bottom shelf, so I pulled up the stool to reach the high cupboard.

There was only one last clean glass remaining—the elephant mug we got from that street vendor outside the Bronx Zoo in sixth grade. I know you remember. Gram had brought us along to see Aunt Ivy in New York. We were so excited to see those elephants. The Erie Zoo never had them, despite Gram baiting us with the false hope that they might come next year—or the one after, or maybe the one after.

We went everywhere on that trip. Coney Island. The Empire State Building. The Natural History Museum. The New York Public Library. The MET. You got that tote bag with a print of Edvard Munch's "The Scream" on it, and Gram and I accused you of being morbid for wanting it so badly. "How about Monet's lilies instead?" Gram asked you. But you wanted that one. "How do you even know he's screaming?" you challenged. You announced that you were quite certain he was actually singing opera. Classic Nova. Always making lemonade out of lemons—always preferring your own humorous version with total confidence and delight.

Before this morning, I'd only cried twice so far since you left. Once after reading your beetle poem and a second time for what seemed like no reason at all as I reached for a gallon of milk in the grocery store. But this morning, perched on that stool holding the elephant mug in my hands, I felt the tears arriving again, beginning as an aching lump in my throat.

I climbed down, delicately clasping the elephant mug like it might be a Fabergé egg, and sat down at the kitchen table. I heard your voice and pictured your face wearing your mischievous smirk.

"How come you never see elephants hiding in trees?"

"Why, Nova…"

"Because they're really good at it."

You snort-laughed at your own stupid joke before I even got it.

I miss those stupid jokes so much. I miss your pranks. And I miss that little smirk. I miss the sound of you practicing scales on your flute in the other room. I miss how you always painted faces out of mustard on your plate. I miss how you always asked me questions about my day that no one else in the world would know to ask. I miss knowing that even when not another soul seemed to understand me, you always did.

I'm trying so hard to hold it all together—to rally even the smallest sense of hope that things will get better, but I still wake up each day with the same sense of paralysis. I feel like I'm in the world's slowest vat of quicksand, and I don't even realize I'm sinking until I look down to notice I've surrendered the use of another body part to the sludge.

I have to get out of here. I mean, get out of Erie. Maybe that's also what the elephant cup reminded me too. There's a world outside this place. I need to remember how to come alive again. A new routine, a new roof over my head, new faces, and a new view out my window each day. Could you find a way to forgive me if I left home without you?

I used the last of my checking account weeks ago on groceries and gas. Now I'm just trying to think up ways to stay afloat for the next month without getting evicted. I took out one thousand and eleven dollars from our joint account, but something about using our savings on rent and Frosted Mini Wheats in Erie feels like profanity.

I need to figure out what to do. Even if I use our money to stay in Erie, a thousand dollars will barely cover a few months of rent, food, utilities, and gas by myself. I can't even summon the motivation to browse job postings. I just can't bear to imagine myself working an eight-hour shift at a checkout line with nothing to look forward to when I clock out. Without you or Gram, I don't know what's keeping me here anymore.

I suppose it's about time I tell you why I started writing you this letter in the first place. Last night I had another dream. It's true that from under my covers, I lied to myself that I was too tired to get up. It's true I didn't want to face the day. But the truest part is that it was my dream that kept me rooted to my mattress for hours after my alarm had sounded. I lay there, half awake, recounting as much as I could, rubbing my feet together as if the dream had given them a mind of their own.

It began as a strange and abstract scene. All I remember is the sensation that somehow my body wasn't a body at all—but instead a flowing, mossy tapestry. It was like I had grown right into the forest floor, a lush, billowing green carpet. Then suddenly, without any warning, I shot up from the ground, emerging as a seedling, and with time I grew taller and taller until finally, I was a beautiful, strong tree with two perfectly symmetrical forking branches.

I felt so alive and capable. I was meaningful to my forest, my roots sprawling out into the soil like long fingers caressing the earth, and my leafy canopy created a natural cover for deer and rabbits to shade themselves. I provided for my fellow creatures in these small ways, and they provided for me too. Life felt simple and harmonious.

Then one day, a dark wind blew, and a storm like I'd never seen before rolled over the forest. A heavy rain hammered at my leaves for hours, but I thought I'd only need to brace myself for just a little while longer, and the storm would finally pass. I heard a sharp clap of thunder just above my tallest branches, and a blinding flash of lightning struck my trunk. In a splintering crack, I watched one half of my forking branches fall to the forest floor in a heap.

Eventually, the storm did pass, rolling away just the same as it had rolled in, but I was forever changed without my missing parts. I didn't know how to exist without my other half, and I wept and screamed so violently I shook all the leaves from what branches remained.

I refused to drink from the soil, and soon I became so brittle and weak that all my bark fell away. As the last pieces toppled to the ground, I realized that underneath I was naked in an entirely new form. I was made of soft skin and warm flesh instead of rigid wood. My roots had been replaced by human hands and feet. And as I stretched out my newly shaped legs, at that moment, I knew it was time for me to use them to walk far away from my forest home.

I walked for what felt like days until gray shapes with sharp, angular edges in the distance began to come into focus. A dramatic cityscape jutted into the sky. I remember that's how New York had looked as we watched it come into view from the train as children. With a mysterious sense of purpose, I continued onward toward the towering shapes ahead. It was as if my legs were navigating all on their own, and the rest of my body was just along for the ride.

At last, I reached the city limits, and before long, I was weaving through concrete and cobbled streets, seemingly magnetized to some location just beyond my view. I thought my legs would never stop, but finally, after what felt like an eternity, my feet planted in front of an old, weathered building. Its door was painted with a face in bright, rich colors. Its mouth stretched into a wide painful grimace, spanning from the doorknob to the pavement.

The expression of that grimacing face feels imprinted on my mind forever. I can picture every detail. Standing before its ominous countenance, I felt so afraid, but I was drawn to it too. Maybe I imagined it, but the door almost seemed to open for me on its own. Cautiously, I pulled the old rusted handle and walked inside. It was only as I stepped over the threshold that I felt a sense of clear resolve. I had not a shred of doubt that this was the direction I was meant to be going. The door closed behind me, and I started down a cold staircase, disappearing into the darkness. That was when I woke up.

Nova, I need to make a plan and figure out my next move. I have a feeling I won't be in Erie much longer. I wish you were here. We could start again together, somewhere new.

Love,
Rosalyn

The Door with the Face

My body was nothing but a bed of moss
undulating under the canopy of an old tree.
It felt like I was a part of every living thing,
and they, too, were a part of me.

Here I stayed for what seemed like centuries
with no other purpose than to exist.
I watched a thousand creatures be born and die,
but Mother Nature was hardy and would persist.

Then one day, I felt my body bursting,
stretching both into the ground and toward the sky.
Overnight, I sprouted deep roots and
a trunk that grew strong and high.

My body forked into two perfectly symmetrical
systems of branches and wide leaves.
I felt such joy to have a purpose, offering
shelter to the animals under my natural eaves.

I passed my days to the circadian rhythms,
passed my years to the seasonal rotations,
and I learned that after every violent storm, we would
again return safely to our peaceful foundations.

But one night, a dark wind blew, and at once
I knew this storm was not like the rest.
The sky grew black, and I braced myself,
knowing I was about to be put to the test.

The sky opened, thunder growled, and a bolt
of lightning struck one half of my forking trunk.
In a flash, half my body died and dropped
away—into the wet ground, it sunk.

The wind calmed, finally passing, and life
went on without another thought of me.
And though I was still standing, without
my other half, I no longer knew how to be.

Soon, my despair turned to rage,
and I knew not who or what to condemn.
I screamed so violently that I shook
every leaf clean from its stem.

I grew brooding and brittle,
refusing to drink even the rain.
No kind of sustenance could
absolve me of this pain.

Too dry to support me, all my bark
began to splinter and fall away.
I emerged as soft, naked flesh in the form
of a human body, and I knew I could not stay.

Leaving my roots behind, I walked
for many days until I saw no more green.
I stood before a city tangled in so much steel
and concrete like I'd never before seen.

To my right, I passed a tall green woman
holding a bright torch high above her crown.
She looked down at me, lowering her flame,
and pointed in a direction across town.

Following her sign, I crossed over bridges
and weaved through street after street
until, at last, my legs brought me to a place
where the city and its outskirts meet.

At last, I arrived at a tall door brightly
painted with a broad, grimacing face.
It unbolted and cracked open, revealing
the outline of a weathered staircase.

The figure's mouth stretched into a wide
black hole, twisting into a painful frown.
I approached the stairs it guarded cautiously,
took a deep breath, and began to walk down.

Two Lions

Sunday, June 1, 1997

Dear Nova,

Sometimes things happen slowly, and then they happen all at once. For the first time in my life, I don't have a single thing left to lose. I did something that might sound impulsive, but the truth is I know it's been a long time coming. I might not know what's next, but at least I know it won't be Erie. I did it. I left. I can hardly believe it as my pen sweeps across this paper. I'm writing you from New York City.

It wasn't much longer after I last wrote that I officially made up my mind to leave. The deliberation lasted no more than twelve hours after I put down my pen. I mentioned it to you here in these pages, and the next thing I knew, my mind was settled. I like to think talking to you gave me courage.

I can't even really call it a decision. The choice was made not unlike getting your appetite. It was a feeling that simply arrived—I took a breath, and the next moment the answer was right there. It wasn't a belabored list of pros and cons. It was simply an urge, like needing to stretch or yawn. Time to go.

Once I was sure I was leaving, it only took a few more blinks to realize New York City was the only destination ever on my list. Where else would I go? We'd been to New York so many times before to visit Aunt Ivy when we were little. It's the only other place we knew besides Erie, and it always felt like anything was possible in a setting like that—even if only for the chance to disappear and start again.

We'd always talked about moving here, but I'd be lying if I said that dream about the splintered tree and door with the grimacing face didn't have an effect on me. I walked to a city that looked just like New York—Statue of Liberty and all. Her likeness punctuated the end of a sweeping skyline of metal and concrete towers, the spitting image of lower Manhattan. If nothing else, it was the extra push I needed to finally pack up and leave—some inner road sign pointing me in a direction I already knew I needed to go. The future felt somehow self-evident, and at this point, I can't afford to ignore intuition any longer. If I hadn't ignored it before, would you still be here?

When I stopped to consider the possibility of staying in Erie, I couldn't think of a single tangible reason for sticking around. I reminded myself it's already been three months since you've been gone now. If Singer had something more to tell me about your case, he would have called already. I don't have faith in him—or anyone else anymore. Singer said himself that the Erie Police don't have the expertise for a case like yours. He told me they'd brought in a special unit from Pittsburgh like it was supposed to be good news—like it was supposed to give me hope. Instead, it just feels like they're passing the buck. Making their problem someone else's.

I didn't even feel the need to tell Singer I was leaving. He's a detective, isn't he? He can find me if he needs to. And if I decide I want to talk to him, I know how to reach him. Before I left, I checked to make sure I still had those two pieces of paper Singer handed me that day in his office—his white business card and the index card with that psychiatrist's number scrawled in Singer's blue all-caps handwriting. I stuffed them both into a credit card flap in the back of my wallet. They're tucked just behind a worn picture of you and me and Gram on The Peninsula. I love that picture of us so much. Your arms are wrapped around me like they always are in photos. Every time I look at it, I still wonder who took it. Had Gram asked a stranger? Was Critter with us that day? Or maybe Aunt Ivy was visiting. It's funny how so often a photograph can stand in the place of memory. Without it, we might not know it happened at all.

If you'd only described that particular day to me, I would have no recollection. But there it is—photographic evidence. I've always kept that picture in my wallet as some sort of token from another time. The sight of the tops of our heads poking up above my driver's license has always comforted me. Even if my wallet was empty, at least my heart always felt full.

When I open my wallet now, even though Singer's card is tucked away and out of sight, I still know it's there, staring right through the underside of our picture. His name and number and the Pennsylvania state seal peer through our backs, all three of us frozen in a constant state of vigilance. The clean cotton paper that bears the name of the Erie Police Department seems to mock us rather than keep watch over us. In that picture, you're still here— still tucked away safely, preserved in an alternate reality of our childhood. The delicate texture of our photograph is pressed against the name of a man who can never bring you back but whose job it is to deliver you justice. Will he keep looking? Maybe I'll never know now that I've left.

All I do know is that it's better if I'm the one who can reach him and not the other way around. I never liked the way he looked at me. He hadn't said it outright, but I know he thinks I'm hiding something. He gave me that shrink's number as if he cared, but I don't believe he's concerned about my well-being—he doesn't trust me. At least our indignation is mutual.

I called our landlord just as soon as I was sure about leaving. I told him we'd be breaking our lease and vacating by the end of the month. Three weeks' notice. I said I understood if he needed to keep the deposit, but he didn't give me a hard time and just asked me when I wanted to do the final walkthrough. Maybe he'd seen your picture on the news, or maybe he just sensed something hurting in my voice. Either way, he seemed to take pity on me and made things easy. I didn't want his pity, but I sure did want our deposit back.

Money has been tight, and the stress has felt like a restless demon pressing down on my shoulders. On the other hand, it's simpler to make decisions this way—easier to trim away the fat of anything that's non-essential. I need to stay flexible and light on my feet. All in all, I have a little over two thousand dollars to my name after selling everything I could: just over one thousand dollars from our joint account, two hundred and six dollars remaining from my savings, nine hundred for selling the car, and I was able to scrape together another thirty-two by selling a few miscellaneous knick-knacks to that thrift store over on Brown Avenue. According to a woman behind the counter with questionable taste in eyeliner, your elephant mug was worth a whopping twenty-five cents.

I would have argued with her over its true value. I would have told her how my sister and I had gotten it together on a trip with our grandmother when we were young, and how neither of you is in this world anymore. But as I stood there, surrounded by overflowing shelves of other people's old junk, I thought I'd be happy enough to imagine a stranger discovering our elephant mug for themselves and momentarily feeling delighted by their luck. Maybe they can give it a new story. I'm sure that place is packed with other people's versions of our elephant mug—a thousand other twenty-five-cent treasures. But no one could ever possibly know just how precious they once were to someone else.

It doesn't matter. I decided straight away that I didn't want to keep any of our things. By the time the landlord came for the walkthrough, all I had left was a backpack light enough to throw over one shoulder. It's comical how you spend your whole life accumulating things that you are convinced matter, yet how easy it is to leave them behind when you lose the few things that actually do.

After all those years of collecting, I can now list my possessions on my fingers: a few old family photos, my buck knife, my Walkman, a twenty-pack case of CDs, my pencil case with a stash of pencils and pens, a week's worth of clothes, and a copy of *The Wonderful Wizard of Oz* for something familiar and mindless to leaf through on the train. I kept our dream journals too—both yours and mine. I'll keep filling these pages and writing you every opportunity I get. As for yours, I still don't know if I'll ever be able to bring myself to read it, but it was your only possession that felt impossible to leave behind.

It might have been easier than I imagined walking away from all our belongings, but it took me a century to sort through them. I thought I'd take a systematic approach and make three big piles—

one to sell, one to donate, and one to trash—but you always think your own stuff has far more value than it actually does. The trash pile began as only a small mound but ended as a moderate landfill. I figured out pretty quickly that I couldn't even pay people to take our things, and by the time I'd finished, most of it had ended up heaped on the side of the road for the garbage trucks.

The other substantial obstacle to dealing with our things was the simple sentimentality of it all—an ingredient I hadn't accurately factored into my time estimate. Nearly every object I picked up was accompanied by a little memory that bubbled up with it. Each item required a small goodbye ceremony, and I had no choice but to just sit with the rolling waves of sadness until they passed.

By far, the hardest thing to get rid of was your flute. An instrument somehow feels too much like an extension of a person—like a piece of their soul or their body—but after some expert negotiation tactics with myself, I finally managed to get it out of your closet and into the donation pile. Later that day, when I went back through your empty room, I could swear I heard you playing scales.

The most tedious effort of all was dealing with all our books. We'd already gotten rid of more than half of them after Gram died, so at least in my mind, our current collection was not nearly the beast it actually was. I counted over three-hundred books by the time I was done sorting them. Enough was in good shape that I thought it would be worth an attempt at selling them to that used book shop on Peach Street, but after all the trouble of transporting them there, they would only accept a few.

I'd lugged an overflowing, boulder-sized box from the back seat of the car and into their store—there was not a chance that box was leaving again with me. The cardboard seams were starting to split, and the books were spilling out the side. They agreed to buy about a dozen, but the rest they wouldn't take. I ended up begging the girl at the register to please just let me leave the rest there too—even if they couldn't pay. After some convincing, she finally agreed, but not without ensuring I had appreciated her exceptional inconvenience. How dare I abandon free books at an institution that just so happens to sell them.

Treasure Island, Charlotte's Web, Wuthering Heights, The Color Purple, Tess of the d'Urbervilles—it was like saying "so long" and "farewell" to a chronology of our adolescence. But that's the fortunate thing about stories. You don't need their physical pages to still hold onto them. Every one of those books is still in me and likely always will be.

I stuck a "for sale" sign in the car's back window right away, but I didn't get any calls, and I soon came to terms with the idea that it would be unlikely I could sell it before I had to be out of the house. At first, I thought maybe I could just drive it to New York and live in it for a few weeks until I found a place to stay, but ultimately I didn't trust the engine to run continuously for over four hundred miles. What if it broke down? A little extra cash would give me more flexibility than a ramshackle hunk of metal.

With only two days left to vacate, I received a lone lowball offer. I folded immediately just to get rid of it in time. A short, mousey guy showed up with a tall friend who must have been over six foot five. Neither of them removed their sunglasses even once. The mousey one asked a disturbing number of questions about the trunk, and the tall one never said a single word. Eventually, when they both seemed satisfied, the mousey one handed me a roll of bills, and the two drove off in separate cars.

A freeloading neighbor witnessed the transaction from their yard and stopped by after to see if I was getting rid of any furniture too. I told him he could have it for free if he moved it within twenty-four hours. All or nothing. He lugged it all out with his son the next day.

Yesterday, I did the final walkthrough of the house with the landlord. Everything seemed in good enough order. At most, the walls could use a fresh coat of paint, and I only had to pay for the broken window pane from when I'd slammed the front door too hard. I was relieved. I had cleaned and cleared meticulously. I couldn't risk any extra charges. Last night before I went to bed, I swept one final time and took out the last of the trash. I slept on the living room floor in my clothes, using my backpack as a pillow and my jacket as my blanket. Lying there on the cold, carpetless floor, I racked my brain for anything I'd forgotten to do.

Canceled the phone. Discontinued the utilities. Closed the bank account. That was when I realized I hadn't told anyone I was leaving other than the landlord. I have no one to tell. I suppose that was always the blessing and the curse of being so close to your sister—you were also the *only* person I was close to. Thanks to school, we learned early on that most other people fall into one of two categories: people who don't bother to understand you at all or people who misunderstand you on purpose just to get in a quick laugh at your expense. Either way, they're not to be trusted. But we never needed anyone else as long as we had each other. Everything between us was always so automatic and safe that most of the time we didn't even require words. Funny how I'm filled with them now.

I woke up just before sunrise to the horrendous, high-pitched beeping of my watch alarm. I was achy and stiff from sleeping on the floor, but I felt alert and clear. All I had to do was get out the door and leave the keys in a lockbox on the fence. A light rain was misting outside, and I was glad I wouldn't have to drag anything heavier than my backpack to the train station. I took Cherry Street so I could walk along the cemetery and see some trees before sitting inside a tin can all day.

It was eerie passing all the wet gravestones so early in the morning, the sun only barely peeking over the trees. It's most certainly mornings like this that earn Erie further rights to its name. I'm glad I never put you in the ground like that. Your dust was scattered on the beach, free to become part of the earth again. What do people think they're really speaking to when they speak to a grave? But who am I to judge? Who do I really think I'm writing to in these letters?

As I rounded the final corner of the cemetery, I thought to myself, in a way, I might be dead now too. I'm nothing but a ghost. No phone number. No address. No bank account. No possessions apart from what I can carry on my back. Does a modern person exist without these things? No one will miss me in Erie, and the only people I miss are already gone for good. There's something terrifying but equally freeing in such complete disconnection.

It was only about a thirty-five-minute walk to Union Station. I arrived with plenty of time to spare and bought my ticket at the window. Amtrak Train 48 departing just before 7 AM. I grabbed a coffee, a banana, and three granola bars for the ride and waited outside the rotunda. I'd gotten a bit damp on the walk, and it was chilly out too, so I stayed on my feet to keep warm. When the train arrived, I was the second person in line, and no more than two-dozen people boarded. My train car was mostly empty for the Sunday ride, and I had my first pick at a seat. I chose a section at the back with two pairs of double seats facing each other so I could put my feet up and keep an eye on my bag.

The conductor muttered something over the loudspeaker, and the train pulled out of the station. I watched Erie glide by through my window until I didn't recognize the scenery anymore. It would be more than eleven hours until I reached New York City—plenty of time to let my mind wander as I watched the houses pass. I don't remember feeling happy or sad or any other emotion I could give a name to. I simply observed the churn of life around me as if I had frozen stiff into place while everything encircling me had come alive with vibrant activity.

When the train stopped in Syracuse, a father boarded from the back of the car with a small boy, maybe only five or six years old. He was carrying a little stuffed animal lion. The father stowed their luggage in the same rear section of facing seats across the aisle from me. I'm not sure why exactly, but the pair immediately captured my attention, and I studied them secretly from under the brim of my hat. Before they took their seats, I watched the father retrieve a ziplock bag full of Goldfish from a side pocket in one of their suitcases. He tossed a handful into his mouth and then extended his hand, offering some to the little boy.

"Which way do we sit?" the little boy asked with outstretched arms, his tiny head falling back to gaze up at his father above. The little boy was referring to either the set of seats facing forward, toward the front of the train's car—and also toward our destination —or to the opposite seats facing the direction we'd already come. The father answered without skipping a beat in a tone that implied the answer was obvious and the question erroneous—even somewhat irritating, even for a small child. "We sit facing the direction we are going," the father said practically.

His answer and his tone took me aback. I'd been sitting the other way since Erie, facing home, watching each second of my past spill backward in the shapes of disappearing trees blurring into the distance. I thought more about the father's answer. Will I keep this up, always looking backward and into the past forever? Will New York really be the clean start I'm looking for? Is there such a thing?

Just before we reached Utica, I looked across the aisle and watched the little boy clutching his stuffed animal lion as he slept against his father's arm. With his free hand, the father stroked the boy's hair affectionately while he rested his eyes too. When the train lurched to a stop to let off passengers and board new ones, I rose to my feet and grabbed my bag by its strap as people rearranged themselves. I sidestepped into the aisle and found a new row of empty seats by the restrooms at the front of the car. I put my bag in the overhead and flopped down, this time facing forward—toward our destination. That little boy's father was right. We face the direction we are going.

At some point, the white noise of the moving train must have lulled me to sleep, and I dozed off with *The Wonderful Wizard of Oz* on my lap and my head pressed up against the cool glass of the window. The last thing I remember reading was the scene when Dorothy finally arrives at the great gates of Emerald City to the Palace of Oz. In the movie, all the characters feel like parodies of the ones you imagine from the book. The cowardly Lion, the Tin Man, the Scarecrow, and of course, Oz.

I suppose it's like that with most movie versions of books, but re-reading the original text of Dorothy's story felt more like some reassuring words that Gram might have said to us as children. "There is no living thing that is not afraid when it faces danger. The true courage is in facing danger when you are afraid, and that kind of courage you have in plenty."[1]

I slept through the rest of the ride and didn't wake up until I heard the sound of bodies shuffling to grab their bags and a voice over the loudspeaker announcing, "Last stop, New York Penn Station." I groggily found my feet and snatched up my bag. The train screeched slowly to a stop, and the doors opened. I stepped out onto the platform and took in my surroundings. The station wasn't how I remembered it from our trips as kids. It felt darker. Dirtier. Lonelier. Had it been like this then too? Trash was everywhere, and a sour smell wafted through the tunnel. The side of my head ached where my hat had been pinned between the window pane and my temple.

It took me a few tries to find the exit. Penn Station is such a maze of underground passageways, and I took wrong turns down three different corridors until I was able to find one that would lead me to the surface. On my way, a man with shoes held together with worn duct tape asked me for some change, and I emptied my pocket into his hand, but by the time I'd rounded the next curve, I'd passed another half dozen people in the same predicament. My heart fluttered, suddenly appreciating the truly extreme nature of New York City. If I don't find a home and a livelihood soon, will I be the one asking for quarters? I'd stepped into the urban equivalent of the Sahara Desert or the Arctic tundra. Without enough resources, are we all marooned—alone in a sea of other humans?

It was early evening when I finally departed the station on Seventh Avenue. I still had about two hours of daylight left to figure out what was next. I'd planned on finding a cheap chain hotel somewhere straight away, but once I'd gotten onto the street, the energy of the city had other plans for me. I wasn't tired and felt rested enough from my nap on the train, so instead, I wandered my way downtown. I zigzagged until I came across Fifth Avenue and knew all I had to do from there was walk in the direction that made the street numbers get smaller—if I followed it straight down, eventually, it would spit me out into Washington Square Park. I still remembered the basics from Gram's never-ending walking tours. She always used to call that park the heartbeat of New York City.

It's Sunday night, and people have work tomorrow—everything feels alive. Couples nuzzling on park benches. A four-piece jazz band playing in front of the Washington Square fountain. Kids huddling together cross-legged on blankets in the grass. I must have spent over an hour just watching people pass. I feel invisible, and I like it. It's as if I'm some kind of lonesome phantom floating amongst people with real lives. They probably have pets and kids, jobs and college degrees, cars and homes. They have so much that I'm missing, but maybe I also have something valuable that they don't. I'm free.

I'm writing to you now from a little coffee shop just off the south corner of the park where I can still watch the nightlife from the street. I can hear live music from a bar a couple of doors down. I think you'd like this place. It's the kind of café with mismatched tables and those French-looking metal bistro chairs. The exterior is painted top to bottom in green, awning and all. I found a table outside on the sidewalk and ordered a black coffee and two napoleons—one for me, one for you. It's dark now, and I've been here for over three hours already. The waitress is giving me a look like she might want to get rid of me unless I order more food or plan on leaving her a fat tip.

It's funny how the mind works sometimes. I'd taken out *The Wizard of Oz* from my backpack and had rested it on the table to read. I was just about to open it after finishing my coffee, but I wanted to catch the waitress first so I could order another. It wasn't until I placed my empty cup on my saucer that I remembered what I'd dreamed about during my nap on the train. It was as if the words of Oz himself had summoned the dream from the folds of my unconsciousness. Or maybe it was the Cowardly Lion.

I was all alone in the middle of what seemed like it should have been a busy New York City block, and I stood in front of a tall marble building with three arches held up by Roman columns. Wide steps descended from its doors into the street where two beautiful stone lions guarded its entrance.

I approached the one closest to get a better look when suddenly I heard the sound of stones grinding, and before I could register what was happening, I watched the lion before me come to life right there on his pedestal. He began to speak. Frozen in shock, I felt more like I was the one who was a statue.

He told me his name was Fortitude, and his fellow companion on the opposite side was Patience. Somehow it sounded like it fit them well. I was so dumbfounded I couldn't do anything but stare back blankly, my lips parted in disbelief as I listened. His speech made him sound more like some kind of debonair oracle—not the words you might imagine from a gruff jungle king.

He went on to describe the meaning of strength, which seemed like a fitting topic, judging by the looks of his broad shoulders and the rippling muscles of his sturdy stone haunches. But he spoke not just of brawn or physical power but about a different kind of strength—a committed determination to overcome whatever heartbreak the days may throw at you. He spoke so beautifully, just like Gram spoke to us in her stories about Astrid. It was like poetry itself. And then, when Fortitude had finished his lyrical counsel, he turned his great maned head away from me and became stone once again as if he'd never been alive at all.

I spun around on my heels to see who else had just witnessed what I had, but I was all alone in the street. There wasn't a soul who would ever believe what I'd just seen. That must have been when we pulled up to Penn Station, and I woke to the sound of the loudspeaker and people shuffling in the aisles to get their things.

It's getting late now, and I still haven't made a shred of progress finding a place to sleep tonight, but truth be told, I'm feeling more inclined to walk around until morning. I can save a chunk of money by sparing myself the cost of a room, and I feel like I need to wear out both my legs and my mind for as long as I can keep them moving. And if I'm being completely honest, something about that dream tells me that maybe I have somewhere I should be in the morning.

Do you remember the New York Public Library from our trips with Gram? I don't know why, but I feel like I need to pay those two stone lions outside its entrance a little visit as soon as possible.

I wonder if their names really are Patience and Fortitude.

Love,
Rosalyn

Two Lions

I found myself standing before a marble
building, spanning nearly twice a city block.
Above six tall columns, "New York Public Library"
was engraved in its facade's smooth rock.

From the street, I noticed two elegant statues
guarding the grand building as a pair.
A duo of handsome stone lions flanked
its steps, gazing forward in a focused stare.

As I walked toward the northern lion, I heard
grinding gravel as if under a heavy truck's tire.
Not a soul was on the street, and for a moment,
I panicked, unsure of what was about to transpire.

But once I'd caught my bearings, I realized
it was one of the stone lions—he had come alive.
"Welcome to our library," he spoke,
"We're the keepers of this hallowed archive."

"My name is Fortitude, and over there,
that's Patience, my identical twin."
The lion had a dapper New York accent
and spoke with a wide, fanged grin.

"You look so downtrodden, young lady,
I see that something is ailing you.
I don't mean to be presumptuous, but if you
need some words of strength, I have a few."

"I've learned a thing or two from all
the brave stories contained within this place."
Fortitude's eyes met mine, his giant snout
so close that his breath warmed my face.

"Each morning, the world wakes to
break your heart in one thousand ways,
but it's a choice to let all that pain instead
strengthen you for the rest of your days.

You see, to fall in love with a purpose
is also to suspend your disbelief,
for its pursuit will be met with sure
suffering and impossible grief.

To become a true warrior is
not to kill, maim or submit—
rather, faith in a worthy mission,
and a humble life to commit.

And if you feel afraid, take comfort
that countless warriors have come before—
inviting you, inspiring you from
the threshold of the next battle's door.

And though you'll feel alone, treading
forth as a single-soldier infantry,
the truth is, you have thousands of companions within
this noble building's volumes of books and poetry.

We're the heirs to our actions—for good
or evil—let only this much be your guide,
and we'd be wise to remember: the master has
failed more times than the student has tried.

Remember that even when the world is
vicious and tears for so long at your seams
that you possess more grit and might
than you can fathom, even in dreams.

I know you seek answers, but have faith
that they all will come with time.
Patience over there can tell you that to rush
your process would be your only true crime.

Take this not lightly—strive to know
truth only through your own eyes,
for it's following the beats of your
own drum that will make you truly wise.

Always be strong and patient with
all that is unsolved in your heart,
for the questions themselves
are like their own kind of art."

With that, Fortitude returned his gaze
forward, transforming back into lifeless stone.
I looked each way for other witnesses
of what I'd just seen, but I was all alone.

A Ghost's Song

Wednesday, May 28, 1997

Dear Nova,

So much has happened in the past two days that I hardly know how to begin this letter. I'm writing from my new bedroom, at least for the time being. I've found a place to stay, and it's not even a hotel or public park.

As I recount the past forty-eight hours, the events feel so surreal. It's like some pre-orchestrated blueprint exists somewhere just beyond my mind's reach. I doubt I could have choreographed things more smoothly, even if I had planned them all myself from the start. I'm trying to feel appreciative of my good fortune—instead of suspicious. After only a day in New York without a strategy, how do I now find myself with a roof over my head? It's like I'm flowing along a river current that has its own destination in mind. I suppose not having a plan is what sometimes leaves room for the impossible.

I was right not to bother with a hotel. I would have surrendered a small fortune only to ricochet off the four walls of a New York-sized room until it was time to check out. As soon as I stood from my seat at the café, I knew I would be too restless to sleep, but if I wandered the city until dawn the next day, I could at least tire myself out—and that's precisely what I did.

After I finished my last letter, I packed up my things, paid my bill, and left an extra few-buck apology tip for the waitress. I tucked a handful of brown sugar packets into my bag for a free snack later and asked a stranger to point me toward the Lower East Side. I still seem to have a decent sense of cardinal direction, and I felt reasonably confident which way was east, but it certainly wouldn't hurt to double-check. I'm fine inside the numbered grid of avenues and streets, but once they inexplicably abandon their ordered logic and are replaced with arbitrary names, I quickly lose my bearings and get twisted around.

I waved down a guy wearing a scuffed leather jacket. We were walking in opposite directions, and he stopped at my request. He had long dirty blonde hair running down his back, and an electric guitar case was slung over his shoulder. "Excuse me, which way to the Lower East Side?" With a question like that, it was obvious I was nothing more than a tourist, but I didn't want to linger, so I asked as directly as possible. Without a word, he pointed down the street in the direction I'd already been walking, then lifted a cigarette from his breast pocket and turned away to light it, indicating his job was done. I felt reassured that my initial instinct had been correct, and I set off to the east with a renewed confidence that I might be a New Yorker sooner than I'd thought.

My loose idea was to weave around the Lower East Side for a few hours, and I assumed that, eventually, I would find my way to Aunt Ivy's old apartment. I thought I'd easily recognize her building's facade when I saw it, and after all, how big can Manhattan really be? My memories of New York with you and Gram have always felt most lucid in Aunt Ivy's old neighborhood, and a pilgrimage back to those same streets felt like the only right thing to do. Do you remember how small her apartment was? The shower was in the kitchen, and it was so tight that even as kids, you and I could barely maneuver our elbows enough to wash our hair without splashing water through the shower curtain and onto Ivy's old, gapped, sloping wood floors. It made our place in Erie feel like a palace.

At first, I thought all I'd have to do was keep an eye out for Aunt Ivy's street name. I knew she was on Suffolk Street. Or was it Norfolk? I always remembered those two streets as a pair because they sounded so similar and ran parallel but, for the life of me, I couldn't remember which one was Ivy's. The longer I walked, and the longer nothing looked familiar, the more I was forced to concede that my memory of Ivy's neighborhood was far murkier than I'd believed.

I must have weaved up and down every block within a mile radius, and after enough frustration, I simply started taking random turns and crossing my fingers. In the end, I got lucky—the strategy actually worked. At last, I rounded a corner and saw a green sign illuminated under a street lamp. Suffolk. I'd made it. I turned right and followed the sidewalk until it ended at a little park, but still, I hadn't recognized any of the apartment building facades. Which one was Ivy's?

We'd visited so many times as kids, but I'd long ago forgotten the actual building number—maybe I never knew it to begin with. I had to rely solely on my child self's visual memory of the front stoop. As I passed entrance after entrance, I realized it could have been any one of those old tenement buildings. We were still so young then, and I suppose at that age, a memory exists more in its sketches than in its finer details—or does the same go for any age? Maybe that's how a memory always works. It's a marvel that we human beings have grown so comfortable with our tenuous dependence on them—so inherently ephemeral and unreliable.

Without any success on Suffolk, I found Norfolk one street over and walked all the way down that one too. When nothing there rang a bell either, I officially gave up on my quest for Ivy's building. After all, I know that apartment is only an artifact of something much more precious but intangible—only a reminder of times we once shared. Those apartment walls had to be around there somewhere, but touching their bricks won't change anything. All the people I love who once gave those walls life are gone now. I know that. I kept walking.

It felt so unnatural to roam New York City as an adult, alone with no chaperones. All my experiences here were shared with you and Gram. It took me hours to adjust to the newness of it all, but once I'd gotten the hang of my solitude, it felt liberating. By around 3 AM, there was almost no one left on the street except drunken bar patrons stumbling their way home and a few unsavory-looking characters who stared me up and down as I passed.

I never felt unsafe, but I couldn't exactly say I felt safe either. That's no complaint. Strangely, I welcomed it. I don't know why, but something excited me about the imminent sense of danger. Though that didn't stop me from taking a knee under a street lamp on a particularly lonely-looking street to fish out my buck knife from the bottom of my backpack and clip it onto my belt. I suspected it might be illegal to carry a knife like mine out in the open of a big city, but if a dangerous enough situation presented itself, better to be prepared, I thought. I was comforted by having it within reach. Its symbolic reassurance felt like enough.

My flannel shirt almost completely covered its leather case, and only the last inch or so poked out over my jeans. I could squeak by without getting arrested, at least for the night. The evening air was crisp, and I felt sharp and clear like some hungry, wild animal prowling her new terrain. I've always been such a night creature, and with the city asleep, illuminated only by the street lamps and neon signs, I felt in my natural habitat.

I think I like the city even more at night than I do during daylight. There's a feeling that maybe you don't even really exist at all. Like you're just a shadow. A specter. I'll never understand how you got the morning gene, and I got the nocturnal one, despite sharing virtually identical genetic code. They call New York the city that never sleeps, but I'm starting to think maybe it just collects sleepless people.

I wandered for hours. I didn't have a specific route in mind, only a vague sense that I needed to keep moving. Instinctively, I let my legs feel their way around the dark streets in search of some new territory that might feel like it belonged to me, even if I couldn't say how or why.

Eventually, I ended up in a public park at the water's edge, and I watched the sun rise over the East River. The rising sun danced over the river's surface, shimmering like the infinite scales of a fish. So much water flows through that river every day—water as old as the planet. Just two hydrogen atoms and one oxygen multiplied billions and billions of times, enough to fill up all the clouds and the rivers and the oceans. What wonders has this water seen? Once upon a time, this same river was ice and vapor, keeping the wooly mammoths company. Now it's here with me, sparkling by the dawn light. What would that river say to me if it could speak? This thought made me lonely as I realized how much I wanted to ask.

"Hello, river. Do you know where your currents are taking you? Do you know where mine are taking me?"

When the sun had stationed itself high enough over the water's edge to signify morning, I knew it was time to start walking again —only this time with a final destination in mind. The night had served its purpose well, granting me the time and space to be alone with my thoughts, and I was glad to have an early start to the day. Despite all the miles, my mind still felt eager and apprehensive. I said farewell to the river and headed back in the direction I'd come. It was time to find the New York Public Library. I was ready to pay those two stone lions their visit.

I didn't know when the library opened—all I knew was that I wanted to be there the moment it did. I figured if I set out early and could at least get myself there, its front steps would be a pleasant place to rest until visiting hours officially began. If I could only get some directions from a benevolent stranger, how far could it be? New York is a walkable city. But by then, I'd been on my feet all night. My legs had started to stiffen and ache. My mind was twitchy and alert, but my body was barely limping along. At a minimum, I knew I'd need to resuscitate myself with some caffeine, and I was able to find an open café within about fifteen minutes. There were only four small two-seater round tables in the whole place, and it looked like they might still be setting up for the day, but they had a restroom in the back that the girl at the counter let me use while she wiped down the espresso machine.

I freshened up and bought a banana, two colossal pastries, and a large coffee. I balanced them all on a small saucer-sized plate and carried them to a tiny table where I devoured them one by one across from only one other customer on the opposite side of the room. I lingered with my coffee until, at last, I felt ready to move again. I brought my dishes back up to the girl at the counter—a polite excuse to request another favor. "Do you know how to get to the New York Public Library from here?" I asked. I took note of how weak my voice sounded. The girl had her eyebrow pierced, wore dark, blue-ish black eye shadow, and was immediately friendly. Maybe she was lonely too. She ripped a sheet of paper from her server pad and started scribbling instructions in slanted handwriting. She was one of those proud New Yorkers, excited to show off that she knew her way around, and I was grateful for the help.

"Houston is the street we're on now," she said. "If you take the easiest route, you'll only have one turn." She told me I'd need to take a right out of the café and just keep walking straight. My first right would be on Thompson Street, and that would lead me to Washington Square. I nodded and said I knew of the park and had been there only yesterday. "Piece of cake. Then the rest will be easy for you," she said. At the top of the park, I'd be back at Fifth Avenue, and from there, keep walking against traffic until I get to another big park about forty blocks away. I'd find the library nestled in the trees about half a block up on the left.

She told me if I adhered to the directions and stuck to Fifth Avenue, getting off track would be nearly impossible. I thanked the girl genuinely and accepted the sheet of paper with her directions, even though it seemed more for her own entertainment than for my information. Thompson Street. Turn right. Fifth Avenue. That was it. I smiled my thanks, and she smiled back.

As I made my way down Houston Street, the morning traffic grew busier and noisier with each passing block. I imagined from the girl's directions that I'd be at the library in a matter of twenty or thirty minutes, but it took me almost another hour before I even hit the bottom of Fifth Ave. I was running out of energy, and my strides had become slow and labored. In my weariness, my pace dragged.

Finding my way was easy. The hard part was summoning the energy to sidestep all the expressionless faces barreling toward me in suits and pencil skirts. Their steps were quick and adrenalized. I imagined them marching into offices with floor-to-ceiling windows and stacks of important papers. To them, I wasn't a person— merely an obstacle. But soon I relaxed, realizing the steady stream of blank nine-to-five apparitions parted around me automatically if I was too slow to dodge their trajectories. Their course seemed pre-programmed. Ships redirecting around icebergs. Planes avoiding turbulence.

I began to imagine Fifth Avenue might be leading me all the way to the Arctic Circle when finally, I spotted a patch of lush green against the expanse of gray concrete. A wave of relief washed over my body as I registered the outline of trees. After another block, the great facade of the library emerged from the street with three massive arches sweeping over its grand entryway, and for the first time, I felt the full impact of my exhaustion. My backpack wasn't necessarily heavy, but it wasn't doing me any favors, either. I reached a hand back into its side pocket and retrieved the sugar packets I'd stashed from the green café. As if to prevent myself from collapsing right there on the street, I delicately tore off their paper corners and poured them into my mouth one at a time as I took in my surroundings.

It was still relatively early, and a few people lingered near the library's entryway, chatting or reading books standing up. I hadn't yet noticed anyone disappear through the front doors, so I assumed the library wasn't open for reading hours. Instead, I seized the opportunity for a small rest and sidled up next to one of the lion statues on the north side of the steps. It was the same lion who had spoken to me in the dream. I tossed off my backpack, leaned against its stone pedestal, and closed my eyes. I have to admit, in my delirium, I almost half expected to hear him speak.

You can imagine my shock when indeed, I did hear a rich, weathered voice address me. It was just like the lion's voice in the dream—though not in a New York accent, but in what sounded like an Australian one. I snapped myself upright, twisting my head up towards the lion, but he was still made of stone, no different than before. It took a moment to recalibrate my attention enough to notice a man with hollow-looking cheeks accompanied by an even more hollow-looking old dog sitting on the steps only five or six feet from me. "Young lady, best to rest with at least one eye open," he said, not in a scolding way, just more in a kind, fatherly tone. "Mister Giuliani ain't watching over your backpack while you squeeze in your nanny nap."

He wore a frayed, light blue seersucker suit with a tattered purple handkerchief tucked into his breast pocket. He looked tidy and put together, but that suit of his had certainly seen better days. It was unclear to me how he had come to be there. I hadn't noticed him when I'd sat down, but he seemed rooted into position as if those library steps were his unofficial watchtower and his raggedy mutt, his loyal enlisted watchdog.

I told him "thank you" as calmly as I could manage, but the sound of his voice had rattled me. The lions from the dream were still fresh in my mind, and in my exhaustion, the lines between dreams and reality seemed thin. My disorientation must have shown on my face.

"You like dogs?" he asked. I gave a weak, cautious smile and nodded, "yes." With that, he made a clicking sound in his cheek, snapped the fingers of one hand, and pointed toward me. His scruffy dog sprung to his feet like a young athletic puppy and scurried to my side. He rested his sweet head full of wiry hair on my lap. He was much softer to the touch than his appearance suggested.

"Not from the city, are ya?" the old man asked, seeming to make small talk, though he didn't really look like the small-talk-type. It was only then that I became painfully aware of my disheveled, sweaty state and realized I might have appeared homeless. Technically, I guess I was. I shook my head "no."

The man motioned toward the two stone lions like a king presenting his court. "That's Patience over there, and this right here is Fortitude," he said pointing, respectively. "Yea. I know," was all I could reply. Their names really were Patience and Fortitude, just like the lion had said in my dream. I can't remember ever having learned that in any books or on our trips with Gram. If only I had told the old man how I actually knew their names. "Yea. I know—because Fortitude came to life and told me their names yesterday," I imagined myself completing the sentence. But somehow by the looks of the old man, I didn't think he'd judge me for my apparent madness. There was something earnest and captivating about him—like he'd seen enough in his life that not much could surprise him. He struck me as someone who might be quite at home with a little madness.

"Looking for some trouble, aye?" he said, gesturing with two fingers to the bottom of my shirt. It took me a minute to register what he was talking about. I looked down in the direction he was pointing and spotted the tip of the leather holster for my buck knife still protruding from under my shirt. I was lucky he was the only person so far who'd noticed. The last thing I needed was to get arrested. I was impressed with how quickly the man had sized me up.

"Good eye," I said.

"Hardly," the man said with a hoarse laugh. "I served for twenty-five years in the Royal Australian Air Force. After that long, you know how to spot a barney from a mile away. It's no different than noticing a freckle on a person's face or a ring around their finger."

"What's a barney?" I asked. He clenched his fists like he was a boxer and raised them to his chest in mock aggression. I smiled and nodded in understanding as I unclipped my knife from my belt and returned it safely to the depths of my backpack. I liked his warmth and gruff humor.

I told the man I was from Pennsylvania and that my great-uncle had given me that knife for my eighteenth birthday. "See now, I could tell right away you were handy," he said affably.

I wanted to tell the old man all about the adventures we'd had with Critter over the years—how the three of us loved being outside together in the peace of the forest. How we'd grown up shooting targets on hay bails in Critter's yard. How he'd taught us everything he knew about bowhunting and fishing by the time we were thirteen, and how you and I even worked at a bow and reel shop for more than five years. How it had started only as a summer job, and we'd only meant to stay until we graduated high school, but before we knew it, we were both working there full-time with no prospects for a way out of Erie anywhere on the horizon. That birthday before graduation when Critter gave us our buck knives was the last time we saw him alive.

I didn't say any of that, of course, although I wanted to. I was surprised by my sudden desire to spout my life's story to a perfect stranger. Once again, I became aware of the dull ache of loneliness. That was when I, too, noticed something clipped to the old man's clothes—a perfectly polished gold pin on his lapel. "What's that pin for?" I said, feeling it was my turn to point and ask a question. He glanced down at it proudly. "Air Force badge. Per Ardua Ad Astra. It's Latin for 'Through adversity, to the stars.'"

It was hard to see the pin's details from where I sat, but I could roughly make out a bird with outstretched wings encircled by a wheel. "I like it," I told him. "Back in Erie, my family had a little Latin saying too. In Somnis Veritas."

"Ahhhh, that reminds me of my other favorite. In Vino Veritas," he said with what could only be described as a twinkle in his eye. I told him I wouldn't mind a drink myself right about now, even if the sun had only just come up.

We sat together in a comfortable silence before the man reached into the breast pocket of his tattered jacket and extracted a small, wrinkled writing pad and a thin gold pen. He scrawled something on a page and tore out the sheet cleanly with a quick snap of his wrist. He folded the paper in half and handed it to me without a word—but with a sly look on his face like he'd just told me a secret.

I unfolded the paper, and a quiet moment passed between us as I held it in front of me without understanding. It was an address. "I don't mean to be presumptuous, young lady," the man said, "but it looks to me as though you might be in need of a safe place to stay. And I don't mean the Plaza Hotel—just someplace more suited for people like us."

"Thank you," I said sincerely. And in a way, I also felt flattered he considered me to be a person "like him." He seemed good-natured and unpretentious. "That's very kind. I just got here yesterday and haven't found a place yet, but I'm not homeless if that's what you mean."

"I didn't think you were," he said. "Just in between," his eyes smiled back.

"The place you're looking for is called The Bardo. The address is on that paper," he said with a nod. "You'll know you're there when you see a brightly-colored door painted with a face. Its mouth is opened wide like a screaming ghost. You can't miss it." My blood ran cold.

"A screaming ghost?" I asked.

"Yes, a screaming ghost, I suppose. That's how I describe it, at least," he repeated.

"Kind of like it's grimacing?"

"Bloody oath, that's a word for it, alright. A grimace. A grimacing ghost," he answered, trying out the word for himself.

His last few syllables hit me like an ice bath. A gri-mac-ing face. Just like the face on the door I'd dreamed about before leaving Erie? I was a tall tree split in half by lightning. I walked for days toward a city that looked just like New York, and when I arrived, I found a door with a grimacing face.

Since you've been gone, maybe a few of my screws have gotten knocked loose, and now I'm looking for coincidences that aren't there. But at that moment, sitting next to the old man, flanked by Patience and Fortitude, the details felt too strange and specific to be chance. I wondered if I was hearing things—or maybe I was dreaming again—but his words were clear, and I was wide awake. At the very least, the old man certainly had my attention.

"How do I get there from here?" I asked.

"It's just over that way across the river," he said, pointing. "I can give you directions if you like. You'd have to be a drongo to get lost."

"Thank you," I nodded.

"Just walk up to that next street and take a left. The subway entrance is right there. You can't miss it. You'll see purple signs for the Seven Train. Follow the arrows to Flushing, Queens. All you need to do is ride for two stops. Get off when you see signs for Vernon Boulevard. When you get above ground, walk to the nearest street corner, and you'll be at 50th Avenue and Vernon. If you see a church on your right-hand side, you're pointed in the right direction. Just keep on walking straight and make sure the street numbers are getting smaller. You can't get lost from there. The Bardo will be about seven blocks down on your left. You'll see the door with the screaming ghost. See? Easy, right? Seven Train. Two stops. Right at the church. Seven blocks. Screaming ghost."

I hoped I wasn't a drongo, whatever that meant. It certainly didn't seem as simple as the man was making it sound, and the very concept of taking the subway intimidated me right away. "Seven Train. Two stops. Right at the church. Seven blocks. Screaming ghost." I repeated softly to myself, committing the route to memory.

"You got it," the man nodded with an approving smile.

"So it's like a hotel?" I asked.

"Not quite," he replied without any further detail. I didn't ask for any more either.

"I appreciate the tip very much," I thanked the man genuinely, although I neither explicitly confirmed nor denied if I'd be taking him up on his suggestion. But in truth, I knew from the second he'd described the door with the screaming ghost that I had to know what was behind it.

I ran my fingers through the fur on his old raggedy dog's head, and he pushed back affectionately against the pressure of my hand. I gave him a few gentle goodbye pats, and he licked my palm as if he were saying a friendly goodbye too.

With that, I slung my backpack over my shoulder, thanked the old man a final time, and found my feet. As I adjusted my backpack straps, the old man winked at me and tapped the Air Force pin on his lapel. I motioned back, tapping my temple with my index finger, signaling that I understood. "Per Ardua ad Astra: through adversity to the stars," I heard the man's graveled voice say again in my mind.

It's funny how these small mantras find us again and again throughout our lives in these moments of fear and directionlessness. "In Somnis Veritas," I heard Gram's voice say too. I hadn't even bothered venturing inside the library, but as I paced away, I had the feeling I'd already found what I'd come looking for.

I paused just before the end of the street to turn and take one last good look over my shoulder toward the two lions. I bid them a silent farewell and let the library slowly fade from my periphery as I turned the corner. It wasn't until then that I realized I'd never asked the man for his name, nor had I offered mine. And though I hadn't said so, I think we both knew the address on the paper would be my next stop.

The Seven Train entrance was clearly marked, and I bought a single ride card from a young woman at the underground kiosk. She looked bored out of her mind, yet at the same time irritated that I had interrupted her boredom. I paid her a buck fifty, and she pushed my change and a flimsy subway card under the glass window. I swiped it at the turnstile and pushed through its greasy bars, arriving at the station platform. I waited only several minutes before I heard a distant rumble and felt a soft, warm gust of wind passing through the tunnel. The air underground was humid and smelled like wet newspaper. Several minutes passed, and a silver train rattled up to the platform edge. A sharp screeching sound echoed as its metal wheels slowed against the tracks. The sliding doors parted, and I stepped over the threshold into the train's car. With that small stride, I suddenly felt like anything was possible.

I found an empty two-seater bench at the far end of the train car and slipped my backpack onto my lap, lacing my fingers over its front so my arms could slacken. The muscles of my left forearm seemed to be in a state of revolt, twitching involuntarily as I attempted to relax. Had I been clenching my fists? I watched my fellow passengers shuffle into their seats along the orange benches or cling to the chrome poles that stretched from floor to ceiling.

"Stand clear of the closing doors, please," a muffled, pre-recorded man's voice said over the loudspeaker. Just before the doors snapped shut, a teenage boy leaped through, only narrowly escaping their clutches. He slid into the empty bench facing mine across the car. He was wearing worn Levi's that looked several sizes too big for his thin frame, and their frayed cuffs dragged along the ground below his heels. Contrary to his jeans' appearance, his shoes looked pristine, as if he'd just slid them on for the very first time before boarding the train—black DC skater sneakers with white soles and royal blue laces. They were too clean for him to be a skater, and he wasn't carrying a skateboard. It feels so easy to study the details of a perfect stranger when you're locked into facing positions only a few feet apart.

He seemed to be studying me too. Although he didn't look at me directly, I could feel him sizing me up out of the corners of his eyes. The conductor announced the next stop over the loudspeaker, his words muttering and inaudible. The train lurched forward, and my torso swayed with the car's movement as we rattled along the track. Only two stops. That had been the man's directions. I'd need to pay attention so I wouldn't miss my station.

I looked straight ahead, out the window of the opposite door, and I watched the dark shadows of the tunnel glide past, feeling momentarily lulled by the clanking of metal against the rails. In a sidelong glance, I noticed that the boy across from me was now looking directly at me, making no effort to conceal his gaze. He waited until he seemed absolutely sure I was looking back at him too, and just as we locked eyes, a bright red stream of liquid emerged from the corner of his mouth. He began clutching his stomach with an agonized expression that contorted every muscle of his face. His brows wrinkled in pain, but he didn't make a sound.

Was he sick? Had he just been hurt? My heart pounded so violently I thought I could almost hear it over the train's thunderous rumbling. I didn't know what to do. Instinctively, I rose to my feet in a panic and looked around the car to see if anyone else was looking. No one else seemed to notice or care.

"Hey!" I said softly, but firmly too, stretching out my open hand, though still careful not to touch him. "Are you ok?" The kid's head slumped to his chest, and more red dripped from his chin and disappeared into his dark blue shirt. "Hey!" I said again, this time loud enough for half the car to hear. I caught the attention of a man in a suit sitting several benches over. He glimpsed up from his newspaper, although only fleetingly, more to convey his annoyance than his concern. He returned to his paper, indifferent to the scene.

I reached out for the kid's shoulder, unsure of what to do next, but before my hand could make contact, his whole body began shaking gently. Was he convulsing? Was he having a seizure? I stepped backward in bewilderment, trying to hold my balance against the movement of the train. As I gripped the handrail behind me, it suddenly struck me that his shaking was not due to some injury but rather stifled laughter. Only an instant later, the kid lifted his head, straightened his posture, and brushed his chin with the back of his hand, wiping away the smudged red liquid into the bottom of his shirt. My panic immediately shifted to outrage.

"So you were messing with me?" I said angrily. I was seething, and the exhaustion in my body was instantly replaced with heat. The kid didn't speak. He just slowly nodded as he chuckled to himself. He spat a plastic capsule into the palm of his hand and shoved it into his pants pocket. It was only a fake blood pellet like you get for Halloween pranks.

The train slowed, and the doors opened once again, shaking me out of my shock and anger only enough to remind me of my journey. One stop down and one more to go. The doors closed again with a mechanical thud.

"Why would you do that?" I demanded.

"Chilllllll," he drew out the word slowly. "Everything's cool. You just needed a little reminder."

"What are you talking about? A reminder of what?" I asked, fury swelling in my chest.

"That's my gift to you today," the kid smiled across at me.

"A gift? The gift of a heart attack?" I shot back. I fell back into my seat.

The kid shrugged. "Maybe that's how you see it."

"How do you see it then?"

"I think it was the gift you needed today."

"What do you mean," I fired with growing frustration, not understanding.

"I could see you stressing over there. Twitching. Sweating. And don't you feel relieved now? There's no emergency here—but you thought there was. And whatever you were worrying about before, I bet you're not thinking about it right now."

"So you just ride around pretending to die and scaring people all day?"

"Not all day. Just every day. You were the lucky one today," he grinned, flashing a perfect set of pearly white teeth.

"Thanks," I said bluntly, making sure my sarcasm was apparent.

We sat in silence for a minute or two until the train again screeched against the rails as it braked. "This is a good city, ya know?" he said with sudden sincerity in his tone. "It's what you make of it."

Something about his voice seemed like it should have belonged to a person twice or three times his age. The train rolled to a stop and as the doors opened, the boy bounded to his feet and sprinted out without another word, disappearing into a throng of fresh passengers. The prophet in skater shoes was gone as quickly as he had appeared.

Two stops. I'd almost forgotten that this was my station too. Regaining my focus, I jolted to my feet, clutching my backpack. "Stand clear of the closing doors, please," the loudspeaker boomed. A massive construction worker as tall as he was wide filed into the train just as I leaped out, and I clipped his enormous arm in my haste, ricocheting off of him and into the handrail. He scowled down at me as I apologized under my breath and slipped sideways between the doors just as they closed.

I stood dumbstruck on the platform as the train pulled away, collecting myself. Right at the church. Seven blocks. Screaming ghost. I was almost there. My whole body began to buzz with a nervous kind of energy. My anticipation of reaching the door with the grimacing face percolated with a force that made me feel ill. I threw my backpack over my shoulder once again and marched toward the signs for an exit. It took all my effort to climb a dirty concrete staircase, finally breaching the underground to the morning light. I was in Queens.

A church was on my right, just as the old man at the library had said there would be. I checked the street signs: Vernon Boulevard and 50th Avenue. I'd only need to follow Vernon straight for seven blocks. I didn't waste any time and started counting off the street corners. The Bardo should be on the left.

The farther I walked, the smaller and less inhabited the buildings appeared and the more sparse the pedestrians. The area seemed almost entirely industrial. What had been a manic morning commute of foot traffic in Manhattan was all but deserted in Queens. A pair of rough-looking characters smoking cigarettes walked a large Rottweiler. Truck drivers dotted the avenue, loading heavy boxes strapped to wooden platforms with forklifts. This neighborhood was nothing but one gray warehouse after another.

I counted off my sixth block and spotted a stout four-story building. When I caught sight of a large, brightly-colored steel door painted with something I couldn't immediately make out, I crossed the street. As I drew nearer, its shapes came into focus. A broad, ghost-like face peered back at me from the door's surface, and I knew I'd arrived at the place the man at the library had called The Bardo. Was the feeling inside my stomach relief? Fear? Or utter famished exhaustion? Maybe all of the above.

I braced myself on the sidewalk, staring back at the face on the door. Its mouth opened into a wide black hole that looked like you could walk right in. Its eyes were open, but they sagged like they were melting into its own cheeks. It was exactly as I remember from my dream. But how can I remember something I've never seen before? I've never been here. I didn't even know it existed until now.

The Bardo's facade was lined with expansive factory windows that from the outside appeared entirely blacked out—or maybe just painted over from the inside. They were dark, unreflective, and completely opaque, but their glass was intact and unbroken, unlike most of the other warehouse windows along the street. From where I stood, the building looked like it might even have been abandoned, but the address matched the one on the paper. Maybe this place had shut down, and the man at the library just didn't know.

I knocked three times, striking my knuckles against the forehead of the grimacing face, but there was no answer. It was no later than 10 AM, and I had no way of knowing if a place like this kept any official business hours—determined, I continued knocking in intervals for another fifteen minutes. I'd nearly resolved to leave and come back to try another day when finally, I heard the bolt of a heavy lock turn in the door. A tall, beautiful woman with hair so blonde it registered as white greeted me. I couldn't place her age, but I guessed she was a decade or even two older than me. Though her physical features seemed youthful and bright, the way she held herself seemed to suggest the effortless confidence found only in someone much more experienced. She looked like she might be the one in charge here.

She wore a black silk kimono embroidered with pink peony flowers and loose leather flip-flops. She apologized warmly. "Good morning. Sorry to keep you waiting. We don't usually get unannounced visitors," she said. "It took me a while to register what all the ruckus was about until I checked the surveillance—and I'm not much of an early bird to begin with."

Surveillance? I was confused, but before I could ask what she meant, she pointed to a small surveillance camera peering down at us, mounted just above the entrance. I had been so focused on the door with the grimacing face that I hadn't even noticed it. The outline of a crude eye had been spray painted around it in white over the brick. "We have our eye on you," it seemed to caution tauntingly.

The woman introduced herself as Zisa and asked who I was there to see. "I'm not really sure," I told her, honestly. How would I explain to her how I had come upon her address? "I know this must sound strange," I began, "but I met a man with a dog sitting outside the library, and he gave me this address." I wasn't sure what to say next, but Zisa smiled knowingly like she knew exactly who I was talking about.

She didn't say a word further about him, and neither did I. I just told her that I'd arrived in New York only the day before, and I was looking for a place to rent a room. I didn't give her any additional details about myself and hoped she wouldn't ask, but she didn't seem struck with any immediate need for inquiry. She did, however, seem to size me up with her glances, not suspiciously, just patiently—as if she were giving all her senses enough time to take me in.

"I wish I could help," she said after a brief pause, "but there's nothing I can do." My heart sank as if it had suddenly become a thousand times denser than the rest of my body. I felt the ground pulling me closer. The strap of my backpack involuntarily slipped off my shoulder, and I did nothing to catch it, letting it hang over the ditch of my forearm.

I don't know what I was expecting, but something about my dream and the man at the library actually had me believing that I was meant to be here—like I'd found myself acting out some preordained role in a mysterious game—all of the playing pieces already set out before me, and all I had to do was show up and make my move. Had some force put me right there at The Bardo's door? I know it's childish, but standing there before that grimacing face, that's exactly how I felt.

The disappointment of Zisa's words physically overtook my body, and my excitement and curiosity instantly dissolved into my overwhelming weariness. I didn't even try to persuade her. Maybe I just felt foolish. "Thank you anyway," I heard myself murmur. I remember feeling shocked by my own words. Was I giving up so easily? But what else was there to say? I was a stranger at her doorstep.

I hesitated before turning away. "Do you know if anything will be opening up soon?" was all I could manage to ask with a final shred of hope. Zisa slowly shook her head "no" apologetically, and I could see in her face that she was sincerely sorry she couldn't help.

I nodded my defeat and turned back the way I'd come, barely noticing my backpack still dangling from where it had fallen on my arm. It wasn't until I'd made it halfway down the block that I gathered enough strength to swing it over my shoulder. My belongings seemed to weigh a thousand pounds. My backpack was top-heavy, its load pressing hard against my shoulder blades. I remembered I was still carrying my copy of *The Wonderful Wizard of Oz*, adding several more pounds to my cargo. In a daze, I squatted to the pavement, unzipped my bag, and reached in to remove the book. I took a moment to thank its pages and say goodbye, propping it respectfully against the side of the building, perhaps only thirty strides from where I'd left Zisa at the door.

I had to collect my thoughts and find a place to sleep. Where would I go next? I was tired and hungry. Maybe a park bench would do just fine for the immediate future, at least if only for a short nap.

That was when I heard a voice behind me. "Hey!" I spun around, unsure if it had been directed at me. It was Zisa, still standing at the entrance with one flip-flopped foot planted on the sidewalk and the other wedged against the door with the grimacing face. She waved, motioning for me to come back. In a weary trance, I obeyed.

As I approached, she angled the door wider as if she were welcoming me inside. "There has been one recent vacancy," she said cautiously. "I hadn't intended to fill it, but I might be willing to reconsider. It's a room in my own loft. Maybe you and your book over there are a sign that I should," she said, cocking her head sideways in the direction of *The Wizard of Oz* on the sidewalk. I don't know if she had taken mercy on me or had simply changed her mind. "You know, it's bad luck to throw away books," she said. I was immediately embarrassed. I hadn't realized she was still watching after I'd walked away.

"So you do have a room for me?" I asked, unsure if I had understood. "Go get that poor book you just orphaned out there, and come in," she said, her eyes smiling once again.

She motioned for me to follow. I nodded my compliance, turned on my heels to scuttle back down the street, and retrieved *The Wizard of Oz* from the pavement. Once I'd returned, Zisa unwedged her flip-flop from the door, and without another word, she gave the door with the grimacing face a little shove with her palm. I caught it with mine. I felt the uneven texture of what must have been years upon years of paint layers under my fingertips. Zisa turned to lock the deadbolt behind us as my eyes adjusted to the dark.

We descended a short flight of steps, arriving at a dimly lit concrete landing with a metal drain on the floor. It felt odd to enter on the ground level and descend immediately into a cellar. At the opposite side of the landing, Zisa withdrew a massive jangling keychain from her kimono pocket, rummaged for her chosen key amongst a multitude of others just like it, and unlocked a second heavy steel door. I felt like I was entering the modern version of an ancient gated city. She might as well have lowered a drawbridge over a subterranean moat.

From what I could tell, this was the only way into the building, and without keys—or apparently, a medieval battering ram—no one was getting in. Zisa waited for the steel door to latch shut, then led me to another flight of steps rising back up to street level on the opposite side of the cellar. Lit only by the dim glow of a red bulb in a rusty, cage-like fixture, we crossed a hallway leading to a second stairwell. By the time we had ascended another four tall flights of wide stairs, I was completely out of breath.

We reached the uppermost landing, and Zisa swung open a heavy fire door opening to a long narrow hall punctuated by a dozen or so sets of facing, paint-chipped doors, each in various stages of decay. When we approached the final set of doors at the farthest end of the hallway, Zisa stopped. "Here we are," she chimed with an air of ease in her voice. The door was freshly painted in a crisp, clean white, unlike the others. She reached back into her kimono for her crowded keychain. This time, in the light of the hallway I noticed a charm of an anchor and ship helm swaying against the white paint as she unlocked the latch to let us in.

As the door opened, my heart skipped a beat, and I summoned every last ounce of remaining energy simply to prevent my jaw from landing at Zisa's feet. The place was as breathtaking as it was unexpected. The building's dismal, industrial exterior could never have prepared me for the sweeping grandeur of its interior. The room was filled at every corner with tall, abstract paintings and potted trees. From the street, the windows had appeared blacked out, either boarded up from the inside or clad in layers of soot—but from within, they were vibrant, elaborately colored stained glass, patterned in contorted faces of a similar style to the grimacing face on the front door.

"One-way stained glass," Zisa explained. They'd been handmade by another one of the residents. A melange of frayed but luxuriously ornate rugs overlapped like a textile collage at the center of the room. Nothing looked even remotely expensive or new, just effortlessly elegant and artfully arranged. Zisa gestured for me to have a seat on a sunken green velvet couch with fraying cushions and requested that I make myself comfortable. I felt every one of my muscles truly relax for the first time since arriving in New York. I felt safe and somehow strangely at home.

Zisa offered me a cup of tea, and I accepted without hesitation. She sauntered over to an open galley kitchen at the far end of the room, and I watched her lift a copper kettle resting on the burner and fill two cups. She returned to the couch not a moment later and handed me a ceramic mug of mildly warm black tea. She must have already boiled the water before she'd been disturbed by my knocking—from where inside she had surveilled me, I was still not entirely sure. She settled herself across from me into a patchwork upholstered armchair, took a calm sip of her tea, and wasted no time getting right down to business. She began with a basic overview of The Bardo.

Zisa told me that her grandparents owned the building while she serves as the de facto building manager. There are currently forty-four occupants in total, now counting me. Some are full-time residents, while others only use the space as a workshop or art studio. The lower two floors are for noisier work, and the higher two are for quiet living. Guests are permitted, but they must be signed in and scheduled with her first in order to protect the outstanding special circumstances of the building.

I asked Zisa what exactly she meant by "outstanding special circumstances." She paused and sipped her tea as she found the right words. She explained that The Bardo had been an illegal living space according to the city bylaws and fire code for decades now. Nonetheless, she was committed to keeping it functioning as a secret sanctuary for artists and tradespeople for as long as possible—and I'm sure for as long as she could keep getting paid for it. Zisa began to explain the accompanying stipulations.

No deposit would be needed, she told me, but rent is always to be paid in cash and on time—no exceptions. There are no phones in The Bardo, but there's a payphone that everyone uses right outside across the street. For mail, we're to get a P.O. Box. Residents are never to let anyone but themselves pass through the front door. And while the rooms are already provided with simple but tasteful furnishings, there are some substantial caveats to living here.

The general welfare of the building itself explains the affordable rent, as well as the qualms with the city's code. There are frequent electrical and plumbing issues—leaks and sinking floorboards. However, with enough tradespeople in residence, everything that needs to get fixed eventually does, but only according to the subjective and often leisurely timeline of the person who happens to know how to fix it.

The stained glass windows and the painting of the grimacing face on the door were done by a resident on the second floor who has been with The Bardo since the very beginning, dating back to the 1960s. There are woodworkers, painters, glassblowers, ceramicists, and writers too. Others, Zisa said, don't have a specific craft to speak of, but are industrious and simply in search of a different way to live.

"Are you an artist?" Zisa paused to ask. "Not that I know of," I said, "but my sister played the flute." Zisa smiled. "Wind instruments are contagious. Are you sure you're not an artist who just doesn't know it yet?" I didn't know what she meant by "contagious." Maybe she'd meant to say "infectious"—or she was just being clever. I smiled politely.

The most important rule of The Bardo is to leave it out of public conversation as much as possible. "Our whereabouts need only be known to the people who live here," she emphasized. The man at the library really had told me a secret after all. Zisa explained that The Bardo had collected a longstanding assortment of self-described misfits and outcasts, all of whom would have significant difficulty finding housing by traditional means in one of the world's most expensive cities. "Don't worry," I told her. "I don't know anyone here to tell. I'm pretty sure I might be one of those misfits too." She smiled sideways like she either thought I was pulling her leg or that she was pleased that I'd fit right in.

"There is only one final rule that must never be broken," Zisa added. "Under no circumstances are you to ever go into my room without being invited. I assume that falls under the category of common decency and respect, but it must be said nonetheless." I nodded dutifully. I was just happy to have my own room. What could I possibly want with hers too?

By the end of the rundown, Zisa had hardly asked me anything about myself, only confirming that I could pay my rent on the first of the month and that I had liked my tea. I was surprised that after telling me so much about The Bardo's clandestine existence, she didn't seem to test me about my background, but maybe she was used to people with stories that were hard to explain. Maybe she just preferred to trust. The less she knew, the better. Whatever her reason, the recommendation from the man at the library seemed to have satisfied her enough. I wanted to ask her how she knew him, but I never found the right moment.

"Do you agree to my terms?" Zisa finally asked, her voice becoming stern for the first time. "I do," I said, unzipping my backpack. I dove my hand into its hidden interior pocket to fish out my roll of cash.

I counted out three hundred dollars in a pile of twenties for my first month's rent and rested it on the wooden table in front of us in a neat stack.

"Any last questions?" Zisa asked.

I paused in thought. Yes, I did have one question. "Why The Bardo?" I asked. "What does the name mean?" Zisa seemed to smile and wince at the same time as her words settled in the air between us. "Are you familiar with the original meaning?" My face must have said "no" because she continued without pause.

"In Tibetan Buddhism, The Bardo is the place between death and rebirth. It's said that in this place, the body is left behind, and consciousness is absolutely free to experience true reality. Hallucinations. Visions. Truth. There are many different names for it. For some, this place is an opportunity to be reborn, but for others who cannot accept it, it can be a great place of danger."

Zisa paused thoughtfully to finish the last sip of her tea and rested her cup beside my stack of cash on the wooden table, already stained with countless water rings.

"Most of the people who find their way here are running from something," she said with a somberness in her tone. "A part of them already died somewhere along the way. But now that a few of us have survived here long enough, we've learned this new home is just as much a place to be reborn. You could say The Bardo grew into its name."

I sensed goosebumps rising on my arms and felt embarrassed and exposed. I hoped Zisa didn't notice.

"I'll have your money ready next month," I said, diffusing my unease.

"I'm glad we have an agreement then," Zisa said. "Welcome to The Bardo. I'll get you a set of keys tomorrow. Don't make copies," and with that, she stood up and led me toward a door off the right side of the living room. "Here's you. Make yourself at home," she said. "I do most of my work from my room, and I'll be around all day if you need anything."

"Thank you," I said. "I appreciate you making space for me—more than you know."

"I think I do know," Zisa said with her coy smile. She opened the door, and I closed it behind myself gently.

My room at The Bardo is plain, but I have a window with a stained-glass face all my own. My furniture is simple: a low, platform daybed, a wooden chair, and a narrow desk. They are all worn but sturdy and well-made. I wonder if someone from the building made them too.

I placed my backpack on the chair, removed my boots, and climbed onto the bed with my jeans still on. I pulled my cap over my eyes to shade the last glimmers of morning sunlight streaming in through the stained glass. I must have fallen asleep the instant my head hit the pillow. By then, it couldn't have been a minute past noon.

The next thing I can remember was jerking myself awake, the way your body saves itself when you dream you're falling. I sat straight up like a board and caught my bearings. I was incredibly groggy, and it took me a moment to recall where I was or how I'd gotten there. I looked over toward the window. The light outside was nothing more than a dusky glow. I'd slept clean through the day.

I regained my senses enough to swing a leg over the bed, but as I touched my toe to the ground, an unsteadiness washed over me. I planted both feet on the floor for balance but was immediately overcome with vertigo, and I was sure I would tumble over. I felt as though I was trying to steady myself on the deck of a moving boat—and with that thought, suddenly, I remembered what had woken me with such a start.

The dream had started as nothing more than a blank abyss. I floated along as if every thought and memory I'd ever possessed had been wiped clean away. But suddenly, the surrounding darkness seemed to shift, and I soon realized the floating feeling was simply the gentle roll of waves. I was alone on the deck of a wooden ship with no land in sight in any direction. I panicked immediately, not knowing my whereabouts or even my intended destination. Surely I would have to bury myself at sea.

I couldn't say how long I went on like this, lost and hopelessly clinging to my ship's mast, utterly unable to grasp any sense of orientation. Reading the winds was futile, and the glass face of my compass was smashed—its needle spun as if possessed. All I had to guide me was the sun moving across the sky, but even that seemed of no use. When the moon finally rose and the stars appeared, they lent me no further clues about my whereabouts. I would be lost forever.

I had all but surrendered to my fate when I heard a faint sound through a breeze. Did I imagine it? I closed my eyes and focused until I recognized the soft sound of music. How could this be? I was all alone and so far out at sea. But then, from the far distance, a faint coastline and the hazy outline of a mountain emerged from out of the darkness. I rushed to set my ship's course toward the shore ahead, hoping my ragged sails could catch enough wind.

The longer I listened, the more sure I became that the sound was unmistakably the song of a flute. It played on mournfully from somewhere far beyond my view. But from where? Who was playing? I couldn't say how, but as the sad melody played on, somehow, I was sure it was you, Nova. It was as real as your own voice calling out to me, leading me safely toward solid land—and toward something else I was meant to find there too.

At last, I reached the shallows and leaped from my ship's deck. I plunged into the cold water, abandoning my vessel. Lit only by the moon and the stars, I ran through the surf and across the length of the beach in frantic pursuit of your flute's song. I paused to listen over my own heaving breath, not immediately understanding where to go next. All I had was your sound.

The open beach ended at the mouth of a thick, black forest, and although the tree cover was overgrown and tangled, I tore a path forward, thrusting myself against the enormous jungle leaves. Branches and vines whipped at my body and scratched at my face, but they hardly slowed me down. Though I could barely see my feet in front of me, I followed your song farther and farther up the bend of the mountain ahead. My heart beat more violently against my chest as your sound seemed to grow closer.

At last, I'd climbed as far as the ground underfoot would take me, and I reached a craggy cliff that spilled into a clearing. In the open air, the quality of your sound had changed, and for a moment, I believed I'd finally arrived at its source. But when I searched the mountain summit, you were nowhere to be found. Where had you gone? I was sure it had been you playing that flute. The way each note hit was unmistakably yours. Instead, I found something else in your place.

A dark hooded figure awaited me at the base of the cliff ahead. Was it The Grim Reaper? The Angel of Death? Whatever name you prefer, surely that's who she was. I knew it even before she spoke.

She was not disgusting, or rotting, or gruesome like in horror movies. It was more like a feeling than an appearance. A coldness. A sense of being close to something unknowable—something from some other world.

She asked me to come nearer. She said she had something to tell me. Her voice was soft but rich. "The truth can be quite dark, my dear," she said in nearly a whisper, "Are you sure you want to know?"

"Yes," I replied.

The next thing that happened is surely what jolted me upright in my new bed. Consciousness slowly faded back as I searched the unfamiliar shadows of my room in a disoriented haze that still clings to my mind like a sort of drunkenness. Even now as I write, I feel uneasy and anxious, stuck in some abstract state of suspense.

Why do I feel so terrified to know the truth of what happened to you that night—and yet so desperate for it too? I've come all this way to New York to escape, but it still feels like I'm just searching for new ways to be closer to you.

Nova, what happened the night you never came home? Why am I at The Bardo? How could I have known about that door before I ever set foot here? I wish you could help me understand.

Love,
Rosalyn

A Ghost's Song

The sparkling stars shone bright above as endless
waves rocked my creaky vessel lost out at sea.
My ship's sails grew holes, whipped by the
battering wind for what felt like an eternity.

With no land in sight and still holding
my smashed compass in my shaking hand,
I had no choice but to beg the fish, the birds,
the night sky to guide me to solid land.

I read the constellations and the moon
to point me in a fortuitous direction.
"How do I get home?"—I begged the currents and
the winds for answers to my desperate question.

Then, at last, in the distance, the hazy,
moonlit shape of a mountain came into view,
and from my faraway ship, faintly, I heard
a flute play—Nova, I could swear it was you.

I sailed closer, moored my vessel, leaped
into the shallow water, and ran to the shore.
The flute song intensified—
"Follow my song," it seemed to implore.

I stumbled through the thick jungle, fiercely
climbing the mountain ahead, toward the sound
until finally, I reached its summit, and though
the music was near, not a soul was to be found.

Exhausted, I stood alone on
the bluff to gather my breath,
when from the cliff's edge, a dark-robed
form beckoned, and I knew I'd met Death.

"Come closer. I have something to tell
you—will you listen?" the voice said.
"Yes. I'm ready," I replied to the cloaked
form waiting on the bluff ahead.

The wind screamed past us as I found
my footing and reached her side.
The mouth of the sharp, craggy
cliff below us opened wide.

Without revealing her face, the hooded
figure motioned to the crashing sea below.
"The truth can be quite dark, my dear.
Are you sure you want to know?"

"Yes. I understand," I told her,
and with that, her cold hand took mine.
"Very well then," she said. "A sun,
after all, needs the darkness to shine."

Grasping my hand, she lurched forward,
plunging both our bodies over the edge.
My heart dropped from my chest,
but it was too late—I'd made my pledge.

Past House

Saturday, June 21, 1997

Dear Nova,

I've lost track of the number of times I've woken up, forgetting where I am and where you are too. It's only for a second, but it happens nearly every day. It's like waking up with amnesia and, each time, becoming more inventive and practiced in delivering the news to myself that you're still gone, and I live somewhere else now. But while my heart still aches every day, I'm starting to notice my mood slowly shifting in its shape and color.

In the mornings, I sense a feeling that begins as a flat, melancholy gray and builds to a sharp, angsty black by the time I get onto my feet. Once I'm dressed and out my bedroom door, it's settled back down again into something calmer and more muted. It's dark but perhaps contains a hint of color—a deep blue or purple, if I had to paint the feeling. In many ways, The Bardo has managed to brighten me somehow, expanding my range of emotion just enough to feel like I might be coming alive again.

It's already been a month since I started calling The Bardo home. I keep to myself mostly, but I genuinely enjoy knowing that Zisa is nearby, even if separated by a wall, and I take comfort in the friendly nods and gentle smiles exchanged with the other residents as we pass in the halls. Since arriving, I've felt little motivation to explore much of the city beyond our little neighborhood, not to mention it's hot as hell outside. I'd probably melt right into the pavement if I tried. New York feels like a kiln. Spending my days under a different roof with different walls and different smells from the ones in Erie has felt like enough.

I've discovered a little shared library on the third floor that's really more like a stack of second-hand books piled against the wall in the hallway. Despite Zisa's initial explanation that the noisier workspaces have been deliberately isolated to the first and second floors, while the third and fourth are reserved only for quiet living quarters, I've come to realize that the clean division is in description only.

In reality, the third floor is much more a mix of both. Although any artist workshops there seem to conduct relatively quiet trades that don't disrupt the full-time residents, the third floor is a bustle of work and creativity, with people in and out of the halls throughout the course of the day. From what I can tell, all the third-floor artists appear to be instrument-less, machine-less, odorless workers such as embroiderers, writers, and illustrators.

This mixture seems to have made the third floor a melting pot of sorts where people from all floors flock, casually congregating for small talk and idea exchange. Typically, this is also where various miscellaneous items of interest wind up. Band flyers, old magazines, books, and household items with notes attached to them labeled "FREE." The third floor has become my Petri dish for understanding both The Bardo and New York City at large without ever needing to actually leave the building.

I've gotten into a new habit of snatching up ten or eleven books at a time from the third-floor treasure trove and ushering them back up to the fourth floor to read alone in my bed. I'm up to almost one hundred pages an hour now, depending on the book, the text size, and my interest level. It's become something of a little competition with myself to see how much I can read in a single sitting.

The other day I read an entire book exclusively about card game strategy just to see if I could do it without letting myself fall asleep. As it turned out, the topic was far more gripping than I'd expected, and now I think I'm even smitten with the idea of learning to play Goofspiel one day. I'd never heard of it before, but apparently, it was invented by a Princeton student in the 1930s who was studying mathematics and game theory. Your bluff is your strongest suit.

Each time I finish a book, I stack it on a little wooden stool that sits outside my door as a reminder to take it back down to the third floor on my way out. On a productive day, my pile is three or four books tall, sometimes five. Zisa seemed to have taken notice of my new monastic reading habits too—not to mention I've barely left the building since I moved in.

I've run errands only a handful of times—twice to the laundromat and several times to replenish my supply of cereal and peanut butter and jelly ingredients, which more or less still serve as my primary sustenance—although as my appetite has grown, I've started stocking up on TV dinners too. Despite starting to feel at home at The Bardo, I try to keep to my own room, and I avoid the bathroom, living room, or kitchen for any time longer than absolutely necessary.

It's not that I don't like Zisa. I do. Maybe it's just that she's not you. Her quiet presence feels familiar and calming—yet unbeknownst to her, she's an imposter. I can never fully relax into our domesticity. I worry that maybe she's offended. Or maybe she just feels a little sorry for me that I'm such a recluse. Whatever the reason, a few days ago, she took it upon herself to try and get me out of the loft.

It was around noon when I heard a polite little knock on my bedroom door, and I heard Zisa's voice ask if I might be interested in an idea. I opened the door, curious about what she could possibly have in mind. "Do you want to come in?" I asked, uncertain of how to host her in her own apartment. "That's ok. It'll only take a minute," she replied. At first, I was expecting a critique of some kind. I left toothpaste in the sink. I keep forgetting to turn out the lights when I'm last to bed. But it was nothing like that.

She told me she had a recommendation for a job, but only if I was interested, of course. She added that she didn't want to be presumptuous about my situation, but she knew of something in the neighborhood that might be a good fit. Although I kept it to myself in her presence, indeed, this was a very convenient offer, as I had not formally figured out how to address a particular pressing issue that happened to concern Zisa very much—I still had no idea how I'd be continuing to pay her rent.

Zisa went on to tell me about an organization called The Moirai, run by three sisters she knew through extended family, though I didn't quite grasp the details of their relation. Together, the sisters ran an extensive private archive of books organized by what Zisa described as "a unique classification system." The Moirai sisters, she said, are eccentric but kind-hearted, and if I liked The Bardo, I would undoubtedly love The Moirai even more. The three sisters' names are Estlin, Ezra, and Eleeza, and all go by shortened versions: Es, Ez, and El. I wasn't surprised to hear that they might be a little strange. With matching names like that, you probably have a birthright to at least some level of eccentricity.

Zisa was also careful to mention that this wasn't the sort of job that would give me deep pockets, but if I wanted to read books all day, I might as well get paid for it. She glanced over to the stool piled with books outside my bedroom door to punctuate her point. She also mentioned The Moirai had only one other employee named Asher, who was also a resident of The Bardo and lives on the third floor. He, too, had been her personal recommendation a few years ago, although for a carpentry job, not as a reader. Zisa said Asher had been out of town since I'd moved in on what she called "one of his frequent walkabouts," but she said she'd be happy to make an introduction if we hadn't made one another's acquaintance at The Moirai already.

Zisa handed me the address on the back of a receipt and told me she'd set up an interview. I wondered how she could be so sure that the sisters would agree to an interview with me—or how she felt confident vouching for a person she'd only just met—but when I arrived at The Moirai two days later, it was apparent to me why it was a low-risk offer for all parties involved. I'm quite certain applicants weren't exactly beating down The Moirai's doors.

I was set to meet the youngest sister Estlin—(Es, as she preferred) —at 9 AM sharp on Monday morning. I left The Bardo early at 8 AM, padding in extra time in case I got lost, but Zisa's directions had been crystal clear. I found my way without any trouble, and when I reached the building that matched the address, I had an additional thirty minutes to spare, so I loitered on the stoop by myself.

The Moirai consists of not one building but three—a beautiful row of connected triplet brownstones. Together, they comprise The

Moirai's physical archive, consisting of thousands upon thousands of books. Zisa told me the sisters have "old New York money," whatever that means. It just sounded like rich, crazy people to me. As promised, I met Es on the stoop of the first building promptly at nine. She looked in her mid-fifties and had beautiful gray hair plaited into a loose braid slung over one shoulder. The first words out of her mouth were a stern request to please call her "Es, and NOT Estlin." Her sisters would join us later for complete introductions, and they also demand their names' informal shortenings. "They won't even respond to the full versions," Es warned.

"Not a problem," I told her, secretly delighted. Things were already getting slightly odd.

Es led me up the steps and into the foyer of building number one to give me the run of things. At a high level, the job is straightforward—cataloging and organizing books that have been either donated or inherited from various private collections all around the city. The sisters seem to have connections everywhere, that's for sure, but they don't seem interested in using their clout for anything but collecting more dusty books than their walls can handle.

Each of the three houses of The Moirai is three stories tall with high ceilings and handmade, century-old details that, for the most part, appear well-maintained and intact. The houses have been loved and cared for over the years—which is quite a different matter entirely from the mess. Every inch of every room and hallway has been outfitted with improvised shelves brimming with volumes of every sized book you can imagine. Some are stacked with careful precision, while others lie in utter mayhem, heaped in piles, their spines jutting in every direction.

Es ambled the halls slowly as I trailed a step behind, and we made our way to a small kitchen at the back of the first floor. She told me to make myself comfortable while she plucked two tea cups from the cabinet, and I took a seat at a rectangular table tucked behind a cliff of books that nearly reached the ceiling.

"Excuse the mingle-mangle, but it's really quite coming along," she piped, filling our tiny cups with steaming water and dropping in a silver tea strainer. I liked her instantly. She reminds me of Gram in some ways, blunt but poetic, proud and unapologetic. She sat down, took a sip of her tea, and folded her hands with a thud on the table while making vigorous eye contact in a way that told me she was about to tell me the catch.

"Few have the patience, interest, or creativity to stick with a job like this," she said matter-of-factly. "And to be honest, we don't trust many referrals these days. But Zisa is special to us, and she mentioned you already act the part."

"I guess so," I said, not exactly sure what I had agreed upon—other than my hermetic tendencies and appetite for the third-floor book pile.

I decided right away it would be best to speak as little as possible and ask questions later. Es proceeded to tell me what made The Moirai's collection so "unique," as she described it. Their manuscripts are not organized by title or author, date or geography, or even by genre, as most libraries or bookstores are, but rather according to a subjective system of the sisters' own devising.

Each sister is in charge of one of the three houses, and each house is home to manuscripts relevant to one of three categories: the past, the present, or the future. Past House, Present House, and Future House, respectively, as they are officially named. According to The Moirai's system, to properly catalog their books, it is essential that the archivist also understands each manuscript's meaning, intention, and context. This, Es told me, is why creating the collection has been taking years upon years.

"I know it might sound daunting, but it will become second nature once you do it a few times," she reassured, although I still wasn't confident I understood. "Let's play a quick game now," she prompted. "I can see from your eyes you aren't quite sure of me yet." Es's own eyes seemed to twinkle. I could tell she was proud of whatever came next.

"Here's how it works," she continued. "I tell you a title that we all know, and you just think about how the book makes you feel. Think about how it applies to your own life, and then tell me in which house it should live. Simple enough. Ready then?"

I nodded. Unreadily.

"*Peter Pan*," she said.

After only a momentary pause, I blurted my answer. "Past House," I said.

"And why?" she asked, awaiting my reasoning.

"Because my grandmother read it to my sister and me when we were children, and that's in my past, I guess."

"Yes, of course," she said, "That's your past. But what then if a child comes to our collection. They're not in the past. It's the present for them, and don't you think they should be able to find that book too?" she pushed.

"No," I said flatly.

"Why not?" she smiled back, looking sly.

"Because *Peter Pan* is never a book for children to find," I said, improvising. "It's a book adults find for children. It's for the ones choosing it. *Peter Pan* will always be a memory of the chooser's past and from their own childhood. They're passing it down from their own memories, just as one day that child will grow up and choose it for some other child. It's a nostalgic book. At least that's how it makes me feel."

Es sat silently across the table, looking very pleased, her eyes smiling. I wasn't sure if I'd passed her test. "So, according to this system," I asked, "it's all up to me to decide where a book goes?"

"That's the idea. It's your choice once you feel you understand your own logic," she nodded. "Just write it in the archive log, and that's all there is to it."

It sounded a bit whacky and convoluted, but I wasn't terribly invested in arguing with her life's work. It didn't matter to me one way or the other how much sense it made. I just sipped my tea politely and told her that it sounded like something I could figure out. Es rested her teacup slowly in its saucer, looking serious and thoughtful.

"You know, people don't look for books anymore these days," she said solemnly. "They're too busy in the bustle. But we're not building a place for people to find stories. We're building a place for stories to find people."

Silence lingered in the air between us. "I think I understand," I said, though truthfully, I still wasn't sure I entirely did. I did, however, admire the sentiment.

"These days, people waste so much energy searching and searching for whatever it is that they seek. They love to 'take' but are rarely open to 'receiving.' What they really need is a place where they can allow themselves to be found. These shelves are a living categorization, and you need to think differently for that." Es continued, suddenly losing her focus, becoming distracted by a fly near the sink. "Our work here is never done. 'Eternity is in love with the productions of time.'[1] Do you know those words?"

I didn't recognize them and shook my head no.

Es stood up sharply, leaving the table to embark on her fly assassination mission.

"It's William Blake," she said, rolling up a stray newspaper as her insect murder weapon. "Don't worry. Not many get the reference these days. But you will learn." I took that to mean I was hired.

That was already a week ago now, and every day since, I've spent my daylight hours buried in more books at The Moirai. I can hardly believe I'm getting paid to read and make up my own stories about other people's stories. I'm like the local lord of temporal significance. I'm the lone arbiter of the final resting place for some of the greatest works of literary history—and many more I've never heard of at all. Past, Present, or Future House. Where will you spend the rest of your days, little book?

I know it all sounds a bit nutty, but to be honest, it's heaven. I'm getting minimum wage. I'm no empress, but it certainly adds up to enough to easily cover rent at The Bardo and then some to save too. I'm even building a little book collection of my own. When I asked Es what to do when I come across duplicate titles, she looked across at me excitedly and exclaimed, "Many paths can lead to the same point, my dear!" Then she glanced at the door for signs of her sisters and added in a hushed voice as if she were sneaking me contraband, "But I don't mind if you hang on to the extra copy." I've taken her up on the offer.

Most importantly, though, The Moirai keeps me distracted. I still miss you day and night, but I must confess that this week, for the first time, I notice moments that actually feel good. And just as soon as I notice, I immediately feel guilty for it too. I know you'd want me to be happy, but I don't deserve it. It's not fair. I'm here, and you're gone. Why should I be having such a grand old time? And it's not just the books at The Moirai that have me so distracted.

Yesterday in Past House, as I was buried in a pile of books so ancient their pages were nearly disintegrating between my fingers, I heard creaking footsteps approaching from the hall. They sounded much too heavy to belong to any of the sisters. I didn't know anyone else was in the house, but I still hadn't met the other employee named Asher who Zisa mentioned in her initial pitch for The Moirai. In the back of my mind, I'd been expecting him to turn up any time now. My gaze was cast down at an odd angle, and I was lying on the floor on my side, propped up on one elbow like I was an open lawn chair knocked sideways by the wind. I turned the pages with my free hand, and my supporting arm was getting tired and little by little giving out.

A towering figure I didn't recognize rounded the corner. He was tall and thin and had thick dark hair. I liked his look immediately. He passed me without a word, and our eyes locked as he walked across the room. He gave me a little smile, and I wanted to smile back, but I can't recall if I did. Was there time? Everything seemed to happen so fast and yet also in slow motion.

Did I look afraid? Surprised? The entire encounter lasted maybe only a few seconds in total (if I'm being generous) but they were seconds I've been clinging to ever since. Just a few seconds from the thousands of meaningless others, replaying over and over in my mind's eye, as if by doing so, I might render a few more to savor before the length of the room pulled our eyes apart.

He didn't say anything at first. He just walked right up to a particularly disastrous pile of books with their bindings turned in every which direction. He ran a finger smoothly along their spines while making a soft clicking noise with his tongue against the roof of his mouth like he was looking for something specific. It was comical. There was no way to find anything in that mess. But when he'd gotten a third of the way through, he snapped his fingers in victory and slid out a book with a red cover like it had been just where he'd left it.

"I'm Asher. You must be Rosalyn. I like your hat. See you around," he said with a playful smile. Then he turned on his heels, left the room again, and that was it. The encounter left my heart pounding, and for the next hour, I re-read the same paragraph, unable to take in its meaning. My mind was so preoccupied with Asher that the words on the page didn't even register as language.

How old is he? Where is he from? What does he do when he's not at The Moirai? Does he like the mountains? Does he like the sea? Does he have a family? Has he been in love? Has he ever lost someone? What do his hands look like up close? How does he like his coffee? And the most interesting question of all—could he be wondering any of these things about me?

Maybe that's all we simple humans really need—just a few seconds with the power to light up our imagination for hours, for days. Maybe even for weeks and years. Just one small moment, out of the multitudes of unremarkable others, to give our hearts and minds a little kindling. A few seconds can destroy us, but sometimes they can also keep us going too. I can't say I've ever reacted like this to someone with whom I've only shared a few breaths of the same air.

My captivation was as immediate as it was bewildering. I've never counted myself as someone interested in romance. I liken a crush to getting the flu—something unappealing and inconvenient that makes you feel unwell. And if the first warning signs ever present, I know what to do. Flee the scene and act disinterested until you actually are.

Flipping that switch has always felt easy—or at least mandatory. We both have had enough bullying to last a lifetime. Do we really need to suffer a crush too? You and Gram were more than enough love in my universe—automatic and unconditional. So why complicate things with another person you can't control? What if they lie? What if they say they care but don't?

Sometimes I think life is just better experienced in our heads. Books and stories are all the fodder I need. I'm happy enough to live vicariously through some other character's love story, and now that I work at a de facto library, I have enough of history's greatest romances at my fingertips to fill my mind until I'm dust. Do I really need one of my own? I suppose if I do, at least those few seconds of Asher's eyes meeting mine from across the room are enough excitement to keep my imagination racing for the next year.

Later that day, I learned from the oldest sister Ez that Asher has been working at The Moirai for three years now, but more unofficially for four. He began as their carpenter, hired on Zisa's recommendation to build the endless shelves throughout the houses. The sisters became smitten with him for his quiet, likable nature—and additionally for his added value of curating pleasant soundtracks for the long days of otherwise silent work. Unrequested, Asher had shown up on his second day of carpentry work with a record player and a copy of Miles Davis's *Kind of Blue*, and every following day he arrived with a new record to add to the collection.

It was pointless suggesting he stop contributing to The Moirai's mess, and soon the sisters came to appreciate the musical accompaniment. It was only when they caught on to the longer and longer lapses in the sound of his bandsaw as Asher snuck in a few pages that they learned he was a bibliophile too, and eventually, the sisters asked him if he'd like to stay on beyond his hired carpentry assignment as a regular employee. Since then, Asher has become a permanent fixture at The Moirai, just the same as the shelves he'd built.

For the remainder of the day, I was entirely distracted in nervous anticipation of the possibility that I could again become enclosed in a room with Asher, but I didn't bump into him anywhere, and I wondered if he'd already left The Moirai. I wanted to ask Ez more about him but felt embarrassed by my rabid curiosity. To pry could be to give away my feelings, and the thought of being exposed felt unbearable—so girlish, not to mention unprofessional.

See? This is what I mean. A crush is such a mightily inconvenient interruption—such danger and yet a thrill in feeling so captivated by a complete stranger—and all without any warning whatsoever. On an unremarkable humid Friday morning, my world is no longer what I thought it was. In a peculiar and painful way, it reminds me of you too. At any moment, our realities can completely change when something we love gets taken away or given to us. We can all be crushed when we least expect it. The term is aptly named.

On my walk back to The Bardo, I was jumpy, wondering if Asher and I might share the same route to and from work, but he was nowhere to be found. By the time I'd made it home, the sun had already set, and a beautiful, perfect last quarter half moon hung in the eastern sky, just above the outlines of the old warehouse buildings—one half in darkness, one half in light.

When I got back to my room, the moonlight seemed so bright it illuminated the stained glass face above my bed, but I'm sure it was only just the artificial glow from the city. I'd been having trouble sleeping all week again, memories of Erie still suspended in my mind. Every time I started to drift off, a little anxious idea interrupted me, like someone tapping through a glass window pane for my attention.

But last night, my mind had a new preoccupation, and instead, I fell asleep, absorbed by thoughts of Asher. I have some immediate gravitational pull toward him that I can't explain. I'm even a little scared by it. I hate feeling like suddenly I want to surrender my natural defenses to someone who's given me all of thirteen words. Would he do the same for me in return? There's so much I don't know—but maybe that's just it. The real attraction is the not-knowing. That's always the addiction of a mystery, isn't it? It's easy to become hooked on filling in the gaps with our imaginations in the absence of the truth.

I went to bed last night sweating from the heat with all my sheets kicked to the floor. A little oscillating fan I'd salvaged from the third-floor pile blew a tiny breeze over my bare arms. The top floor of The Bardo gets unbearably hot, and the night does little to cool things off. When I awoke this morning, I realized that somehow I'd managed to turn myself around in bed completely without any recollection of doing so, and my feet were on my pillow. It was my very disorientation that jogged my memory, and immediately I recalled my dream. I even tried to fall back asleep in an attempt to return to its plot. It felt incomplete, and I needed more. But it wasn't about you this time. It was about Asher.

In the dream, he was only a young boy, unrecognizable except for his swath of dark hair, and yet somehow, I still knew it was him. I watched from a distance as he ran through a wide field of tall grass and wildflowers and arrived at a little tree house painted all in white. He scrambled up its ladder and emerged from a round lookout window with a fox horn. Pressing his lips to its mouthpiece, he let out a series of quick, pulsating notes that seemed to trumpet something urgent was afoot. Then gazing into the horizon, he waited until another young boy, much smaller and with a plume of red hair, came running toward him from the opposite side of the field. Asher leaped down from his fort, and the two greeted one another in a warm embrace, like best friends or even brothers. The two looked nothing alike, but their kinship was obvious.

The red-headed boy reached into his pocket and retrieved a tarnished skeleton key nearly as big as his own hand. He held it gingerly like it was some kind of prize. Then the two boys looked at one another knowingly and set out back across the field. I slinked behind in a guarded pursuit, careful not to let them see me following. We walked for what felt like miles, weaving through suburban neighborhoods until the sun had lowered to nothing more than a shadowy glow.

Finally, the boys' pace slowed to a shuffle, and they soon stopped in front of an old abandoned house. Its roof and porch were sunken, its shutters falling off their hinges, and its yard was overgrown with weeds. Suddenly, their mood shifted, and even from where I stood, I could see their dispositions become somber and nervous. But Asher quickly composed himself, standing up straight and tall as if to physically embolden himself, and he nudged the red-headed boy with the side of his elbow. With Asher leading, the pair marched up to the house's collapsing stoop and paused before its spooky door. The red-headed boy looked as pale as a sheet.

Asher extended his hand, and the red-headed boy placed the old key obediently in his palm. Slowly, Asher inserted its stem into an old mortise lock and unlatched the door, and within seconds, both the boys had disappeared inside. Dusk blackened into night, and not a single light could be seen from the windows. I drew closer through the weed-tangled yard and noticed the words "Past House" carved on a beam over the door, though the building looked nothing like the Past House of The Moirai. I don't know why, but I couldn't let myself lose those boys. Throbbing dread surged inside my chest. Cautiously, I climbed the steps to the stoop, pushed open the old door, and followed inside.

My heart raced in my temporary blindness as my eyes adjusted to the darkness. When my surroundings finally came into focus, I realized the house was overflowing with a maelstrom of books, piled in disorder just as they are in the real Past House—except something here was all wrong. Something was unnatural. I struggled to translate my senses. What was it? I couldn't comprehend how, but the space was alive. It moved.

I jumped like a startled cat, stretched out both my arms for balance, and braced myself, crouching with my feet wide on the planked floor. The walls and all their shelves seemed to rearrange themselves, changing shapes and configurations right in front of me like some kind of living Rubik's cube mixed with an M.C. Escher drawing. Some walls seemed to duplicate, while others inexplicably disappeared, and in a sudden flush of fear, I wondered if I'd be trapped inside this place forever, unable to find my way back out again. The front door that had been just behind me only moments ago was now a solid wall.

It was then I heard a grown man's voice, and instinctively I walked toward its sound. I followed it into a new room that unfolded itself right before my eyes like origami, and as I stepped through its doorway, I found a tall figure slumped in the corner in a heap. I drew closer. It was Asher—but he was a grown man now, just as I'd met him at The Moirai the day before. He was disheveled and sickly looking, and he was weeping silent tears. His face was wet, and sweat plated his black hair against his face in wild strands. He seemed trapped in some kind of delirious fever trance.

With tears dripping from his chin, he looked up at me with the saddest eyes I'd ever seen and told me that he and the other boy had come here long ago looking for answers. What he said next confused me—and yet, somehow I understood it too. He said they'd come here to search these countless pages for clues that might explain how evil people can act the way they do—as if all the endless stories of fiction and history books alike might lend some blueprint or formula that could make sense of it all. But after all their years of searching, it was futile. Even if a person could read every manuscript ever written, still, there would never be a satisfactory answer to such a question.

Then, with anguish straining every angle of his face, Asher gazed up at me from the floor as if his soul itself had just shattered. His desperate eyes seemed to plead with me, but his next words were calm and toneless. He said that not even all the knowledge within these books could keep him from losing the person he cared about most.

What did he mean by that? The red-headed boy? Were they friends? Brothers? Is he real? Where had he gone? Was he a grown man now too—or did Asher lose someone from his past just like me? And what "evil people" was Asher talking about?

I woke up feeling ashamed and tense—like I'd accidentally seen someone taking off their clothes in a dressing room or trespassed on someone else's property. I'd seen something personal that didn't belong to me. I'd violated Asher's privacy, even though I knew the whole thing was just an invention of my own mind. I don't even know Asher. I've only met him once.

And yet, this morning, I feel close to him in a way I can't quite articulate. It's like I already know him, though rationally, I know I don't. From the confines of that dream, I knew his loss and the incurable torment of missing someone.

I'm sure my newfound infatuation has simply taken hold of me from the depths of my subconscious. Of course, I want to feel close to Asher. Of course, my mind would want to try and justify that possibility in any way it can. But today, I still can't help but wonder if somehow there might be even one morsel of truth to that dream. I've dreamed of truth before, haven't I?

The wolf and my twisted reflection with her warning. The broken tree that lost half her branches and then walked her way to New York City. The door with the grimacing face and the two stone lions who led me there. The Bardo's door is real. I open it every day. What now am I to make of this? What's happening to me?

I need to find a way to put all of this out of my mind. I can't appear paranoid at work over a bad dream. How exactly do I think I would even begin to ask Asher any of these questions anyway? I don't even know him, and I would sound like an insane person. Not exactly the introduction I'm going for. I know I need to let it all go, but today it's occupying my every thought. My mind is up to something—I just wish I understood what.

I miss you, Nova. I miss having someone to love. But to love someone so completely is to always live with the possibility of a broken heart. I think I always took that for granted before.

Love,
Rosalyn

Past House

On the horizon, I saw a young boy running—
he was tall and skinny with long, wild black hair.
He loped through a wide field toward the forest's
edge, all smiles, seemingly without a single care.

There, he scrambled up a ladder, disappearing
into an elegant little tree fort all painted in white,
and only moments later, he emerged from a window
with a fox horn, blowing with all his might.

Perched from his lookout, he lowered the horn
and scrupulously studied the horizon, waiting.
Many empty minutes passed, but the boy did not budge,
squinting into the distance, concentrating.

Finally, from the far end of the field, a small
figure appeared, no more than a tiny speck.
And as it drew closer, I could see it was a second boy
with bright red curls falling all down his neck.

The first boy shouted out a short name I could
not quite distinguish at the top of his lungs,
and in a rush, he leaped down from the ladder,
skipping the last half dozen of its rungs.

The two boys met, embracing breathlessly,
slapping each other heartily on the back.
The black-haired boy slung his arm around his
friend while the other reached into his knapsack.

Grinning, the red-haired boy presented
an oversized key that looked worn and old.
He held it like it were something deeply precious,
laid with diamonds or plated in gold.

The two set off toward the outlines of houses,
synced in a perfectly matching stride.
And as the sun set, I trailed them in secret,
all the while, they remained glued side to side.

We passed sprawling house after house that
looked like they belonged to people with clout,
but for some reason, this place filled my heart
with uneasiness—an unplaced fear and doubt.

Finally, the boys stopped in front of a dark
ramshackle house with a yard overtaken by weeds.
The black-haired boy nudged his companion—
I could tell he was the one who always took their leads.

He marched with confidence to the porch,
motioning to the red-haired boy to follow,
but his comrade's face looked stricken,
his skin pale and his eyes suddenly hollow.

The black-haired boy was not dissuaded, and he
fetched the key and turned it in the door's latch.
Facing one another, I saw both boys jump in
surprise as they heard the deadbolt catch.

The knob turned, and the door swung open,
offering only a wall of pitch black.
The boy with the dark hair stepped forward,
but the one with the red hair took a step back.

"Come on," the black-haired boy called,
"We both know we need to find the answers inside."
And with that, they vanished into the dark
as I looked on from the street, petrified.

I wasn't sure why, but this house felt like a trap—
like a prison in some sort of camouflaged way.
Even so, I couldn't abandon the boys—I could only
heed my instinct's instructions and obey.

Stepping over the threshold, I saw the words
"Past House" carved in the transom overhead.
The door slammed behind me with a crack, and my
chest became gripped with a sudden sense of dread.

My eyes hadn't yet adjusted to the dark,
and I groped blindly in the air, unable to see.
I fumbled behind myself for the doorknob
but found it had already locked behind me.

Unsure of what to do next, I waited for my
sight to acclimate, listening for the boys,
but instead, I heard a sound like timber
splitting—it was an unmistakable noise.

As the outlines of the space came into view,
I saw nothing but books heaped wall to wall.
They were piled in chaos, all over the floor
and snaking in teetering stacks down the hall.

Suddenly, I placed the sound, my mouth
gaping open in awestruck hypnosis.
The frame of the adjoining room started to
split and separate like cells in mitosis.

I heard a voice from one of the newly
formed rooms, and I followed the sound.
As I rounded the corner, I jumped in astonishment,
not yet understanding what I'd just found.

Hunched over a book, the black-haired boy was now a grown man,
his long hair beaded in sweat and plastered against his skin.
He whispered to himself frantically as tears
streamed down his face and dripped off his chin.

In a fevered trance, he looked up from
his book, his eyes bloodshot and wet.
He spoke to me softly in a calm but
exhausted monotone as our eyes met.

"As it turns out, Past House is haunted—
not by ghosts—but by our own looping memories.
I lost my way out of here years ago, and by now,
it feels like I've been locked in here for centuries.

We came here thinking that this many books
must be able to give us some sort of answer.
Maybe we could learn to understand the evils
in this world that eat away at us like a cancer.

Surely, all the volumes of history could help us
comprehend the motives of the wicked people we knew.
And by studying the works of literature's finest, maybe we
could finally grasp why evil people do what they do.

But even all these books couldn't tell us why—
or keep me from losing my best friend.
However, locked away in here all these years
I did learn one important thing in the end.

The past isn't just an idea you visit only in your
mind's eye, for it too can also be a physical place.
And it's not so hard to become its prisoner, locked
away inside forever on some impossible chase.

"Come on," I said, reaching for his hand.
"Let's get out of here and find freedom after all."
But just then, a cracking rumble spun me around—
and the exit behind us transformed into solid wall.

The Laws of Physics

Tuesday, July 22, 1997

Dear Nova,

As you well know, it's easier to open a clam with a piece of wet spaghetti than to get me to wake up voluntarily any earlier than absolutely necessary. However, the fourth floor of The Bardo is essentially a tropical torture chamber, and I often have no choice in the matter. It's a sauna in my room by sunrise, so when I can't fall back asleep, I've taken to sketching and doodling from my desk in the mornings. It's the perfect time to write you.

For the most part, I've learned my way around The Moirai and found my own sort of understanding with the sisters. They are sharp and funny, good-natured and feisty, nurturing but tough. All three of them, each in their unique ways, remind me of Gram's sturdy temperament, and I feel at peace in their presence. They're free-spirited and maybe even a little kooky, but they certainly don't seem crazy—as I'd first imagined. They're hard workers too— there's no doubt about that. I enjoy watching them throw themselves so enthusiastically into an undertaking I never once considered could even be an occupation until now. They're a reminder that work isn't just a paycheck. It's that which you pursue.

When I arrive each morning, the sisters are already out on a pickup or otherwise running around the houses, dusting shelves or stacking piles of books into haphazard towers. By the time I leave for the day, all three of them are still at it. They approach their work with a vibrant and genuine curiosity that's refreshing and invigorating. At first, I wondered if all the commotion was in some haste to soon open their precious archive to the public, but it didn't take long to surmise that the simple act of creating their work is enough for them. Their resolute dedication is truly energizing, at least if you can consider turning pages while lying around on a divan like a house cat all day energizing. But my mind feels ignited. Getting lost in other people's stories has been a pleasant distraction from thinking about my own.

Some days, I still can't believe I live in New York City—though it's bittersweet. None of it happened the way it was supposed to. We were going to move out of Erie together—you'd pursue your music, and I'd write. In the end, I guess I am writing after all. What a dark comedy that is. New York is the place people come to make their ambitions come true, but I feel like I've failed before I've even begun. I ran away from Erie, not toward a dream. That distinction makes all the difference.

If I'm counting correctly, it's been just about seven weeks since I arrived, and not a day has passed that I haven't thought of calling Singer. He's my only link to news about your case. His business card is still tucked away in my wallet—but I just can't bring myself to dial the number. What am I so afraid of? That they've found something? Or that they haven't? Singer said they were working with that special unit from Pittsburgh. Surely seven weeks has to be enough time for some kind of progress. But if I really want to know, I have to be the one to pick up the phone. I wonder if Singer even knows I've left Erie. Back home, I was so eager to beat down his station's door and demand answers. In New York, I feel too afraid even to make a simple call. Each time I think I might have worked up the nerve, I feel my face twitch, and I tap Singer's card back into my wallet.

Fortunately, my growing infatuation with Asher is proving to be an ever-increasing diversion. I'm embarrassed by how much I like him, despite knowing him so little. However, I'm beginning to get the impression he might enjoy my company just as much as I enjoy his. The pleasure of his quiet companionship always feels mutual, although it's not lost on me that his effect is only a smokescreen for avoiding thoughts of you. I feel guilty for letting something as frivolous as a crush overtake my sensibilities, but it also feels entirely out of my control.

As far as personal details go, Asher and I still seem to know only the surface details about one another, but this only adds to the intrigue. So far, I know that he's originally from upstate New York, about three hours north of the city. He went to a trade school to study carpentry instead of college, and he has the most extensive recall of song lyrics I've ever encountered in another human being. He collects records, books, old typewriters, and polaroid cameras. He's missing part of his ring finger on his left hand, which he lost in a mishap with a table saw when he was young, even before carpentry school, and I've come to notice that when he's thinking, he rubs the top of his stub with his thumb.

As for me, I've made it a point to surrender only the bare minimum of information. He knows I'm originally from Erie, and I'm brand new to the city. At first, I kept my hat on around him, but as I've grown more comfortable and the days have gotten more humid, I started leaving it on my backpack when I read. I explained how I wear my hat out of habit to avoid recounting the subject of my birthmark to strangers. Funnily enough, he's never asked about it. He knows I live one floor above him at The Bardo in Zisa's loft, and he knows I cringe every time he puts on country music.

Otherwise, his inventory of my personal details is exceptionally low, and for now, I prefer to keep it that way. I know any inquiry into my past will eventually lead straight to you in a matter of a few questions, and that's not who I want to be to him right now. Not as some spectacle or a cause for pity—not as the twin sister of an unsolved homicide case. Not as someone sad. And certainly not as someone on the verge of losing her mind. I couldn't blame him for thinking so. If only he knew half of what I think about these days.

Instead, things remain on the surface. Simple. Superficial. And I'm always careful to keep this journal zipped in the back pocket of my backpack so as never to be mistakenly picked up and sorted as one of The Moirai's books. Can you imagine? What's worse—Asher reading my innermost thoughts or my blather on the shelves next to Proust?

The only other miscellaneous fact Asher knows about me is that I can speak some elementary French. It's only a few assorted phrases, but I'm still surprised by what vocabulary I still recall. It's not a detail about myself I would ever volunteer out of the blue, but the other day, Asher and I opened a heavy box of recently donated original French classics, and I couldn't hide my enthusiasm. Balzac, Hugo, Camus.

Usually, books written in any language other than English we box up and stack off to the side to deal with later, but in a moment of vulnerability, I told Asher how I'd always fantasized about going to Paris one day. I told him I'd preemptively started teaching myself a little French years ago and that I was trying to learn a little more. One day I hoped I'd still make it to the Latin Quarter, Notre Dame, and the Louvre. I didn't elaborate on the details. How could I without telling him about you? Paris was our shared ambition—we'd either do it together or not at all. I asked Asher to leave the box open for me. At least I can still go there at any time in my mind.

Carpentry school and a typewriter collection. Basic French and wears a hat. These small, innocuous details about each other represent the limits of Asher and I's acquaintance. I feel so hungry to learn more about him, but I'm cautious about asking too much too quickly.

At least once a day, in the midst of skimming one uninteresting passage or another, my eyes start to grow heavy, and as I fight to stay awake, momentarily, I lose hold of my surroundings. Reality slips away, and for a brief second, the bookshelves of The Moirai seem to close in around me. In an instant, I'm transported back into my dream again, trapped inside that shape-shifting house with the sight of Asher distraught and hunched on the floor. What was haunting him in that maze of a house? What was he trying to answer with all those books? Is he somehow trapped in the past, just like me? Maybe we have that much in common.

My mind must be working overtime to fulfill some twisted wish for us to share something meaningful, even if only some wounded part of ourselves. Isn't that what happens with a crush? A yearning to make something far away feel close? A hidden longing to be fully known and accepted by another?

For the most part, Asher and I barely even speak, each immersed in our thoughts. We're busy solving our own little riddles, assigning the appropriate home for the latest book at hand, and rationalizing their themes into something that can fulfill the sisters' logic. But sometimes, I'll glance up and catch Asher's eyes already looking at me. Sometimes, he'll catch mine. Our rapport hardly involves conversation but rather a silently negotiated footing in one another's wordless company. It feels safe. Comfortable. In some ways, it's the same feeling as being at home with you—just so satisfying to be alone together.

Asher and I almost always sort from the same spot in Past House—the main salon between a small entry foyer and the little kitchen in the back. It's where the sisters typically drop the new donations, so we always know where to find each other. It was nearly noon yesterday when Asher finally joined me. He was wearing a roguish, asymmetrical smile across his face in lieu of a verbal "Hello." I was buried in a pile of German language translations perched in a small window seat, which I've established as my own territory.

He walked over to his record player, selected an album from the crate in the corner, and carefully slid the disc from its cover. My eyes followed his hands as he slotted the disc expertly over the spindle. He lowered the player's arm, and after a few cracks and blips, the sound of a piano filled the room. I immediately recognized it as Beethoven's sonatas.

Do you remember when Gram brought home our first record player? She'd gotten it from that secondhand store right by the library before picking us up from school. I think she was even more eager to set it up than we were. Among the first members of our new record collection were Duke Ellington, Sarah Vaughan, Herb Alpert, Joni Mitchell, The Doors and then the outlier: Beethoven's sonatas. That was the same year you announced that you wanted to learn the flute. The verdict is still out whether or not that record had anything to do with it, but I distinctly remember a flute sonata in B-flat major on repeat in our house.

Asher's eyes darted in my direction after the first few notes floated across the room as he waited for my evaluation. It's become a ritual that every time he changes the record, we look over at one another and, without saying a word, sign our approval or disapproval with nothing more than a wrinkle of the eyes, a smile, or a playful nod —yay or nay.

When he's feeling more experimental with the day's musical accompaniment, sometimes he can seem so sheepish in his body language, like he's showing me a secret he's not yet sure I will accept. I find it endearing and sweet, especially from a guy of his size, who at all other times of the day seems to take up so much space, radiating confidence. I can tell he cares what I think of his selections as if through his musical offering, he's giving away something private about himself. In a way, this feels as close to a proclamation of affection as I need.

As the first few lively notes of piano and flute danced together from the speakers, I smiled across the room and nodded my approval. Asher asked me over the music if I'd determined the final resting place for the book I was currently working on. I didn't answer. Instead, I just read him the line I'd been reading and re-reading so as to commit it to memory.

"Love consists in this: that two solitudes protect and border and greet each other," I recited.[1] "Who's that?" Asher asked.

I told him it was a translation of Rilke, a poet born in the 1800s in Prague who wrote in German. The line was from a letter correspondence to a young aspiring poet in Vienna who was trying to decide between a future as a writer or as an officer in the army. I told Asher that Rilke, too, had once been mentored by a famous artist, the sculptor Rodin in Paris when he was not much older than the age of the young poet who was now asking him for advice.

"Rodin. That's *The Thinker* guy, right?" Asher asked, propping his head on his hand and his elbow on his knee, mimicking the statue.

I nodded "yes" and smiled.

"So, if love consists of two solitudes that border and greet each other, where does that put your book, little thinker?" Asher asked. "Which house for Rilke, the romantic?"

Love. Discussing the subject with Asher made me nervous. I stammered and suddenly felt my face turn hot. If I could see myself, I'm sure I had flushed to a shade not dissimilar from a ripe tomato. Love consists of two solitudes that protect and border and greet each other. Asher and I, each a solitude—each quietly offering a distant love from our borders. Can he feel it too?

"Present House," I said, trembling. I wasn't sure if he was reading between the lines.

"I see," he said, with what couldn't have been mistaken for anything but a flirtatious smile. Had he picked up on my hidden rationale? "And why, might I ask?" he pressed. Was he baiting me to confess my feelings?

I paused to think of any other answer than: "Because I think I'm falling in love with you—now! Presently!" But of course, I never could have said that. I wouldn't have had the courage. Besides, it all feels ridiculous. How can you fall in love with someone you hardly know? I must admit, I felt so tempted to show him a few of my cards, if only just to see if he'd show me any of his.

Instead, I kept my distance from the topic but said something else that felt true too. "We may consist of solitudes when we come into this world and when we leave it too, but love is always here with us in the present moment—either inside us or just at our borders, reminding us who we are and what we truly care about."

We both grew quiet as if each of our minds had drifted off somewhere else. I was remembering you. Somehow it felt like he was remembering someone too. His usual mercurial composure sunk into something more somber and reflective. What was he thinking about? Or who?

I tossed the Rilke book into a thatched basket beside me, the designated receptacle in which we collect books to carry over to Present House later. I scribbled my post-rationalization for why Rilke belonged in Present House in our log and wondered if I'd ever tell Asher the whole truth. A sonata ended on the record player, and Asher again lumbered to the other side of the room to look for a new album. He walks like a tall, sleepy giant. With his back turned to me, he flipped through the crate, lifted his next selection, and delicately inspected each corner of its cover.

I watched him stall like this as if he was still deliberating over his choice until finally, he turned his head over his shoulder to look back at me with one eye, then gently slid the disc from its jacket and placed it into position. Again, he lifted the spindle as before, but this time he took an unusually lengthy pause, staring down at his outstretched hand.

Then, almost inaudibly and without looking up, he asked something that took the ground out from under me. "Rosalyn, why are you so sad?"

I didn't know what to say or how to start. Is it so obvious? I know I come across to others as reserved, but is my sadness so transparent? Or can he just see into me somehow? A part of me wanted to tell him everything right then and there. He had given me the opportunity, after all. I wanted to let it all spill out—but I couldn't. I wasn't ready to try and explain what I can't yet understand myself. Instead, I let a few moments of silence speak for me. Maybe he understood the speechless abyss of loss too.

He seemed to accept my answer in its wordlessness, and he lowered the spindle. A strong but haunting woman's voice floated over the room, and a slow, subtle bass joined in. We both sat quietly, dodging one another's glances as the lyrics unfolded.

I shifted uncomfortably as a woman's sultry voice washed over us. Not daring to look at Asher, I found a place on the floor to fix my eyes as I listened to the lyrics unravel. The words felt as though someone was, at last, understanding me—as if Asher understood too by letting the song speak for us both. I later discovered it was Nina Simone covering Peggy Lee and Victor Young's "Where Can I Go Without You" after I secretly dug up the liner notes tucked inside the record sleeve.[2] Where can I go without you, Nova? It was a love song, of course, but love songs aren't reserved only for lovers.

When the track ended, Asher looked meekly in my direction, timidly taking stock of how his song's selection had landed with his audience. This time, I was the first to speak.

"Do you ever remember your dreams?" I asked, diverting the topic.

"I try not to," Asher answered flatly.

"What about you? Why are you sad?" I said, returning his question. I could tell he wasn't expecting it, and I even surprised myself by asking it. His jovial, self-assured demeanor only runs so deep—a delicate mask that clings only to the surface. Underneath, I can see there's something soft and more fragile. This time our eyes met, and Asher's expression seemed to beg me from across the room to leave the topic alone, but all he said was, "I'll tell you another time."

"Ok, another time. Maybe in Future House," I said, struggling for a Moirai joke.

"I think it would be better in Past House," he said. This time I read between his lines. I nodded in a weak demonstration that I understood. Something did happen to Asher in his past. Now I can be sure. But what, I still can't fully imagine.

When I returned home to The Bardo, I felt exhausted, even though all I'd done all day was sit around like a barnacle. My brain felt frayed, and my conversation with Asher once again filled my mind with memories of you. Defying my cardinal rule of not lingering in shared spaces, I took a long soak in our bathtub, attempting to clear my head. The full moon was perfectly situated through the bathroom skylight, and it seemed to hypnotize me as I marinated. I must not have realized how much time had passed, but it was long enough that Zisa had to politely knock on the bathroom door to see if I wouldn't mind wrapping it up soon so she could get ready for bed too.

Mortified, I shot out of the tub, sending a wave of bathwater over the edge. I was embarrassed I'd been so thoughtless. Zisa must have been waiting for ages. In a mad dash, I scrambled to towel off both myself and the drenched floor. As I threw a T-shirt over my head, I caught a glimpse of my face in the mirror at an unexpected angle, and I all but jumped out of my skin. For just a split second, I didn't recognize myself and thought that somehow someone else had gotten into the room with me. It was one of those bizarre, dissociative moments like when you touch your own hand after it's fallen asleep. You feel the warmth of your skin under your fingertips, and yet your touch may as well be a stranger's. I was me and someone else at the same time. It was unnerving, but I shook off the feeling, knowing how tired I was. My mind was playing tricks.

I hurried past Zisa like a small, damp, and profusely apologetic human cyclone. She was calmly waiting outside in her kimono and smiled back in her composed, unbothered sort of way as I bumbled back to my room. The night was especially humid, and I knew the hot, rising air from the rest of the floors would have me tossing and turning for hours. My state of mind certainly wasn't doing anything to help.

I slid on top of my sheets, situating myself as comfortably as one possibly could whilst simultaneously roasting like a kebab. I was physically worn out, but the suggestion of sleep only awakened my mind with questions. What's happening when I close my eyes at night? What are all these fragments of storylines I've seen in my dreams? I've never dreamed so vividly in my life.

As I lay in bed, I couldn't shake a nagging thought. Are my dreams nothing more than breadcrumbs leading me along some coded trail? Alice down the rabbit hole. What else might I find? Why were you leading me to that cliff with your flute's song? What did you want me to see? Something beyond death? Something supernatural? Something inexplicable. And what does Asher have to do with any of this?

All I can say is that I feel close to him somehow, though I can't say what exactly I mean by that. My affection is immediate, but is it really love? Or do I only miss having someone to love? Perhaps I'm just lonely. Afraid. Attaching to the nearest possible subject of my admiration. Is he a crush or simply a crutch?

This philosophical quagmire was the last thought I remember before finally drifting off to sleep. I didn't catch a glimpse of the clock, but I'm sure by then, it was long after midnight. When my alarm went off the next morning, I woke up without any struggle, as if I'd gotten much more rest than I knew I had. I was unusually clear and eager to get the day started—I felt swaddled by a vague sense of resolution, though I was skeptical of what could have possibly been resolved in the unconscious darkness behind my eyelids. It wasn't until I was brushing my teeth in the bathroom this morning that I understood why. As I stared back at myself in the mirror, last night's dream came flooding back, and a momentary feeling of peace seemed to wash over me.

I dreamed I was alone in the forest with nothing to light my path but the glimmer of a full moon, illuminating the shadowy terrain just enough for me to find my way over the uneven ground. I'd only walked for a short while when I spotted something in the distance catching the moonlight. I approached cautiously, soon recognizing that the strange object before me was a full-length mirror standing plumb in the dirt as if it was growing right out of the soil like a tree. I was baffled and frightened, but I couldn't resist my curiosity. I stepped close enough to study my reflection, quizzically inspecting the contours of my face. Something felt wrong. Off-kilter.

I searched my face, uncertain of what I was looking for. I lowered my chin. I furrowed my brow. I pursed my lips. Something about my reflection didn't quite seem to match my own expression. Squinting, I turned my head to the side, but my reflection only stared straight ahead, and suddenly the face gazing back from the mirror became stricken with a look of intense gravitas. Slowly, it spoke to me, yet I was not speaking. My blood rushed to my stomach. I thought I might be sick with shock.

As if it were an entirely separate person, my reflection said she'd been waiting to talk to me for some time. "I" or "she," I'm not even sure how to describe the encounter. She spoke, and I listened. Then she listened, and I spoke. There, alone in the forest, my reflection and I calmly had an impossible conversation. I wish I could say it felt like talking to you, but in the dream, it felt more like a dialogue with another piece of my own mind. We seemed to both agree and disagree simultaneously, the same way it feels to wrestle with different parts of yourself.

My reflection would argue one side—then I would make my case for the other. Afterward, each of us would concede some portion of the other's truth. We spoke in double meanings and abstract terms, but nonetheless, I felt we'd understood one another's intention.

I'm headed back to The Moirai for another day of sideways glances with Asher in an hour or so. I wish so much that I could tell him everything about you—and about my dreams too. Is there a chance he wouldn't think I'm mad? Tentative and cautious as our relationship is, he's still the closest thing to a friend I have.

Right now, everything feels like a mystery, but there is one thing I know for sure—I'll have to trust myself before I can ask someone else to do the same. Until then, these dreams must stay between sisters.

I miss you so much, Nova. A person can only talk to themselves so much.

Love,
Rosalyn

The Laws of Physics

The forest was dimly illuminated by
a full moon despite the cover of night.
In the distance, my eye caught an unfamiliar
object reflecting the silver moonlight.

As I grew near, I realized it was a tall mirror
standing upright in the dirt as if it were a tree.
I met my reflection and studied my face, but
something was strange—it was not entirely me.

I turned my head to the side, but my
reflection did not imitate my motion.
Instead, it stared forward and suddenly
appeared overcome with strong emotion.

"I've been waiting to talk to you,"
she said, "ever since your sister died.
Now that your other half is gone, it's time you
learn to replenish that missing piece from inside."

I lowered my head, for though she did not
explicitly say it, I knew what she meant.
"You're right," I said, "but I don't know how—
all I feel is loneliness and discontent."

"When you lose your heart's counterbalance, it's only
instinct to steady yourself with whatever support is nearest.
It's merely the laws of physics pulling you together, fooling
your heart when it's still broken and not seeing clearest."

I paused and heeded her words but still
her logic did not rest well with me.
"But what does it matter your heart's reason?"
I countered softly. "Is a heart not wild and free?

And mine has already nominated its new subject—
my feelings for him are unmistakable and clear.
After all, when a storm rolls over the canyon, we don't
ask why—all that matters is that the storm is here."

The face in my reflection was quiet
and thoughtful as she furrowed her brow.
"Yes, I suppose you're right too, but still, it's
important to give credence to the 'why' and the 'how.'"

"Fair enough," I warmly grinned back,
"So then we can agree that it's a little of both.
The world is not black and white, and we must
find comfort in the gray if we seek growth."

With that, I looked my reflection in the eye
and gave her a feeble but agreeable smile.
"You're right," I said. "I may need to find my
own way, but that will surely take a little while.

In the meantime, though, I need some company, and
it's not up to me to decide who will fill that role.
You see, my heart already chose someone to love,
and for now, at least, he can help me feel whole."

"I understand," she said. "We all need a little
help until we are strong enough on our own.
And besides, perhaps he can lend a hand
so you don't have to solve your mystery alone."

In silent understanding, we nodded at each other
simultaneously, each knowing what had to be done.
Then in unison, my reflection and I walked toward
each other, and our forms merged into one.

The Egret

Saturday, August 9, 1997

Dear Nova,

I'm writing from the middle of the woods on a porch that wraps around the circumference of what can only be described as an adult-sized tree house. Its main structure is a humble but beautiful cabin on an elevated platform like an exaggerated beach bungalow on stilts, and the entrance is about fourteen feet off the ground. Two flights of stairs lead to a screened porch that seems to float over the forest below. I'm surrounded by trees, and New York City is three hours over my shoulder. It's afternoon now, and believe it or not, I'm with Asher.

He's diligently whittling away at a piece of wood several feet to my left as I write. You can hide your most secret thoughts in plain sight with a journal. It feels so risky to write like this in Asher's presence—like my private words might animate right off this page, leap across the porch, and whisper themselves into his ear.

I'm not sure how to say this, but I think I might know something about the person who killed you, and you're the only one in the world who I can tell. I need to start from the beginning.

It's been nearly three weeks since I last wrote, and every sleep has been nothing but a blank curtain of temporary darkness. I wake feeling heavy, frustrated, and flat. I'm anxious for something I cannot see or name but have somehow come to expect when I close my eyes at the end of each day. Yet night after night, I'm met only with more of that bumpy kind of sleep, as if I'm floating over windy chop in the middle of Lake Erie. It wasn't until last night a new dream sailed in from the distant edges of my mind—and so, here I am with my pen, Asher only a few feet away, trying to recount my days in the hopes of making sense of things.

Not a day passes that I don't think about the investigation back in Erie. It weighs on my mind constantly. I wondered if there'd been any new breaks in your case, though I still haven't been able to work up the nerve to call Singer. Each time I pulled out his card from my wallet, I pictured his face—and that wary way he'd study mine before scribbling in that little pad of his. He doesn't trust me —and I don't trust him. There's something he's withholding from me, and I have the distinct impression that any conversation with him will only leave me feeling worse off than before. I tapped his card back into the folds of my wallet. No more Singer.

Instead, I wondered if I could acquire an update on your case by some other means. Your story had been all over the local news back in Erie. If there'd been a meaningful headline, there must be a way of finding it on the Web. The week before last, I asked Asher if he knew of any cybercafés nearby, and after a few minutes of head scratching, he mentioned a little place he'd been to before over on Avenue A in the Lower East Side. Putting his suggestion to good use, I sucked up the cost of a cab and took a three-hour lunch break to scour the Internet, hoping I could learn something on my own.

The café was nearly full, and a three-piece jazz band was setting up in the corner. As I waited for a computer, I felt a nervous flutter in my stomach, anticipating what I might learn. When a woman with jet-black hair and purple glasses finally stood up and offered me her seat, I flopped down appreciatively with my coffee and went straight to AltaVista's Web site. I searched for your name. I searched for Erie murders. And I searched for "Detective John Singer" too—but after only a half hour of scrolling, it became apparent there wasn't much to find—just the original stories transcribed from The Erie Times back in February and March and a few sickos with their own personal speculations on a site entirely devoted to nationwide unsolved crimes. I found another site whose owner had written a flowery ode of appreciation to Singer for tirelessly tracking—and eventually apprehending—her husband's assailant after over three months at large.

Nothing of use. Only enough to know that if there'd been an arrest by now, it would have hit the news—at least somewhere. I paid and left, feeling testy—like I should have guessed it would be a waste of time.

Despite my preoccupations and lackluster mood, work at The Moirai has been quiet, pleasant, and predictable. Asher and I have turned out to be quite the team, and now we even walk to and from The Bardo together. We're two peas in a pod, even if our idea of flirtation is limited to conversations about books and music. Everything between us lives just below the surface—in ambiguity and pun, lyrics and metaphor—letting the content of our songs and stories say all the things we don't dare say ourselves.

Asher picked up on my most recent fit of melancholy and appeared to be doing his best to keep my spirits high in his own subtle way. Upbeat rock and roll were on repeat—not a note of depressing Bach or The Smiths. Mysteriously, my pile of Victorian realism and Russian literature was nowhere to be found in my book mound, even though it had been full of them only a few weeks before—nor did it escape my attention that the missing titles had been neatly replaced with a sprinkling of humorists like Mark Twain and James Thurber, even a few of Shakespeare's comedies.

Yesterday, I woke up early and couldn't get myself back to sleep. I didn't need to be at The Moirai for hours, but I figured I might as well get a start on the day rather than stare languidly at my bedroom ceiling. I packed my backpack and headed straight outside without stopping to meet Asher on the third floor, as has become our custom. I arrived at Past House more than two hours earlier than our usual start time, but when I stepped into the kitchen, Asher was already making a pot of coffee with a tidy stack of books on the table, ready for the day's sorting. With his back still turned to me, he announced that he'd made me a cup of coffee too.

"Couldn't sleep?" he asked.

"Nah," I confirmed.

He fussed in the cabinet for what felt like too long and finally turned to me with a royal blue tin camping mug. He strode over to the table with his head slightly tilted and his eyebrows pinched together into an expression like he knew something I didn't yet. He placed the blue mug in front of me with one hand and, with the other, set down the small serving cup we often used for milk.

He returned to the kitchen counter, slouching to prop himself up on an elbow while he sipped his own coffee and watched me out of one eye. I reached suspiciously for the serving cup to add a splash of milk to my mug, and as I poured, instantly, I realized the reason for his questionable behavior. The milk he'd provided was bright blue. I threw a dubious look in Asher's direction, and a wide, mischievous smile stretched across his face.

"I think there's something wrong with my milk," I said, stating the obvious.

"Nothing wrong with the milk. You've just got the Robert Johnsons," he said diagnostically as if he were a physician pronouncing I'd caught the common cold.

"Come again?" I said.

"You know. Robert Johnson, the blues singer from the 30s. Cross Road Blues. Walkin' Blues. Me and the Devil Blues," he said from across the kitchen. "You've got the blues. Thought we might as well make your coffee to match," he said like it was the most natural solution to a foul mood there was. I felt my lips curl into something like a smile. He wasn't wrong. His tactic was working so far.

He asked if I was ever going to tell him what was eating me, but I only lowered my eyes into my blue-ish black coffee. I wanted to tell him everything. How I'd lost you and Gram and why I came to New York in the first place. How I found my way to The Bardo and everything that pointed me here. But I still wasn't sure how to begin a story that's never found a conclusion. I can barely make sense of it in my own mind. So what can I tell Asher? The only story I have to offer would only be a patchwork of nonsense, exasperation, and despair. Sometimes I feel like the only intelligible account of these past few months is right here in this journal.

Asher and I glanced across the kitchen at one another, and I took a long sip of my blue coffee. When I rested my cup on the table, I felt my mouth part like I was about to speak, and for the briefest moment, I thought maybe everything about you and Erie might spill out without my mind's permission. But with a quick, shallow inhale, I caught myself before the words escaped.

"Yes?" Asher asked expectantly, sensing I was struggling to speak.

Instead, what I said was this: "Where do pencils go on vacation?"

"Wherrrrre…?" he asked, dragging out the word as he squinted over his coffee.

"Pencil-vania," I said, straight-faced. That was one of your dumb jokes. I hope you don't mind I borrowed it.

"Wow," Asher said, shaking his head with an incredulous half-smile. "I can't say I was expecting that from you." My burst of playfulness felt so out of character, but I knew it was only a deflection from the truth. I wanted to shake my head too, conceding my small absurdity, but instead, I tried to enjoy the moment of making Asher laugh.

When it feels right, I hope I will tell him everything, but I have to know I'm ready. For now, I need things to stay uncomplicated. Surface level. Clean. And telling Asher the whole story is far too messy. I could ruin whatever closeness we do share. It's not much, but it's certainly something. So, for now, I let it rest.

Maybe it's like my reflection in the mirror had said: "We all need a little help until we're strong enough on our own." Simply finding myself in Asher's presence seems to soothe the heartache of missing you. It helps just having someone I care about in the same room. I want Asher to know my whole story, but what's the point if it only turns out to be an admission of my insanity?

I can tell you, though—that's what sisters are for. It always felt like you and I could figure anything out as long as we did it together. So, for the time being, you're still the only person I can trust.

Asher turned toward the sink to clean out the French press as I studied him from the table. "OK then," he said with his back again to me, "I know I've lost this battle. You're not going to tell me now. But when you're ready, how about we make it a trade? Deal?" he asked as he tapped the coffee grounds into the trash.

His offer caught me off guard. A trade? A trade of what? Could he mean he'd share something personal in exchange? It's hard to resist any invitation to learn one of Asher's secrets. My relentless curiosity about his past is a force to be reckoned with, and I'm still desperate to know if that red-headed boy is real. But yesterday morning, over my blue coffee, even the temptation of Asher's proposal wasn't enough to budge my still unwavering reluctance.

When we'd emptied our mugs, Asher rinsed them in the sink while I leafed through his books on the table. He hung our cups on the little countertop drying rack and loped toward the kitchen door with his long, slow, faltering strides. Then, out of nowhere, he turned his head over his shoulder, told me to grab my things, and kept walking down the hallway. At first, I didn't think I'd heard him correctly.

"Do what?" I asked, confused.

"We're skipping today. It's Friday. Self-proclaimed holiday," he said lightheartedly. Skipping? Skipping what? Work? What was he talking about?

"We can do that?" I asked skeptically.

"We can do whatever we want," he chimed from halfway down the hall. "Use the bathroom or finish up whatever you need, but let's blow this popsicle stand in five-ish minutes, yea? Don't worry. The sisters will be fine," he said. "We're going on hiatus. I'll wait for you outside."

"We're going on WHAT?" I almost shouted after him, but he kept walking as if he hadn't even heard me. That was when I remembered what Zisa had told me about Asher before my interview at The Moirai. She'd said he was away on one of his "frequent walkabouts," though I had no idea what that meant at the time. First blue coffee? Next, an inquisition into my mood? Now a "hiatus." What was he up to? I was flustered, but he didn't give me time to argue. And to be honest, I didn't want to. Everything about it was exciting.

I didn't need to use the bathroom, and by the time I'd grabbed my backpack, Asher was already waiting at the front door with his keys in hand. He stepped onto the stoop, and I followed, speechless. He locked the door behind us. "Ready?" he said, seemingly more to the fresh air than to me, as if he were addressing freedom itself. We were newly released animals back into the wild.

"How can I be ready?" I said. "I don't know where we're going." With the aftermath of a smile still lingering on his face, Asher looked over at me, paused, then traced a line with his index finger under each of my eyes just above my cheekbones. The physical contact made my heart race. "Now you're ready," he said, inspecting my face. With a satisfied squint, he gave the brim of my hat a little tug.

"What did you just do to my face?" I asked suspiciously. He didn't acknowledge my question.

I followed on his heels for several blocks until we turned onto a deserted-looking street with nothing but tumbleweed candy wrappers and yellowed newspapers wafting along the curb in the wind. He sidled up to an old, white, beat-up pickup truck with several pieces of ragged lumber poking out the back of the cargo bed, and he told me to hop in.

Asher unlocked the driver's side and leaned over the cab to pull open my door from the inside. The lock popped open, and I lifted myself in. It smelled like mold and sawdust inside. The passenger-side foot space was littered with parking tickets crumbled into little balls. I brushed them into a pile with my boot to make a place for my bag. "Sorry for the mess and the smell," Asher said. "Lois doesn't get many baths these days."

"Lois? So your car's name is Lois?" I asked, not sure if I'd heard him correctly.

"Yea. Lois Lane."

Asher's delivery was completely dry. I snort-laughed involuntarily on the spot. My own sound surprised me so much that I started laughing at my snort—and then I laughed even harder at the fact that I couldn't stop laughing. I couldn't control myself, and soon hysterical tears were streaming down my face. I don't even know why. It wasn't that funny. But once I'd started, I couldn't stop. It was like a nervous tick—like a dam had cracked open. It felt more like maybe I needed to cry, but laughter was what came out instead. The whole scene surprised Asher too, and he just looked across the stick shift at me, amused, and said, "Well, right on."

"So you named your car after Superman's girlfriend?" I asked once I'd managed to compose myself.

"Obviously," he said with a smirk.

The whole thing, right down to that smirk, felt like something you would do. Asher looked at his hands on the steering wheel and let out a little chuckle, but I worried he looked more bewildered than humored—like maybe he thought I'd suddenly gone nuts. If only he knew.

It felt so good to let out a genuine belly laugh, not just some well-mannered appropriation of what you think a person should sound like in polite company—a little performance you put on for other people, so you can get through the day. Laughing there in Lois's passenger seat felt like rediscovering a whole vocabulary I'd forgotten existed. You were always the one who could really make me crack up like that.

Asher started the ignition, and I adjusted my hat's brim against a blinding sheet of sunlight pouring through the windshield from a gap between two warehouse buildings. I flipped down the car's visor to block it out, catching my reflection in the little rusted mirror attached to its inside flap. That was when I noticed two finger-width blue lines on the top of each of my cheekbones, just like a football player with grease marks before a game. Asher must have snuck food coloring onto his fingers in the sink before he left the kitchen and painted my cheeks with it when he'd touched my face on the front stoop. He's just like you—master of pranks.

Asher looked over at me, seeing that my new warpaint had finally been revealed. "The Robert Johnsons don't stand a chance," he said matter-of-factly. "You're a blues warrior now."

"Born a warrior," I corrected, emboldened by our banter, attempting to match Asher's brand of jesting overconfidence. He nodded to himself with a grin as he put Lois into first gear and flipped on her prehistoric stereo. We pulled out onto the empty street. I thought of asking him where we were going, but it occurred to me that I didn't want to know the answer. Maybe it was my mood or the accumulated melancholy from the week, but something felt more appealing about just letting things unfold.

The first few bars of "1979" by the Smashing Pumpkins resonated from the radio.[1] The rattle of the drumsticks and the haunting melody of the first verse always gives me goosebumps. It's upbeat and sad at the same time. Billy Corgan's voice has that contradictory quality of being soft and rough simultaneously. Asher tapped his ring finger stub on the steering wheel to the beat as he drove straight through a stop sign.

I remembered the song's music video on MTV with the kids riding around in that old Dodge that seemed to be about the same age as Lois. It had a bumper sticker that read, "Proud parents of a 'D' student."[2] That part always amused me—but it broke my heart too. We always got straight A's, although I know we both would have traded them in for D's any day to have proud parents. 1979 was the year mom and dad died, and we moved in with Gram. We were four years old.

Asher pulled up to another stop sign, and this time, he hit the brake gently. I liked the sight of him in the driver's seat and how he propped his long left leg up against his door at an angle in between hitting the clutch. I watched him from the corner of my eye as he mouthed the lyrics to himself. I knew them too.

I recited each verse in my mind as I bobbed my head shyly along to the beat. It was as if Asher and I were harmonizing, and he didn't even know it. When the last line drifted from Lois's speakers, I wished the song would start again from the beginning. The final chord faded, and the drums pattered out as the next track cut in under the DJ's voice. All songs must come to an end.

We merged onto a busier road and climbed a long ramp that lifted us to a massive bridge of rusted, bolted metal. Asher seemed to know the route well. He asked if I'd ever driven over the Queensboro Bridge, and when I admitted that I hadn't, he added, "So that means you've never seen Roosevelt Island from above." A long, thin island came into view—perfectly situated in the middle of the river, halfway between Queens and Manhattan.

"There's a building down there at the very end called the Octagon," Asher said, reaching his arm over my lap to point out the passenger's side window. "It's been abandoned since the 50s, but it used to be the New York City Lunatic Asylum. I hear they want to turn it into apartment buildings one day. I guess they finally caught on to the fact that everyone who comes to New York is crazy, so you might as well start charging them rent."

"Makes sense," I said, looking out the window and scanning the tops of the buildings. It was exhilarating watching the sprawl of skyscrapers float past from a car.

Once we'd made it over the bridge, we followed a highway along the water, and by the time I started to see signs for another bridge, I was sure we were leaving the city.

We rolled down the windows to let the draft keep us cool, defying the summer heat rising off the concrete. The radio DJ expounded upon Kurt Cobain's curtailed genius as we crossed a massive, two-level bridge suspended high above the water—we were at least twenty stories in the air. Asher expertly changed lanes, gliding through traffic as the bridge fed into a highway, and before long, our new world came alive around us, the silhouette of the city growing smaller behind us in the distance.

I took off my hat and rested it on my lap, letting the wind of our motion tangle my hair. I felt peaceful on the road in the company of both Asher and our new radio DJ sidekick. We stopped only once after about an hour and a half into the ride for gas station food and to refill Lois's tank. It was the first time I noticed how the air outside felt not only cleaner and crisper but a good ten degrees cooler than in the city. Asher paid the cashier, and we shared a bag of Cheetos Checkers. I licked my fingers clean. Asher wiped his on his jeans. We climbed back into our seats, still without any further inquiry into our destination.

By the time we'd been back on the road for nearly another hour, I started to wonder if the entire purpose of our excursion was nothing more than a joy ride. Even so, that would have been plenty enough adventure for me. But just as soon as I'd convinced myself of my new theory, Asher took an abrupt left and turned onto a packed dirt road with a stripe of weeds running down the middle between the tire tracks. Soon, we were completely enveloped in green, and I felt a tightness in my chest release that I hadn't even realized had been there until it was gone. "We're close," Asher said over the music, and only an instant later, the dirt road spilled into a wide clearing with tall, wild grass that stretched nearly the length of a full city block. At the clearing's edge, I spotted what appeared to be a small elevated house on stilts emerging from the trees.

We bounced over the jagged terrain as Asher plowed through the rippling sea of grass and parked Lois in a patch of uneven gravel under the raised platform of the house. "Welcome to hiatus," he said whimsically. Asher proceeded to explain that right under our feet was a small plot his parents had bought decades ago when the land was cheap. Asher raised his left hand in the air and wiggled his ring finger stub. This is where he had his little incident— "Bloody Sunday"—as he amusingly called it. "Rest in peace, old friend," he added for comic effect. Asher said he built the house himself when he was young with his father and his younger brother.

My pulse seemed to flutter. "You have a little brother?" I asked. "I didn't know that..." I wondered if he'd picked up on the quake in my voice. Asher opened the car door and swung out his left leg. "Had," he corrected, before closing the door after himself without another word.

Asher had a brother. Had. Past tense.

I opened my door too and stepped out, sensing from Asher's body language that this wasn't the right moment to press on with my spontaneous flood of questions. What happened? What was he like? What color was his hair? Could he be the same red-headed boy from my dream? My heart raced. I followed close behind as we climbed two flights of steep but beautiful steps with irregular raw edges, leading us to a screened entryway that sat below the house like the hull of a ship. Every surface of the main structure was painted in a soft whitewash, just enough for the original wood grain to show through.

Asher dove his hand into his pocket and retrieved another set of keys while I absorbed my surroundings. Above the door frame on a smooth wooden panel, the words "THE EGRET" were painted in all capital letters in a sharp black paint, contrasting the soft white all around. The lettering was impeccable—perfectly straight, executed with not only care and craftsmanship but also a touch of personality. The house did, in fact, look very much like an oversized egret bird, its brown stilted wooden legs supporting a handsome, slim white body peering over the treetops.

Inside, The Egret cabin was tidy and austere. Much of the furniture looked to be hand carved as well. A stack of logs was arranged neatly by a soot-covered hearth, and wood shavings were piled into a basket adorned with woven geometric patterns wrapping its circumference. A low, built-in bench stretched the length of the room, lined with at least half a dozen old typewriters and two or three times as many vintage-looking polaroid cameras. A healthy heap of hardbacks, garnished with two gray rocks as their bookends leaned against the side of an orange couch. The house's structure consisted of no more than a single open space with two tall sloping panels of roof that met in an A-shaped peak.

"Hey, make yourself at home," Asher said in a warm tone. "It's impossible not to feel good out here. The air is different." He sauntered over to the built-in bench and dropped his keys into a wooden bowl next to one of the typewriters. "Like my collection?" he said with his back to me, admiring the spread of beautiful machines before him.

"I started picking them up at estate sales out here over the last few years. I guess after working around so many pages of other people's stories, I thought one day I might have something of my own that's good enough to commit to ink. They're kind of romantic, don't you think?"

I nodded my timid agreement. The mention of romance made me nervous in Asher's presence.

I slumped into a lumpy-looking chair draped with a patchwork quilt of rich browns, oranges, and yellows. In the comfort of its sunken bucket seat, I hung my hat over my knee and closed my eyes. Behind me, I heard the sound of Asher shifting around the house, swinging open window cranks to air out the humid mustiness of summer, followed by the sharp snap of two bottle caps popping off somewhere in the kitchen. My whole body slowly began to relax, muscle by muscle.

A soft breeze passed through the length of the house, and the sound of birds in the surrounding trees lulled me into an effortless sense of calm. My head fell back over the neck of the chair, and I hadn't even realized I'd fallen asleep until I became aware that the birdsong had morphed into another sound I didn't immediately recognize. When I opened my eyes again, I discovered daylight had already dimmed to dusk, and the chattering of birds had been replaced by a colony of frogs announcing nightfall with their croaking symphony. In my confusion, I thought I might have been transported back home to Erie. Asher was right. The air here is different. And there are few sweeter sounds than the wind through leaves.

I knew I was tired, but I hadn't fully registered just how truly exhausted I'd become from the accumulated weeks of broken sleep. It wasn't until the hush of the forest offered a contrast to the industrious drone of city noise that I could fully appreciate the extent of my fatigued unease. I shifted in my seat, surprised at myself for being such a comatose guest. Asher was lying on the couch a few feet away with a book on his stomach and his fingers laced together across his chest. He looked like he might have been asleep too before my stirring had woken him.

"That's the most peaceful I've seen you in weeks," Asher announced. "Sweet dreams?" he asked. I hadn't dreamed, but I nodded and thanked him for letting me sleep. I tossed my hat onto the floor, and that's where it stayed for the remainder of the evening.

"Hiatus is all about going with the flow," Asher winked over at me. He gestured down to three empty beer bottles resting on the floor next to the couch. "Hey, speaking of flowing, a couple of Belgium's best just so happened to flow their way into my belly while you were sleeping. I don't think Lois would approve of a drive right now. Are you up to spending the night here?"

"I'd like that a lot," I told him. I have to admit, from the moment we'd opened the door, I'd hoped we could stay a while.

"You were lights out before I could offer you anything. Thirsty? Hungry?" He was a natural and unfussy host.

We assembled a makeshift dinner as best we could from the gas station provisions we'd picked up earlier and supplemented our junk food feast with some old canned vegetables from the pantry. We ate on the porch under the stars, and though our scenery had changed entirely from the city, our pastime hardly did. We stayed up late into the night doing much of what we normally do at The Moirai—reading and peering up bashfully at one another in between pages—only this time, we were on the deck of The Egret listening to crickets and the wind instead of distant sirens or the rumble of construction trucks.

When the balm of the summer night had finally weighted our eyelids to their limits, we went back inside, and Asher offered me the bed as he walked in the direction of the couch. I pictured the image of him from earlier, lying there with his feet hanging over the arm. He was over a foot taller than the length of the couch. "You're going to hurt your back sleeping like that all night. We can both fit in the bed, right?" I said shyly, looking over at what appeared to be a double-sized mattress. Truthfully, I was worried about his back—he looked like a Saint Bernard sleeping on a pin cushion. But I have to admit, I also wanted an excuse to be close to him.

We crawled onto the bed together, fully clothed, each wearing what we'd arrived in except for our shoes, and we didn't bother turning down the quilt. We lay on our backs, rigid and motionless, each afraid to let our limbs go limp and drift toward the other. We fell asleep side by side, staring at the ceiling like mummies.

In the morning, I awoke with an anxious gasp, my heart racing, forgetting where I was. A dream had woken me, and my wide eyes met Asher's only a few inches away. We must have both rolled onto our sides to face one another in our sleep, and my socked foot had drifted from my half of the bed over to his and was resting against his shin. Had we been this close all night? My gasp must have woken Asher too, and he smiled across the quilt drowsily. A few sleepy moments of silence passed. I was the first to find something to say.

"Do I still have blue on my face?" I asked.

"What's blue and wrinkly and has a long nose?" he answered instead with another question.

"Glad you think so highly of me," I shrugged into the pillow.

"An elephant. I lied about the blue part."

An image of you sitting on my bed telling your stupid jokes flashed through my mind, and my own laugh confused me until I realized I was really crying. I wanted so desperately to tell him everything, but I couldn't find the words to begin.

"Still blue," he said softly, wiping a tear off the top of my cheek with his thumb. I couldn't tell if he meant the food coloring on my cheeks or the Robert Johnsons.

"Still blue," I repeated, trying to hold back more tears.

We've spent the morning quietly drinking coffee, nibbling on canned green beans, and listening to records. I've had more time to explore the details of the cabin, which are something between kitsch and true artistry. It's no longer any mystery to me how Asher came by his trade, and his carpentry skill seems to be more of a genuine passion than just a way to make a buck.

Asher's been steadily chipping away at a piece of wood with a whittling knife, and I watched a bird's shape materialize in stolen glances in his direction. It wasn't until he expertly brushed away the carvings and I noticed the creases of its long graceful beak emerge that I suddenly remembered the morning's dream that had woken me with such a start—it made me gasp again just to relive it. Asher's little whittled creation must have jogged my memory, and that instant, I shot to my feet and fished my journal from my bag to write you.

I dreamed I met an egret bird who could speak just as well as you or me. He told me something that has had my chest feeling as tight as a drum. It was only a dream—and about a talking bird, no less—but I think I might know something—something that possibly even the police don't know.

I can't begin to understand where this information could have come from or how it could be true—I think I have a clue about the person who killed you.

Love,
Rosalyn

The Egret

Nova and I were girls again—we must
have been no more than seven years old.
We danced playfully around a bonfire on
the lake, keeping ourselves from the cold.

I felt so complete and at home
with my twin counterpart by my side.
"Why don't you ever see elephants hiding
in trees," I asked, but no one replied.

I turned to Nova, but she had disappeared,
and I found myself suddenly and painfully alone—
until I looked down to where she once stood to find a
graceful egret bird who spoke to me in a calming tone.

"I can see you're feeling lost and stuck
and are searching for some kind of release.
Your world has been shaken, and there
is no justice—there is no peace.

But what disturbances are made will always
find their way back to a balanced state.
Scientists call this the Equilibrium Law,
while others simply call it nature or call it fate.

You don't need a microscope or a caliper
to see that everything is connected.
When something falls out of balance, the forces
of the universe will have it corrected.

Pay attention—for you might discover
that sometimes you are that very force.
You could be the right to the wrong,
helping the Equilibrium Law take its course.

You may wonder what invisible power is pushing you—
and you'll surely have your doubts and your fears.
And deciphering the instructions of that inner
voice may take many months or even years.

But your demons are yours, and yours
alone to surrender to—or to slay.
You must trust what might seem like
mad intuition so it can show you the way.

Sometimes it's just a feeling or coincidence
and sometimes, it's a dream.
And it may lead you to a ghastly
underworld, or so it may seem.

But never forget, every time something
dies, something else is born.
Shapeshifting is a painful business—
and really, it's the change that we so mourn.

Of course, the hardest of all is when
we ourselves, to be reborn, must also die.
And this must happen countless times
in a life before we say our final goodbye.

I tell you this because the difficulties
that lie before you will be your truest test.
You will need to become a new version of
yourself to fully embark on this dark quest.

Each of us has our own boogeymen,
Achilles heels and our own Kryptonite.
But we have in common a shared
obligation to do what is truly right.

I'll leave you with this final clue
to help you do your job ahead.
For you will find the man who spilled your
sister's blood and made Erie's soil run red.

Wise ones say the foundation of the universe
is love and all that love can create.
But your clue is this: the man's name who
killed your sister translates to 'I hate.'"

Memento Mori

MEMENTO MORI

Sunday, August 10, 1997
Dear Nova,

What's it like where you are now? How does it smell? What colors do you see? I wish you could be here instead—or at least I wish there was some way you could write me back. I miss you.

The disorienting, though welcome novelty of a life away from constant reminders of Erie often has me hopeful that a happier existence is possible—but for the past two nights, it's clear that such hasty optimism is premature. I only feel stuck on some purgatorial loop. Either my dreams are playing tricks on me, or I'm coming closer to some dark secret that feels only just beyond my reach. I often think of the photographs Singer showed me at the police station, their gruesome images seared into memory and haunting my thoughts.

As I write, I'm still with Asher at the cabin. We decided to stay another day, but ever since those strange, cryptic words from that talking bird, I haven't been able to relax again. It feels like my brain is on fire, and I'm racing around to find a hose as covertly as possible in Asher's presence. My whole body is tense once again. I'm fairly certain Asher has picked up on it too, although he does seem to enjoy the sight of me engrossed in my journal.

"If you talked to me half as much as you scratch into that book, we might really turn out to be soul mates," he joked yesterday morning after I'd finished writing to you. I know he's being sarcastic and cheeky, but his choice of words always seems to venture into flirtation. It wouldn't be half bad to have a soul mate like Asher.

We spent the rest of the day on the porch together, listening to the trees while I secretly tried to see how many breaths I could count without my mind clawing its way back to thoughts of you and Erie. The egret dream has shaken me. It's that same aching feeling of foreboding that stuck to me the day you were killed.

The bird had said the name of the man who killed you translates to "I hate." What does that mean? Even if I were to translate a list into every language on the planet, where does that get me? It doesn't make any sense. At first, I thought maybe it was only the intoxication of all this fresh air making my mind do strange things —or perhaps simply the influence of Asher's Egret house nudging me to invent surreal scenes in its likeness. But last night, I had a second dream that only echoed the one from the night before.

Yesterday, Asher and I found ourselves so comfortable on the porch that we decided if only we could make a quick drive into town for more appetizing dinner provisions than the old canned vegetables in the cupboard, it would be worth spending another day and night with the trees—not to mention we'd save ourselves the headache of Sunday traffic back to the city. Around five o'clock, Asher drove us to a small local grocery store he knew of about twenty minutes away, and we took turns naming ridiculous dishes we would make for dinner. Angel food cake sandwiches. Cream-chipped beef with beef jerky instead. Peanut butter and jelly burritos.

When we pulled into the parking lot, Asher told me my assignment was to pick out our dessert while he found our dinner, and we'd surprise each other back at The Egret afterward. We checked out separately, trying to conceal our spoils under our T-shirts or behind our backs, but my secret was revealed when it started melting from the afternoon's still oppressive heat. I licked the sticky residue off my fingers from the leaking pint of Ben & Jerry's vanilla ice cream as I rearranged it in the paper bag. Asher managed to keep his dish fully classified until I smelled it cooking from the porch. Curry chicken with rice. He's a surprisingly excellent cook.

We ate outside, savoring the clean air in the cool cover of night, and jokingly agreed we'd have to be good citizens by not wasting any food, which unfortunately would require us to eat the entire pint of ice cream right away. We did so without difficulty, passing the carton back and forth from our chairs, sharing the same spoon. Asher's warm disposition is such a comfort, contrasting the cold, gloomy interiors of my mind. We went to sleep the same way as we had the night before—fully clothed and careful not to breach the invisible barrier that was supposed to separate our sides of the bed—although slightly more at ease. The past twenty-four hours with Asher have cemented a new level of closeness between us that feels genuine, regardless of my sheepish, self-conscious crush. As my eyes grew heavy, I allowed my body to sleep the way it wanted to fall, and if my hand or foot were to accidentally brush up against Asher's arm, so be it.

This morning, I awoke in the same way as I had the night before— in a jolting start—but this time, I didn't appear to wake Asher right away. He slept soundly beside me. I took the opportunity to study his face in all its details for the first time since meeting him. He has a small light scar on the left side of his cheekbone and dark, spidery eyelashes that seem far too long for a man. He has a slight curl to his lips at their edges, even as his face rests.

It comforted me to see him sleep. Awake, despite the guise of his good-natured nonchalance, there is always something brooding and sad about him that underpins the lines on his face. What happened to the brother Asher had mentioned when we pulled up to the house? Is he gone? Estranged? Or has Asher lost someone too? Asleep, his face shows none of his subtly masked sadness. I wondered what he might be dreaming.

It's hard to describe, but in a way, resting next to Asher feels like I'm back home somehow. It's so good to care about something real —and right here in front of me. Everything else I love only exists in a memory of the past. When Asher finally woke, I pretended to have just woken up too. He inhaled and held his breath as he stretched out his long limbs like a cat, then released his stretch with his breath simultaneously. Our eyes smiled at each other. With our cheeks against the quilt, the world was on its side, and he and I were the only ones upright. "Don't worry," he said, "No stupid jokes this morning. I should have known my jokes were so bad that they induce spontaneous tears."

The weather was warm but pleasant, and once again, we spent the day outside on the porch. The porch is the main event out here. Coffee, books, and whittling. If it got too hot for my taste, I'd roll up the legs of my pants and let the breeze roll over my skin. Asher seems unbothered by the heat. Maybe he's used to it after all these years. I've never even so much as seen his feet without socks.

We alternated between listening to the serenade of birds or playing records inside. Asher always knows how to choose just the right album for just the right moments. Radiohead's *The Bends*, Bob Dylan's *The Times They Are a-Changin'*. Whatever the hour,

Asher's choice always seemed to read the room. Sometimes, as a particular verse would strike him, he'd rat-a-tat his index fingers against a table or chair like tiny drumsticks in an outburst of his appreciation. His lips moved without sound, and I knew he was reciting the lyrics to himself, even though he never sang aloud.

"Time for another classic," Asher said, rising from his chair as the last notes of The Smith's *The Queen is Dead* floated from the speaker. He swung open the creaky screen door and disappeared inside. I used the natural pause to stand and stretch, watching Asher across the room from the doorway. Within seconds he'd made his selection and swapped out the discs as if he'd already planned his follow-up soundtrack. A strutting voice I recognized rang through the cabin, accompanied by a catchy piano riff and twangy 70s-style guitar. In addition to his lyrical recall, I'm learning Asher also seems to possess an impressive repertoire of obscure music trivia.

Asher lowered the volume after the first few verses and gazed down at the album cover as he held it in the tension between his open palms. It was the iconic image of shirtless David Bowie, his plume of burgundy hair silhouetted against a white background, his eyes closed with a red and blue lightning bolt painted across his face, running all the way from the middle of his forehead, over his right eye, and onto his cheek.[1]

"Most people don't know the story behind this album," Asher said over the music. "Did you know David Bowie had a half-brother named Terry who killed himself? Terry struggled with schizophrenia his whole life. His condition declined, and eventually, he stopped taking his meds. The day he got out of one of his stays at a psychiatric hospital, he laid down on the train tracks."

"That's so awful," I replied, surprised by such a suddenly weighty topic.

"Bowie wrote this album in between shows when touring for Ziggy Stardust, long before his brother's condition had gotten to its worst. Most people think this album is just Bowie's newest incarnation of a glam rock stage character."

"It's not?" I asked, intrigued.

"The album is called *Aladdin Sane*," Asher said before dialing back up the volume as if the song were answering the rest of my question for him.

"Who will love Aladdin Sane," Bowie sang.[2]

"Who will love a-ladd-in-sane," Asher repeated. "A. Lad. Insane. It's a common theme in many of Bowie's songs—struggling with the fear that one day he might go insane too, just like his brother. Even when Bowie wrote this album, he didn't yet know his brother's fate," Asher said, running his finger along the edge of the record cover. "It's only the Greats that can entertain you while also feeding you true art," Asher added approvingly as he paced back toward me by the door and returned to his perch on the porch. I followed, feeling a somberness trailing on our heels. I settled back into my chair, concentrating hard on listening to the lyrics of Bowie's opus, my eyes fixated on the swaying trees.

When the record ended, the room fell back into the quiet sounds of rustling leaves, and I wondered if the lull was offering me the right moment to ask Asher about his past. "What happened to your brother? Why did you say you HAD a brother, not HAVE?" With every small opportunity our newfound domesticity provided, I paused on the brink of a question, then lost my nerve again. Why is this so hard for me? Just ask the question.

"I'll do it when he changes the next record," I'd tell myself. "I'll do it when we finish our coffee and wash our cups together in the kitchen. I'll do it when we just so happen to look up from our books at the same time."

But I know how this works. Trust is always a trade, just like Asher said. Those were the exact words he used. "How about we make it a trade then," he'd said at The Moirai. I can only ask him about his brother when I'm ready to talk too.

I thought about the little boy on the train to New York. "We sit in the direction we are going," his father had told him. I've come all the way to New York to get away, to start again, and to keep on moving. But I know I'm not done with the past, and it's not done with me. Every time I speak your name in my mind, my heart breaks again. My silence feels like the only thing preventing me from shattering right here on the floor at Asher's feet.

"You have to keep breaking your heart until it opens."[3] It's a line I read in a collection of poetry last week at The Moirai, and my mind has since refused to let it go. A mystic poet called Rumi wrote that over eight centuries ago, and though he could never have imagined all the ways in which the world would have changed when he penned those words, he still understood one thing well. No matter the epoch, the world will have no shortage of ways to break your heart. After the accumulation of enough cracks and fissures—or maybe only just one smashing blow—we ultimately give in to the truth that brokenness is only evidence of life. There's no use trying to patch things over and pretend all our surfaces are smooth. Only with this realization can we allow our hearts to open freely.

But I don't know how my heart can break any more than it already has. What more must it take? Why can't I open up to Asher? "My twin sister is dead and gone forever. My best friend. My universe," I imagine myself saying. But to speak those words aloud surrenders them as final and irrevocable—and I'm not ready.

Or is that my excuse? It's more than just those few words—it's everything that comes along with them. The unimaginable circumstances of your death. The open investigation. Singer and the special unit from Pittsburgh. And my dreams too. Am I starting to believe them? Am I willing to question my entire understanding of reality? These are weighty questions to share with someone who doesn't even know my last name.

Would Asher listen? Or will he go with the easier assumption—I'm just traumatized? Someone to pity. Superstitious. Gullible. Or even mentally ill. Nothing but a lad insane.

Bowie and I aren't so different, both fearing for our fragile sanity. We even have the lightning scars on our foreheads to match. Who will love a lad insane? Am I coming unhinged, or does my inner mind know something my outer one can't yet see? Are my dreams phantoms of reality, or is it the other way around? All I know is that I need to be clear on these matters before I can say a word to Asher.

I have something else to tell you too. It's why I'm writing again so soon.

This afternoon in a sudden flash as I pushed open the screen door to the porch, I remembered what had woken me with a shudder beside Asher. You were calling out to me, pleading desperately for help. I searched but couldn't find you anywhere—though I found something else instead.

If I'm not completely delirious—if these threads between dreams and reality are somehow real—I might just have another clue about the man who killed you. I think he wears a strange ruby ring. I can picture every detail. It's not much, but maybe it's something.

Love,
Rosalyn

Memento Mori

I found myself kneeling on my hands
and knees on a cold stone floor.
An echoing passage stretched before me,
lined with heavy door after door.

In the distance, I heard a woman's voice
crying, though I could not tell from where.
Her frightened wails echoed down the
endless hall in agonized despair.

As I gained my senses, I realized
it was Nova's voice crying out to me.
I leaped to my feet and lunged at the
closest door, but it was bolted securely.

I heard her desperate scream, "Sister, help!
He wants my teeth—don't leave me here alone!"
It was then I noticed above each door
a twisted face was carved in its keystone.

Again, I tried another door, then another,
but they, too, were firmly locked shut.
There had to be a way inside—some key,
some secret, some kind of shortcut.

Though I can't say why, I opened my mouth, took hold
of my tooth, and wrenched it as if I were possessed.
With all my strength, I ripped free my canine
and closed it in my palm against my chest.

When I opened my bloody fingers, I found
it had transformed into a long skeleton key.
In a daze, I raced toward the nearest door
and thrust it into the padlock urgently.

The lock turned, and the door swung open,
but there was nothing but a wall of stone.
Painted on its surface was the image of an
exotic bird so realistic it could have flown.

I slammed the door and charged down
the hallway to give one more a try.
I ripped another tooth from my mouth,
letting out a blood-curdling cry.

A second tooth revealed a second key
and I opened the door to step past,
but again, there was only a wall adorned
with a bird more richly plumed than the last.

Nova's pleading cry grew closer,
and unyielding, I followed her sound.
Now ten teeth, ten keys, ten wild birds,
but Nova was nowhere to be found.

At the end of the hall, I approached one last
door, its surface painted with a grimacing face.
With a mouth full of blood, I tore out a final tooth
and awaited the key that I'd find in its place.

When I unlatched the door, it opened, not
to a wall, but to an empty beach at night.
There, I realized the screaming belonged only
to the wind, for there was not a soul in sight.

Emerging from the sand
stood a tall silver candlestick.
A slender candle rose from its base,
a crescent moon glowing atop its wick.

In the sand at my feet, something
shiny and metallic caught my eye.
I stooped to retrieve a silver ring with a
jeweled skull and held it up to the twinkling sky.

Inscribed inside the band were two
words that at first I could not quite see.
Squinting harder into the dark, I finally
made out the words "Memento Mori."

I knew the Latin saying well, and
suddenly I seemed to lose my breath.
The skull's ruby eyes peered back and seemed
to whisper its translation: "Remember death."

Everything You Need to Know

Tuesday, August 12, 1997

Dear Nova,

I'm back in my room at The Bardo, and right now, I have two choices. I can sit here and willingly suffocate in my own apparent lunacy, or I can write. For the third night in a row, I've had vivid dreams about you, each one more disturbing than the last. I feel some sort of momentum building, like a story coming together across time and space. I don't understand. It scares me—tortures me to the point of sickness. It all seems so real, and yet I know they're only dreams.

We stayed at Asher's cabin until yesterday afternoon, following through with our plan to avoid the weekend traffic back to the city. The majority of our drive was smooth until the inevitable honking snapped us back into the fray as we neared the west side of Manhattan. Besides a brief moment of mild road rage from Asher, our car ride was calm and pleasant.

Asher's disposition is almost always even-tempered, but the more time I spend with him, the more I'm becoming attuned to his small quirks and mood shifts. When he's frustrated, he's hardly ever outwardly angry, but his body language tightens, and the left side of his lip pulls back toward his ear, just on that side. When a blue Honda cut in front of us, although I couldn't see his face, I knew he was doing it. I could feel his energy shift next to me, and I was sure that little snarl was making an appearance.

Apart from his lumbering walk, the rest of his fine motor skills are effortless and expert—but when he's agitated, his movements become momentarily erratic and clumsy. It's like that too when he's driving, and for a second, I thought he might slam Lois right into the back of that blue Honda. I wondered if a fluctuating mood like this one might be how he lost the end of his finger. But just as quickly as his spurts of anger arrive, they settle down again with equally as little warning.

By the time we arrived back in Queens, the sun had set, and the asphalt was beginning to cool in the evening air. Asher found a parking spot a few blocks from The Bardo, and he masterfully parallel parked Lois between a VW van with cardboard duct taped over the back window and a rusted delivery truck that looked like it probably didn't even run anymore. I grabbed my backpack, and we lingered by the car to stretch our legs in the street.

It was surreal finding ourselves again surrounded by concrete after three days enveloped in green. We each seemed filled with a silent mutual gratitude for our little shared adventure, but there was a tinge of bittersweet wistfulness too. Just as the sun melted into the silhouette of midtown skyscrapers in front of us, a sense of nostalgia melted over us. Our weekend together began its inevitable transformation from a living experience into the outlines of a memory.

We walked back to The Bardo in matching stride, and when we arrived, Asher took so long to unlock the door with the grimacing face I could tell he was just buying any time he could to append to the finale of our adventure story. Eventually, he succeeded, and I slid inside underneath his long outstretched arm above my head. When we reached the third-floor landing to say our goodnights, I, too, suddenly became aware of another part of myself screaming her refusal to let Asher go. I didn't want our time to end. After our shared weekend, the thought of my empty room felt so painfully lonely, and I took notice of my lingering desire to sleep next to him once again. It's juvenile, I know, but I'm afraid of what happens after I close my eyes at night. It feels so much safer to witness the darkness with someone else close.

There, on the third-floor landing with Asher, I had no choice but to acknowledge my overwhelming terror for the night's sleep to come —at least if only to myself. I felt like a child again, afraid just like you were of your beetle dreams. Yet, I felt strangely desperate for them too. What would I see next? Am I finally getting the answers that Singer was never able to give me? The answers I've been pleading for?

Asher swung open the fire door and wedged it open with his boot. "The Robert Johnsons are looking much better," he announced proudly. "Thanks for joining me on hiatus. Lois and I really enjoyed the company."

"Thanks to both of you too," I stammered. "I might not be any good at showing it, but it really was the best time I've had in months."

"Not to pat myself on the back, but somehow I believe it," Asher quipped with that trademark smirk. He looked down at his boot still chocked under the door and drummed his fingers on the doorframe like he was killing time as he waited for the right words to arrive. A sincere, and perhaps even slightly meek, out-of-character smile peeled across his face. "I really do hope you're feeling better, Ros," he added. "Let me know if you need anything." He gave the door a little shove with his toe, said goodnight, and started to lope his way down the hallway with his sleepy giant walk toward his apartment.

As the door eased shut, I felt my heart sink to the pit of my stomach, and in its place, a new nervous energy percolated under my sternum. Just before the latch caught, I grabbed the door's handle, yanked it back open, and whispered Asher's name into the distance between us as loudly as a whisper permitted.

"Asher. There is something you could still help me with." I couldn't believe I had summoned the words. He shifted on his heels, looking back at me sideways from the hall, his body tilted mid-step as he waited for me to finish my request. I had to push the rest of the words out one by one like unwilling skydivers forced from their tiny plane into freefall.

"Would… it… be ok… if… I… slept next to you again tonight?" I whispered after what felt like an excessive pause.

"Not a problem." His voice was warm but hushed. "I didn't hate it so much myself." I couldn't see through the dim of the hall, but I knew that smirk was back once again.

I ran upstairs to deposit my backpack and freshen up before heading back down to Asher's. Zisa had already retired to her room for the night, and the living room lights had all been turned off. I showered as quickly as I could manage and stole out of our loft in a pair of sweatpants and my old Siamese Dream T-shirt, my hair free, my hat abandoned. I felt like a teenager sneaking out of the house. When I arrived at Asher's apartment, I knocked so lightly I doubted he'd hear, but he was already standing by the door waiting. A sheet of dark, wet hair stuck to the side of his face.

Several untamed strands had broken free and curled across his forehead. He'd showered too.

The moment felt special somehow. People always seem so exposed with their hair wet like that. It reminded me of the way your hair would go wild on humid summer mornings after swimming in the lake. I suppose mine must have looked just the same. It's funny how I can still forget that looking at you is like looking in a mirror. Your hair like that always felt important somehow—like it could never lie. It had accepted its true nature and circumstances and was free to exist exactly as it was, tumbled by the wind and pinned to your face like an abstract sculpture.

Asher led me to his room off the left side of the living space. His loft has an identical layout to Zisa's and mine upstairs, only reversed. His room was tidy and minimalist like I imagined a sailor's ship bunk might be. He had nothing but a neat stack of books on the floor, a low, plain platform bed frame with a sunken mattress, and a chipped wooden dresser. A chair with a fraying woven rope seat was tucked under a scuffed secretary desk with metal legs. Every surface was threadbare but also rich in its simple, textured materials. He had no excess possessions, despite having lived there for years.

We hadn't eaten dinner, and neither of us had enough of a grocery stockpile to concoct a meal. Instead, Asher procured a secret stash of a half-empty box of cinnamon and brown sugar Pop-Tarts from his desk drawer. He tore open the silver packaging, and we silently devoured its contents in an instant.

Asher's bed had a single-sized mattress, not a double like the one at The Egret, and I made myself as narrow and rigid as possible, pulling my arms in tight against my body so he wouldn't get the wrong idea. It was virtually impossible to prevent our bodies from touching. The tension was so thick you could have sliced it with my buck knife, but I did truly just want to sleep, and I think Asher did too. I have to be careful with him—careful not to ruin things between us. It just feels so good to be close to someone and not have to explain myself.

We unfurled a thin, neatly folded blanket from the foot of his bed and pulled it over ourselves. Asher reached toward an old library-style lamp with a green rectangular shade on the floor and switched off the light. I fell asleep to the sound of Asher's breath, his head so close to mine I could hear each steady inhale and exhale in my ear. It may as well have been the soft waves of Lake Erie lapping at the shore.

I can't recall stirring even once through the night. The morning, however, was a far less tranquil scene. I awoke clutching my side and panting like a wild dog. I felt like I was tumbling off the edge of the earth, and all I had to hold onto were the reigns of my own breath.

In. Out. In. Out. Breathe.

I woke Asher too. He just rested his hand on my forehead as you do with a feverish child. "Bad dreams again?" he asked. I didn't need to answer.

The dream was immediately fresh in my mind, and I was relieved to have arrived back to the waking world, safe again next to Asher. I remembered everything instantly, unlike the others, which were often elusive far into the following day. It felt no more complicated than slipping through an open door. On each side of its threshold existed separate but perfectly contained realities—the one of my dream and the one of waking. But even with the door of sleep slammed securely behind me, there was no way to forget what had existed just on the other side only moments before.

I dreamed it was night, and I overlooked Lake Erie from the beach. It was hauntingly quiet. I felt the hair on the back of my neck raise, though at first, I wasn't sure why. Some sixth sense seemed to alarm. Things were not as they should be. Some looming danger felt near.

Only an instant later, I felt a hand over my mouth from behind and the cold, sharp pressure of a blade at my throat. An electrified terror overpowered me as a warm body pressed against my back, and a man's graveled voice spoke slowly against my ear. I couldn't see anything about him—I only felt his force against mine. I sensed he was strong but wiry thin and much taller than me.

"You have a choice," the low, guttural voice spoke. I could feel his vocal cords vibrating against my neck. "I can slit your throat right here, or instead, you can choose a second route. But only if you give me your permission—I'm a gentleman, of course," the voice said. What the second route was, he would not say. "So what will it be, then? Choice one? Or choice two?"

My heart beat frantically. My only thought was survival. "One?" he repeated with a low growl. He took a long pause. I remained perfectly still. "Orrr twwwooo?" he said, drawing out the words. I nodded my head in his clutches to indicate my selection, knowing that "two" was my only chance of staying alive.

"Good choice," he said, his jaw still pressed hard to my ear. Instantly, he released his blade from my throat and tossed it to the ground, tightening his grip over my mouth so forcefully I thought he might snap my neck. He raised his newly freed hand back toward my face and gently petted the top of my forehead with the tips of his fingers like my skin was some fragile, precious material.

Then, as if he were executing some practiced ceremony, he traced an invisible path starting from the top of my hairline—first, over the top of my birthmark, then down the middle of my forehead between my eyes, and finally along the bridge of my nose until he reached its tip. When he'd arrived at the skin between my nostrils, he paused, then dragged his fingers lower to meet his other hand, still clasped tightly over my mouth. He seemed to pinch and adjust a glinting object wrapped around his index finger.

The night was dark, but I strained my peripheral vision enough to make out the clear outlines of a silver ring. Even from the imprisonment of the dream, I was somehow keenly aware that it was identical to the one I'd seen only two nights before in an entirely different dream world—a silver skull with ruby eyes on an engraved band.

He swiveled the ring on his index finger, redirecting the angle of its skull charm under the base of my nose, pointing it just below my nostrils. With a flick of his thumbnail, he unlatched a tiny hinge in the ring's pendant, and the face of the jeweled skull popped open, revealing a small compartment inside. From the fringes of my vision, I could see it was filled with what looked like a fine white powder. What it was, I didn't know, but the sight was enough to send another jolt of pulsing fear through every nerve in my body. I tried to slow my breathing, careful not to inhale any of what was inside that ring's hidden chamber.

"Don't be frightened," he whispered as I shifted in terror, futilely struggling to break free. I knew that something terrible was about to happen. In one smooth, calculated motion, he cupped his other hand over my nose, pinching both my nostrils shut.

My chest heaved for air, but none could pass—both my nose and mouth were tightly covered. I clawed at his forearms with my nails, hysterically trying to pry away his grip, but he had the advantage of both strength and position. A rage seethed inside me, and I summoned every ounce of energy to kick and buck and toss my body from side to side. I dropped my weight to the ground as if I were an anchor casting myself out to sea, but still I could not break free. I felt my life force draining with every passing second. Would this be how I died?

Had it been a minute? Two? Three? I no longer had the strength to struggle, and I felt my field of vision closing in. Every instinct screamed for me to fight, yet a deeper intuition told me that this was the end. I had no choice but to succumb to the creeping darkness. But just as soon as I had resigned myself to my grim fate, I felt the hand pinching my nose suddenly release, and a heaving wave of dusty air filled my lungs through my nostrils.

"That's better now, isn't it?" he whispered in my ear, still clutching his right hand over my mouth. I gasped uncontrollably through my nose, recuperating as much oxygen as I could. As I panted in the fresh air, the dizziness of oxygen deprivation dissipated, but some other clouded feeling rushed in to take its place.

What was happening? Something was not right. I felt a chalky film inside my sinuses and a bitter, chemical taste in the back of my throat. What had been inside that ring's compartment? Whatever it was, it was now coursing through my veins. He'd rigged it. He'd poisoned me. Trapped me. Forced me to breathe it in.

One moment I was sure I would die of suffocation, and the next, I was overcome with a new terror of what unknown fate now awaited me instead. Even before I could recover my breath, I felt something immediately shift in my body—like when you're a kid and fall to the pavement hard, your adrenaline pumping so fiercely that although you are sure you've been hurt, you cannot yet tell how or where.

I sensed the dull sting of the ground meeting my face as I slumped to the sand in a thudding heap, and even in my bleariness, I began to understand what was happening. I could no longer feel even my own skin. I was numb and paralyzed, hazy—yet still vaguely conscious. It was as though my body had detached and simply levitated somewhere else nearby. I could not move or speak—all I could do was lie there helpless, waiting for what he would do to me next.

The night was dark, and from the angle that I'd fallen, I could not make out the details of his face, but through the shadows, I did see well enough to know that he had retrieved his knife from the sand. I watched the silhouette of his profile several feet away as he wiped its blade on his pant leg, then licked it clean. He knelt where I'd fallen and spoke in a sinister but calm tone, describing to me the option I had chosen. He drew so close his lips almost touched my cheek. I braced myself as best I could in my immobilized and altered state.

I was so terrified I wished death would take me right then, but nothing came to my rescue. Instead, I felt a dull pressure in my abdomen, followed by a slow, intentional pull, and though I did not feel the sting of pain, I knew the sensation was his knife in my side. I closed my eyes in sorrow, understanding what had befallen me. I'm not sure if it was the drugs he had given me or delirium as my blood began to leave my body, but when I opened my eyes again, I couldn't tell if I was already dead or merely hallucinating. Your face stared back at mine, our cheeks pressed against the sand, mirrored eye to eye. Your face was bloody and pale. With tears streaming from your tired eyes, you told me something that I still don't understand. That was when I woke up, panting and holding my side next to Asher.

Is this how you died? Was that white powder in the ring's hidden chamber the ketamine that Singer said they found in their report? Were you poisoned? Numbed? Paralyzed and tortured? Were you alive and helpless in the sand as your killer cut away what he wished? Could this possibly be what happened to you in your last moments on Lake Erie's beach—or am I just imagining this entire horror show?

Singer's pictures must really have done a number on me. My mind must be making things up again. I feel like some lunatic grasping for answers from the empty air. It's just a dream—just a nightmare —all too deranged to take as truth. But what else do I have? There's been truth to my dreams so far, hasn't there? Right now, the only possibility that feels crazier than believing them is ignoring them. Piece by piece, dream by dream, is this how your story finally unfolds? It doesn't seem fair. Why must I get madness instead of justice?

A name that means "I hate." A silver skull poison ring with ruby eyes, the words "Memento Mori" engraved on its band with ketamine powder inside. Are these all clues? All fragments of the real story? Either I'm finally starting to collect enough pieces to put together what really happened that night, or I've amassed some convincing evidence that perhaps I'm slowly losing my mind. If there's any possibility in this universe that these dreams could be true, I suppose now the only thing to do is wait for sleep to teach me more.

Love,
Rosalyn

Everything You Need to Know

The waves on Lake Erie's beach were
calm, just barely lapping at the shore.
I felt a strangeness in the air, and the hairs on my neck
stood on end, though I didn't yet understand what for.

Despite the thick cloak of silence all around,
something inside me knew that I was not alone.
It was then I felt a hand over my mouth and a knife at my
neck as a graveled voice spoke in a menacing tone.

"You have an important choice ahead of you—
it's up to you to decide how this will all play out.
Either I can slit your throat right now on
this beach, or you can choose a second route."

"So what will it be? One?... Or two?" he snarled,
awaiting a sign indicating my verdict.
I felt panic course through my body, and the pressure
of his knife caused my throat to constrict.

"One?" he repeated, as a silenced pause passed—"Or two?"
I knew the second would be my only chance at life.
In his cold grips, I nodded my selection of option two
and felt a momentary wave of relief as he tossed away his knife.

His free hand rose to meet the other still over my mouth,
and he turned his ring to rest just under my nose.
He unhinged its skull charm like opening a tiny box,
and against my heart's pounding, I regretted what I chose.

Though the night was dark, I distinguished a fine
white powder inside the compartment of his ring.
Then without warning, he pinched his free hand over
my nostrils before I could process what was happening.

Both my nose and my mouth were
covered, and no air could get past.
The more I fought and flailed to get free, the more
I realized the oxygen in my lungs might be my last.

The walls of my periphery began to close in
and defenseless, I knew it was too late.
I no longer had the strength left to fight and
feeling my body go limp, I realized my fate.

But suddenly, I felt a wave of fresh air rush through
my nose and fill my lungs as he released his hand.
Yet something was wrong—a chemical taste stuck in my throat,
and the earth seemed to drop like I'd stepped into quicksand.

"In the end, you're all the same," he whispered,
"Afraid of death, like frightened fools."
But I'm here to save you from this bitter world—I need
only a small trade, more precious to me than fine jewels."

Slumped in the cold sand, my mind was clear,
but my whole body was heavy and motionless.
Awaiting his brutality, my chest sunk
into sorrow, fear, and hopelessness.

"You're paralyzed," he growled, "but because I'm a gentleman,
these drugs up your nose will dull the pain of each slice.
You made your choice, but don't fret—once you're on the other
side, your souvenirs to me will seem but a small price.

You see, you're a unique creature, and to me, you've earned
my gift of the greatest freedom you've ever known.
All I ask in exchange is to watch the blood drain
from your face as I cut your flesh from bone to bone.

And once I've released you from all this mortal suffering,
I'll keep some mementos from you to remember our time.
Each life I free is so special to me, and to let it
be forgotten would be my only real crime.

Such rare and remarkable beings like you
should not be trapped in this cruel life.
You see, that's where I come in, relieving
you of all this worldly strife.

And when one day I've done my share of good work, I'll meet you
and all the other creatures I've freed on the other side,
but until that day, Memento Mori—for it's the one
guarantee that in the end, none of us are denied.

With that, he retrieved his knife from the sand,
wiped it on his thigh, then licked its blade.
There, on the cold packed sand,
I'd never been so helpless or afraid.

He knelt above me, his face still too
shadowed to see in the moonlit night,
and slowly, he plunged his dagger
into my side with a cackling delight.

I pleaded for death to take me right then,
but I could not speak or cry out.
"I'm in no rush," he hissed. "This will
take us some time—I have no doubt."

Then, in a flash of wild fear, I saw Nova's tear-streamed face,
and though her eyes were tortured, her voice was calm and low.
"Sister. Find the man who did this," she whispered.
"I'll show you everything you need to know."

Tooth Collector

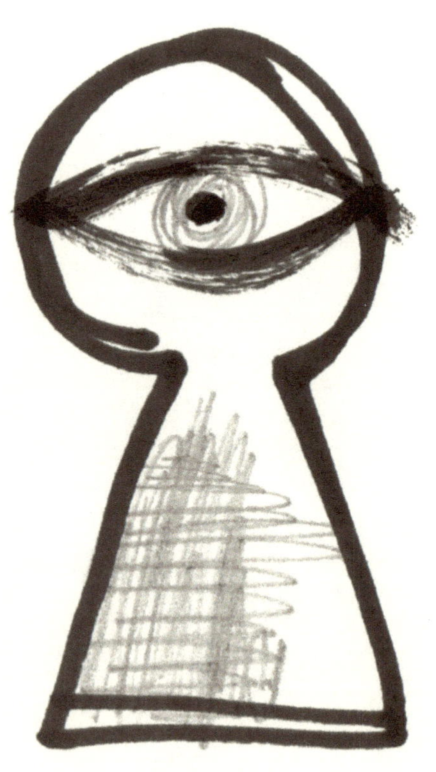

Friday, September 5, 1997

Dear Nova,

I'm sorry I haven't written. My mind is swimming. It's been weeks now since Asher and I returned from The Egret, and while I've been trying my best to play the role of a sane person, I'm not sure I'm living up to the part. I've been distracted, using my time at work more for research purposes than for the items of my job description, treating The Moirai more like my personal investigation facility than my place of gainful employment.

It also has come as no surprise that while the sisters' methodology is quite useful for stumbling upon the unexpected, it is nearly impossible to find something you are actually looking for. Nonetheless, I made do, starting with the obvious when I found a long section of bilingual dictionaries in Future House. Their logic's description was scrawled into the log in Asher's handwriting. It read, quite simply, "Wouldn't it be nice to speak more languages one day?"

I went through each one by one, translating the words "I hate" into every language I could find.

Je déteste: French.
Odio: Spanish.
Ich hasse: German.
Vihaan: Finnish.

The full list went the length of a yellow pad page, but none of it seemed to jog any ideas. The other day, from over my shoulder,

Asher caught me staring at it from the kitchen table. I should have been more clandestine carrying around a pad of paper with the words "I hate" written in all caps at the top with a long list running down the page, but all Asher did was pat me on the shoulder from behind and offer to change the music. "I can put on some Black Sabbath or Slayer if that's more your speed today." He grabbed an apple from the fruit bowl and walked right back out again, unfazed.

When the list didn't seem to get me anywhere, I read up on the background of poison rings in a book I found in Past House about the history of warfare. All I learned was that they seemed to have originated in India as a vessel to store tiny keepsakes, eventually making their way west as part of the "holy relic trade," and later became popular in Europe as a way to slip poison to enemies in their food or wine. In other cases, they were a convenient way to commit suicide if one was facing inevitable and painful death, but all that cheerful material still didn't seem to help.

Once I'd exhausted myself researching translations and poison rings, I took a step back and started reading about dreams in general. I didn't quite know what I should even be looking for, but psychology and anthropology seemed like good places to start. These kinds of books were much harder to find by chance, but several weeks ago, a large donation had come in from a university professor who had passed away. We seemed to share the same interests. I was in luck.

I learned that in Aboriginal culture, there is a belief called "Dreamtime." According to Dreamtime, Earth's original inhabitants were large spirit beings that could travel from one sacred site to another. It was when all the patterns of life first took shape. Now, although the original spirit beings no longer walk the Earth, a human can still access this entire lineage through their dreams.

In "The Dreaming," as it's also called, all worldly knowledge is granted through ancestors, even across space and time. All beings already exist and continue to exist, both before and after their physical life. Only when a fetus moves in the mother's womb is it believed the spirit has entered into the form of a human body. I liked this concept right away. Are you one of our ancestors now, your wisdom forever accessible through "Dreamtime?"

The Ancient Egyptians recorded their dreams on papyrus paper. They believed dreams were like oracles, delivering messages from the gods. In ancient Greece, a physician named Hippocrates believed in the simple theory that during the day, the soul receives images, while during the night when asleep, it produces them. In some Buddhist literature, multiple people sometimes shared the very same dream as part of a collective dream consciousness. Dreams could be seen as premonitions, and in some instances, Buddhas from different eras had reported identical dreams despite living in entirely different generations.

Then there were the classics of psychology. Freud, of course, believed that dreams were merely manifestations of a person's deepest desires and anxieties, and he often tied them to repressed memories from childhood. One afternoon, while engrossed in his *The Interpretation of Dreams* masterwork, I wondered what Freud himself might have to say about me and my own childhood. Would he say I was melancholy? Morose? Repressed? Traumatized?

There, with Freud's seminal work resting in my lap, I even considered the possibility that surely, in a place like New York City, I could find a shrink of my own who knew all of Freud's tricks. I wondered what it might be like to talk to someone here who could interpret my dreams into something more manageable.

I still had that card with the number for that shrink Singer had given me at the Erie police station. Dr. Hilma Molina. I have to admit, on my most tormented days, the concept of confidential and impartial help felt overwhelmingly tempting. Once, in a moment of desperation, I actually dialed her number from the payphone across the street from The Bardo. No one picked up, but I got her answering machine. The voice on the recording was poised and velvety. When I heard the beep, I froze. "My name is Rosalyn… uhhhm, Detective John Singer gave me your information…" I started, but nothing else would come out. I hung up, feeling stunned and helpless. I tore up the index card into thin slivers and poured them into the trash.

I can't talk to a shrink. It's a waste. What if there's nothing for her to interpret? Just a tangle of nonsense—spaghetti soup inside my skull. And then that same question comes crawling back—but in a different way. What if there's nothing for her to interpret because my dreams are true, just as they are? No interpretation necessary. What if it's not all some elaborate allegory that can be analyzed and organized into neat little psychological boxes? What if my dreams are more like an open window, not a delusional mirage— just like the Aborigines and Egyptians, and Hippocrates believed? What if they're a trail of real clues that not even Singer could find?

Sometimes I feel like I have nothing left to lose in believing this version—except perhaps the end of my wits. Is this how Astrid felt in Gram's fairytale too?

I turned over all these questions countless times, brooding in my little window nook at The Moirai, but still, nothing that even vaguely resembled an answer paid me a visit. Instead, an even more terrifying thought sidled up to me. What if I sat down in some shrink's armchair and shared all my questions, fears, and foreboding dreams, and their conclusion wasn't an interpretation at all, but something else entirely? What if they thought I was the one who killed you? Is that what Detective Singer thinks too? And is that what Asher would think if I ever worked up the nerve to tell him the whole story? Was I misreading Singer's aloofness and mistrust when all along, it was outright suspicion?

No shrinks. No detectives. I can't make matters worse. No one else can help me. No one else would believe me—except for you.

"I'll show you everything you need to know." That's what you said to me in the dream, your eyes filled with anguish as you lay paralyzed in the sand next to me. What did you mean? What do I need to know? How can you show me?

I feel like I'm slipping away into some dark abyss. This week, I must have heard Gram's voice a hundred times in my mind telling us the story of our names. "A sun, after all, needs the darkness to shine," she would always say. "The darkness, my dear, is nothing to fear, only something to tend to like its own sort of garden." I'm trying.

If all of Gram's Dream Eye stories were true, what then am I supposed to do with that truth now? How could I have witnessed these things in my dreams that I could never have known in my real life? It's like I was seeing through your eyes the night you were killed, a spectator to your experiences. I was me, and I was you at the very same time.

What am I even talking about? Tormenting myself is just an excuse to delay the real and only truth there really is: you are gone, and I'm alone.

I wish I could snap my fingers and vanish all my questions like fairytale magic. "It's just nightmares, Rosalyn. You're an adult," I tell myself. I could just get on with life. Learn to be happy. Pursue ambitions. Become closer to Asher. It's as if I'm afraid if I move on, I'll lose every last piece of you. Will the memory of you slowly slip away until there is nothing? Or can I learn to find peace in the heartache itself?

Day after day, I try to calm myself with the notion that maybe this acceptance is mine to choose. Yet still, the dream residue sticks to me like a heavy film that won't wash off. Everyone has nightmares —I know that. But what I've experienced runs deeper. They're clues. They have to be.

I felt agitated all morning. I can't even recall waking up, I just remember sitting up in bed sweating. I was only vaguely aware that I was no longer asleep, though not yet fully conscious either. Today I feel fragile, like at any moment, the world as I know it may fracture into something between memory and the spirit world.

On the way from The Bardo to The Moirai, Asher and I stopped for bagels. We ate across from one another in the kitchen, our crunching dampened by the sound of a sad trumpet playing on the record player from the other room.

"A Baker, but not of bagels," Asher announced. It was another one of his quips, a warm personality feature he employs in lieu of small talk, which I always appreciate. It feels light and connected but not labored. The look on his face told me he was pleased with his joke, but I didn't get it. "Chet B-A-K-E-R. One of the best trumpeters and voices of all time. Classic," he elaborated.

When I recognized his association with our baked breakfast fare, I parted my mouth to make a little "ahhh" sound of understanding and took another bite of my bagel. His cleverness deserved a better-humored audience, but I was feeling too distracted and gloomy. Asher rested his foiled, half-eaten bagel onto his plate and looked across at me, wearing a serious look like I'd never seen before.

"You know," he said, "I used to be just like you when I was younger. I spent all my time digging around in books, looking for answers to questions that had none. I don't know what it is you're going through right now, and I don't know what you're looking for, but if I've learned one thing in life, it's that some things are just beyond a logical explanation."

He paused and rubbed the nub of his finger on the table beside his plate. "You can spend your whole life living in the past, but one day you'll look up and realize that while you were at it, you've forgotten all about the people right in front of you who care." It took me a moment to place the emotion on his face. He looked hurt.

My appetite evaporated, and I lowered my bagel to my plate too. We sat together in a sort of understanding silence. I wondered if it was finally the time to tell him your story, but before I could begin, Asher was the one who spoke—and longer than I'd ever heard him speak in a single sitting before. I'll do my best to retell his words. I hung on his every breath, immediately forgetting my own mood and self-absorption.

"I had a little brother once," he began. "I think I mentioned that to you before when we were on hiatus. He was the one who helped build The Egret with my dad and me when we were kids. His name was Fisk. He was a half-brother, and we looked nothing alike, but he was as much of a brother as a brother could be. He had bright red hair—RED-red, you know? And back then, mine was even darker than it is now.

We looked funny together, and people used to call us the licorice brothers because they thought we were stuck together like those pieces of red and black licorice you buy at the drugstore. Fisk was born with a sixth finger on his left hand—apparently, lots of kids are born with extra fingers, but Fisk's was the rare kind. Believe it or not, it looked pretty normal until you actually counted. After my accident, we'd always joke that one day he'd donate his extra one to me. He really would have too.

Fisk was small and sort of frail, and I was tall and strong for my age, but we still did everything together. We had the same mom but different fathers. Our dad is the one who raised us, but he's not blood to either of us. He's a good guy and brought us up like we were his own boys. My biological father was never in the picture, but Fisk's real dad was still around, and Fisk would stay weekends with him once or twice a month. He seemed like an OK guy in the beginning, and he had a respected career as a family doctor in the next county. The arrangement seemed to work until it didn't.

One summer, when I was fourteen and Fisk was ten, his dad was in a fairly serious car accident and almost didn't make it out alive. He lost a leg, damaged some organs as far as I can remember, and was in a coma for weeks. Fisk and I were even at the hospital when he woke up. From that moment forward, it was clear something wasn't right. A wire had gotten crossed somewhere, and nothing the doctors did could put it back in place.

It took almost a year for him to recover enough to take care of himself on his own again, and eventually, Fisk resumed his weekend sleepaways. But every time his dad picked him up in front of our house, there was a nervousness about him that I'd never seen before. It was like, all of a sudden, he was scared to be left alone with his own father, although I could never get him to admit it outright.

The first few times Fisk came home from his reinstated visits, he just seemed spooked and jumpy. Then he started coming home with a few bruises here and there. Nothing major. When my mom and I asked about it, he would just cheerfully brush it off and explain they'd been playing catch in the yard, and he'd tripped. Something didn't feel right, but we didn't know to worry yet. He was a little boy, after all. Boys get bruises.

It wasn't until one weekend when Fisk came home with a bloody lip and a missing tooth on the side of his mouth that we were sure something was really wrong. Mom was inconsolable for two days. We begged Fisk to tell us what had happened, but he wouldn't speak a word of it. Our mom must have called Fisk's dad fifty times demanding an explanation, and each time she hung up without a believable answer, she was only more furious. She threatened to call the cops, and our stepdad even got close to going over there himself to wring out the truth with his fist. How could neither Fisk nor his father know what happened? They were keeping a secret, and we all knew it.

That was the turning point. Mom forbade the weekly sleepovers, at least for as long as she could. Legally, they shared custody, and eventually, the visits cautiously resumed.

That was around the time Fisk took a strong interest in the library, and I suppose that's where my interest in books began too. At first, it just seemed like Fisk was looking for an escape to occupy his mind, but as the older brother, I started catching on to new themes in his interests. He devoured murder mysteries and books about criminal psychology, cognitive science, and history in general. Let's just say it seemed like pretty heavy reading material for an eleven-year-old.

Fisk was always a sweet and gentle kid. He was nerdy, no doubt about it, but he wasn't dark or morbid. I knew, somehow, all of this had something to do with the weekends at his dad's. I tried to ask him about it again and again—I asked if he'd seen anything that had upset him, but each time he just turned pale and changed the subject. The most I ever got out of him was only a question: 'What do you think makes good people turn bad?' he asked. That was enough for me to read between the lines.

Our mom managed to go to the courts with her suspicions of some kind of abuse, but even the tooth incident wasn't enough to get the visitations completely suspended. Somehow the 'good doctor's' reputation went a long way with the judge, and mom was only able to get visitations reduced to holidays. In the end, that wasn't good enough.

The Christmas before Fisk turned twelve, he went to stay with his dad for Christmas Eve. We'd made a tradition of doubling up our celebrations so Fisk could do something special with both sides of his family. We would get him for Christmas Day and had planned a whole day of a tacky light tour and ice skating on our neighbor's lake. None of that ever happened.

The story his dad gave the police was that Fisk had run onto the snow-covered train tracks near the house and slipped. That's how it happened. A cargo train around noon on Christmas Eve.

To this day, it still doesn't make sense. Fisk was neither dumb nor a daredevil. He knew the tracks were back there. He didn't even like the snow. He would never have been playing out there in the first place. After all these years, I'm sure the only explanation is that his dad had pushed him—or something worse. Somewhere along the way, Fisk had seen something he wasn't meant to see. I'm certain of it. I don't know exactly what, but I do know Fisk was hiding it —and had been ever since he lost that tooth. Maybe even before. That's what I think all the books were about—a little kid just trying to make sense of what was happening around him. What could make the good doctor turn bad?

In the end, there wasn't enough evidence against Fisk's dad that we could put forth to the police. It was our word against his. 'Just one of those tragic accidents,' they called it. It wasn't long after that though that his dad packed up and moved. People around town thought he left from a broken heart, but ever since that car wreck, I don't think the guy had a heart left to break. I've never heard anything about him since, and I never want to either.

After Fisk died, something broke in me too. I withdrew completely and lost myself in books and music, just like Fisk. Maybe a part of me felt like I needed to continue his search. What makes good people turn bad? His question became mine. I spent years shunning the world after Fisk was gone. I felt helpless to an injustice against which I had no recourse. Making sense of it all somehow felt like the only antidote. I finally understood why Fisk was always buried in those books, but in the end, no book could explain to me what happened to my little brother, and no book ever will."

Asher looked across the table at me as I stared back in rapt silence. No words arrived to form a reply. I didn't even realize tears were streaming down my face until I felt their warmth on the back of my hands in my lap.

Asher had lost someone too. The little red-headed boy in my dream was his brother. He was real. But how could I have known about Fisk over a month ago? I knew none of this then.

Asher slid his right hand out across the table toward me, his palm down and his fingers spread. "I hope you find whatever answers you're looking for, Ros. I really do," he said. "But promise me that you'll also consider what it might look like if you don't." I extended my hand past my half-eaten bagel and wove my fingers into his.

"Thank you for telling me," I said, nearly choking as I held down more tears. "I promise. I'll think about it." Neither of us finished our bagels, and we cleaned up our dishes quietly with the sound of Chet Baker's sad trumpet still floating in from the other room. I rinsed my plate in the sink and laid it on a towel on the counter to dry next to his. Asher stood next to me at the edge of the counter and wriggled out of the flannel button-up he was wearing over his T-shirt. On his way out of the kitchen, he turned to hang it on a hook between the refrigerator and the parlor door.

I caught the image of his shirt dangling against the wall in my periphery and did a double take. There was something about it. The vague outlines of some scene I recognized flitted across my mind. It felt like déjà vu. The image of a leather jacket hanging against a wall in a dingy room floated to the surface.

"See you in there," Asher called from our reading room. "Be right in," I called back, my voice trembling as my knees went weak. A sudden avalanche of memory poured over me, and in an instant, last night's dream was as fresh as powdered snow.

Love,
Rosalyn

Tooth Collector

I awoke in some seedy hotel
suite, all squalor and gloom,
dimly lit only by a single lamp
in the far corner of the room.

A weathered black jacket dangled from
a hook on an otherwise empty wall.
The air was dust-filled and stale,
and smelled of grain alcohol.

I seemed to be alone, my only company
a faint screaming wind outside.
"Anyone here?" I asked the cold walls
anxiously, but nothing replied.

Though the room was vacant, I sensed
it wouldn't stay this way for very long.
I needed to watch my back, for I could
feel that something here was all wrong.

Across the room, I noticed several objects
on a desk that I couldn't quite discern.
I approached the scattered forms, and as
I did, I heard the lock in the door turn.

I panicked, my heart beating so hard
against my chest, I could barely think.
I darted forward, the objects coming into view:
teeth, a needle, and a vial of black ink.

I threw myself in a closet and peered through
the keyhole, fearing my cover wouldn't last.
The hotel door opened, and a hooded figure
entered, retrieving the jacket as he passed.

Arriving at the foot of the bed, he spread
open the jacket after turning it inside out.
Its fabric was lined with hundreds of teeth—
and they were human, beyond any doubt.

From the bedside drawer, he procured
what looked to be a small electric drill,
and he reached into his pocket, retrieving yet another
tooth, the sight sending me into a violent chill.

Pinching it between his ringed index
finger and thumb, he drilled a small hole.
Then he threaded a needle at his desk
with well-practiced control.

Returning to the edge of the bed, he ran his fingers
over the jacket's teeth like it was Braille,
and he threw his head back, letting out
something between a laugh and a wail.

Finding a spare space in the fabric,
he steadily sewed in his new trophy,
and when he'd finished, he robed himself with the
jacket, as if it were something precious and holy.

Then, as if he'd known I was watching all along,
he turned toward the closet and walked in my direction.
Blindly, I groped in the dark, but there was not
a thing within my reach to use as protection.

The door creaked open, and there he stood,
grinning at me as if I were an expected guest.
"What nice timing you have—I was hoping
for a few more pearly whites to add to the rest.

How funny—I just finished someone who looks so much
like you, I could almost swear you had a twin."
With that, he ripped the door from its frame
and seized my neck with a wide, sinister grin.

The Removable Leg

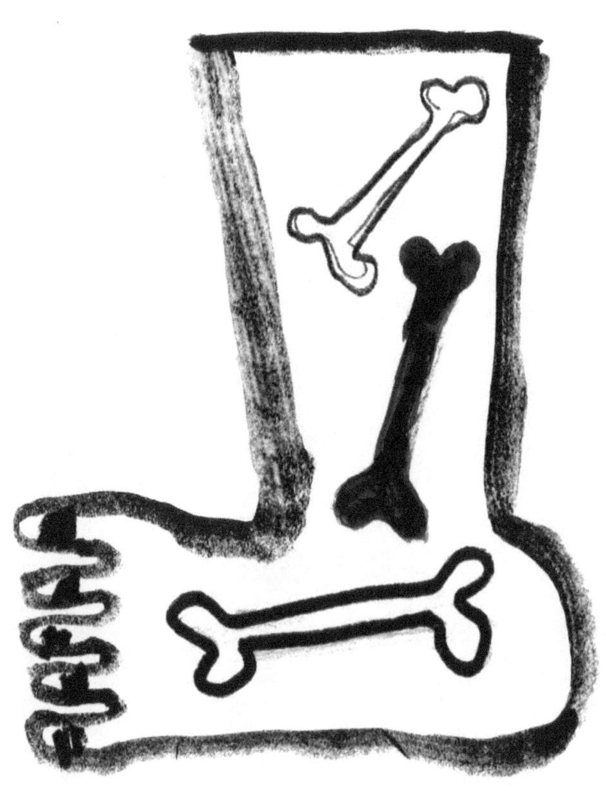

Thursday, September 18, 1997

Dear Nova,

All I can seem to do lately is pace, tracing a small figure eight along the uneven, creaky floorboards in my room. When I go on like this for long enough, I see a shadow flicker in the stripe of light under my bedroom door, and I know Zisa has come to check on me. Sometimes she'll softly ask if I'd like some tea, but mostly I just see the uncommitted movement of her feet, and I wonder if she has her ear against the door. We both stand motionless as we wait and listen for each other's footfall, and eventually, the light becomes solid again, and I'll know she's walked away. Once it gets late enough, the white stripe finally turns black as she flicks off the living room light and goes to bed.

After I last wrote, I can't tell you how relieved I felt to wake up in bed, still alive and in one piece. But with the relief came a steady edginess. I've been such a nervous wreck it's almost comical. Is it the untiring clutches of grief? Or simply the reminder of guilt? Why am I still here and you're not?

When pacing my room isn't enough, I leave for the street and slink along the warehouses by the river until I've tired my body enough to quiet my mind. I've been doing this every evening after work for a week now. Last night I left The Bardo long after the sun had already set, and I let my legs choose their course. Before I knew it, I was already at the Queensboro Bridge, and I thought if I was already there, I might as well walk over it. Once I'd gotten over, I thought, well, I might as well walk through Manhattan.

It didn't feel so different from the very first night I arrived in New York with all my world's possessions strapped on my back and not a soul in the world who was missing me. I guess it felt natural to haunt the streets at night when my own head felt so haunted too. I floated over the pavement, guided by instinct rather than by intention. I didn't have a plan—I just knew I needed to stay moving.

The September air is becoming cool again, and it makes walking feel effortless. Once I'd meandered my way beyond a mess of high-rises, I decided I wanted to see how Queens looked now that I could see it from the other side of the water. I wandered for miles along the walking path that follows the East River, immersed in my thoughts until I passed a four-hundred-meter running track and tennis courts.

It must have already been well after midnight by then. The streets were dead, and for the first time, I realized how vulnerable I was out there all alone. That's the thing about cities—there's always that false sense of security in the constant company of other bodies nearby, not only on the streets but also locked away right beside you as you sleep in row after row of sardine-sized apartments. A city is really nothing more than a collection of people and their props—suits and penthouses, guitars and mohawks—all of us mingled together, bearing witness to one another's lives. It all seems to come with some hubristic sense of safety in numbers when really, we're all just alone together. Is it this deceptive comfort that blinds our defenses?

I wasn't satisfied with my walk until I found the very same park bench overlooking the East River where I'd watched the sunrise on my first night here. I removed my backpack and settled down, stretching my legs out straight in front of me on my heels. The water looked so peaceful at that hour with just a hint of the city glow flickering over its surface. I sunk my head back, letting the top of the backrest fall under the nape of my neck, and I sipped in a few deep, slow breaths—in through my nose, out through my mouth. The air itself seemed to make me drunk.

I hadn't meant to fall asleep, but the next thing I knew, it was dawn. I woke up in the same sitting position with a neck ache, a ravenous appetite, and a chill nipping my extremities. A pleasant breeze floated over the promenade, but my body temperature had already grown too low to enjoy it. I had a strange feeling—like somehow I'd just used one of my nine lives. My backpack was still resting beside me, just where I'd left it. I was a sitting duck all night, but miraculously, no one had bothered me. Maybe no one had even passed by. I was lucky.

I wondered how I would get back to The Bardo in time to shower and still make it to The Moirai without being too late. I'd already skipped two days with Asher for our excursion, and I didn't know how much more I could push my luck. Maybe Asher had earned his long leash, but I was still new. I hadn't had any intention of staying out all night, and I wasn't even wearing my watch, but from the feel of things, I'd be cutting it close. Walking back wouldn't be an option. I reached into my bag to see how much money I had left, hoping I could spare the extra cost of a cab. As my hand groped around for my wallet, it found a little granola bar instead, and I immediately tore open its wrapper, relieved by my good fortune. I was famished from all the miles, and I'd forgotten to eat dinner before I'd left.

Two pigeons took notice of my meal, and their hunger seemed to surpass my own, for they had no fear marching right up to my feet like begging dogs. A third pigeon caught wind of all the fuss from a few benches away and flitted over to mine. The image of him bobbing toward me with his sights set so intently on my snack triggered something, and in a burst of memory, the disjointed details of a scene began to congeal in my mind. A shiver rattled through my body, head to toe. I'd dreamed again, right there, resting on that park bench. And once again, I saw that same man from the other dreams—the one in the hotel room with the jacket full of teeth—the one who poisoned me, then dove his blade into my side.

But this time, I was not me. I was a seagull, flying high above a wide body of water just like Lake Erie, and I was searching for my morning meal. The water was empty except for a small rowboat I spotted in the distance, and my compelling appetite ordered me to fly closer to see if there were any tasty morsels on deck that I might steal. As I glided overhead, the features of a man came into focus. He was seated in the center thwart spanning the boat's small hull, slowly slicing away at the surface of the water with two oars. He was stripped down to his underwear with sweat rolling off his shoulders, though the morning was cool. I flew even closer for a better look. There was no mistaking—it was him.

My eyesight seemed so much sharper as a bird, and from above, I could see beyond any doubt that on his index finger, he wore the very same skull ring as from the other dreams before. Until now, I'd only heard his voice and seen the shadows of his face, but in the early morning light, I could now discern far more of his physical details. Finally, I could get a good look.

He was thin and sinewy, his collarbone and ribs protruding through his skin. His feet, thighs, and calves appeared covered in a collage of black ink markings that looked like outlines of animal skeletons and miscellaneous bones in various shapes and sizes. I remembered the needle and vial of ink on the desk in the hotel from my last dream and wondered if he'd made the markings himself, like some sort of crude, homemade tattoos. The Bone Man. Or at least that's how I've started referring to him in my own mind.

I was nearly ready to fly off and try my luck somewhere else when I noted something unusual and stiff about his posture. I swooped in for one last closer look, coasting above to spy. In the last moment before I'd finally flapped away, I watched the Bone Man grip his thigh with both hands and yank, detaching his leg from just below his hip. He tossed it to the side, right there in the boat, freeing his severed stump. The Bone Man has a prosthetic leg.

A black leather jacket with human teeth sewn inside. Tattoos of bones in every shape and size. A removable leg. Are these all clues? But with each new piece of this nightmarish puzzle, I only feel more paralyzed. How can I possibly transform these outlandish visions from mere night terrors into concrete evidence? It all feels preposterous—as if meant only to torment me.

Who is this Bone Man? Is he real, or is he just some monster in my dreams?

I can't begin to imagine how to find absolute proof of either, but until I do, I will remain a reluctant but obedient scribe—writing all that I learn in these letters.

I'll keep searching for the man who killed you in the only way I know how. And if I do ever find this Bone Man, he will pay for what he took.

Love,
Rosalyn

The Removable Leg

It was nearly dawn, and my belly was
alerting me it was high time for some food.
Some fat herring or goby would do
quite nicely for my gluttonous mood.

I flew circles around my usual breakfast spot
just past the place the waves break from the shore
when I spotted a rowboat with the outline
of a man slicing the water with each oar.

While he was occupied, I flew closer to see
if he had a snack or two that I might steal.
For a seagull, a piece of stale bread
would indeed make a mighty fine meal.

I swooped lower to take inventory, but as
I did, my instincts screamed at me to fly away.
Something told me this creature was not safe, and
though I was hungry, perhaps he was the one out for prey.

His pants and shirt were draped over the seat,
and he was stripped down to his underwear.
His wiry legs were covered in strange inky markings—
his skin was nearly translucent it was so fair.

I remarked to myself that a creature with such
a pallid complexion surely only comes out at night.
It must be a rare sighting to find a nocturnal
animal like this out in the early morning light.

My natural instincts for a predator alarmed
as he raised a knife and waved it in the air,
and as I plunged low for another look, he scowled
in my direction with a cold-blooded stare.

"Just because you can fly," he yelled,
"doesn't mean you're really free.
You stupid bird, you're not even worthy
of me putting you out of your misery."

And though I knew I should leave, my curiosity
commanded me to stay for just another moment to spy,
when I noticed something unnatural and
stiff about his leg, starting mid-thigh.

"Just one more look," I thought to myself, "and then I'll
find another fishing spot and leave this maniac alone.
I swooped once more, this time clearly discerning each
marking on his legs was in the shape of a bone.

The morning sun caught a silver shape on his finger—
it was a jeweled ring in the shape of a human skull.
And just as I flapped my wings to fly away, I saw him
detach his leg from his thigh and toss it in the hull.

The Workshop

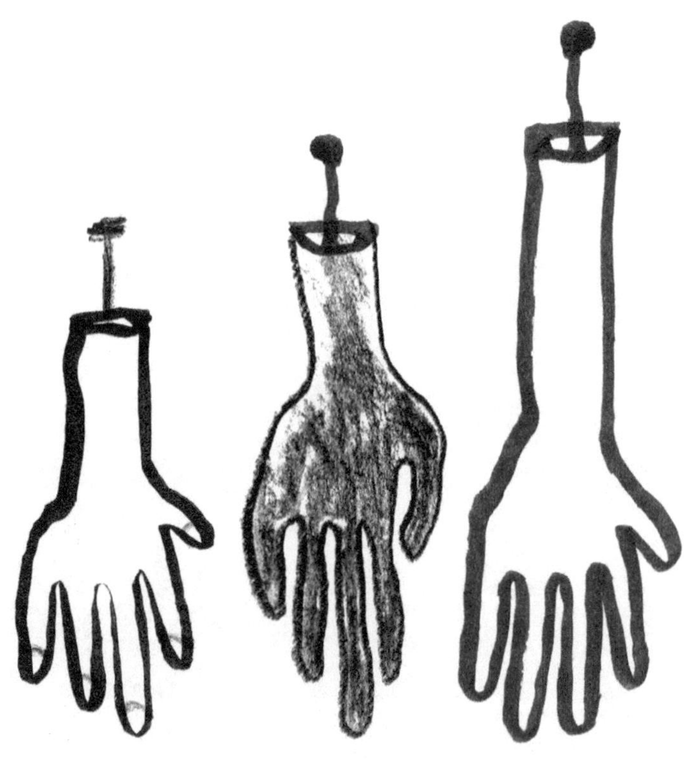

Thursday, October 16, 1997

Dear Nova,

Time has begun to drag. The waking days themselves seem like a bad dream. I'm tired and irritable, and my nerves feel like a thousand tiny frayed live wires. I know my mood must radiate off me like an odor that takes over the whole room.

The function of sleep no longer serves any of its intended purposes of rest and repair. Instead, I can only think of it as some sort of aperture I wait all day to slip through, hoping that by night I can step into some other place that will offer me more answers than the one I'm in now. Just maybe, I think, I'll awake with some new idea —some new information—that I didn't have before I closed my eyes. Day after day, I catch myself believing in this fantasy, my irrational hopefulness for this possibility propelling me forward, even as my logical mind remains passionately skeptical.

I do my best to stay occupied with the routines of the day. Sometimes I'm able to forget about everything for as long as a few hours at a time. Still, inevitably, the thoughts return again, gaining strength and momentum, spinning themselves in intrusive rumination. It goes something like this: my dreams are real. They're giving me clues. And the details are as follows.

One. The man who killed you has markings on his legs and feet. Tattoos of bones and skeletons, I think—and likely ones he's made himself.

Two. He has a black leather jacket that looks normal enough from the outside, but inside it's lined with hundreds of teeth, each drilled with a tiny hole and sewn in like embroidery beads. Hidden from external view, no one could possibly imagine what twisted keepsakes lay within. A collection of traveling trophies for a monster.

Three. He wears a poison ring decorated with a skull and two ruby-colored jeweled eyes. The words "Memento Mori" are engraved on its band. I've seen it in four different dreams now. I'm certain of it. If I can somehow find him, I'll know it's him by that ring.

Four. And the most concrete clue so far. He has a prosthetic leg from an above-the-knee amputation. I clearly saw him remove it from his rowboat. His real leg ended somewhere mid-thigh.

Five. The Bone Man's name translates to the words "I hate."

I have five clues about the man who killed you. Five clues, all of which were dredged from nothing more than the recesses of my own dreaming mind. It would be so much easier to dismiss them —that is, of course, if only I hadn't felt so many compelling traces of their truth already. The wolf with her teeth torn away, just like yours. And how could I have seen the door with the grimacing face or Asher's brother Fisk before I knew either was real? I wish I could shrug everything off. Every day I wish for that. But I can't.

So what happens next in this mystery? How would I even begin searching for a person like the Bone Man? And what would I do if I found him? When I catch myself in the midst of these thoughts, I almost have to laugh. This is the stuff of comic books and fantasy novels, superheroes, and vigilantes. Or just people who have gone insane. I'd say my chances of the former are slim.

To make matters worse, something else is going on too. The other night Zisa asked to speak to me in the living room before she headed off to bed. She hadn't made tea, which she always does before she asks to speak. Zisa looked serious—not at all her usual mercurial self.

"Let me start by just saying I don't need you to explain yourself after what I'm about to tell you," she began. It wasn't off to a good start. "A man with a mustache came knocking downstairs this morning. He asked if I knew of anyone by the name 'Rosalyn Whitman.'" Zisa paused, searching my face for recognition.

"I don't think I know anyone with a mustache here," I said honestly.

"He left me this," Zisa said, holding out a clean white business card in front of me, awaiting my reaction. "He asked me to give him a call if I meet or remember anyone by that name."

I reached out and took the card. "Detective John Singer." My chest clenched.

"So you didn't tell him I was here?" I asked shakily, unsure of what exactly Zisa was telling me.

"I told him I wasn't aware of anyone by that name," Zisa repeated.

"So you lied?" I asked, shocked.

"I didn't lie. You never told me your last name. I said I wasn't aware of anyone by that name," she said, crossing her arms.

"Like I said, I don't want you to explain why you think a detective might be looking for you. All I want to know is that you pay your rent and you follow the rules for as long as you're here. It's very simple."

Zisa's voice was calm but direct and firm. "I use discretion in who I choose to tell what. It wouldn't take much to shut us down, and I'm certainly not about to give a detective an open invitation. We're operating illegally as it is, and I don't need a mess. If you're carrying around any dirty laundry, clean it up or keep it far away from here. Otherwise, you can find a new place to stay effective immediately."

"I understand," was all I could muster. I needed to diffuse the situation as quickly as possible. I couldn't imagine what horrible things Zisa might be thinking of me that would prompt a detective to grace us with his presence, but I wasn't about to defend myself. There's no reason why Zisa needs to know what happened back in Erie.

"I went out on a limb for you when you showed up on our doorstep," Zisa said in a steady tone. "I didn't have to let you in. Please don't make me regret my decision," she added with her characteristic cool-headed sincerity. She made her point clear enough. Don't make my past The Bardo's future.

I should have been relieved to hear Singer was looking for me. Did he finally have a break in your case? A lead? What could be so important to bring him all the way from Erie to New York City? At first, I wondered how he'd even found me. I didn't tell anyone I was leaving, much less where I was going. I didn't even know that myself.

Then I remembered the phone call I'd made to Dr. Molina almost a month ago now. I'd left my name on her answering machine and said Singer had given me her number. She must have called Singer and asked if he knew any "Rosalyns" so she could call me back, and then he traced the number from her office back to the payphone across from The Bardo. I'm such an idiot.

There's no way Singer traveled all this way out of the goodness of his heart just to personally deliver me an update. He's not a social worker—he's a cop. He was here to ask more questions. I know he was—but there's no way I'm talking to him anymore. The thought is enraging. No more Singer. I have enough to worry about right now. For all Singer knows, I was just passing through the neighborhood and used the payphone. I have to stay focused on the clues without imploding.

Asher is still my only source of solace, but unfortunately, he is also the one who bears the brunt of my foul mood. I hadn't thought it was possible for his unflappable nature to become flapped, but I have indeed managed to achieve the impossible by finally exhausting his patience.

Yesterday at The Moirai, my concentration and distraction were in a gruesome duel. I was nearly ready to give myself a lobotomy with Es's knitting needles. I'd been trying to get through a volume of poems from an ancient Roman poet named Catullus, and I wasn't getting anywhere fast. "I hate and I love," he wrote. "Why I do this, perhaps you ask. I know not, but I feel it happening and I am tortured."[1] The words seemed to levitate off the page. I hate and I love and I feel tortured. At least some things are universal across time, culture, and language.

From the opposite side of the room, Asher caught me staring off into space and winked at me playfully in yet another determined attempt to lift my spirits, but yesterday I was feeling so cantankerous I can't even remember if I acknowledged his gesture. I hadn't meant to be cold. It's just that anything that doesn't feel relevant to my questions about the Bone Man has started to feel invisible—even Asher at times.

When the record ended, Asher got up from his book to flip through his record crate and find us a new album. He dug around for longer than usual, announcing his decision with a chef's kiss to the air, his good spirits still intact. He turned his back to me, concealing his selection, then lifted the record from its cover and switched out the discs in an exaggerated covert operation.

He raised the needle and paused, "I dare you to be in a bad mood by the end of Robert Smith's finest work," he announced, sounding genuinely impassioned. These are the very moments that make me most enamored with Asher, but in my current state, I had neither the capacity to be charmed nor the ability for even basic manners.

"Can't we ever just have SILENCE?" I shot back in something of a shriek. My tone was frenetic and abrupt. After the words left my mouth, I had to pause to allow my mind to catch up and understand that the sound in the room had actually been my own voice. It was as if I had just heard a recording of someone else emerge from my own body. If only I could take it back. I'd never spoken to Asher like that, nor him to me.

As the silence I'd just requested filled the room, I could see Asher's posture become stiff and bristled. Suddenly, he looked a foot taller than his already towering frame. It had been a harmless enough comment, but it was my tone that had finally snapped Asher's good nature. Death by a thousand cuts, or in my case, bad moods.

"You know, Rosalyn," he began in a low, steady voice, his back still to me. "You've been acting like a black cloud for weeks. I know you keep your private matters close, but if you're not going to tell me what's going on with you, I'd appreciate it if you tried a little harder not to contaminate everyone else's attempt at a decent attitude. You act like you're the only person around who's ever had a bad day in their life." He looked not only bruised but angry too.

I hung my head, immediately ashamed. Why couldn't I just tell him about you so he could understand? So I could be understood? I'd never seen him like that, and I felt sorry that all these weeks, my mood had been so affecting him underneath his cheerful veneer.

Asher turned his body to square mine, his face growing pale. "Past House is just a brick building in Queens. You are free to step outside and beyond its walls whenever you like," he said with a weight to his voice. His words were punctuated as if he were speaking either through pain or through the restraint of wishing to shout them at me instead. It was like he was talking to me in song lyrics again, his deeper meaning wrapped in their poetry, but I understood what he meant.

Everyone has their own version of Past House, and it can be easy to get trapped when you venture too far inside, forgetting the front door is not locked, nor has it ever been.

I felt that tingling sensation that arrives deep in your sinuses just before you are about to cry, but I fought against the tears, struggling to stay composed. Asher had shocked me right back into the present. I felt my words gathering in my chest. I took a deep breath to let them out.

"My sister was killed and is never coming back," I wanted to scream, but the words were still stuck just behind my teeth. I felt like I was teetering on the edge of a tall building, ready to fall either forward or backward, and it was up to the wind, not me, which way I'd go. The words pleaded with me to let them spill forth, but before they were granted their chance to escape, Asher shoved the unplayed record back into its cover, flipped off the speakers' power switch, and stormed into the kitchen to retrieve his overshirt from the hook on the wall.

Was he leaving? I felt as if my brain was processing with a ten-second lag. I heard the heavy tread of his boots from the kitchen through the main hall and all the way to the front door. "I'm going for a walk," he shouted from the foyer. He didn't wait for the possibility of an apology. The door slammed not a moment later.

Asher is right. I'm free at any point to stop writing to an apparition in these pages. It's up to me to decide if healing might look different from justice. Sometimes you don't get any of the answers you believe you deserve. If I choose, my past doesn't have to be a physical purgatory. I'm free to walk beyond its walls and watch the sun kiss the edge of the horizon at the end of each day, and rise again the next, knowing that each of Earth's rotations is a fresh lesson in letting go and starting over. There are no steel bars or padlocks forcing me inside the Past House where we work, nor in the Past House that exists only in my own mind. When The Moirai sisters gave Past House its name decades ago, I'm sure they didn't envision a prison.

Lately, everything has felt like a confusing tangle of raw emotion and rational thought. It wasn't until I heard the latch of the front door close behind Asher and echo through the parlor that I felt my first dose of clarity in a long while. The truth is, knowing that Asher is nearby has felt like my only anchor in life, even if I've never remotely had the courage to articulate this to him. He reminds me there are still other people in this life to care about. How can I let myself push him away?

You and Asher are not so different in the ways you keep me grounded. I always felt like you and I were less identical twins, but more like harmonious forces—little subatomic particles with the same mass but opposite charges and spin, keeping one another in a balanced orbit—and now that your energy is somewhere beyond this world, mine is spinning wild. I never meant for it to happen, but I've found some new kind of unexpected symmetry in Asher.

The other week when I'd been searching The Moirai for books about dreams, I came across one called "Einstein's Dreams."[2] It appeared to be a work of fiction that imagined young Einstein troubled by his dreams as he worked on his early theory of relativity. I liked the writer's concept right away—how it married dreams and science. Even in his real life, Einstein's theory of relativity had come to him in a dream, and he spent his lifetime trying to reconcile it with his other theories of quantum mechanics. Einstein's quantum entanglement theory states that once two particles become entangled, they stay connected even across all of space and time. He called it "spooky action at a distance." If the spookiest laws of physics can be true, almost anything seems possible. Sometimes I wonder if that's what you and I are. Entangled particles, at a distance.

Maybe that's all karma is, in a way. A good deed offered in one life, rewarded in another. An unabsolved wrong from one time, punished in a different time. The universe keeps track of the state of things, even if we can't. If any of that is true, all I can say is that right now, the universe is unbearably out of balance. Where is the karma you're owed? Where is the justice? The answers? In science, you get a reason. There is always a "why."

So why were you killed? What possible reason could there be? Is the Bone Man sick? Has his mind been scrambled, just like Fisk's father after his accident? Or must pure evil exist in the world simply as a violent counterforce to balance the purest good?

> "Wise ones say the foundation of the universe
> is love and all that love can create.
> But your clue is this: the man's name
> who killed your sister translates to 'I hate.'"

That's what the egret bird had told me in the dream at Asher's house over two months ago now. Yesterday, I flipped back and must have read that poem fifty times. Those words have been ringing in my ears. "The man's name who killed your sister translates to 'I hate.'"

I waited all day in Past House for Asher to return and stayed an hour after our normal wrap-up time to see if he'd make an appearance. When he didn't show, I checked every corner of Present House and Future House too, before finally deciding to call it a day. I walked alone back to The Bardo and stopped on Asher's floor to knock on his door on the way to mine. No one answered.

When I got home to our loft, Zisa was cooking with an artist who I recognized as Asher's neighbor a couple doors down. They were concocting something that smelled garlic-y and delicious, but the very thought of eating made my stomach cramp. Zisa offered me dinner and asked if I'd like to join them, but I thanked her and declined as politely as I could. The only person I wanted to share a meal with was nowhere to be found.

Before bidding each other goodnight, I took the opportunity to ask the other girl if she'd seen Asher around their floor. She shook her head "no" apologetically. "Help yourself to the leftovers," Zisa added. She seemed to have recovered from Singer's visit, or at least she wasn't visibly holding a grudge. Unsatisfied and restless, I went back to my room and climbed into bed, expecting to stare listlessly at the ceiling and think, but I must have fallen asleep right away.

This morning I woke up without an alarm, just as the rising sun had started to glow through the stained glass face over my bed, painting saffron oranges and azure blues onto the walls as I regained my senses. My head felt clearer than it had in days, and I allowed consciousness to return to my body at its own gentle pace. By 7:30 AM, the stained glass face was completely beaming with light, and as I studied its features in more detail than I think I ever had before, a sudden realization washed over me. I closed my eyes, and the traces of last night's dream came pulsing back into focus as if summoned by the sunshine, its pleasant warmth instantly interrupted by a shooting chill that ran all the way to my toes.

As the dream's details replay themselves in my mind now, for the first time, I have the feeling that maybe I have something concrete. Has last night's dream delivered a final clue that makes all of this real? If what I've just seen is somehow true, I might have the proof I need to track down the man who killed you.

I'll know whether or not I'm going insane soon enough. I think I know the Bone Man's name. He's been to The Bardo. And I think there's a good chance he could be back again.

Love,
Rosalyn

The Workshop

I awoke in a cold room with high ceilings
and generous windows paned in colored glass.
In the corner were over two dozen full-sized forms
of human bodies cast in plaster, marble, and brass.

From the ceiling hung countless beautifully
sculpted arms and legs of every color and size,
and the walls were paneled with life-like floating faces
so realistic they might have blinked their eyes.

At the far end of the room was a long
table strewn with a mess of metal parts,
and in haphazard piles were stacks of various
sketches and electrical circuitry charts.

Below on the floor was a massive tangle of wires
like a gigantic mechanical tumbleweed.
Notes were scrawled on every surface in hurried
handwriting that I could barely read.

In the center of the clutter were three different
right arms, all in varying stages of creation.
Their synthetic skin was peeled back
to reveal their machined articulation.

I reached to touch one arm's artificial skin,
and as I did, its fingers moved and twitched.
These sculptures were living prosthetics that
had been painstakingly and robotically enriched.

I was as curious as I was spooked and
instinctively took a nervous step back.
I bumped into something behind me, and it
clattered to the floor with a loud crack.

On the ground was a leg covered toe-to-thigh
in images of bones that looked like crude tattoos.
My stomach flipped as it struck me—souvenirs
kept right on your skin are impossible to lose.

I reached for a tag tied to its toe
like a corpse with my trembling hand.
In black ink, I read the word "Odi,"
and suddenly, felt I could barely stand.

"Odi et Amo"—the words of the ancient
Greek poet Catullus once lyrically stated.
It was then I knew I'd found the killer's name—
"I hate and I love," the Latin translated.

My heart pounded so hard in my chest
I feared it would give my whereabouts away.
The owner of this strange workshop could return
at any moment—it was clear I could not stay.

I sped toward the exit, hoping to steal
away from my trespass without further trace.
I closed the door behind me—it was
painted with a broad grimacing face.

Poacher's Prize

Friday, October 24, 1997

Dear Nova,

Do you remember when Gram was in the hospital, and we sat around in that waiting room with the sad-looking striped beige wallpaper for hours? The chairs felt like torture devices, and everything smelled like rubber and disinfectant. We were so worried we refused to leave, and the nurses would take turns coming over to suggest we consider going home for at least a warm meal and a shower. Remember how I used to chew my dry cuticles so badly they bled? I thought I'd broken that habit years ago, but my thumbs once again look like Prosciutto.

The last few days have been an angst-ridden waiting game. Asher was still missing, and Zisa was mostly out of the loft until late into the evenings—I wondered if she was avoiding me. Either way, their absences left me to my own devices, and my anxiety had flamboyant free rein, having its way with gnawed thumbs. I was consumed by my new question. Are there any workshops in the building that meet the description of my dream? Robotic, artificial limbs and a mess of electrical wires and scrap metal. The workshop's door had been painted with a grimacing face, just like the one at The Bardo. That detail had to mean something, but I've never seen any workshops like that around here—and trust me, I've already attempted loitering on every floor for hours at a time to see what doors might swing open long enough for a peek inside. So far, nothing but messy art studios and confused neighbors.

But what else could I do? Break and enter? Knock on every door and ask for a personal tour? I'm already in deep water with Zisa since Singer came by, and I can't make things worse by adding munitions to the rumor mill. If people start whispering about me, and Zisa catches wind, I have a feeling it will only be a recipe for my immediate dismissal.

It quickly became apparent that my only option was waiting out Asher's disappearance. He's the only person I trust enough to ask about that workshop—I'd just have to bide my time for his return. By the second day of his absence, I assumed he'd gone to The Egret for some space, but by the following Monday, when he didn't show up for work, I worried his latest sabbatical might be indefinite. All I could do was to stick out the siege. I certainly didn't expect almost an entire week to pass, and I was running out of diversions to occupy my twitching mind. Patience is a virtue, just not one of mine. At least I had my cuticles to shred.

The day before yesterday, I was perched on Zisa's green couch in the living room, cradling a volume of Edgar Allan Poe's poetry. I read and re-read the same four lines, unable to absorb more than a single verse in my anxious preoccupation.

> In visions of the dark night
> I have dreamed of joy departed—
> But a waking dream of life and light
> Hath left me broken-hearted.[1]

Poe was onto something. The waking dream of life hath left me broken-hearted too. Zisa had already retired to her bedroom for the evening, and the loft was all mine. Eventually, I rested the book on the floor and closed my heavy eyes. I didn't open them again until sunrise, the morning light spilling onto the wall from our biggest stained glass window facing east. I hadn't meant to fall asleep, but it was magical waking up to the light like that. The room's colors slowly transformed from a soft, amber glow into a luminescent sheet of white, and as I sipped in my first deep breath, I spoke out loud to the day as if I thought it might reply back. "Nice to see you," I whispered to no one, nor was there any reply—just a small voice in my own head: "Go look for Asher. Apologize. Talk to him and ask for the help you need."

That morning, I waited again in the third-floor stairwell where Asher and I always meet, but still, he didn't show. I walked to The Moirai alone, scanning each street corner like he might be anywhere. What was this unbearable feeling—so familiar and yet so foreign too? The suffering of missing someone? That one, I already knew well. Or was it the agonizing uncertainty and doubt born of any timid affection that has not been explicitly requited? Or perhaps simply the pain of distance that comes with withholding the truth.

Asher is all I really have left to care about. I can't lose him too. I rounded the last bend of our route, hoping I'd finally find him a few strides ahead, but instead, the only sign of life on the empty streets was an old car slowly pulling away. I could have sworn it was a brown Buick with Pennsylvania plates. Sometimes I truly can't tell if I'm hallucinating.

When I got to Past House, the door was already unlocked. My heart leaped. I smelled coffee brewing, and from the foyer, I could see the sleeve of Asher's plaid overshirt hanging from the hook in the kitchen. He was back. He must have come straight from The Egret.

My footsteps on the creaky, planked hallway floor broadcasted my arrival before I'd said a word, and when I reached the kitchen entryway, Asher was already turned around at the counter waiting. I didn't know what there was to say that could adequately articulate my overwhelming relief in simply having him near. Instead, I walked straight up to him, let our eyes meet for just a beat, and wrapped my arms around him as tightly as I could, letting my actions speak all the things I didn't have language for. I pinned his arms to his waist, not even giving him the chance to reciprocate. It was only a hug, but it was by far the grandest gesture of affection I've allowed myself toward him since meeting. I don't believe words exist that can describe the solace I felt at the sight of him standing there over the steaming French press. Two strangers alone together again.

"What do you call an elephant that doesn't matter?" I asked.

"Uh oh, ladies and gentlemen, she's come back to the land of the living," he said, smiling. "What?"

"An irrelephant," I said, borrowing another one of yours.

Asher shook his head in mock disapproval. A grin peeled across his face, though it surely wasn't owing to the caliber of my joke. It was my best attempt at an apology in the costume of a wisecrack, but Asher seemed to accept it, and almost instantly, we fell back into our quiet companionship. He handed me a cup of coffee, and as I extended my arm to accept, I realized the words I was so afraid of were already making their preparations to leak out.

"Asher…?" I asked with a wobble in my voice.

"Rosalyn..." he replied, imitating my cagey delivery. He slung back the last swig of his coffee and lowered his caffeine accoutrements into the sink, turning on the faucet to rinse them.

"I think I could use your help with something that might explain a few things about...," I began. The sentence had started with confidence, but my voice had trailed away by the time I'd reached the second half. "About...why I've been acting... the way I have."

"Shoot," he fired back warmly. A few suspenseful seconds passed as I took a seat at the kitchen table, anchoring my trembling body to the nearest fixed object.

"I'm finally ready to tell you why I'm so sad," I said, referring to the question he'd asked months ago that I'd left unanswered. My whole body felt electrified with a nervy skittishness, though my voice fell flat and lifeless. Asher turned off the faucet, leaving his half-washed cup in the sink. His hands were still dripping as he joined me at the table. I wasn't sure how to begin. I didn't know if there was a right way to begin. I took a deep breath and summoned my courage underneath the refuge of a long blink. It was time. I was ready. I let the words tumble out in whatever formation they pleased.

"I'm here because I'm lost," I began. "That, I'm sure you figured out on your own. But that's only part of it. I'm not just lost—I lost someone. My twin sister. Back in Erie. Her name was Nova. She was murdered in January of this year, and they never found her killer."

Asher's eyes stared back into mine. His face was expressionless, frozen in rapt attention.

"I came to New York to try and forget—to start over," I continued. "I needed to find a way to escape all my unrelenting questions, but without Nova, I wasn't sure I even knew who I was anymore. Most people can never understand what it's like to be that close to another person." I paused. Asher was silent. His eyes were clear, his mouth slightly parted in focused anticipation, still waiting for me to say more.

"The next part is the hardest to explain," I continued. "Somehow, I think I was supposed to end up right here all along. I don't just mean in New York. I mean at The Bardo—and with you too. Now that I'm here, I'm starting to believe that maybe I was never lost in the way I thought I was. Somehow, I think I was meant to be here." I searched Asher's face for a reaction, bracing myself for what I knew I would say next.

"I don't know how to explain it, but I think I've found the man who killed my sister—or at least somehow… something is leading me to him." Asher's eyes widened, and I watched his countenance shift. I took another grounding pause. "And now I need your help," I said. "I've never said any of this out loud to anyone before."

My body flushed with the heat of exhaustion from prying forth the long-guarded truth. Asher leaned his body forward in his chair, sliding each hand out to either side of himself on the table, splaying his fingers wide as if to catch his balance, even though he was already sitting down. A solemn hush descended over the room as my words trailed away. His face didn't seem shocked or grieved, just somber. "I'm so sorry this happened to you, Rosalyn," he said, lowering his eyes. "You're right. That does explain a few things. I don't know how I can help with something like that, but I promise I'll do anything I can."

With just those simple words, my relief physically rearranged my posture. A great weight felt lifted, and each of my vertebrae took a stretch in my spine. It wasn't simply the offering of help. It was all of it. Acknowledging what happened and speaking the words aloud to another living person—and not just in these pages.

Asher looked expectantly across at me. "What can I do?" he asked gently. It was a big question, but at least I knew where we had to start.

"Do you know of any artists at The Bardo who might have kept a workshop for human robotics or prosthetic limbs?" I asked, uncertain how exactly to phrase my question. "Fake faces, arms, legs—that sort of thing?" I said not quite in a whisper, but not exactly in a speaking voice either.

Asher's face looked momentarily puzzled, then suddenly brightened, as if a flash bulb had gone off behind his eyes.

"Frankenstein…?" Asher piped.

"Who…?" I fumbled. He couldn't possibly be trying to make a joke right now.

"I think you might be talking about Francesca, but everyone calls her Frankie or Doctor Frankenstein. You know…with all the body parts and stuff. I'm pretty sure 'Frankenstein' pisses her off though," he elaborated. My heart raced. The workshop is real. Is everything else from my dreams real too?

"Her workshop's on your floor, actually," Asher added. "I guess she was grandfathered in and never moved. She's one of The Bardo originals. Most of the old-timers knew Zisa's grandparents from back in the early days when they first bought the building. Frankie's probably known Zisa since she was a kid."

"What's she like? Have you talked to her before?" I asked.

"I've never even seen her. Known by reputation only. She's more like Bardo legend, and from what I've heard, she doesn't come around much anymore. I guess she lives somewhere else and just hangs onto her workshop because she can. My roommate claims that once he saw her in the hall on Halloween holding a hack saw, but he was probably just pulling my leg. Are you saying she has something to do with your sister's killer?"

"I don't know," I said cautiously. "All I know is that I think he's missing his left leg, and I suspect he might come to The Bardo for his prosthetic. It must be with Frankie. What else do you know about her?" I asked, my chest pounding.

"You got me. She's pretty elusive. If anyone would know more, it's Zisa. She keeps tabs on anyone coming in from the outside. Gotta clear strangers with her to make sure The Bardo stays tight, ya know?" Asher paused and drew circles on the table with his stub.

"What do you mean 'keeps tabs?'" I asked.

"Keeps schedules, manages datebooks, signs people in—that sort of thing. She makes sure she has a record of everyone's name who's in and out."

I remembered Zisa telling me the rules of The Bardo on my first day. Guests were permitted, she had said, but they needed to be signed in with her first. My brain seemed to spasm as it suddenly became aware of a possibility. If Frankie has ever had an appointment with someone named Odi, Zisa must have that written down—that is, of course, if only he gave that name.

"So what's the plan, and how can I help? Are we going 'vigilante-style'?" Asher asked, his sarcasm only a weak disguise for his obvious concern.

"Something like that," I said flatly, acknowledging the utter ridiculousness of the situation. "I need to find a way to talk to Frankie and see what she knows about someone named Odi. I don't have any physical proof he's a murderer, but I might have an idea for how to get some," I said. The leather jacket. Had he really collected his victims' teeth and sewn them inside? It's the stuff of horror fiction. Now the question is if it's the stuff of reality.

Asher stared across the table at me in silence. The invisible circles he was tracing with his stub transformed into figure eights. "And why is it again that we can't just go to the cops with all of this?" he asked. "Isn't finding criminal evidence their job?" It was a valid question. I've asked myself this many times too.

"Because the way I've come across this information is…" I paused to find the right word, "unconventional."

"You mean illegal," Asher replied.

"No, I mean more like… unusual. Not immediately believable," I clarified. How could I possibly explain that I dreamed it all up? "It won't help the police—I know that much," I said instead. "Besides, we can't have them poking around The Bardo unless we're sure. We could get it shut down."

"I see," Asher said, withdrawing a hand from the table, and moving it through his hair, scratching his scalp slowly in thought. "And you're really not going to tell me how you know all this?"

I lowered my eyes, knowing I couldn't answer. Asher nodded gently to himself in unresisting acceptance.

"Well, at least you're back to making terrible jokes again." Asher stood up from the table resolutely. He took a step toward me and paused, reaching to give my shoulder a gentle squeeze. "Rosalyn, I'm really sorry to hear about your sister. I know it feels like it'll never get better."

Asher returned to the sink and finished cleaning up the coffee paraphernalia. I could tell he was disoriented. I was too. I watched him snap the plastic lid onto the tin of coffee grounds and place it in the refrigerator instead of the cabinet with the mugs where we usually keep it. The new information was sinking in for both of us. I could tell he was exerting extra effort in a performance of acting natural, but it wasn't enough to camouflage his unmistakable bewilderment.

We spent the rest of the day in quiet contemplation, all our unspoken questions levitating over the room like prognosticating spirits. There seemed to be a new understanding between us that cemented our wordless coexistence. We know each other in a way that few others in this world can—joined in our loss—his of Fisk, and mine of you.

We didn't speak any further until our walk back to The Bardo that night when Asher asked me quite simply, "So what's next?" I was caught off guard, realizing that sincerely I wasn't sure of the answer. "I guess I have to convince Zisa to help. Ask her if she could make an introduction to Frankie somehow." I hung my head. I knew that wasn't a solution. I was already in deep water with Zisa.

"Yea. Maybe. Just be careful how you put it. Zisa's not a fan of probing, especially not of Bardo veterans," Asher warned. "She's very protective."

The crisp October air was beginning to nip at our cheeks, signaling an early winter. Maybe it was our new coalition of trust, or maybe the cold had just hastened our strides into lockstep. Our legs seemed to synchronize perfectly. We rounded the corner, and the grimacing face of The Bardo door stared at us from across the street. I dove a hand into my backpack for my keys and looked up at Asher, his soaring frame just barely blocking out the setting sun to the west. "Thank you," I said awkwardly. "For what?" Asher asked back. All I knew was that I felt grateful.

We said our goodnights on the third-floor landing as we always do. I was bleary-eyed as I climbed the last flight of stairs and paced home, propelled only by my yearning to collapse into a weary heap on my bed. Though the day's confession had buoyed my spirits, it hadn't done much to assuage my unraveling nerves. By the time I'd pushed open the front door to the loft, it was clear that rest would have to wait. A military-style duffel bag was sitting by the coat closet, and Zisa was in the kitchen spreading jam on a piece of buttered toast. "I'm headed out of town tomorrow morning, and I'll be gone for a few days," she shouted over her shoulder in a sing-song voice. She seemed to be in a good-humored mood. I was about to ruin it. If I was going to ask her for an introduction to Frankie, I couldn't waste any time with my question.

I hung my jacket by the door and took my time pretending to rummage for something in my backpack while I stalled and collected my thoughts. How could I ask Zisa without inviting further scrutiny and suspicion?

Zisa nibbled on her toast with one hand and flipped gingerly through an old issue of the Village Voice with the other as she kept watch over the kettle simmering over a low flame. I slowly sauntered to the other end of the counter.

"Oh, that's nice. Going to any place special?" I said, trying my best to pad my inquisition with some polite conversation, but Zisa just looked at me sideways. By the expression on her face, it was obvious she'd instantly seen right through my act. I might as well have said hello, levitated, and spun my head around three times. Since when did I care what she was up to? That's the problem with a consistent antisocial track record. You can't go from snow leopard to golden retriever overnight. I'd never once voluntarily used any of our common space for their intended purposes of human-to-human social contact, but I didn't want to appear desperate or pushy with my questions. I knew almost nothing about Frankie's workshop beyond what Asher had told me, and maybe I wasn't supposed to know. Maybe no one was. I knew I'd need to approach the topic gently.

Zisa humored me with a few questions, offering only vague answers, seemingly for her own entertainment. Then, when she'd had enough, in something of a mothering tone, she called my bluff. "So, Rosalyn, is everything ok with you?" as if the small talk was just as physically painful for her to witness as it was for me to perform. Something must really be wrong if I was willing to subject myself to casual mingling. I was relieved she let me off the hook, though at once, I dreaded my real question even more than the harmless prattle. Would she help me talk to Frankie? Or would it be a dead end that would only make my situation with her more delicate than it is already?

"Uh… oh, nothing," I fumbled. "I was just wondering... Have any of the artists here ever kept a workshop for human robotics or prosthetic limbs?" I asked, playing dumb. "I heard there might be one on our floor, and I'd really like to talk to the owner."

Zisa's mood instantaneously shifted to cold trepidation. "Now, what could you possibly want with Frankie?" she said in a low voice. "You seem to have all your limbs at the moment."

"Oh, I was just interested in talking to her about a personal matter," I stammered, uncertain how to convey my request. It was apparent from her tone and body language that this was not a welcome topic, and now she knew I'd already asked around.

"I don't mean to be rude," she said, "but it seems like you might need some help clarifying a simple concept. You didn't seem too upset about me turning away that detective, isn't that right?"

I nodded.

"I wasn't born yesterday. I know you know who he is. If you don't appreciate people prying into your business, you might not want to pry into others. That makes sense, doesn't it?" Zisa said with a firmness I'd never heard from her before. I nodded again. She took a long, pensive breath.

"The rules here are very simple, and I believe I've made them clear from day one. Beyond those rules, my philosophy has always been to extend a great amount of trust to our residents. I believe that when we are given such a gift, most people are grateful and treat it with the utmost respect—but the moment that trust is broken, there's no repairing it. I don't feel I need to spell this out, but in your case, maybe I do." Her voice wasn't threatening, just direct. I was speechless and knew I had no room to argue. I was walking a thin line. I wouldn't be getting to Frankie through Zisa—that much was clear.

The kettle screamed as a cone of steam shot from its whistle, and Zisa fixed her tea as I ambled awkwardly to my room. "Good night," she said over her shoulder before I closed my door. I felt defeated, even though I had to admit the outcome was self-evident all along. Even Asher had warned me to be careful, and he doesn't even know about Singer. Besides, how could I argue with her point? I respected the privacy she kept for The Bardo's residents. I was its benefactor too, after all—but I needed to talk to Frankie, and I'd do anything to make that happen.

I climbed into bed feeling agitated. My head was filled with static, and I tossed and turned all night. My only other option would be to stake out Frankie's workshop from the hall and simply hope that I might intercept her before she slipped inside. It was a weak prospect. There was no telling when she'd be back again. It could be tomorrow. It could be next year. Whatever I decided to do, I knew I'd have to be careful. Zisa has her eye on me, and I can't get kicked out of The Bardo. It's my only connection to the man who goes by Odi.

The next morning when I opened my bedroom door, Zisa was already clamoring around the kitchen again, and I smelled the remnants of fried eggs. The chime of the toaster oven rang, and Zisa lifted a piece of crispy toast, holding it with her mouth as she grabbed a stack of papers with one hand and her keys with the other.

"Remember what I told you," she said instructively through her teeth, and with that, she marched toward her duffel bag and swung it over her shoulder. The front door creaked closed after her. I listened to her footsteps grow fainter, and as soon as I made out the feeble clank of the stairwell fire door latching, I peeked into the hall to make sure the coast was clear. There was one last possibility. If there was any way to contact Frankie, my best bet would be somewhere in Zisa's bookkeeping.

I started my investigation in all the obvious places. The living room, the kitchen cabinets, the bureau by the front door, the top shelf in the coat closet. Nothing but household junk. I felt guilty for snooping, but Zisa had already correctly assumed I might try ferreting about, and the common spaces had all been tidied before she left. All surfaces were bare, all drawers completely void of personal affairs. Nothing but books and plants and bric-a-brac. Within only twenty minutes, I knew what I was about to do, and I didn't like it one iota.

I approached Zisa's bedroom door and gazed down at its aged bronze lock, remembering her words from the first day we'd met. "Under no circumstances are you to ever go into my room without being invited." I reached out my hand and turned the knob. Locked, of course—but I had been expecting that.

Right away, I determined it was only an old single-lever skeleton key lock, just like the one on the back office door at Orly's. It was as basic as they come. We must have picked that thing a hundred times when Jack would lock himself in there to drink and end up passing out on the couch before we'd had a chance to close out the register. If we didn't pick that lock and get the money in the safe, we'd be there til morning otherwise.

I raced over to the bureau in the foyer and fished through the bottom drawer where I'd remembered a scattering of tools—screwdrivers, scissors, loose nails, nuts and washers, and most importantly, an incomplete set of Allen wrenches. I lifted the smallest two from their case and ran back to Zisa's door like I was sliding into home base. I inserted the first wrench into the keyhole, my hand shaking as I groped around for the lever. At last, I felt its ridge and managed to lift it just enough to pry in the second wrench and pop open the deadbolt. My heart pounded as I resigned myself to my imminent transgression. I was in.

Picking the lock was easy. The problem was, once inside, there wasn't much to find—just a tidy bed and secretary desk no different from my room or Asher's. The only noticeable difference was a small black and white TV displaying the surveillance from The Bardo's front door camera sitting on a large army green filing cabinet in the far corner. I approached and tugged the first drawer pull, but it only lurched with a rattle against a long silver metal plate—what appeared to be some makeshift security measure. A metal bar had been hinged and soldered to the entire length of the cabinet, preventing any of the drawers from sliding open, and a heavy four-digit combination lock hung from a latch at the top.

This had to be where Zisa kept The Bardo's records. I didn't even know what exactly I was supposed to be looking for, but with all of Zisa's talk of privacy, I knew whatever it was would have to be somewhere in that filing cabinet. The only problem now was that lock. If I clipped it and broke in, there'd be no going back. I'd be out of The Bardo the minute Zisa returned. My only option was to crack the combination—but there could be thousands upon thousands of possibilities. How would I even begin to start guessing?

I scanned the room, frantically racking my brain for ideas. Four numbers. It could be anything. On top of the filing cabinet beside the old TV was a little shrine of photographs in a haphazard stack. Earrings in a shallow dish, miniature art pieces, and tchotchkes. A bundle of dried flowers in a tiny vase. A ballroom mask. Mardi Gras beads. A smorgasbord of personal mementos. The long side of the filing cabinet was strewn with Post-its and notecards scribbled with what looked to be unimportant personal reminders and unlabeled phone numbers, but nothing that looked useful for the incumbent mission of deciphering that lock's four-digit code.

I was nearly ready to give up entirely and steal back out of Zisa's room to find another plan when suddenly my eyes fixated on an old postcard taped to the side of the cabinet amongst the mess of other paper scraps. It was an image of a painting—a door standing tall in the middle of a daylight scene on a beach. There were no walls to support it—rather, it floated upright in the sand. The door was ajar in its frame, opening to what seemed to be another world entirely.

On the other side of the threshold, it was night, and a crescent moon rested atop a long candlestick as if it was the candle's flame. To the right, two wide jungle leaves as tall as the door hovered impossibly in the air, and ten exotic birds twirled against their waxy greens. The image stopped me in my tracks. The scene felt familiar. Where had I seen that before?

Exotic birds. A door that opened to another world at night. A candlestick alight with the crescent moon. I took a breath and closed my eyes, sensing a fog beginning to clear in my mind—and suddenly, as if I'd just opened the door myself, I remembered where I'd seen it.

The dream I'd had months ago. I was in a long corridor lined with heavy, bolted doors, and you were screaming out for help. Intuitively, I ripped my teeth from my jaw, and one after another, they transformed into keys that fit their locks perfectly. Door by door, I unclasped their locks, and behind, I found paintings of huge, exotic birds, each one more magnificent than the last. Your voice seemed to grow closer, but when I swung open the final door at the end of the hall, it opened not to you but to an empty beach. A tall candlestick rose from the sand, and the crescent moon lit its wick. None of it had seemed to make any sense, or at least not until now.

Carefully, I untacked the tape from the postcard and turned it over. "Le domaine enchanté, 1953, René Magritte."[2] I vaguely knew the artist's name. He was a famous surrealist painter who ran around with the likes of Dali and Picasso. I looked down at the lock, then again back up at the postcard's caption. "Le domaine enchanté, 1953." My heart hammered against my ribs. I adjusted the lock's dials. 1-9-5-3. I tugged. The shank popped open.

A rush of adrenaline overtook my faculties, not only due to my trespass but also my disbelief. I could barely operate my fingers. I was trembling so violently that the metal scraped and clattered as I clumsily unhooked the padlock. I swung open the bar from its hinge and slid open the topmost drawer. I peered in, careful not to disturb its contents before I was certain I could return everything back to its original place. I'd discovered the motherload of Bardo secrets. This was where Zisa kept track of all the building affairs, and I knew if there was anything to find out about Frankie, it would have to be here.

Slowly, gently, I began sifting through the drawer's articles. A stack of bundled receipts, a zippered pouch filled with cash, composition notebooks, yellow pads, and paper-clipped piles of loose envelopes. Finally, in the back, I found a set of beige hanging folders with clear plastic tabs, each label marked by unit number. The first one was ours, Unit 4AB. I pulled it out to inspect. A list of five or six names that had been scratched out ran down the front cover in different colored pens. "Rosalyn" was written in blue at the bottom, "Whitman" scrawled in a messier version of the same handwriting, presumably added later. I flipped open the cover, and a crisp white business card fluttered to the floor. I craned to retrieve it, recognizing it immediately as I brought it to the light. "Detective John Singer." I suppose Zisa hadn't made up her mind about protecting me from Singer after all.

I was still trembling, causing the folder to quiver in the exaggerated extension of my hands. I felt clumsy and scattered. I returned Singer's card to the folder and shoved it back into place in front of the others. I flipped to the next, and to the next, and to the next until my breath froze in my lungs. "Francesca, Suite 4J." I yanked out the folder. It was awkward and much heavier than the others, I soon realized, owing to a black leather-bound notebook that had been tucked inside. I flung open its jacket and turned its aged pages slowly, my heart leaping for what I might find.

The top of the first page was labeled "July 1971." Names, dates, times, and short notes ran down the lined paper in chronological order. It was Frankie's datebook. I was staring down at decades worth of appointments, each page representing a month. I skipped ahead in a frantic rush. The names and entries grew sparser and sparser as time wore on. I neared the current year, scanning the nearly empty entries more slowly, forcing my eyes to focus. If the datebook was accurate, what Asher had said was true. Frankie hardly comes by The Bardo anymore. There were only a handful of appointments over the last few years, each visitor's name inscribed in Zisa's curly handwriting.

I neared the current month. August. Nothing. September. Blank. October. Also blank. November. All was blank too—save a single entry at the bottom of the page. My air halted in my chest. My eyes re-adjusted, my mind not yet trusting the shapes of the words. "O. Cairan / left transfemoral / socket replacement and hydraulic tune-up / November 17, 4 PM." Left transfemoral—that's for a left leg.

The Bone Man. It has to be him. He's real, and he'll be at The Bardo in just over three weeks.

Fixated, I flipped through the remaining pages of Frankie's datebook, but future month's entries were all blank as well. I felt so overwhelmed I thought I might burst into tears and collapse on the floor, my own madness finally subsuming me. Or did I actually have proof that I am, in fact, quite sane?

When I reached the back sleeve of Frankie's datebook, I discovered a piece of folded, lined paper. Carefully, I opened its crease. Thick, smeared pencil handwriting stared back at me—a phone number and what appeared to be a location. CR 515 and Buck Pond Trail, Stockholm. In a mad dash, I ran back to the living room and grabbed a pen and the copy of Poe's poetry I'd been reading the day before. I transcribed the numbers and names into the inside cover and shoved the paper back into Frankie's datebook, then the datebook into Zisa's labeled folder.

I scanned the contents of the drawer, checking that I'd returned everything to its proper place. I couldn't be sure if I had. I slammed the drawer shut nonetheless, closed the cabinet's homemade locking hinge, and refastened the padlock, hoping my intrusion would go unnoticed. I shut Zisa's bedroom door behind me and crouched to relock its deadbolt, my quivering hands barely able to grasp the wrenches. At last, I heard the latch catch back into the strike plate, and I leaped to my feet to return the wrenches to their drawer before fleeing to my room, my breath rising and falling at the same furious pace as my racing mind.

A phone number. A street name. And a city all the way across the Atlantic. Was it a partial address? Is this where I'd find Frankie—a quarter of the way around the globe? The only Stockholm I know is in Sweden, but the street name wasn't in Swedish, and the phone number looked to be local—only ten digits. There was only one way to find out.

I waited for my breath to calm before grabbing my backpack and my book of Poe. I stole down the hallway like a bandit, slinking through the stairwells. When I breached the door with the grimacing face to the electric daylight, I darted across the street, taking cover under the hood of the payphone opposite The Bardo. I grabbed the receiver, opened Poe's poetry, and dialed the number.

There was no answer. I let it ring. Finally, a recording picked up. "Leave a message, but only if I know you and only if you have a good reason." It was a thick smoker's voice belonging to an older woman. I slammed the receiver on the hook. If that voice belongs to Frankie, there's a good chance that street name belongs to her too.

I was hours late to The Moirai. I ran every step from the payphone to the front stoop, and I found Asher already at work in the salon. I was out of breath and sweat beaded on my forehead. My shirt reeked with the stink of stress. I looked like a wreck.

"What happened to you," Asher asked at the sight of me. I didn't immediately know how to reply.

November 17th. Just over three weeks until Odi will be at The Bardo, and before then, I have to find a way to speak with Frankie in person. All I had was a street name, a city, and whatever CR 515 meant. It had to be a location. But even if I do somehow find it, how can I be sure Frankie will be there? Who knows what I'll find? I knew I needed help—and I also knew Asher was the only one who could offer it.

"I have reason to believe my sister's killer will be making a trip to The Bardo in three weeks," I blurted, "but I have to be sure."

"How'd you figure that out? ..." Asher replied, his own answer slowly sinking in. "Oh no... you got into Zisa's stuff, didn't you?"

I looked at my feet in shame. "I had to," I said in a hushed mumble.

"I hope you covered your tracks," Asher said in disbelief. He didn't look disappointed in me, nor did he seem particularly impressed. It was more like his mind was still trying to catch up. "Your days are numbered with Zisa once she figures it out. Too bad. I've really liked having you around," he said, his face looking long. "So what are you thinking next?"

I opened Poe's cover and showed Asher my transcription. He pointed to CR 515. "Well, CR means 'county road.' I think that's in New Jersey if I'm remembering correctly. It connects to the New York state border," he said softly. "And I'm pretty sure there's a Stockholm somewhere nearby."

"Think you can help me get there?" I asked, a bead of sweat rolling from the tip of my nose and splattering onto the open page.

"One thing at a time," he said. "Let's get a map later, and we can look it up to make sure."

"Later" seemed so far away, but it would allow me some needed time for my mania to subside. Asher and I feigned work for several more hours, but it was obvious neither of us could focus. As soon as the clock hit five, we abandoned our books and grabbed our jackets. We walked back to The Bardo in a spooky kind of quiet. My mind was spinning, and I think Asher's was too, but I feared for entirely different reasons. Does Asher think I'm crazy? Right now, I'm not sure if I even care. I need to find out who O. Cairan really is.

Our walk home felt miles longer than usual, and as Asher fished his keys from his pocket, I mustered a request. "Would it be OK if I stayed in your room again tonight? I could use the company." My question seemed to clear Asher's daze, and he reached down to cup his hand over the curve of my shoulder affectionately. "Missed you too," he said, but his smirk was only at half tilt. At least our flirtation was still alive, even if just barely.

We went our separate ways for the first half of the evening, then reconvened to pick up a pizza and bring it back to Asher's room. He insisted we eat off real plates like civilized people instead of out of the box, and I set the table on his desk by folding flimsy pizzeria napkins into little diamonds like we were at a fancy restaurant. We tapped our first pizza slice together as if we were toasting pints of beer. It was late by the time we switched off the lights and crawled into bed side by side.

With my cheek pressed deep into my pillow, I tried in vain to summon sleep. Through the darkness, all I could make out was the outline of Asher's silhouette, his eyes still wide open, gazing up at the ceiling. He couldn't sleep either. Eventually, the shape of his profile transformed into a wild mess of hair as he turned his head to face mine, his breath so close it warmed my face in the cold air. "I know it's not the same thing," he said, "but if I thought I had a way to put Fisk's dad behind bars forever, I might spend the rest of my life trying too. For all I know, he's still out there practicing medicine and doing who knows what to innocent people." I found Asher's arm under the covers and gave it a "thank you" squeeze.

We rested just as we always do—parallel and barely touching, but this time I allowed my hand to stay clasped to his arm.

I listened to Asher's breath become heavy, and when I felt his fingers twitch over the sheets as his body finally relaxed, I knew he'd fallen asleep. I lay as still as I could, but darting thoughts still ricocheted against the walls of my skull. For the first time, I feel so close to answers. Who is this Odi? O. Cairan. My mind was caught in a loop again, just like one of Asher's old records, still spinning even after the last song has come to an end.

Why Nova? Why Nova? Why Nova?

Why Odi? Why Odi? Why Odi?

I couldn't sleep. I tried to instead concentrate on the inhale and exhale of my own breath to relax, but the pace of Asher's breath beside me soothed me more than my own, like an external pendulum for my mind to trace. Soon enough, I had drifted off too.

The next morning a clap of thunder woke me, and I heard the sound of diagonal rain knocking against the window in tiny cascading thuds. Somehow Asher was still fast asleep. I was so warm under the covers with his body only a few inches away, and yet an iciness seemed to cling to the back of my neck. I listened to the rainstorm as I studied Asher's face, and my questions found me once again. "Why you? Why Nova? Why my sister?" But you can't find an answer if one doesn't exist.

When we were kids Gram's way of explaining the world to us was through her stories. It was always through the power of imagination, metaphor, and morals. The story of how we earned our names. The story of Astrid and her foreshadowing dreams.

"Everyone has their own special story," Gram would say. "Some people show their uniqueness on the inside, some on the outside, but no two people are ever truly alike, not even identical twins," she would tell us. She wasn't wrong. We were always so different in our very nature. At first glance, we may have appeared as human replicas, but even that wasn't really true.

I thought back to the day I went to the police station in Erie, and Singer had asked me about the way we looked. I told him the usual explanation—we were mirror twins, and it was just the luck of the draw that we happened to have unusual features. Gram always tried to make us feel proud and special for that, reminding us of how slim the chances were to be built like us.

Why Nova? Why Nova? Why Nova?

Why Odi? Why Odi? Why Odi?

The rain stopped, and it was the absence of sound that seemed to finally wake Asher. His eyes opened, and he caught me staring at him. His pupils were beautiful black rings, fully dilated as they adjusted to the light. He gave me a gentle smile. "G'morning," he said, his vocal cords raspy. "Morning," I said back.

He pulled an arm out from under the covers and cradled the side of my head. Softly, he tilted my face and lifted his lips like he was about to kiss me on the forehead, right on my birthmark. I should have been delighted, but the sight of his face mere inches from mine sent me into a fluster. At that very moment, last night's dream came flooding back, and I jerked my neck reflexively, ripping my head away from Asher's hand.

"I'm sorry!" he apologized abashedly, recoiling his hand. "I shouldn't have done that," he said, lowering his eyes.

"No!" I said emphatically. "It wasn't that. It just… it surprised me. It made me remember something. I had a dream, and I guess it came back to me just now."

"Oh. Yea, I know. I'm a dream guy," he said looking relieved, adding his usual charm and levity. "Glad I could jog your memory." His confidence didn't take long to rebound.

"So, what was it about?" he asked. "A nightmare?"

I took a deep inhale. "It was about the man who killed my sister," I told him honestly.

"Not the kind of dream I was going for," Asher said, taking a pensive pause. "Do you dream about this guy a lot? About how it happened?" he asked cautiously.

"I have before," I said. I knew Asher was asking from personal experience. I'm sure he's both dreamed and imagined Fisk's last seconds countless times too. I didn't need to tell him about all the hours I'd spent obsessing about exactly the moment he was asking about. I didn't need to tell him about Singer's pictures or about the dream when the Bone Man had plunged his blade into me the way he did to you. Asleep or awake, I'm sure every person has their own way of coping with the last breaths of their loved one, whether they are there to witness them or not.

Why Nova? Why Nova? Why Nova?

Why Odi? Why Odi? Why Odi?

"So, what did you dream this time?" Asher asked gently. I pinched my eyes shut. An image of a monstrous vermilion chair flitted across my mind. Instantly, I felt transported somewhere else.

I was in a room filled floor to ceiling with taxidermied animals—life-size bodies on pedestals and game heads mounted to every inch of wall. Rare ones, endangered ones, and many others I knew it was illegal to kill. The Bone Man was there too. He even spoke from his scarlet throne.

Why you, Nova? Why were you killed? It was there the Bone Man finally explained his answer, according to his own twisted rationale.

It makes no sense. And yet, in my dream last night—there in that room with Odi—his purpose was clear to his own raving mind. How can even the vilest among us justify such reasoning?

After all this time, is the explanation for why you're gone truly so crude—the crooked logic of evil so primitive?

Love,
Rosalyn

Poacher's Prize

I found myself alone in a cold, echoing room,
a violent rain beating the roof overhead.
Not a single piece of furniture adorned the space, save
a tall leather chair, upholstered in a bright coxcomb red.

Through the patter of rain, I heard a grizzled throat
clear, and suddenly the chair swiveled around.
Sitting across from me was Odi, with a
depraved look on his face as he frowned.

"Oh, hello again—I wasn't expecting company,
but I suppose I should welcome it nonetheless.
While you're here, allow me to elaborate—
I think you misunderstand this little mess.

I've been to every corner of this earth,
I've skinned every species—I've hunted it all.
Elephants and eagles, tigers and leopards—
every rare game I've killed, great and small.

They call me a poacher, a villain, a murderer, but my
work is a gift—a relief from all this worldly affliction.
Not everyone in life appreciates your good deeds—
and sometimes, even charity can be an addiction.

For years, I hunted every type of game there was,
but soon, I needed new prizes to satisfy my taste,
so my palette expanded to human sport—after all, not
to save a few of my own kind would be a terrible waste.

Long ago, I earned the name Odi
because people think I'm filled with hate,
but what they don't seem to comprehend is
that I'm driven by quite the opposite trait.

You've got me all wrong, for it's my
overwhelming love that makes me do what I do.
You see, I love the rarest, the most unique kinds
of beauties—just like your sister and you.

I love them so much that I collect
their teeth to keep forever with me.
And besides, I'm not taking their
lives—I'm setting them free.

For creatures with uniqueness like yours are far
too special to deserve this horrid mortal plane,
for there are limits to our prosperity here—it's only
after our last breath that true freedom is ours to attain.

For haven't you noticed the
state of the world we live in?
The ones supposed to keep you safe
are overrun with corruption and sin.

Maybe it's just always been part of my nature to turn
out like this, but in the end, who can really say?
What I do know is this—you know too much,
so now I'm afraid you cannot stay.

If only I'd known there were two of you from the beginning,
you best bet I would have left Erie with a second prize—
with not one but two sets of teeth from skulls crowned
with those beautiful, wide-set, blue and brown eyes."

With that, he lunged from his chair, and
suddenly everything around me went black.
I lost the gravity beneath my feet, and I heard the
sound of my head meeting the floor with a crack.

Another Nova

Sunday, November 2, 1997

Dear Nova,

Things have taken a turn. I woke up no more than a half hour ago and lay in bed listlessly until my anxiety was finally too much to keep me horizontal. I gave in, threw on socks and a sweatshirt, and here I am again at my desk, wielding my pen like some wand that might reveal answers if only I can chant the spell just right. Things started out on the right track—but as of now, everything feels like one big mess after another, and I don't know what to do next.

Believe it or not, Asher and I tracked down Frankie. We've even spoken with her. But things did not go as I intended—and it wasn't until this morning I woke up with an awful realization. I have to think, and I have to do it fast. I'll try my best to explain from the beginning and hope the act of writing will somehow reveal my next moves.

Just as promised, Asher helped me locate the cross street from Frankie's datebook on a map. Buck Pond Trail and County Road 515. The following Monday, he and I made a detour to a nearby gas station before work. The only other vehicles besides Lois were several enormous freight trucks and oversized moving vans. Asher filled up the tank while I ran inside to pay, and I picked up a pack of M&Ms and a AAA New Jersey / Pennsylvania State road map while I was at it.

When I got back to Lois, I offered Asher the M&Ms, and he poured a healthy helping of breakfast chocolate into his mouth. "Route 515's not too far from The Egret," he said as he chewed.

"It's just south of the New York / New Jersey border. I know the area pretty well, but it's been a while. We used to hike Wawayanda State Park when Fisk and I were kids. The Appalachian Trail runs right through there." Asher planted a finger on the map. "See, here's The Egret." He traced an invisible line, dragging his finger along the map over a snaking line that I assumed indicated a major road. Craning his neck closer to study the map's details, he then drew a wider circle. "I don't see anything called Buck Pond, but this is Route 515 right here. Stockholm, New Jersey. It has to be in this general area, but I don't see it marked on the map. Maybe it's a private road."

"Thanks, Superman," my latest bad joke of what seems to be a newly developing survivalist tactic. A cover for my discomfort—levity to balance the embarrassing weight of the situation that I've now put both of us in. "Happy my powers can be of some use," Asher quipped.

Our plan was simple enough, though it would require improvisation. We'd leave that coming Saturday morning, and if we could just find the cross street, the rest we'd have to wing once we got there. There was no way of knowing what awaited us, but one thing was obvious—if this was indeed where Frankie lives, we could be quite sure we'd be unwelcome guests. Our only goal was to persuade her to speak with us face to face for just long enough to find out more about Odi. Will this be his first appointment? If not, how long has he been coming? Does he wear a leather jacket? A skull ring? Does he have crude tattoos in the shapes of bones? Where is he now? Has he ever said anything in his visits that seemed suspicious? Or even confessional? Anything that alluded to his crimes? What else did Frankie know? And most importantly, would she help us get him to the police—that was, of course, if we could confirm proof of his criminality? My torrent of questions seemed endless, and when Saturday morning finally arrived, Asher, Lois, and I were ready early, itching to get on the road to see what our journey would have in store.

The weekend traffic out of the city was horrendous, and in my impatient anticipation, every minute felt at least three times as long. I was both nervous and hungry, and the confusing mix of the two only made me feel sick to my stomach. Over Lois's low, staticky radio, I was sure that at any moment, Asher might start to probe me with some of his own questions. *How did you learn that Frankie is working for your sister's killer? How did you find out he only has one leg? And what are the chances that you end up living at The Bardo, just a few doors down from where he'll be in a matter of weeks?* The list went on, but Asher only drummed his fingers softly to the radio.

I still haven't uttered a single word to him about how I've dreamed my way to my suspicions of Odi or discovered Frankie and her workshop, but the longer we drove, the more sure I became that he wasn't going to ask me after all. Maybe he doesn't want to know these answers. Maybe they scare him. Or—maybe the explanation is much more uncomplicated. Has he simply chosen to trust me?

Once we'd made it out of the mess of Manhattan and onto Interstate 80, the rest of our drive was relatively smooth. The havoc of crowded on-ramps and merging lanes was soon behind us, and after about forty-five minutes, we followed the map to our first exit. The landscape shifted to a bucolic backdrop of rolling farmland interrupted only by thick curtains of forest. Our drive felt much like the one to The Egret, only this time, the lush summer greenery had transformed into the rich shades of fall. Patches of spruces and pines colored the roadside in a deep green, contrasting the reds and oranges of various oaks and alders. Many others were completely bare, their gray, spidery branches already dormant for the season. Fallen leaves danced behind us in the windstorm of our spinning tires.

We passed only a few others on the road, mostly old, weathered pickups much like Lois. It seemed like we might cruise on like this forever until we hit the Great Lakes, but as we neared an intersection marked with a blue pentagon-shaped sign, Asher slowed. The number 515 in bright yellow signaled our turn. We were close.

According to the map, we'd entered from the southernmost end of the county route, and if we kept driving north, we'd find ourselves in New York State before long—which also meant that if Buck Pond Trail did exist, it would have to be on this stretch of road. We each kept watch from our respective windows, and after only a few minutes of scanning the passing scenery, I started to feel dizzy. I couldn't tell if it was the car's motion, the anticipation of our arrival, or the uncertainty of what might transpire if we ever got there—but I didn't have much time to dwell. In less than ten minutes, Asher spotted an unusual placard on his side of the car, and we pulled over to get a better look. The signpost was unlike the others—handmade and mounted to a stone pillar. The words were chiseled into a dark stained wood, its recesses filled with white paint. "Buck Pond Trail." We looked sheepishly across the armrest at one another as if to say, "OK, here we go. No going back now."

Asher made the turn onto a gravel road. We climbed a steep incline that snaked around a gargantuan boulder and a craggy rock face, and after several bumpy minutes, our path abruptly ended at a tall stone wall with a metal gate. We'd arrived. Though to what, I was not yet sure.

Without a word, we unlatched our seatbelts and pushed open Lois's doors. Absorbing our new surroundings, Asher and I approached the barricade to search for our way in. The gate itself was colossal, towering at least several feet above Asher's head. An impassable grate of thick steel bars spanned the length of the door, each of its individual pickets so wide I was unable to fully clasp my hand around, my thumb still more than an inch from my other fingers. The top rail was a wide, flat mantle, and instead of traditional finials, its surface was spiked with what looked to be a series of bronze sculptures in evenly spaced intervals.

I squinted to study their forms. They consisted of nothing more than bizarre bodiless metal heads that guarded the rampart like grotesque human gargoyles. There were seven in total, each at least twice the size of our own skulls. They were as intimidating as they were entrancing. I didn't know how to feel about them. Were they delightful or menacing? I was spellbound. They wore helmets like ancient gladiators, each crowned with a single tall pointed spire, and between each figure were only more rows of individual spikes. Together, they created a thorny blockade that made it impossible to scale and climb over the gate without surely impaling oneself—a more artistic and diabolical approach to barbed wire.

Unsure of what to do next, Asher and I glanced over at one another, then back up at the seven heads above. "Uh. Okaaaay,"

Asher said, shaking his head in a tone of amused bafflement. "Be right back. I really gotta take a leak." He turned his back to me and took a few steps toward a small tree on the other side of the road. Soon, I heard the sound of trickling water.

"Is there a buzzer or anything?" Asher shouted over his shoulder.

"I don't see one," I said, inspecting the tall stone posts on either side of the gate's runged metal door. "I think we might have to…" I began, but before I could finish my sentence, all seven of the metal heads seemed to spring to life, suddenly animating in unison. I nearly peed too. With the mechanical sound of gears turning, each of the heads rotated on their metal necks and settled at varying angles, their gazes pointed to exactly where I stood. Their engraved eyes peered down at me as if they could see through their copper-colored pupils.

"That's a red oak, not a toilet," a voice said, emanating from all seven of the bronze helmets. It took me a moment to understand that each statue had been outfitted with a tiny loudspeaker. I felt like I was in an amphitheater, a single voice multiplied simultaneously across seven sources. Its fullness wrapped around me.

We were being watched, but I couldn't spot a camera anywhere. I recognized the raspy voice. It was the same one I'd heard on the recording when I called the number from Frankie's datebook—a woman's deep smoker's voice, powerful and commanding. Was it Frankie? And how was I going to get her to let us in? I had to think fast. I looked back at Lois and her dented, rusted truck bed against the swath of forest behind her. "Sorry to bother you," I said to the seven heads above. "We're taking firewood orders for the season.

We noticed you have quite a bit of land. Would you be interested in either buying or selling?" It was a long shot, but it was all I could think of on the spot.

A staticky silence emanated from the speakers. "Come in," the voice finally spoke. "I'm about a mile down the dirt road." The gate's latch snapped loose, and its heavy door swung open automatically. I heard Asher zip up his pants from behind me, and I turned to see his reaction. While I was speechless and unnerved, Asher seemed more entertained. "Oooohhh yeah. She's DEFINITELY Bardo material," Asher smirked, walking back toward the car.

We hopped back into Lois, and Asher started the engine. He turned to me, tilting his head sideways toward the tiny tree he'd just baptized with his urine with an expression like he was about to say something profound. "Next year, that red oak will be twice the size as the others. Just wait. Frankie can thank me later." I didn't laugh at his joke, my growing unease anesthetizing my sense of humor. Asher gently hit the gas. It was time to meet Frankenstein.

We drifted over the strange gate's threshold and made our way down a packed dirt road under an overhang of bare trees, the last of their foliage still clinging to their stems. The road gradually widened, and eventually, we spilled out into a vast orchard that sprawled into the distance as far as the eye could see.

A beautiful single-story terra-cotta house soon appeared. Its minimalist concrete porch overlooked a rippling pond no smaller than an Olympic-sized pool. Everything was so perfectly manicured it looked as though it may as well have been painted into the scene. The fallen leaves had already been cleared, a feat that must have required a small army.

A nearby row of swaying weeping willow trees seemed to beckon us toward the house, their naked branches gently swaying in the breeze. Without leaves, they looked slightly ominous, like their ropey vines might be ready to entangle us and never let go. As Asher switched off the engine, a woman who looked to be in her mid-fifties emerged from the front door of the house. She had long, thick waves of red and gray-streaked hair, loosely gathered into a messy plait that spiraled down to the small of her back. She waited for us by the door, one hand akimbo on her hip.

If this was indeed Frankie, I couldn't help but wonder how a person who keeps a workshop at a place like The Bardo could afford such a magnificent, expansive property—not to mention the long private road which led us there. She must quite literally be able to charge an arm and a leg for her work—or at least have enough lavish customers for the money to flow downstream. But more importantly, I wondered what could make a person want to live an existence so untouchable and secluded, cloistered away down miles of an unmarked road and behind an impenetrable gate with spying gladiators. Was living like this simply a personal preference, or was it an intentional effort to keep one's home far removed—and protected—from one's work? What sort of people was Frankie involved with? People like Odi?

"So," she began as we approached the door, "I see we've got two traveling salesmen," she said snidely. Two massive black German Shepherds flanked her sides. Her voice was deep and rich, and she had a nondescript accent like it might have been a combination of a few—maybe British or French, even South African or Eastern European. I couldn't place it. I wondered if perhaps she'd moved around when she was young.

I shifted my weight on my hips, my heart pounding. "Hi, I'm … Sylvia. This is Walter," I fumbled, attempting manners. They were the first invented names I could think of.

"And I'm guessing you already know who I am, Syl-vi-a," she said, exaggerating her enunciation. "You might be interested to know, Sylvia, that Zisa already called to warn me that a young woman around your age named Ros-a-lyn was asking around about me. I can see you're not a very good liar, and I don't appreciate uninvited guests."

A spear of panic shot through my throat, momentarily paralyzing my capacity to speak. I was caught off guard, but perhaps I shouldn't have been so surprised. Had Zisa also figured out I'd been in her room too? Or had she simply called Frankie after I'd asked about her that night in the kitchen? At least now, we could be sure we were at the right place. For better or worse, we'd found our Frankie.

"These days, I've got plenty of time but not patience. You've got five minutes to tell me what this is all about." She must have known who we were from the moment we'd pulled up at her gate.

"And please stick to the things I don't know yet," she directed. "I know you're not cops, or else The Bardo would have already been shut down by now."

"We…" I stammered. I caught my breath to adjust my tact. "…We could use your help." It was already clear that immediate candor was our best and only approach. "It's about one of your clients," I began, glancing at my feet. "We suspect he's a serious criminal."

"Not specific enough, honey," she said dryly, turning her back to us as she walked inside the house. "Do you know why I let you in?" she asked as she strode ahead of us without waiting for a reply. The two German Shepherds trailed dutifully on her heels. "It's brass monkeys out. Are you coming?" she added over her shoulder.

We climbed the stoop's concrete landing and followed her into a foyer, spilling into a magnificent lofted living room. A matrix of beautiful wooden beams supported a tall pitched roof that opened into a massive pyramid skylight. Pottery, carvings, drawings, etchings, paintings, mosaics—any kind of visual art form you could imagine—lay strewn over nearly every inch of floor and wall. They all appeared in varying degrees of completion, yet were arranged with such intention that the space did not give the impression of a mess. Though there was not a single plant inside, the room felt as alive as a luxuriant garden.

Frankie ushered us to a sitting area with a deep leather couch that sloped into a single, long sculptural horseshoe. It must have been able to seat ten people. In my dream, the sight of Frankie's workshop had been a heap of disarray with piles of discarded machined parts, hundreds of plaster molds, and a mess of metal and wires. But while her place of work struck me as chaos, her home was a carefully curated masterpiece that appeared to be in a constant state of deliberate change and creation.

While she took a seat alone on the massive couch, she gestured to the opposite side toward two elegant armchairs with soft leather stretched over their metal frames. "Sit," she commanded, crossing her legs and folding her hands over her lap. They were strong and veined and looked like works of art themselves. I felt her studying us from across the coffee table as we settled into our chairs and her dogs found their places at her feet. "And?" she prompted. "About this client of mine?"

"I believe… you've worked on his leg?" I started again nervously.

"Darling, what did I just say about being specific?"

"Sorry," I apologized. Her imposing straightforwardness made me tense. I was having trouble getting my words out. I could feel Asher shifting in his seat beside me, likely wondering if he should intervene.

"You might ALSO be interested to know that Zisa shared another piece of information. A detective came by The Bardo asking about you," she said unprompted. I was so shocked I nearly toppled over in my chair. Asher's head whipped toward me. I still hadn't told him about Singer. Now I would have to answer to Asher too.

"The only reason I let you in was to make it abundantly clear that you are not to talk to the police or interfere with me or any of my clients—I don't care what you may or may not suspect of them. If the police start snooping around The Bardo, they'll get the whole thing shut down—that's a guarantee, even if only as an unfortunate side effect. You, me, and everyone else will be gone faster than a toupée in a hurricane. But much worse, it'll be open season for law enforcement to start poking into everyone's business."

Frankie squinted across at us, letting the impact of her words settle in. It was abundantly clear that she was now running this interrogation, not me. "I have to know about Odi Cairan," I said no louder than a whisper.

"It seems you have a problem with your ears," Frankie snapped back.

"Please," I said, my determination dampened but not broken. "What do you know about him?" I pushed.

"You need to understand one simple thing. I don't ask questions that don't need to be asked in my line of work. My clients are all individuals who are in need of new body parts. Some were in accidents, but plenty weren't accidents at all—if you catch my meaning. Very often, the people I serve have a few loose wires upstairs, and I'm not interested in tripping over any of them. As I said, most things just aren't my business—and I'm not thrilled when people force things to become my business," she said with a sideways look that implied that we'd better not fall into that category. Her voice was low and unflinching.

"Please. Anything. Does he wear a leather jacket?" I wasn't leaving until I knew something about the Bone Man. Is he even real?

"What don't you understand?" Frankie fired back, an incredulous look in her eyes. Her dogs raised their heads, sensing the tension in her tone. Asher seemed to squirm next to me. I wondered why Frankie wasn't already escorting us back out, but I could tell she wanted something from us too.

"You need to explain why I shouldn't turn you away right now and contact Zisa on your way out. I'm quite certain she didn't tell you where to find this house. What do you two think will happen when I tell her you went fishing through her affairs," Frankie said as she reached into her pocket to retrieve a silver Zippo and a perfectly hand-rolled cigarette. She flicked open the lid and struck the flint wheel, taking a long draw into the flame with visible pleasure.

"I need confirmation that your client Odi Cairan is the man I'm looking for. It's a personal matter," I explained as vaguely as I could. Frankie took another lingering drag. She had a power about her.

"My concern is not for your personal matters," she finally said, exhaling smoke. "It's for keeping my business functioning and the police out of it. I provide goods and services for which I am well paid. I consider my work the finest available. I don't choose who commissions my work—they choose me, you understand? I don't care who you might have business with. You just better not be costing me mine."

I nodded obediently. "We're not asking you to do anything to compromise your business. Please, just anything you can tell us about him."

"Ha!" Frankie scoffed to herself. "Remind me again. Why on God's green earth would I want to help you two little snoops with anything at all?"

"Because..." I fumbled for a reason. There were none. "Because... you want to do the right thing," I said in desperation.

"Oh honey, I most certainly do not."

What could I say? I had nothing to offer. Nothing to bargain with. Exasperation welled up in my chest.

"Does he have tattoos on his legs? Does he wear a silver skull ring on his index finger?" I shrieked, feeling myself becoming erratic. Asher looked over at me, bewildered. He'd never heard me mention any of those details before.

"A ring? Is this the Hope Diamond heist now? I see I'm not getting through to you," she said with a stony leer. She paused to re-cross her legs and study my face, meeting my mania with an eerie calm. Her long eye contact made me squeamish, but I stared back, furiously holding her gaze.

We watched her smoke the last drag of her cigarette thoughtfully in silence as if we weren't even there. She put out the butt in an ashtray that looked like she might have sculpted it herself and spread her arms to her sides over the top of the sloped couch like outstretched wings. "Well then, I see our meeting is over," she said, rising to her feet to escort us out.

I bolted upright too. How could I change her mind? In a sudden avalanche of emotion, I realized I hadn't prepared myself for the possibility of her refusal. She had to help. It was the only way. I froze. I wasn't leaving without something on the Bone Man, but I didn't know what to do or what to say—and so I said the only thing that was left.

"My sister was murdered. I believe your client Odi is the one who did it," I said. "You have to help me," I demanded.

I watched Frankie halt mid-stride. She was motionless, her back to me. Slowly, she turned, and I watched her expression shift. Her stiff posture softened into disarmament, but she didn't immediately say anything in return. I stared back intently. This time I was the one demanding her eye contact with mine. I noticed her eyes wrinkle ever so slightly like she was noticing something for the first time.

"You know, where I'm from, the old timers used to say that eyes like yours can see into other worlds. My grandmother would tell me that when babies were born with different colored eyes, it was because a witch had come in the night and swapped one of her own with the child's. The witch possessed part of the child's sight and the child part of the witch's."

"Maybe a witch swapped one of mine with one of my sister's," I said. "Hers were just like mine too."

"Maybe so," Frankie said solemnly. "I'm sorry to hear about your sister," her voice sounded kinder, though still firm. "That's a sad tale. If it's true, that's a tragedy, but if it's not, it's a pitiful lie. A nice try, I'll give you that. But help you? I don't have to do any such thing. I gave you my answer, and you gave me none of my assurances. Zisa can take care of the rest from here." She gently tapped her Zippo against the top of the leather couch and squinted. I felt my rage boiling over. How could she refuse to simply confirm Odi's existence?

"I know you're seeing him on November 17th," I bellowed at the top of my lungs. It was like some more powerful version of myself had suddenly commandeered my body. Frankie's posture bristled. Suddenly, she seemed to inhabit the athletic figure of a woman half her age.

"So you've been in my datebook too, then? Meddling is supposed to get you your way?"

"I'll take the whole Bardo down with me!" I screeched. "I know he's coming to see you. I know you have the answers to my questions!" I was shaking with rage. Frankie's temper was equally apparent, but her body was steady, and her voice was so calm it was more terrifying than if she had screamed the same words.

"Someone named Odi. A man you say you've been looking so hard for and yet seem to know so little about. How would you know to snoop for him in my appointments in the first place? What about your tall, silent friend over here? Does he know?" I could feel Asher's eyes on me, anticipating my answer. I didn't reply. I just stood there, crazed and trembling.

Frankie slapped her hand against her hip, and her dogs scrambled to her side as she marched toward the front entrance. She yanked open the door and gestured with her hand toward the front porch, indicating our meeting was over and that we were no longer welcome. We followed, not knowing what else there was to be said, stepping onto the landing in silence. I paused, my body refusing to depart without the answers I'd come for. I turned to square Frankie, and our eyes met. She seemed to examine my face as if she were turning over some distant thought.

"I can tell you one thing," she finally said coldly. My heart leaped. Had I changed her mind at last?

"If I were you, I'd start looking elsewhere," she said under her breath. Frankie's eyes seemed to sparkle knowingly. "This Odi of yours won't be anywhere near The Bardo any time soon, I can tell you that much. And you best stay far away from my workshop, my home, and my affairs. I never want to see either of your faces again," she warned.

I didn't know how to react. Could I believe her? Was she bluffing? Protecting herself with a red herring? Inventing a diversion to keep the police from descending upon The Bardo? At least she had finally confirmed his existence.

"When you get to the gate, I'll let you out," she added bluntly. With that, I turned to the door to leave. Asher followed. Together, we stepped back into the grass in silence and walked past the leafless weeping willows in the direction of Lois.

Asher opened the passenger side door for me to get in, as if out of chivalric habit, but I could see something in him fuming just beneath the surface. He walked his ambling, sleepy giant walk to the other side of the car, let himself in, and started the engine—still without a word. When we reached the metal gate with the strange seven heads, as promised, it unlatched automatically like we were being watched. Its door swung open slowly, and Asher braked, waiting for our clearance.

"Why was a detective looking for you at The Bardo?" Asher finally said, looking dazed as he accelerated through the open gate. "Why wouldn't you mention something like that?" His voice sounded as hurt as it did suspicious.

"I'm sorry I didn't tell you. I'm sure he just wanted to ask me more questions about my sister," I said, knowing my answer would be unsatisfying. It failed to satisfy even me. Why had Singer followed me all the way to New York just to ask me more questions? Was he there for me? Or is he on the same trail as I am—on the search for Odi?

"What are you not telling me…?" Asher's voice trailed off. It was a question, but he seemed to ask it more of himself than me. We hardly spoke again until we'd made it back to the city. Asher felt miles away across Lois's armrest.

I spent the ride in something of a contemplative haze. If Frankie is lying, the Bone Man will be at The Bardo in just over a week. If I miss my chance, who knows how long it will be until I can figure out how to find him again? In my dream, the Bone Man had said that long ago, he had "earned the name Odi because people think he's filled with hate." If that's true, Odi likely isn't even a real name—just some alias or epithet. How would I begin tracking him down a second time without so much as a legal name? It's not like I can just look him up in the phone book. November 17th at Frankie's workshop is my only chance—but then again, if Frankie was telling the truth, the Bone Man could be anywhere. There's no way to know for sure unless I stake out her workshop and wait. But then what?

Trap him? Kill him? The mere sight of those words on this page confirms their absurdity. And besides, I need physical proof of Odi's crimes before I even imagine drastic measures against someone who I've only so much as dreamed about. I have to get my hands on that leather jacket somehow. If there are human teeth inside, I'll know I've found the Bone Man—and only then can I call the cops. Otherwise, I can be quite certain I'll be the one locked in a cell—only my walls will be padded.

Asher found a parking place a few blocks away, and we made a deli detour for pastrami sandwiches on our way back to The Bardo. We ate on a cold cement stoop nearby, the crinkle of wax paper the only sound between us. We finished our meals and ambled to the door with the grimacing face in awkward silence, and when we reached the third-floor stairwell, we said an uncomfortable goodbye.

"Thank you for everything today, Ash," I said timidly. "OK," was all he said back in a faraway voice. His face was tense, expressing none of his typical ease and buoyancy. There is a canyon between us—so much I've kept from him, and now he knows it too, more than ever.

We parted ways in the stairwell, each of us retiring separately to our own rooms, alone with our thoughts. It was only nine o'clock when I felt drowsiness tugging at my eyelids, and I happily acquiesced. The cognitive load of the day seemed to have exhausted my faculties, and I don't even remember undressing for bed.

I hadn't realized I'd already slept through the morning until I heard Zisa playing French 1940s jazz in the living room, as was her Sunday afternoon custom. She was back—and if I'd made it thus far without being served my eviction, I knew Zisa hadn't detected my break-in or heard from Frankie—at least not yet.

The dampened sound of a woman's sensuous voice filtered through my door, and I wriggled myself upright, leaning against the bedframe. The muffled French lyrics reverberated through the walls. I squeezed my eyes shut with a feeling that I was forgetting something important. I sucked in a few long, slow breaths—and in a flash, suddenly I remembered.

I feel sick, Nova. I don't know what to do next. I don't know how to make sense of any of it. I thought writing you this letter might help—force me to calm down and recount my steps—but as I write these words, all I feel is panic tightening again in my chest.

Last night I dreamed I saw the Bone Man again, but this time I knew exactly where we were—and it wasn't at The Bardo. It was Paris, and a terrified and helpless woman lay at his feet.

Was this in the past? Or is this something yet to come? And how could I begin to find out? It's not like dreams come with a postage stamp.

Will Odi kill again, only someone else's sister this time? I have to find out. But how? If I wait for Odi's appointment with Frankie on the 17th, it could already be too late.

I need to think.

Love,
Rosalyn

Another Nova

When I opened my eyes, I knew
I was looking at the river Seine.
I'd seen the City of Light's landmarks in books, and I
recognized it immediately, though I'd never been.

Through the dark of night, rising from the Left Bank,
I could see the twinkling lights of the Eiffel Tower.
The moon was a perfect glowing disc radiating
over the city with its full moon power.

It must have been even later than I realized,
for there was not a soul on the street.
I began to walk in urgent haste, though not sure
whereto—I simply followed the direction of my feet.

I must have made a dozen turns—somehow,
my legs knew exactly where they wanted to go.
A winter storm was on its way, and the cobblestones
were blanketed in a soft, gray snow.

Soon, I'd completely lost my bearings
and no longer knew my orientation to the river.
When my feet finally stopped, my whole body
was overcome with a bone-chilling shiver.

I found myself in an old alley, and though I felt
some kind of other eerie presence, I was utterly alone.
Instinctively, I took a step backward, my footprints
revealing an engraving in the street's old stone.

I bent down to brush away the snowfall,
exposing each cold, carved word.
I didn't realize I'd spoken its message aloud
until I surprised myself with what I heard.

"Arrête! C'est ici l'empire de la Mort," the words
hung in the air with the steam of my breath.
My French was weak, but I knew its translation:
"Stop! Here lies the empire of Death."

A stone relief of two skulls flanked the words,
the recesses of their eyes forming a sort of grip.
I slid my fingers in like a bowling ball and pulled,
but the wet snow made it difficult not to slip.

With a possessed strength, I strained my weight
against the slab, and at last, it gave way.
Below was a pitch-black hole, and a faint voice
I recognized echoed: "Bonjour encore. Entrée."

Feet-first, I descended into the dark on a crude
ladder formed by short, protruding metal rungs,
and as I lowered myself step by step, the air
changed, and a rotting mustiness filled my lungs.

I knew I'd found the bottom when my feet
hit a pool of freezing black water.
I couldn't turn back now, even if I was
leading myself straight to the slaughter.

From the murky depths, I took in my surroundings
by a faint light flickering in the distance.
All the cavern walls were stacked with skulls.
Shaking, I waded toward the glow in persistence.

When I reached the far end, I came to a turn, and
from the water rose a set of uneven stone stairs.
On either side, the cavern walls were meticulously
laid with bones arranged in symmetrical pairs.

I followed the passageway until it opened
into an expansive, skull-covered room.
And there, a hooded figure turned to me,
waiting in this elaborately constructed tomb.

He spoke without pause, "Bienvenue.
Salutations. You've found me once again.
As you can see, the mood down here is sublime,
and makes for my favorite hunting den."

As the candlelight caught his face,
I could see it was Odi, just as I'd feared.
"Isn't this place exquisite? It has that
certain… je ne sais quoi," he sneered.

Slumped at his feet was a paralyzed
woman—her terrified eyes met mine.
"I'm a little busy now, as you can see, but I'll make
sure you join her—you'll just have to wait in line."

Battlecry

Sunday, November 9, 1997

Dear Nova,

It will be another two hours until the sun rises, and everything here is quiet. My bag is packed, and when I finish this letter, I'll close the door to my bedroom for what will likely be the last time.

For all these months, I've hoped to condense my world into these pages so you could follow—and so I wouldn't have to be alone. I know my feeble words can never be enough to convey an absolute picture—although I've tried, nonetheless. How could anyone possibly understand through only these small glimpses—this patchwork of stories and feelings and clues? But then I wonder if maybe you've been by my side all along, even without these letters.

Since I last wrote, every waking minute has been a test of tolerating my own psychological torment. The image of the Bone Man crouched over another helpless woman's body is seared into my mind's eye. I replayed every small moment over and over until the edges of each detail felt tangible. If I could at least try and recreate the scene as clearly as I'd dreamed it, then maybe, I thought, I could understand it too. Maybe I'd know what to do next.

Asher took notice of my visible preoccupation, but he's been brooding just as much as I have. I feel heartbroken for the divide between us, but I know it's all my own doing. I've strained our trust with all my secrets—and after this week, I'm worried I've tested our bond to its limit.

Cutting Asher out is agonizing and lonely, but it's also the only way I know to carry on in the midst of these latest developments. He still doesn't know anything about my dreams—he only knows a detective was looking for me and that I hid it from him. What more might I be hiding? He wouldn't be wrong to wonder. How would he react to the truthful explanation of how I've really arrived at my information? Would he think I'm inventing some desperate excuse for my behavior? Some pathetic justification? Or think that I'm simply delusional. Would he recoil? Question everything between us? I can barely stomach the thought of losing him entirely.

For a week I've desperately turned over these questions, all the while knowing that, right now, those answers don't matter. There are only two questions worth my energy, and I have to answer them on my own—without Asher. Is Odi preparing to kill again? And can I stop him?

Here is what I know. In my dream, the Bone Man was in Paris. I'm absolutely sure of it. I saw the river Seine and the Eiffel Tower. They were unmistakable. The street names were all in French, and the Bone Man even spoke in French phrases too. And as for those underground, bone-covered corridors where I'd found him? They must have been the tombs of the catacombs. I've read about their history before. I could never forget those pictures—the strangeness of their skull-laden passageways, the mosaics of bone after bone, piled into heaps like altars—the final resting place for millions of Parisians. I wondered what else I could learn, and after half a day of searching The Moirai, I was able to dig up a dusty black, leather-bound book about graveyards all over Europe. The second chapter was dedicated to Paris and included a useful historical overview that was worth remembering.

Between the 17th and 19th centuries, countless haphazard and even illegal mines had been constructed throughout Paris's southern hillsides in order to extract the limestone used in many of the city's grandest buildings. The Louvre, the Place de la Concorde, Les Invalides. But once the mines were depleted, they were often abandoned and forgotten. By the end of the 18th century, much of Paris's suburbs sprawled into the previously mined areas, and unsurprisingly, both homes and streets began to sink into its hollowed-out underbelly. A series of collapses prompted a mass inspection of the mines, and Paris soon began to consolidate their passageways and reinforce their underlying masonry in order to support the streets above.

In the meantime, Paris's cemeteries had been overflowing with the dead for centuries, and conditions worsened year after year. To make room for new burials, the bones of the long-dead were exhumed and packed into the cemetery walls. Sometimes, the disentombed bodies hadn't even yet completely decomposed, reduced only to large deposits of fat called "corpse wax," and it was often collected and turned into candles and soap for the living. Imagine bathing in your neighbor's dead body. By the end of the 18th century, some burial grounds were nothing more than towering six-foot-tall mounds of earth packed with old skeletons, and eventually, these derelict cemeteries were condemned as a better solution gained urgency. This is how the catacombs were born.

By the 1780s, it was decided that the millions of Paris's overflowing dead would be relocated from the bursting cemeteries into the newly renovated and reinforced mining tunnels—and by 1785, the idea was law. The mines were now tombs. For the first several decades of use, the tunnels were nothing more than a disorganized repository for bones, but by the early 19th century, they had been transformed into a mausoleum open to the public.

Femurs and skulls had been arranged in intricate patterns lining the catacombs' walls, and large stone tablets with ominous inscriptions were later added to warn its visitors. Today, only a small area is open to the public, with another nearly two hundred miles stretching in every direction beneath Paris's streets, many of which remain uncharted.

I ran my fingers over the book's black and white photos, absorbing their features. I'd seen these same bone-covered caverns in my dream. Operating according to some instinct I still can't understand, I lowered myself rung by rung deep below the cobbled streets, and when, at last, I reached the end of my crude ladder, I was surrounded by bone-laden tapestries affixed to every wall, just the same as in those pictures. I vividly remember how their outlines had been illuminated by some dim light in the distance. The dark, echoing passage was so flooded with icy, black water that I nearly had to swim. Nonetheless, I pressed forward, wading slowly, step by step. I must have been too afraid to feel the cold.

I felt as if I was willingly climbing into my own grave, no more than some helpless creature tumbling to the bottom of a well with no possibility of rescue. Once inside, I imagined myself being swept away by a torrent of groundwater, carrying me off to join the millions of others buried forever in this crypt. Even now, as I recall its scene, the hairs on my arms stand on end. I'm overcome with stabbing claustrophobia, and I can barely regulate my breath.

I've been manic all week, anguished over what to make of any of this. The Bone Man of my dreams won't rest for long before he needs to feed his appetite with some new trophy. He said himself his deeds were an addiction. But what could I do? I only know two dates pertaining to his whereabouts—one in the past and one in the future—February 22nd in Erie, the day you were killed, and November 17th at The Bardo, the day he may or may not show up at Frankie's workshop. Everything before, in between, and after is a mystery. My questions would not leave me alone. How could I begin to understand the logic of this dream? What could I be missing? What was I not seeing?

I replayed every triviality. The cobbled streets. The twinkling lights of the Eiffel Tower. The full moon, a perfect glowing disc, its reflection shimmering over the Seine. It was only yesterday when I recalled this particular detail that suddenly, I got an idea. I remembered seeing a copy of an almanac on the third-floor book collection and raced down to retrieve it. I flipped to the moon cycles in the farmer's calendar. The next full moon is in only five days from today. November 14th.

Another detail flitted back into view. A light snow had been falling. I remember it clearly. I had to brush the flakes away with my hand to read the inscription on the stone slab covering the entrance that led underground: "Arrête! C'est ici l'empire de la Mort." Stop! Here lies the empire of death. That's when I got another idea.

Yesterday was Saturday, and with nothing to occupy myself but my own obsessive thoughts, I took a cab back to the same internet café I'd been to before. I bought a coffee and shredded my thumbs near a cluster of tables as I waited for a computer to open up.

Eventually, I sufficiently irritated another patron with my hovering enough that he cleared his things in a huff to finally surrender his table. I slid into his seat in an impatient frenzy and began typing into AltaVista's search bar. Weather. Local Paris weather. November Paris weather. I'd dreamed of both a full moon and a light snow. How many times a year could Paris possibly get both?

The page seemed to take forever to load. At last, the local news and a forecast flickered onscreen. November 14th. A prediction for an early winter snow. I could feel my pulse in my temples. What could this mean? Coincidence? Or is it possible I had dreamed about the future?

I wish I could just change the channel somehow—hop into someone else's life and take a nice, long intermission. In just five days, there will be both a full moon and an early snow in Paris on November 14th. Will the Bone Man be there too? And three more days after that, if Frankie's lying, will the "O. Cairan" from her datebook arrive at her workshop with some new keepsake lining his jacket?

For days I flitted from one plan to another, gripped by responsibility and utter fear. Each time I thought I'd settled on a solution, some new wild idea would take me in a new direction. If I believe my dreams are true, could I live with myself knowing I've allowed the Bone Man to kill again? It would be like letting you walk out that door a second time.

From that cold, flooded passage, my path too dark to see even the steam of my own breath, somehow I summoned my body onward —toward my fear and not away. And though a paralyzing terror gripped my logical mind, some incomprehensible force propelled me forward. I inched closer to the voice I knew belonged to Odi, petrified of what scene might unfold when I reached its source. What would the Bone Man do to me? And what might I be powerless to do in response? Death felt near—but I pressed on nonetheless. I have to find a way to hold onto that same courage now.

Who was that helpless woman slumped at Odi's feet? Someone's daughter? Mother? Someone else's sister? Another person's Nova. I did nothing to stop you the night you left and never came home. I can't remain actionless a second time.

My original questions soon spawned and multiplied in droves. Can I go to Paris and hunt down the Bone Man myself? And if he's even there, am I capable of stopping him? According to that book, there are over two hundred miles of underground passages—he could be anywhere. How will I find him? I don't even know where to find an entrance. Does anyone? How do I expect to scour such a sprawling and treacherous labyrinth alone in the pitch black with nothing to defend myself? An army of doubts—and it only gets worse the more I think.

Even if I am right about Paris—and even if I do somehow track him down—surely I'll end up as his next souvenir. But if I don't try at all, am I simply a passive accomplice to another Nova's death? The idea of doing nothing is a far more unbearable notion than even the thought of losing my own life.

Yesterday afternoon I felt so nauseous with indecision I pilfered one of Zisa's cooking pots from the kitchen and laid down next to it on my bedroom floor in case I lost my lunch. Do I stay? Do I go? Have I simply lost my mind? Is any of this real at all? Just when I thought I'd finally landed on the right answer, I'd turn myself right back in a circle again.

I've weighed everything a hundred times—asked myself a hundred questions. How will I confront a seasoned killer—a deranged poacher addicted to his trophies? It goes without saying the Bone Man is dangerous, and I have nothing to threaten him with. What could he possibly fear losing? A man like that holds nothing in this life sacred with all his talk of seeking freedom from it. Could I even bring myself to kill him if I had to?

The answer might not matter. All I have to defend myself is my buck knife. What good will it do up against the likes of Odi? Tracking a deer is not even remotely the same as defending myself against a practiced murderer. A hunter and a killer are two entirely different things. If the version of the Bone Man I know from my dreams is real, he'll be more than happy to slice me up and take me apart without another thought. And I imagine if somehow he and I ever do come eye to eye, surely he'll recognize me—if not as your twin, then certainly as your ghost.

Nonetheless, I called the airport last night from the payphone to check the regulations. Blades under four inches are permitted. My knife just passes. I'll have to make it work, at least for now. Maybe I can find something better once I get there, but I can't count on it. With every new consideration, I only feel more unglued.

Smothering swells of fear passed through me, but when I stopped to ask myself why, I realized it was not the fear of losing my own life, only the fear of making the wrong decision. Of letting you down. Of letting myself down. A fear of failing, again and again, to listen to that part of myself that always spoke the truth. And now the final cost is allowing Odi's evil to continue.

New York or Paris? I only get one choice. I might not get the luxury of both. If I stick around in New York to wait for the possibility of Frankie's appointment, it could be too late—the Bone Man may have already slaughtered someone new. If I go to Paris to stop him, it's true I might become another one of Odi's trophies, but perhaps it's just as possible I could finish things too. I don't yet know how, although I think I'm willing to find out.

I can't possibly figure out all of this now. Maybe I don't have to. All I can really do is make a choice and have faith that I'll know what to do next when the time arrives—some new clue lighting my way when I need it. I'm no superhero. I'm no prophet. But I can't deny what I've seen in my dreams. What if all the stories Gram told us as kids weren't just about an imaginary girl who lived in a small village centuries ago? What if Astrid's story belongs to all of us? This must be what she felt too.

Last night I couldn't wind down for bed until hours after midnight. I was so agitated it felt like I had centipedes crawling in and out of my ears. My whole body was twitchy, and I knew sleep wouldn't come easily. When I finally crawled under my covers, I only alternated between erratic spells of staring at the ceiling and the inside of my eyelids.

By the time the ceiling reappeared, I realized I had indeed managed to drift off, though I wasn't sure if it had been for hours or merely minutes. I swung my legs over the side of the bed and brushed the ridges of the wood floor with my feet, feeling the margins of another dream just within reach. Where had it gone? Only a moment ago, it had been right there with me.

I waited, gently tracing the gaps in the floorboards, guiding my big toe over each crevice. Left. Up. Right. Down. Left. And slowly, I felt the dream clotting together like a heavy cream gathering at the top of a perfect black coffee. Suddenly, there it was—every vibrant detail as if it were a memory from yesterday.

And finally, I realized that as I'd dreamed, I knew my answer.

Now awake, I know this answer too.

My urgent sense of debate and deliberation has left me, and for the first time, I feel eerily clear about what has to be done. I'm leaving just as soon as I finish writing you. I have enough money saved for a one-way plane ticket, and I should still have some left over to get around for a few days. Maybe even enough to get back to New York later—that is, if I'm lucky enough to try. In a way, I feel a final sense of relief. After all these months tangled in impossible questions, I feel at peace.

There is, however, only one last question my heart can hardly bear. I know better than anyone the pain of questions left unanswered. How can I abandon Asher with more? Where have I gone, and why did I leave? Will I ever come back? Why couldn't I tell him? I can't leave him with yet another aching mystery, feeling as though I never cared about him enough to be honest. That couldn't be farther from the truth. It frightens me somehow to commit these words to ink, but Asher is the only person left in my life who I can say I truly love.

I know he cares about me too, or he would never have done all that he has for me. He took me under his wing when I had no one. He gave me glimpses of humor again—just like you always used to do for me. He went along on this goose chase with me on nothing but blind trust. I'm not sure how to articulate what that has meant to me. He deserves to hear all this face-to-face. I only wish I had the courage. But even if I did, now there isn't the time. The whole story is much too long—and it's a story's details that are sometimes the most important.

In some indescribable way, I can't help but feel like he and I were always meant to intertwine, even if only in this strange, quiet, dark way. We don't always get to choose the ways our lives irreversibly enmesh with another's. You and I, us and Gram, me and Asher, our stories always destined to overlap, suddenly discovering ourselves in one another's orbit, irreversibly entangled. I wonder if a human mind can ever really understand the true mechanics of these connections. All I know is that I'm grateful for them.

I've gathered my things and stacked them neatly into my backpack. My clothes. My walkman. My buck knife. And then there it was again. Your Dream Eye journal, every last page filled. All these months later, I still haven't read another word. I wondered what I might learn about you if I did. That's when I had a thought. What if there was still a way to tell Asher what he's always meant to me? A way to leave him with the entire story—every last detail, even my dreams. Maybe all along, these letters for you were meant for Asher too.

It would be simple enough—stop by The Morai before I go and leave this journal for him beside the French press with a note. He couldn't miss it. But getting your letters in Asher's hands is the easy part. Letting them go is another matter altogether. I've fought so hard to protect all my secrets since I left Erie, only now to cast them off into the great wide open. And yet, it's all that's left to do.

These letters say all the words I was never brave enough to speak aloud. I only hope Asher can understand. Over these last few months, we've invented our own kind of shared language, speaking our hidden feelings through the veil of book quotes and song lyrics —but those were other people's words, not ours. It's time Asher finally hears my own. Even if they can't come from my lips, they can still come from my heart.

Maybe Asher will never believe all that I've written here, but at the very least, it might help explain why I've acted the way I have. If anyone can understand the irrational ways a person becomes tormented after losing the person they love most, it's Asher. After all, he's been in these shoes too. We don't always have control over the illogical ways our grief manifests, and we certainly don't choose the questions that haunt us. The good doctor turned bad. The Bone Man. The boogeyman. Maybe there's no difference in the end. Asher never got his explanation, and maybe I'll never get mine.

Hours have already passed since I started this letter, and the sun will be up soon. I won't be able to write you again here, but maybe I can find some other way. Sometimes I really do think you get these letters. I hope this isn't goodbye. I love you, Nova. Please forgive me for leaving our private letters for someone else's eyes, but if I know Asher like I think I do, he'll take good care of them.

Asher, if you're there, I always thought I was coming to New York to run away, but maybe it was always something else that I was running toward—my dreams nudging me along the way. I can't help but feel like you and I were always meant to meet. In the end, no one has to understand my choices except for me, but I still hope you can try. You're never really lonely so long as you're understood.

You were right when you said, "Past House is just a brick building in Queens. You are free to step outside and beyond its walls whenever you like." Maybe leaving you with the story of my past is the only way I know how to be free. Thank you for holding onto it for me, so I don't have to anymore.

I think that's what you taught me most. I know I may not have made the most of the present when we were together. I was still so trapped in the past, and now I can't even imagine what a future might look like—but if there is one, I hope to meet you there one day and try again. And if I'm not able, maybe you can at least keep one of those old typewriters of yours busy with a story that you've helped write too. You've meant more to me than you know. Thank you for trusting me. I know you would have done the same for your brother.

Love,
Rosalyn

Battlecry

I found myself at the bank of a lagoon,
surrounded by tall, swaying reeds.
A regal figure rose from the water wearing
a tunic embellished with sparkling beads.

In a daze, I realized it was Gram
dressed in a beautiful draping gown.
She spoke to me as fireflies encircled
her head like a living, glowing crown.

"When you think you know something vital—
but aren't sure how—it's important just to trust.
You always had this power, whether or not you
knew it—and now it's time to do what you must.

You will go to Paris and stop Odi from
doing what he did to Nova to someone new.
There is no one else who can find him
in time—the only person who can is you.

In life, sometimes the task ahead may feel meager while
others may feel much greater than you think you can hold,
but it's taking the first step in this kind of hard work
that's worth so much more than accolades or gold.

Each of us arrives in the world in the very
same way, just as one day, we each will die.
But until that day, you must fight to honor your
own heart's truth—and this is your battlecry."

With that, she raised her open hands
and thrust them toward the full moon,
and suddenly, her body disintegrated into dust,
the wind carrying it away over the lagoon.

Afterword

From the author

I put this rhyme here so you'd know
it's a poem: to you, from me,
but how many more poems right outside
your door did you forget to see?
The crack in your leavened bread,
the froth on your milk,
the fresh rain on the glass,
billowing as if it were silk.

Not all poems arrive
arranged in perfect lines.
Plenty you can't see, but you'll know
are there if your heart aligns.
And though they may not yet
be built from verse or word,
they'll wink at you to shape them into
the music of your inner songbird.

And when your heart breaks,
or when the day is long—
when there's only rubble left, and
you think you must simply move along,
the poet in your soul will cry out
and raise her hands to the sky,
"This is your poem, and if you don't
claim it, it's only your own heart you deny.

And if you feel lost and
you forget your truth,
just sink into the dream place,
for it will give you your proof
that your answers are
within you, every last one.
Just wait for the darkness
behind the sun.

For when the moon is full,
or when she is new,
remember, our bodies are water,
and the tides will tell you
that dreams are not fiction—they
are merely a sharper looking glass
to examine the truth to come,
and has already come to pass.

So if you have something to do, say,
or make, no better day than today to start.
It's your obligation to follow only those
pursuits which truly vibrate your heart.
Be patient with your journey and remember
that all things that matter also take time.
That's one of the many tricks of poetry,
forcing you to slow down with its meter and rhyme.

For every bold act, every roaring
protest for what's right,
there are boundless quiet revolutions
not always as obvious to plain sight.
For these, we need our poets, our dreamers—
to touch both our spirit and our mind
so we can keep what truly matters
alive for all humankind.

It's the intention of a good tall tale
to awaken that sleeping warrior in you.
Courage is simply believing what in
your heart you already know to be true.
It's the ability to do something that frightens
you so much you'd rather leave it undone.
And it's why so many of history's greatest true
warriors never once wielded a weapon against anyone.

Dreams can't always solve dark crimes
or spare the world from the evil powers that be,
but they are the poetry of your subconscious,
and hold the clues that can help you truly see.
A dream, after all, is simply an idea that arrives
to your conscious mind only as you sleep.
And it's ideas that change the world forever,
inviting humankind to take the next bold leap.

Gratitudes

Thank you, David Bowie,
for your Spiders from Mars.
Thank you, Frida Kahlo,
for your self-portrait memoirs.

Thank you, Mary Oliver,
for "The Summer Day."
Thank you, Kurt Cobain,
for "Something in the Way."

Thank you, Homer,
for your enduring hymns and epics.
Thank you, Hilma af Klint,
for your mystical canvas relics.

Thank you, Maya Angelou,
for your lyrical prose.
Thank you, Nina Simone,
for balladeering your woes.

Thank you, Vincent van Gogh,
for "The Starry Night."
Thank you, William Blake,
for "Tyger Tyger, burning bright."

Thank you, Billy Corgan,
for "Siamese Dream."
Thank you, Janis Joplin,
for that soulful scream.

Thank you, Radiohead,
for "Lotus Flower."
Thank you, Patti Smith,
for "People Have the Power."

Thank you, Robert Smith,
for "The Head On The Door."
Thank you, Pablo Picasso,
for reminding us there's always
another way of seeing left to explore.

It's thanks to intrepid
dreamers like you
that any of us dare
to try it too.

Thanks, About, and Notes

Mom

Dear mom, you've been
by my side through it all.
Failures and success
of all ilk, great and small.

From art classes to doctor appointments,
homemade meals and all-nighter homework—
not to mention enough teenage rebellion
to make even the sanest go berserk.

And now you've done it again,
still by my side, even as an adult.
You're my rock and my guide,
always there when I need to consult.

For the past six years, you've been
my trusty editor-in-chief,
cheering me on to the finish of this bloody
book whenever I got stuck in disbelief.

Dad

Ever since I was small, you were always the designated
concert chaperone—there to feed my creative appetite.
You've always stoked my love for art—even hosting (and
Eugene-sitting) when I needed a retreat to get away or write.

Emily

Emily, it's no secret that having a sister I adore
as much as you was this book's greatest inspiration.
How wild that after it was written, you had twin girls too—
Ada and Iris, you're our star twins for the next generation.

Mile

Mile, my king, thank you for
your partnership, humor, and love.
I'm so lucky to share a life with
someone I will always stand in awe of.

Your feedback, ideas, and encouragement
pushed me to a new height.
You're a true artist who knows if you have
a dream, never let it out of your sight.

You've seen me at my best but more
importantly also at my worst,
and when I need support
you're always there first.

And if that wasn't enough, you still
found time to help me edit and design.
Please forgive the cliché, but always
know I love you until the end of time.

Barry

Barry, thank you for gifting me Pirsig's seminal work—
our friend Phaedrus gave me the confidence to go my own way.
And it was your honest feedback that prompted a much-needed
rewrite of the old ending—which was quite far-fetched, I daresay.

Uncle Rob, A.K.A. Critter

Uncle Rob, your vast knowledge and love for both wildlife
and the outdoors helped me with a much-needed revise.
Thank you for all your factual corrections so every
real bow hunter won't be completely rolling their eyes.

Frank

Frank, thank you endlessly for somehow making sense
of the first draft of what, at the time, wasn't even a book.
I still don't know how you did it (wine?)—but without
your sage feedback, this manuscript would be gobbledygook.

Tina, Lys and friends

Tina, Lys, dear loved ones, family and
friends—(you all know who you are),
thank you for being my steadfast cheerleading crew—
if I need a pick-me-up, I never have to go far.

Hunter, Michael, Frank, and Mary

Hunter M., Michael V., Frank C., and Mary C.—
ye brave friends who have published books before—
thank you for shining your light on my path and
helping me uncover the right channels to explore.

Dave and Michael

Dave and Michael, thank you for
all your generous audio advice.
You're as kind as you are professional, offering
decades of expertise without even thinking twice.

Hollis and Holly

Hollis, Holly (and Oats—woof!),
my true and trusty denizens of Erie,
thank you for your priceless fact checks
and helping answer my every local query.

Eugene

My sweet little Eugene, you're the greatest
snuggle buddy that there ever was.
You've purred on my lap for all those late nights of writing—
what would I do at 3 AM without your impossibly soft fuzz?

About

The Rosalyn Letters was written, illustrated, designed,
and published in New York City by an artist named Sara Blake.
This six-year project helped her learn to listen to her dreams, and
now she mostly makes art quietly in the woods beside a small lake.

She sewed every stitch
and drew every line.
She pushed every pixel
and wrote every rhyme.

She wrote these words because
they told a story she needed to hear.
And now those words are for you too,
whenever you are ready for them to appear.

Mission

To all our fellow humans, what a gift it is to be here with you.
Lend an attentive ear to your dreams, but also to one another.
It's not idealism to hope for a future where regardless
of race, gender, or religion we all act like sister and brother.

In Somnis Veritas—in Latin it means
"In Dreams There is Truth."
Dreams aren't just for sleeping, so remember, it's never
too late to seize those truest dreams of our youth.

More for readers

www.therosalynletters.com

MEMENTO MORI

Disclaimer

This is a work of fiction. Although its format is that of a series of autobiographical letters, it is not one. While this story is set in real places, certain establishments, geographic locations, and landmarks are not real—with the exception of those establishments, geographic locations, and landmarks which are real. Certain long-standing institutions and agencies are mentioned, but the characters involved are wholly imaginary. The author has taken care to ensure moon cycles are correctly represented, though the historical accuracy of weather in certain places at certain times is, indeed, fictitious, though some readers may still consider it accurate in its inaccuracy. Please do not plan your trip back to 1997 according to this work's meteorological descriptions.

Unless otherwise indicated, all names, characters, businesses, places, events, and incidents in this work are either the product of the author's imagination or used in a fictitious manner. Any resemblance to actual persons, living or dead, or actual events is purely coincidental and the opinions expressed are those of the characters and should not be confused with the author's. There are many references to books, songs, poems, and historical happenings. Some of these stories are true. However, they are retellings through fictitious characters according to their fictitious recollections. And as evidenced by the length of this disclaimer, this work was completed in the year 2022, not 1997.

Notes

The Door with the Face

1. AURELIUS

A translated quote from Marcus Aurelius, who lived from 121-180 AD and served as Roman emperor from 161-180.

"Loss is nothing else but change, and change is Nature's delight" (Aurelius).

Aurelius, Marcus. Meditations: A New Translation. Translated by Gregory Hays, Random House, 2003.

Two Lions

1. BAUM

An excerpt from Frank Baum's *The Wonderful Wizard of Oz*, written in 1900.

"There is no living thing that is not afraid when it faces danger. The true courage is in facing danger when you are afraid, and that kind of courage you have in plenty" (Baum).

Baum, L. Frank. The Wonderful Wizard of Oz. Oxford University Press, 2010.

Past House

1. BLAKE

A line of poetry from William Blake's The Marriage of Heaven and Hell, composed between 1790 and 1793.

"Eternity is in love with the productions of time" (Blake).

Blake, William. "Proverbs of Hell." The Marriage of Heaven and Hell, Chelsea House, 1987. Line 10.

The Laws of Physics

1. RILKE

An excerpt from Letters to a Young Poet, written by Rainer Maria Rilke to Franz Xaver Kappus in a series of letters composed between 1902 to 1908.

"Love consists in this: that two solitudes protect and border and greet each other" (Rilke).

Rilke, Rainer Maria, 1875-1926. Letters to a Young Poet. San Rafael, CA, New World Library, 1992.

2. YOUNG

A reference to the song "Where Can I Go Without You" composed by Victor Young and originally performed by Peggy Lee, later covered by Nina Simone on her album Forbidden Fruit.

Young, Victor. "Where Can I Go Without You." Performed by Nina Simone, Forbidden Fruit, Colpix Records, 1961.

The Egret

1. SMASHING PUMPKINS

A reference to the song "1979" written by Billy Corgan and performed by The Smashing Pumpkins from their album Mellon Collie and the Infinite Sadness, released in 1995 by Virgin Records.

The Smashing Pumpkins. "1979." Mellon Collie and the Infinite Sadness, Virgin Records, 1995.

2. SMASHING PUMPKINS

A reference to the music video for the song "1979" by The Smashing Pumpkins, directed by Jonathan Dayton and Valerie Faris.

"1979." Directed by Jonathan Dayton and Valerie Faris, performed by The Smashing Pumpkins, music by The Smashing Pumpkins, Virgin Records, 1996.

Memento Mori

1. BOWIE

A reference to David Bowie's album art for his 1973 album Aladdin Sane, photographed by Brian Duffy and released by RCA Records.

Bowie, David and Duffy, Brian. Aladdin Sane. RCA Records, 1973. Photography artwork for vinyl LP.

2. BOWIE

A reference to David Bowie's title track Aladdin Sane for his 1973 album by the same name, released by RCA Records.

Bowie, David. "Aladdin Sane." Aladdin Sane, RCA Records, 1973.

3. RUMI

An excerpt from Jalāl al-Dīn Muḥammad Rūmī, a Persian poet and Sufi mystic who lived from 1202-1273 AD.

"You have to keep breaking your heart until it opens" (Rumi).

Jalāl al-Dīn Rūmī and Coleman Barks. The Essential Rumi. 1st HarperCollins paperback ed. San Francisco, CA, Harper, 1996.

The Workshop

1. CATULLUS

A translated excerpt from Gaius Valerius Catullus (Catullus) c. 84 - c. 54 BCE, a Latin poet of the late Roman Republic.

"I hate and I love. Why I do this, perhaps you ask. I know not, but I feel it happening and I am tortured" (Catullus).

Catullus, Gaius Valerius. Odi Et Amo: the Complete Poetry of Catullus. Translated by Arthur Swanson, Bobbs-Merrill Liberal Arts Press, 1959.

2. LIGHTMAN

A reference to Alan Lightman's 1992 novel "Einstein's Dreams," published by Pantheon Books.

Lightman, Alan P., "Einstein's Dreams." New York, Pantheon Books, 1992

Poacher's Prize

1. POE

An excerpt from Edgar Allan Poe's "A Dream," written in 1827.

In visions of the dark night

I have dreamed of joy departed—

But a waking dream of life and light

Hath left me broken-hearted (Poe).

Poe, Edgar Allen. "A Dream." Complete Stories And Poems Of Edgar Allan Poe, Doubleday, NEW YORK, 1966, p. 769.

2. MAGRITTE

A reference to the painting "Le domaine enchanté."

Magritte, René. Le domaine enchanté. 1953.